Praise for Kris Radish

"*The Year of Necessary Lies* is a memorable and beautifully written story about reinvention, standing up for your beliefs, and staying true to yourself, no matter what the cost."

—Kristin Contino, author of *The Legacy of Us*

"Radish unrolls a rollicking yet reflective read that adds to her robust repertoire of beloved fiction. What's a reader to do but relish the ride."

—BookPage on *Searching for Paradise in Parker, PA*

"Kris Radish creates characters that seek and then celebrate the discovery of women's innate power."

—*The Denver Post*

"Radish's characters know how to have a good time on their way to matriarchal nirvana."

—*Kirkus Reviews*

"Through the women in her popular novels, author Kris Radish reveals what has value and meaning in her life—friendships and a passion for living."

—*Albuquerque Journal*

"In Radish's book, everything takes on a meaning that is larger than life . . . Radish's books are also a little like cliff-hangers of the 1920s, with one page pulling you to the next."

—*Lansing City Pulse*

"A funny and provocative attempt to nudge numb, stagnant, and confused souls in a new direction."

—*Capital Times*

"Slyly comic . . . Radish is a good writer to get to know, creator of terrific characters and warm and tangled relationships, and a world that's a pleasure to visit."

—*Sullivan County Democrat*

"A rallying cry for the empowerment of women. Radish's book is also a celebration of the strong bond that exists between female friends."

—*Booklist*

THE YEAR

of

NECESSARY

LIES

THE YEAR

of

NECESSARY

LIES

A NOVEL BY

Kris Radish

SparkPress, A BookSparks Imprint
A Division of SparkPoint Studio, LLC

Published by SparkPress, a BookSparks imprint,
A division of SparkPoint Studio, LLC
Tempe, Arizona, USA, 85281
www.gosparkpress.com

Published 2015
Printed in the United States of America
ISBN: 978-1-940716-51-0 (pbk)
ISBN: 978-1-940716-50-3 (e-bk)
Library of Congress Control Number: 2015935422

Cover design by Julie Metz, Ltd./metzdesign.com
Interior design by Kiran Spees
Julia's Journey Map by Mike Morgenfeld

Also by Kris Radish

Fiction:

The Elegant Gathering of White Snows

Dancing Naked at the Edge of Dawn

Annie Freeman's Fabulous Traveling Funeral

Searching for Paradise in Parker P.A.

The Sunday List of Dreams

The Shortest Distance Between Two Women

Hearts on a String

Tuesday Night Miracles

A Grand Day to Get Lost

Non-Fiction:

Run, Bambi, Run: The Beautiful Ex-Cop and Convicted Murderer Who Escaped to Freedom and Won America's Heart

The Birth Order Effect: How to Better Understand Yourself and Others

Gravel on the Side of the Road—True Stories From a Broad Who Has Been There

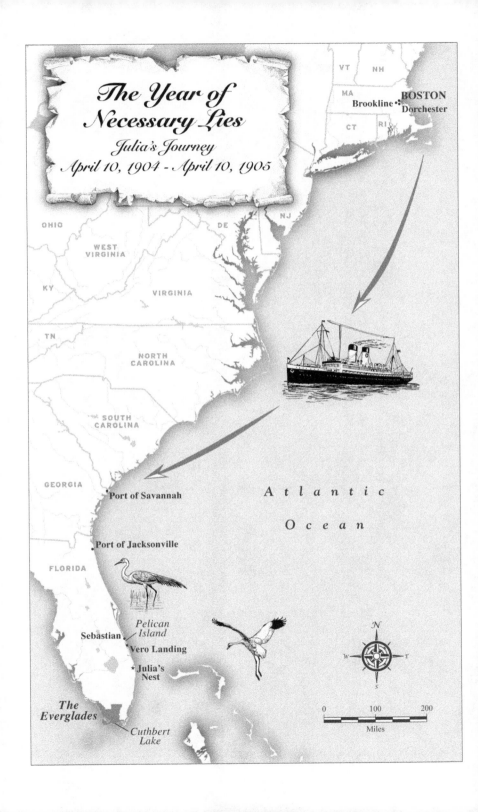

Author's Note

My lifelong love of all things bird probably started when I was a little girl and my father brought home a duck or a pheasant he had shot and then wanted me to eat it. This was also probably the day I decided to become a vegetarian. I also tried to release my mother's pet parakeet numerous times and I still don't understand why anyone would want to put a bird in a cage.

There's something magical about winged creatures and something magical also about the men and women who swam against the tide to put an end to plume hunting and to help establish all of the refuges and parks that now grace our country.

This book has been humming (yes—just like a bird) inside of me for a very long time. I've always wanted to write about birds and strong women and to honor the sacrifices and risks they took and this novel really sprang from a very special place in my heart. It's so easy to forget how women like Julia risked it all to do something so amazingly important. Change always requires risk and boldness and I believe it's important to celebrate those who sacrificed so much so that we could live the way we do, with so many choices, and in a world that still has such expansive slices of wilderness.

Julia is not real but to me she is and this remarkable, brave, and true woman is a composite of so many women who blazed trails that are now well-worn paths that many of us take for granted. I did extensive research for this novel and many of the men and women mentioned really did exist and they changed the world. I stood in the quiet jungle surrounding the very first National Wildlife Refuge and saw flocks of gorgeous birds and one amazing ghostlike vision of the woman who became my Julia. I cried when I circled near the islands where thousands of birds had once been slaughtered and where women and men braved the hunters and the elements and helped form the backbone of the Audubon Society. And I stood in many quiet places where I could hear the wings of beautiful birds fluttering in the wind and where my own notion of always keeping my eyes to the sky gave me countless doses of inspiration.

In the end what I wrote is an amazing love story on many levels, which I hope will become an example about the importance of following your own heart, designing your Year—no matter how long it takes, and for living a life that is written by no one but you.

An Honest Introduction
by the Great-Granddaughter

There's a sweet moment, I think, when we all cross an invisible line and stand for a few minutes in the shoes of adulthood—just to see what the shoes feel like or how close they might be to actually fitting our growing feet. Call it a dress rehearsal or a serendipitous glimpse into the future, or a simple moment of childhood brilliance.

My moment came in 1969, the first time I remember hearing about what we all ended up calling "The Year." I was just a young girl, but in a family littered with strong, vocal, and really opinionated women, it was impossible not to be an occasional good listener. I'm also positive that there had been other family conversations about this topic, but this time, when I was just beginning to understand the importance of female connections, shared secrets, long audible sighs, and treasures that are passed from one generation to the next, was the first time the enormity of what I was hearing started to seep inside of me.

I was sitting on a long covered porch in a place that is miraculously now mine, my back slanted against old, weathered wood that has since been replaced three times, the warm wind in my face, the sounds of the constant roll of waves sliding into this small bay over and over again, and a view of the sky that is as brilliant today as it was that late spring afternoon. I like to think it's the same slice of sky, the same revolving set of clouds, the same occasional gust of wind that my great-grandmother, Julia Briton, claimed as her own too.

This is mostly her story, one year of her story anyway, and as you will see, it's also my story. All those years ago when she sat with her

1

eighty-eight-year-old legs up on the porch railing, tilted back her head, and rambled on about "that year, that year," it may have been the first time I actually listened to what she was saying with sincerity. Mostly I listened in disbelief. Everything she said seemed extraordinary, wonderful, dangerous, fairly unbelievable, and absolutely stunning.

And it was.

Now that I am grown woman who has lost and loved and sacrificed and lived, I can rappel back through the special moments in my life, as if there is a slide projector running those important moments over and over again. The afternoon when my cousins, aunts, grandmother, my two sisters, and my own mother and I listened as Great-Grandma Julia recounted what I later found out were selected and heavily edited portions of her incredible year. Even though I vividly remember closing my eyes as she spoke, I saw her.

I saw her as she was in mid-1904 when her story started and when she crossed so many borders and boundaries that even now it seems almost unbelievable, perilous, dangerous, and perhaps even slightly insane. I saw her dashing through streets, riding wild horses, shooting a rifle, bouncing across the ocean on the bottom of a filthy ship, meeting famous men and women who I later studied via my history books, chopping through a sea of swamp grass, and causing a familial riot via behavior that could have gotten her institutionalized. And, as I was to discover, that was only part of her story.

When I dared to open my eyes halfway through her tale, the woman telling the story wasn't the dashing, beautiful heroine I had seen in my mind's eye. Instead, there was the matriarch of our family, whose weather-beaten face looked as if it could tell its own stories. There was the woman who could not walk past me without running her hands through my hair and telling me she loved me and that I must remember I was born to do great things, take huge risks, and "carry on, carry on." That day, and until I grew older and realized what she was talking about, I thought she meant carry on because I was her namesake. My name is Kelly Briton, and Julia's maiden name was Kelly.

She paused as I was staring at her that afternoon, looked me in the eye, and I'm certain she sensed my bewilderment. How could the woman in the shortened version of her life story that she was sharing be my great-grandmother? How could this tiny, shrinking-before-my-eyes *lady with snow-white hair, old-fashioned rimless eyeglasses, and a penchant for storytelling be the same woman in her story? Then she smiled at me and winked.*

I blinked, and when my eyes focused again, my great-grandmother was a beautiful young woman. Her brown hair was braided and looped around the top of her head and pinned in place with a long, silver comb. She had on a soft red blouse, buttoned to the waist, that showed a speck of her gorgeous white throat. Her black skirt fanned out like a dark flower, and I could see the tips of shiny brown boots at the very bottom.

I saw the woman she had been slowly fade into the woman she was then, and if she had not coughed loudly, on purpose to startle me, I may have fallen off the porch.

That sweet moment changed everything for a few years of my life. I became enchanted by history and I hung on every word Julia said. I spent weekends with her, slept next to her in bed, made her tell me her story over and over again until I could almost repeat it myself. Gradually, she told me more, and gradually, she showed me more, and even more gradually, and to be honest gradually in my life means about forty-plus years, I came to realize not only about "carrying on," but also about the importance of legacy, of what I had been given and what I must do. But Julia, I'm certain, would have said, "I had my year and as long as you get there, Kelly, it doesn't matter if it takes you a lifetime," which indeed it almost has.

During those special conversations, I thought I had learned all about her life before she married and launched herself into a year and into a life of epic proportions, but I was wrong—there was so much more to know, and Julia had been selective in her sharing. For years and years, I loved hearing about the bits and pieces of her life, and Julia Briton, in spite of her age, had an incredible memory. But then I turned into a teenager.

In 1974, I was fifteen years old, Julia was ninety-three, and if you believe anyone who knew me back then, I was also a lot of trouble. My father had announced he was no longer in love with my mother, and for an entire summer my two sisters, my brother, and I were deposited, or "dumped" as my siblings and I liked to say, at Julia's house, while my mother, with the help of her mother, tried to walk her through the loss of her marriage and near-crippling depression. Thankfully, we all lived in the same town, Vero Landing, a way-too-small-for-a-fifteen-year-old burg that wasn't bad except for the location of Julia's house. She lived on the St. Johns River on a rather isolated twenty-acre parcel of land that may as well have been in Africa as far as I was concerned. Julia was not feeble then, but it wasn't wise for her to be alone either, and so there we were, four teenagers and an ornithological and environmental legend, left to our own devices.

I was the youngest, and jobless, and the most horrible. I learned how to smoke and drink and would have had sex if anyone had asked me. I probably would have also robbed a bank, taken off in a stolen car, or moved to Canada, too, if the opportunity had presented itself. I moped, mouthed off to the one woman who had been a constant source of nothing but love in my life, and once, in a fit of teenage rage, I came an inch away from pushing Julia down the same porch steps where I had sat and listened to her tell stories.

Then one day, searching for my older sister's hidden stash of marijuana, I discovered something else. I stormed into Julia's bedroom because I had looked everywhere else in the entire house. She was sleeping on the downstairs sofa and her hearing was definitely fading by then, and eventually I pulled open the bottom drawer of her bedroom dresser and discovered a silver box about the size of a large notebook. I quickly pulled it out, set it on the bed, opened the box, and discovered a tape recorder.

It was still the 1960s, and cassette tape recorders, 8-track players, indeed anything besides an old record player and a boxy television set, had not yet been invented or mass produced. I had never before seen a tape recorder except in magazines, and I was mystified and a bit thrilled at the same time. The machine was silver and covered with a black leather case and engraved with the words, Steelman Transitape, 1959. It was a reel-to-reel machine, about the size of one of my school notebooks, and there was a tape loaded and ready to play, as if it had been expecting me to come along at any moment. It wasn't hard to figure out how to use it, even for an insolent girl, and I pushed the play button and there was Julia speaking.

She was tentative, testing the machine with a soft, and very sweet, "Hello, hello, this is Julia," and I laughed when I heard what must have been her fingers tapping the microphone to see if it worked. But then she *started to talk and I didn't laugh again. I knelt in front of the machine, like someone might kneel at an altar, while the first reel played. When she said, "Tape One," I folded my hands, took in a breath, and closed my eyes.*

And I listened.

Tape One

A Loss of Great Proportions
Boston—April 10, 1904

The heavy gold drapes were open, which I immediately mistook as a sign of great hope. The other times, they closed the drapes and left me lying there in the darkness, totally alone and absolutely fearful. It was a cave of black that allowed me to disappear and to imagine that if I stayed there long enough, wrapped in my physical and mental pain, the world would float away and perhaps take me with it. The drapes stayed closed for what seemed like forever the second time, for three entire weeks, and when I thought I was ready, I rose slowly, walked to the long covered window, grabbed the heavy, stiff fabric in my hands, and pushed the drapes aside so the bedroom was filled with light again. It was a sign for me and for everyone else in the house. A sign that I was back, that I would try again, and that I must go on. One must always go on.

So the third time, when I woke up, which I later found out had followed twelve fitful and semi-delirious hours of sleep, and saw the drapes already pulled open, my heart became as wild as one of the powerful storms that often lashed out across the bay and pounded down the Charles River. But before I called out, or thought to listen for the sounds of life down the hall, I lay still, relishing what I assumed would be the last moments of this portion of my life. Everything, now, of course, would change.

I surveyed my room. It was not just my room, but a room I also shared with my husband when he was not at late-night meetings, traveling on business, or discussing politics on the porch or down in the parlor with a variety of men who would often only acknowledge my existence when Charles demanded it. Charles was the same as them but so very different. He was kind enough not to enter this bedroom if it was too late, if he had passed his tolerable limit of Irish whiskey, or if I had been unkind and lashed out during what I perceived was one of my many moments of ignorance or societal clumsiness. This room, however, was clearly my domain, even though his mother, Margaret, had done everything from selecting the carpets to hanging family photographs on the wall. She had at least asked me before she placed everything where it was—the huge chest across the room, the clear vases for fresh flowers on the dresser against the back wall, lamp stands on either side of the bed, a soft run of the most beautiful snow-white lace I had ever seen that she had set on the windowsills, a hint of yellow in the bedspread, the walls, the sheets. "The color of the morning sun," she told me, "so that you will always know the feeling of hope, of promise." The day she took me up to the room for the first time with Charles quietly following behind, she stood by the door before she opened it, turned toward her only son, and said, "You will never wear your shoes in this room or scatter your things about, and you must always remember that this is Julia's room first and yours second."

I was stunned! But Charles did not hesitate to answer, "Of course, Mother," before she motioned for me to enter first. I did not know that this space would be the only thing I was allowed to manage or call my own. Already blinded by my good fortune for marrying into this family and to such a man, I almost dropped to my knees when I saw the bedroom as large as the two bedrooms and the entire kitchen in my own family home. I wondered if I would ever get accustomed to this life, to my brazen mother-in-law, to this odd world with its customs of propriety that was unlike anything I had ever really known before. But there I was not so many months later, lying in a lovely bed surrounded by soft cotton, my precious books on the table where I could glance at them without moving, the drapes open and not closed, and I had a sense that I had finally accomplished something grand and expected.

Outside my window, I knew the gardener would be busy with

spring planting, pruning, digging, and moving in the precise manner that Charles had outlined before he left for work that very morning. There was not one movement, one decision about the running of this household that Charles did not direct. The world, he told me time and time again, can be perfect if it is organized and there is someone in control. The yard and roof might require his attention on a daily basis, but I was holding in a secret about my own intentions concerning the management of the household that I would one day spring on him at the appropriate moment. Margaret had even been helping me with my plan, which would require more than passing thought and quick discussions in the kitchen, but then it was also a comfort to know that everything, including the blades of grass, had been tended to and were in just the correct position.

The downstairs too, I was certain, would be running smoothly. It was possible that Margaret was there herself right that second, making certain the hardwood floors had been polished, the windows shined clean, the welcoming parlor readied for the guests who would surely be paraded in and out during the coming weeks. She would not be busy with this work herself. The mere thought made me giggle and push my head under the covers lest someone hear me and discover that I was awake. Margaret, who let her close friends call her Maggie, directed life, as did her son. She pointed and looked over shoulders and often stood with her hands on her hips, while the girls she sent over to clean and cook silently took her direction.

Margaret was confusing to me. In the few years since my marriage, I had come to realize that I might never know how to act or what to expect when we were together. Sometimes she would take me aside and share something personal and almost extraordinary. "I have often wondered what my life might have been like if I had never married and lived freely," she whispered to me with her eyes closed one morning while we were drinking tea in her formal dining room. Such an intimate revelation was shocking and also lovely to me, but then a day later she spoke to Charles when we were in the same dining room as if I were not even there or alive. "Your wife has a lot to learn, sweet Charles," she said, leaning into the table, almost as if he were a lover and not a son. "Let's hope she can fulfill your promises to me." I simply lowered my head and stared at my feet, fighting the urge to rise up, leave the room, and slam every door in her magnificent and terribly perfect house. Promises? How many secrets did this family and my own husband have between them?

I hoped that everything would settle into a new place. Promises and secrets would not matter. Margaret would become Maggie to me and I would grow stronger and bolder with each passing day. I would stroll through the yard and into the back stable without worrying about who would see me or what I would say that might be wrong or misconstrued. I could sit on our wide but tiny front porch and rock no matter what time of the day it might be or who might be strolling past.

A bird suddenly appeared outside the middle window as I was trying hard to push thoughts of Margaret from my mind. The house remained so incredibly quiet that I could hear wind passing through its feathers, and I managed to lift myself off the pillows to get a better look. The bird was not an early spring arrival, one of the bright colored cardinals or yellow hummingbirds that were due back any second. It was a seemingly plain wren or sparrow, but the little brown-and-gray speckled bird was illuminated by one spot of sun and it looked as if it were dancing in place just for me. I held my breath and the bird turned in a circle.

I could see the wind pushing back its feathers and it looked as if the tiny thing was throwing back its head and laughing. My precise eyesight narrowed in on its beak, which was open so I could also see a sliver of light passing from one side to the next. It was impossible for me to determine how or why the bird could stay in place for what now must have been almost an entire minute. I had never seen anything like this and was close to shouting for someone to come and be a witness to something that was already seeming more and more like a miracle, a sign, some kind of heavenly gift, but I wasn't yet ready to relinquish the last few moments of my solitude.

It struck me, as the bird hovered, that this was perhaps the first time I had stopped to admire the beauty, grace, and aerial poise of creatures of the air. My father at one time had been somewhat of a bird watcher, although his life did not afford him much time to sit in place and stare at the sky. I had some far-reaching memories of him pointing, standing as still as a statue, and moving his head back and forth to follow flocks of birds moving across the sky. However, I was more intent on watching him as a little girl because he was a rare sight to me.

I began to wonder if that would happen with Charles as the bird fluttered away and left me with a pounding heart. Would having a child change him? Would he be a doting father who bounced his son or daughter on his knee, paraded his child through the streets of Boston with pride and deep affection, and eagerly rushed home each evening, or would things remain as they were? Would he be preoccupied with his business, careless in remembering the importance of the needs and wants of those he loved, or would the Charles of the Heart, as I sometimes dared to call him, blossom even more?

Charles of the Heart was gentle and kind and without pretense yet strong and fierce at the same time. This Charles did not show himself often and I was still unsure of how to coax this part of him out even further. I was terrified that if I said something wrong, did something inappropriate, moved incorrectly, the tender part of him would disappear and I would be left with just the Charles everyone else seemed to know. Even though I knew he had risked everything to claim me, to marry me, to challenge so many parts of the world he brought me into, I still walked tenderly and timidly in every room of my life. And I still had not discovered a confidant, a friend, a woman who could help me traverse the passageways of a life that was still as foreign to me as this very room where I was waiting.

And what about me? Was I ready for this? I rolled over slowly and felt a wide pain move from the base of my hips, through my pelvis, and down both legs. I put my hand into my mouth, closed my eyes, and bit down on my fingers to keep from yelling out. The pain took my breath away and for a moment I thought I might faint. I slowed my breathing, relaxed, and then opened my eyes. The bird was back! I smiled and felt something sure and calm come over me, as if the simple sight of this creature was a healing tonic. How beautiful this gray bird seemed to me, and how absolutely extraordinary that it came back! "Hello, little sweetheart," I dared to whisper as it circled and circled outside of the window as if it were looking for a place to land. "Do you have something to tell me? Tell Mama, what is it?"

Mama.

Was it finally true, and if it was, why did I not feel different?

Suddenly, knowing was all that mattered and I started to call out, "Hello? Hello? I'm awake... Come to me! Please, bring me my baby!"

The drapes were open. I said this to myself over and over again. The drapes were open, while I heard noises below and then the sound of someone coming up the stairs and down the hall toward me. I was listening for the cry of my son, my daughter, the voice of Charles cooing to a baby, our baby.

The person who came was unfamiliar to me, a large woman in white, her hands held close against her chest and her face pinched so tightly that her lips had disappeared. Her eyes were buckets of black, dark as coal, a cavern of sad bleakness that I will never forget.

She said nothing but stood with her head lowered, and I rolled onto my back, forgetting the searing pain, and screamed, "No, no, no," over and over again as the bird dipped from sight and a new pain, the pain of loss, of having to keep living, of utter grief, fell upon me and branded me with an open wound that I knew would never heal.

I was barely twenty-three years old, married to an up-and-coming millinery owner who was a descendant of one of the wealthiest families in Boston, and I had just miscarried my third child in thirty months.

The Great-Granddaughter
Does Not Know Everything

Thankfully the tape ended, because by the time I heard her admit that she had miscarried three babies, I was sobbing so uncontrollably I couldn't have gone on. How could I not have known this and why did she never tell me? Did my mother know? Questions were ricocheting from one side of my head to the other and I was trying to remember if I had simply forgotten this part of her story. And I wondered why she was taping this, where she had even gotten a tape recorder, and finally, the tiny remaining flame of kindness that had not been obliterated by my teenage angst and horrid disposition rose up, and I wanted to run to her and kiss her face.

But I didn't do that because I was beyond selfish. In fact, it would be a long time before I was anything but that, and I didn't want her to know I had found her secret stash. The marijuana was no longer attractive to me, but I knew I would be back to listen to the other tapes that were stacked next to the recorder. I didn't count them, but it looked as if she were still recording because there was a pile of them waiting to be used. Listening to the tapes would become an addiction that thankfully resurrected itself decades after I first heard her on the recorder that summer so very long ago.

I didn't know it then, but finding the box in her drawer probably did save me from a life of high, instead of just medium to low, crime. I had been blessed with the good-looking Briton genes—brown, wavy hair, forest-green eyes, a small frame that laughed at other things people worried about like excess weight and sagging skin, and a set of *cheekbones that might have made us all model material if we had not been so damn short. Julia was still a very good-looking woman until the day she died, and that summer I was coming into my own. My brother's friends started to linger in the kitchen when I was there, I was followed down to the beach all of the time, and I'm almost certain my brother grabbed at least three of them by the throat and told them to get lost. All I could think about were those tapes and the truth is, at first anyway, I found it hard to be around or even look at Julia because I felt as if I suddenly had no idea who she was. I felt as if she had lied to me all those nights when we had snuggled in her bed.*

I brooded, which I was very good at, and I tried to remember what she had shared of her life, not just that year, but before that as well. Thankfully, writing in the diary I stuck under my mattress each night had been a bit of an obsession with me, and every other young girl during the sixties, before I had allowed my hormones to get the best of me. There were pages of information about my Kelly ancestors and a slew of old newspaper clippings in Julia's library from her book tours, appearances, and there were interviews with her long-dead friends and siblings. I became a spy and did not realize how I was already beginning to parallel her life. It was very easy, at first, to fit some of the pieces of her life into place. All I had to do was page though stacks of books, magazines, and newspapers and read.

Julia was born into a working class Dorchester, Massachusetts, family on a day in March, 1881 that her mother remembered as being brutally cold and remarkable because, as numerous reporters pointed out, Julia was her fifth baby, her fifth live baby out of ten pregnancies, and she made my great-grandmother promise never to tell her siblings a lovely secret. "You were the most beautiful baby I had and when I saw you, so perfect, so healthy, I thought perhaps I had died." Julia had apparently loved talking to reporters and me about her own mother, a woman she clearly loved and admired. I found it interesting that the loss of so many babies was mentioned without comment but as part of the reality of childbirth back then and vowed never to have babies myself. Thankfully, that was one important vow I broke.

I was a bit stunned when I read an article from 1965 in the Boston Women's Magazine focusing on women from Dorchester—a part of the greater Boston area, who had become famous. In the article, Julia said that her mother, my great-great-grandmother, told her the story of the day of her birth over and over again when they were alone, and how she would close her eyes as the soft, calm voice of her mother outlined the beginning of her life. She believed that her mother told her this story so many times because Julia was her last baby and her entrance into the world signaled a huge change in her own life. Terrified of bearing another child, of the possibility of losing another baby, of the physical struggle involved in childbirth, of yet more heartache and loss, she never slept with Julia's father again after the day Julia was born.

What? I hadn't even been kissed yet but couldn't imagine not sleeping with my husband for fear of getting pregnant. I'm certain this fact helped me not feel sorry for myself for at least an hour or two and offer up thanks to something or someone for not having been born prior to the advent of accepted and medically safe birth control.

Julia and I were both the babies of the family. Her three older brothers were already apprenticed by the time she was born, and her sister was in school. She recalled in one story that it seemed as if the moment the house went quiet, her mother would start talking to her about that "magical day when you became my sweet gift." Julia told the reporter she would close her eyes as she recounted the exact words her mother had said. "You were sitting so high, so close to my heart, that I knew you were a baby girl. I felt light with you. It wasn't like any of the others, all my loves too, you know, but everything was easy when I was carrying you. Some day, when you are a mother yourself, you will understand what I am telling you. You will also know how the sweet burden of pain is worth it all, so worth it all."

Like all mothers, mine included, her mother apparently never sat still when she talked. Julia said it was almost as if the constant movement helped her remember that the pain of bearing children, and losing them, was worth it all, but it was really because she had no choice as there was always work to do. Her mother had to run the household and she took in mending and sewing for extra money. I couldn't even imagine such a thing because simply dusting and vacuuming were exhausting to me, but for Julia's mother, it was a rare moment when she was at rest. She was always moving, bending, cleaning, cooking, and when she got to the end of some chore or task, it was time to start over again. I moaned about everything, even breathing, so when I read, "There was never complaining, never an angry word about what surely must have seemed like an endless cycle of labor, never a moment either when I did not feel loved and wanted," I felt more than a twinge of embarrassment. It's one thing to read history books and watch television shows about hard times, but when you read about your own family, someone you can actually reach out and touch, well, it becomes tangible and very real. But there was more and I found myself tearing up again.

"That remarkable feeling, knowing you are loved, gave me great courage as I grew older and I often wondered if it weren't for that, for the strength one can gain from something so tender and real, if I might not have been able to have taken so many risks. There were many times to come when that was all I had, an intangible inner feeling of sureness that burned inside of me, and I was certain that feeling helped keep me alive during my many adventures. I assumed so many things when I was a young girl. I thought everyone was loved like I was loved. Surely, as the baby of the family, I was spoiled and treated in ways that must have made my brothers and sister jealous, but if that is all one knows, then there are assumptions abounding in all directions."

Well, there you have it. She could have been talking about me, sick at heart because my parents, like half the parents I knew, were breaking up. I was still very loved even if it would take me half a lifetime to realize it.

Julia had once told me that she thought everyone had a father who worked long hours and came home with thick dust in his hair and hands that were swollen and calloused. She also thought everyone had brothers who were pulled from school to work at the Norway Ironworks and then apprenticed to businesses all over the city. And that it was only the girls who could go to school well into their teens and then decide what would happen next in their lives or specifically whom they might marry. She believed that everyone in the world was Catholic and that if they were not, they would burn in hell because they were sinners. And, of course, she thought every street in Boston was like Victoria Street where she grew up, all but isolated from the rest of the world. Apparently, I didn't have it so bad after all, big baby that I was.

I suppose it was during these weeks of investigation, reading everything I could find and even slipping off to the library to find more in those pre-computer years, that it may have also dawned on me how seriously famous and well-loved Julia had been. Julia had always been special to me and until some evil spirit invaded my body, I had considered her my muse, my guiding light, mine and mine only. Some girls had aunts or a friend of their mother's or their Girl Scout leader or a teacher to help them into their first pair of big-girl shoes, and I had Julia, so I thought, all to my own. Seeing her face on magazine covers, and in full-page feature articles made me think, back then anyway, that our relationship was not as sacred as I had thought. Even though I was hurt, too young to realize how real and true she had always been to me, I could not release my obsession with the tapes and with her real past and with all those magazines and newspaper articles. I kept reading while more days passed, and some of what I read ended up helping me understand why she had been so driven.

I read about how Victoria Street was a hardscrabble corner of Boston in Dorchester, a tight-knit, working-class community that may as well have been a continent across the sea from Brookline, where Julia ended up living as a young wife. Her street was a long road of small wooden houses tended by women like her mother, who scraped and saved and sewed and cleaned and occasionally left to work in the shops and millinery outposts in the heart of Boston, where high society, unbeknownst to them, was flourishing. And on the verge of changing the world in ways that no one in her neighborhood, especially Julia, could have imagined. They were all busy working very hard to keep the world moving forward. The men on Victoria Street were the men who built and maintained Boston. Julia's father, my great-great grandfather, was a brick mason, like his father and like two of her brothers. Other men were carpenters, factory workers, street cleaners, farriers, dock hands, ferry boat workers, and a few, very few, were clerks and assistants in the banks, stores, and businesses in the shopping and business districts scattered near Boston Common.

Most of the Dorchester boys knew their days catching baseballs and sneaking out to the Mount Vernon cow pasture to throw rocks and gaze out to sea were numbered unless they were some of the lucky few who could finish high school and maybe go to college. According to Julia, life wasn't any less predictable for the girls on Victoria Street or on the neighboring streets like Mayfield, Pearl, or Thornley. In the early 1900s, girls were still burdened by tradition, social circumstance, and by the often limited expectations of their families. They could marry, enter the convent, become teachers, or if they were on the lower end of any of our streets, go to work in the sewing factories that were part of the thriving millinery business in Boston. Julia and her sister Isabelle were lucky to have been born on the south end of Victoria Street, where the houses were barely a foot longer than at the north end but a measure of more than just size. They joked about this all of the time, as Julia recounted in a scene I discovered in a Good Housekeeping magazine article from 1953.

"We could have been Northenders, Julia," my sister would whisper to me in bed at night. "The girls up there are ugly, they talk nonsense, and you know their dads will send them off to the convent as soon as those terrible nuns will have them so they won't have to feed them any longer."

"Izzie," I would answer slowly, because I was always delighted when my big sister confided in me, "they won't all go away and they are not all ugly. Will father send us away? What will become of us? I don't want to marry a smelly old boy. I don't want to work in the mills or sew like mum."

"You are a fool! Of course you will marry because you are beautiful and smart, and we will visit each other and our children will be best friends until the very day we die."

"We are lucky, then, to be who we are, Izzie, yes? Is that true?"

Julia said her sister's laugh was always the perfect answer and she would simply nod her head. And on the days when she was feeling sweet and not angry that she had to share a bed with someone six years younger, Izzie would tuck her under her arm and she would fall asleep dreaming about the men she saw in her mama's magazines and the handsome man with the tall hat who came on the first Monday of every month to collect their rent, but mostly about what it might be like to have to live with a stinky boy.

Sometimes, Julia said, Izzie would slip out of bed on her tiptoes so no one would hear her, walk to the small dresser, and bring back the mirror that her grandma had given her. She would hold it up first to her own face for a long time and then pass it on to Julia. "Look at yourself," her sister ordered. "Some day a boy will kiss your lips and then a man will

17

kiss your lips, and before you know it, you will be in love and the world will be grand, just so grand!"

Julia's heart raced picturing such things, and it was impossible, she said, to imagine then how their lives would unfold and how two sisters who once held each other in a sagging feather bed, combed each other's hair, and shared brave secrets could end up so differently. When she looked into the mirror, she did not see a beautiful girl. "I saw me, just me," she said quietly, always looking off into the distance. "A girl with dark-green eyes, a tiny nose, hair the color of burnt straw, high cheek- bones that made my face seem too long, and lips that curved upward and seemed to me as if they were preparing to fly off my face. I dare not look further for fear that my slender arms and even thinner legs would make me disbelieve everything my sister was telling me. I was small, 'a tiny bird,' as my father often called me, and any sense of beauty or pret- tiness would take years to unveil itself. When it did, my sister would have long since left my bed for another and I would be racing for my own unpredictable destiny."

I was absolutely mesmerized by all of these revelations. It was almost impossible to think of my great-granny as a sexual being, as someone who may have had the exact same feelings, longings, and desires I was having. But there it was. She had once been in the same emotional posi- tion as I was when I was reading all of the articles—tentative, excited, yearning, and scared half to death. Love, life, and adventures were waiting for both of us. Neither one of us knew, at that moment—me sitting in her library and Julia perched on the edge of her bed in faraway Dorchester decades earlier—what was already unfolding in our young lives.

I admit that my immaturity at the time made me feel glad to know that my miserable, or so I thought, family life was apparently an inher- ited condition. Julia had been honest when she shared the fact that her years in the Dorchester house were not always grand nights and days of lively love and tenderness. I could so relate to this, considering I had just spent the past two years listening to my parents scream at each other, while secretly promising myself that I would never get married. Julia revealed that her brothers took turns causing both her mother and father tremendous amounts of parental anguish. There would be a fight, a lost job, someone asleep on the front step after a night at the local pub, a visit from the neighborhood policeman concerning something that Julia was never allowed to hear about, and later, the sudden appearance of a niece and a silent sister-in-law who could never look her mother or father in the eye. The boys were much older than Julia because she had come after those lost babies. It was so easy for her to ignore their transparent failings because they treated her either as a sweet toy or as an invisible part of a world they were about to escape. My own mother would agree, especially during the coming years, that it wasn't always the boys who made hair go gray.

And there was the anguish of her ever-tired father. A little girl growing up in a small house where the mother and father do not share a bed has no choice but to grow up a bit confused, so that would make two of us. My parents had been sleeping in separate rooms for quite some time, which I would use as an excuse for many things during the coming years. Being young and overly anxious about anything having to do with love, which mostly meant sex to a fifteen-year-old, I brazenly dared to ask Julia about this one day.

She was sitting outside with her trusty binoculars in one hand and a notebook in the other, gazing out across the small field. There could not be a lawn, for God's sake. Because the birds needed a field for nesting purposes—it was all about the birds. I sat next to her because, after all, I was a spy and I was not about to quit. Being me, I got right to it and I lied a bit too.

"You know Mom and Dad haven't even slept in the same room for a long time, which, you know, is kind of odd."

Julia didn't even bother to put down her binoculars. "Yes, sweetheart, I know."

"Didn't you say once that happened to your parents, too?"

If she knew she had never said a word about this to me, she did not give it up. "Well, yes, but I didn't even know about it until after I was married. Back then we didn't speak of things like that. But it tore them apart, both of them. They loved each other very much, but it was about the babies, you know. My mother couldn't handle another pregnancy."

Then she reminded me of the "kissing rule," which my family had abandoned exactly two years ago. This family tradition started with Julia's mother who raised all of her children to kiss everyone in the house hello and good-bye because, as her mother explained to her and mine explained to me, "What if you never come home? I need to remember you with a touch of love, with the softness one can only gather from the gentle moment when there is a sweet kiss, when we are close enough so I can feel the beating of your hearts." She lowered the glasses before she continued and her voice became very soft. "But when my parents kissed, there was nothing simple and sweet about it. My father would take my mother in his arms, close his eyes, lower her toward the floor, and then raise her slowly to his lips, and the kiss lasted a very long time."

I could actually see this happening and I thought Julia might stop talking, but she didn't, and if I had been older and wiser, I might have urged her to keep going, keep remembering, but I didn't.

"The kiss was often followed by whispers and then my father's raised voice, and then my mother would close her eyes and say, "I am so sorry," over and over. Some things one does not forget, no matter how old and tired the brain might become."

And there was more.

This was about the same time Julia remembered her father started to walk at night, which she never understood until much, much later. When she would ask her mother why he was leaving, because he was clearly exhausted, her mother would shush her and say that he simply needed to take in some air.

I couldn't stop myself. "Did he meet someone or was he simply walking off his, you know, physical desires?"

Julia said she never knew for sure because her life changed so quickly not so long after those years and she would never get the chance to ask her mother or her father. She told me she never forgot the silence after the door closed behind him and her mother quietly disappeared into her tiny bedroom.

"It was such a different world and time and I was on the verge of, you know, The Year," she said, finally turning to look at me. Her eyes were cloudy then but still shining with what I would one day realize was the look of sweet love. "The gift of age helped turn me into a woman who knows the importance of the joy of the flesh and of the unspeakable word—sex. My parents were in love, but they were lovers separated by the cruel fate of time and place, a fate that almost befell their youngest daughter," she whispered, "almost."

I felt as if someone had just hit me upside the head, and I imagine my eyes were as big as one of her beloved bird's eggs. This revelation about the joys of sex was mind-blowing. I had to get back to the tapes after that, and I excused myself and ran into the house, while praying to God a flock of long-legged and terribly rare flamingos would make a surprise visit and keep her busy and out of the house for a very long time.

Tape Two

Grieving Be Damned
Boston—Through April, 1904

There was no place to hide after I realized I had lost yet another baby and no place to go but the bedroom, and for the next fourteen days, it became my refuge. Charles had all but disappeared from the house and *especially* the bedroom. I had not seen him in five days. It is also safe to say that I also disappeared and wished to stay missing for an extended, perhaps eternal, amount of time. I am not even certain if I can adequately describe what the past two weeks had been like for me. I am not ashamed to say that I wished for my life to end so that I could fly away and hold those three lost babies in my arms.

The moment after the woman in white, a nurse as it turns out, spun on her heels to leave the room, I forced myself from the bed, wincing in pain, so I could close the drapes and burrow into the bed, hoping that when I woke again, my nightmare would be over. I prayed and willed it to happen, but when I did awake again, hours later, nothing had changed. I was ill, childless, and swept into a river of depression that was unlike anything I had ever experienced.

All of that was about to abruptly end. The window was popped open just an inch and I could hear Margaret down below, bellowing orders to her driver. "Stand by and do not overfeed the mare until I return." My stomach lurched south a bit. Something was about to happen and within five minutes, it did.

"It is Sunday and time enough," Margaret declared as she pounded into my bedroom. I closed my eyes the moment I heard her shrill voice, willed her to disappear and to leave me alone with my almost unbearable well of sadness, but that was apparently not going to happen.

"Enough," she all but shouted, and I was forced to open my eyes and look at her. She was standing a foot from my face, one hand on her hip and the other waving back and forth as if she were about to conduct an orchestra. "Your time in this bed is up, missy."

I hated her, and I did not move or bother to acknowledge that she was even in the same room with me.

"Get up," she ordered.

I still did not move.

"Do you think you are the only woman who has lost babies? The only woman who has felt empty and alone? The only woman who would love to lie in bed, crying for the rest of her life?"

I pushed myself up on my elbows. Was she talking about herself?

Margaret's occasional bursts of tenderness and sharing had been few and far between since my marriage even though I longed for something more. My own mother had sent me a short letter concerning the loss of the baby that someone had slipped under the door, but Margaret's appearance now marked her first visit since the day I had lost the baby. I had been left alone to recover, or so I thought. Her son had only bothered to stop in three times, briefly touch my arm, and then wordlessly disappear. I had never been or felt so alone in my life, and this was also the first time that anyone had raised his or her voice to me. It was unsettling and I had to focus so I would not burst into tears.

Margaret continued shouting and I pushed myself into a sitting position. "You have obligations, Julia Briton, and your time up here is over. Do you understand?"

I nodded my head, but I refused to speak to her. I felt as if the only thing I had left to myself was my voice and I was not about to share it with someone who was shouting at me.

"Dr. Langdon is downstairs and I am going to send him up in ten minutes so he can talk to you. I want you to put on your dressing gown and prepare yourself, and when he is finished, the nurse will draw you a bath, you will dress, and meet me in the kitchen to discuss the new routines of your life."

She did not bother to wait for a response but turned and swept out of the room, gathering up her skirt in one hand and making certain to slam the door with her other hand just hard enough so I could see she was still very angry. It took me a few moments to realize I simply had no choice. I could not stay in bed. I could not run home to my mother. I could not lie in the arms of my husband and pour out my heart and explain how empty and lost I felt. I could not reverse the hands of time and give back this life, this house, my husband, and all the demands I had accepted as part of my marriage. I could not do anything but put on my dressing gown, walk to the chair by the window, and wait for the doctor.

The doctor knocked lightly a few moments later. I managed to say, "Come in," and the soft yet serious look in his eyes must have been a way for him to prepare me for what was to come next. Dr. Langdon had been with me when I lost the baby, and unlike the women on Victoria Street and the other side of town, I had been lucky to have him assist me and tend to me following the birth. All of that remained a blur in my mind, and I had absolutely no idea what he was about to tell me. He closed the door behind him, took three steps into the room, and asked me how I felt.

"Tired and sad."

"That is normal and it will pass. Do you have any pain?"

"A little bit, but I have been eating and walking about the room a bit."

"Good. That's very good, but now you must get on with everything, and I am suggesting that you walk outside in the fresh air, every day, a little farther each day to regain your strength and…"

He hesitated and took a step closer so he could reach out and touch my shoulder lightly while he spoke.

"This loss was very difficult and when the baby came, there was damage, I'm afraid very severe damage, Mrs. Briton."

I was staring at him in disbelief. Now I wanted to speak and when I tried, nothing came out. I could only form the words and move my lips. *What are you saying?*

The doctor squeezed my shoulder as he continued, perhaps hoping to keep me in place least I faint or try and climb out the window. His face, outlined in a black-and-gray, neatly trimmed beard and moustache softened even more, and I thought for an instant that he might cry.

"I am not certain you will ever be able to have a child, and I am suggesting that until you heal or work out some arrangement that you refrain from having relations with your husband."

My heart stopped briefly and I swayed away from his hand, but then he grasped me tightly to keep me from falling over.

"I'm sorry," he whispered as I took it all in.

"What am I to do? What can I possibly do?"

"I wish there was something I could do to help or say that might be of assistance, but for a time, abstinence is best until you heal and then…"

He hesitated and closed his eyes for a moment as if he were praying or asking for strength or guidance.

"There are women who might help you if you know where to look but I am legally bound and cannot say anything else, and you must promise me never to mention this part of our conversation. Do you agree?"

"Yes."

"I know this doesn't seem fair to you now, but no one can know what might happen tomorrow or the day after. The body is a miracle, Mrs. Briton. I see miracles every day and I pray that your sadness is one day wiped away by one."

"Does Margaret know? Does Charles know?"

He nodded yes and I dropped my head in embarrassment so that my chin was touching the top of my chest.

"You must be strong now. Walk. Eat well. Listen to Margaret because she has been where you are and you must keep a happy countenance. Look to the sky when you are out walking my dear."

I wanted to smile at this kind man, but I was fighting back tears and could barely muster a soft "thank you" as he turned to leave. Before he could open the door, I rose and touched his arm.

"The baby?" I asked with emotion breaking up my words. "Was it a boy or a girl?"

"A boy."

"And the other two? I never asked you. They all just disappeared. Please tell me!"

"Girls."

"Where are they?"

"You will have to speak to Margaret. She took care of everything. Ask her. Do not be frightened. Ask her."

I found Margaret an hour later following my bath and my stoic but false acceptance of yet another uncontrolled phase of my life. She was dismissing the nurse and did not see me standing behind her in the kitchen. She pressed the door shut and then leaned against it with her hands parallel to her head. I was absolutely stunned to see that she was crying. Her body began to shake and her head was resting on the door and her sobs were so severe that the door began to shake, and I was paralyzed.

If Margret had been my mother or my sister, I would have not hesitated to run to her and take her in my arms and share the sorrow that was in my own heart. But clear lines had been drawn in this family, my new family, and I was uncertain of what to do and how to handle the situation given how she had acted in my room just a short time ago. Ashamed, I quietly took one step back and then another so that I was standing at the bottom of the steps leading to the second floor of the house. I wanted her to think that I was just coming into the kitchen and had not seen her crying and in an emotional state. I was confused and unsure and when I heard her blow her nose, I finally walked back into the kitchen and stood in the doorway.

She looked at me through eyes that were now rimmed in red, and I struggled to control myself.

"You are dressed," she said, tucking her handkerchief behind her back.

"Yes."

There was a short pause when an unspoken conversation took place. I knew that she knew about the babies and what I must now do and not do, and we both knew that the grieving would go on and on until it was replaced with only a lesser kind of pain. This was all new territory to me and I had no choice but to trust her. I tilted my head to the left, and I wanted her to know that it was okay to cry and not be stoic, but we were not yet ready to speak of such things. Her shoulders dropped after a few moments, almost as if she were about to surrender, and I seized the moment and took a few steps toward her. If only she could have taken me in her arms! If only Charles of the Heart had been there to help me sort through all of this, but he had disappeared and finally I had to speak.

"Where is Charles?"

"He is with his father on a buying trip," she said without hesitation, straightening back up.

"I find that terribly odd."

She bristled a bit and all of the lines in her face went tight.

"This is not just about you. He has also suffered a great loss and a great humiliation. There is no son. There may never be a son. And now he cannot come to you as a husband should."

What a fool I was! It would always be about the men and their needs and never about a woman's loss or a woman's needs. I had grown to love the intimate aspects of my marriage, probably more than I ever cared to admit. Charles was sweet and caring in bed. It was the one place where I had felt as if we were equals, and now that would be gone. In a very short period of time, I had become like my mother and was suddenly terrified that Charles might find pleasure in another bed. How much more could I take?

"I want to see where they are buried," I blurted out.

Margaret suddenly paled and I did not give her a chance to respond or even take in a shocked breath.

"They were my babies and I need to see where they are resting. You owe me that."

I had no idea what Margaret might say. The emotional fog in the kitchen was so thick it was a wonder we could both stand. These were her grandchildren too, I realized, and Dr. Langdon had let slip that Margaret had suffered more than one loss of her own, which would explain why there was only Charles and no brothers or sisters. Margaret hesitated for what seemed like an hour to me. She pursed her lips so they disappeared inside of her own mouth, nodded up and down, and then dismissed me with the wave of her hand even though we were standing in my house and not hers.

An uneasy truce erupted for the next week and there was a blur of expectation, for Margaret had left me a note that informed me we would visit the gravesites of my children the following Sunday. Her note also outlined my expected household duties and while I waited for the time to pass, I failed miserably at the seemingly simple task of pulling myself together. My depression was startling and endless and I woke every night in a heated sweat, always searching for a lost baby and for the man whose absence made the depression even worse. How was I ever to be certain who was ruling my life? Two full-time workers, a cook, and a housekeeper had been hired and I quickly felt as if I had more in common with them than Margaret, Charles, or anyone else I had met since my marriage. They were young women, Ella and Ruby, and I all but forced them to sit with me and talk about their lives, about the world they lived in, about their hopes and dreams.

A short note also arrived from Charles that totally ignored the obvious. He said he would see me soon, wished me well, and told me to rest and recover. I so wanted and needed more from him, but I was also struggling to understand what this loss might mean to him. Should not a husband and wife be sharing the hard and the good times? I was absolutely confused.

Ella and Ruby became my medicine and in Margaret's absence during that week, I gladly became the mistress of the house and told them they must obey me. I said it with a wink and made them come into my room and sit on the bed, wishing the whole time that I could fetch my sister and pour my heart out to her. Ella and Ruby were sweet, open, lovely young women who thought of me as Cinderella, and I dared not reveal my true feelings and life story. They did not know what had just happened to me and I thought it best to let them have the false picture of my life they seemed to need. They were young enough, as was I when I met Charles, to believe in fairy tales and the hopeful rising up from one class to another. When I asked them to drink tea with me on my bed, I could not spoil the illusion with the truth that what I was merely trying to do was survive until Sunday.

Sunday.

It was so lovely when I woke and realized that I had slept the entire night without waking or a restless dream. I shifted in bed and could not believe my eyes. There was another bird hovering outside my window! This time it was a bight yellow hummingbird, its wings beating so rapidly it sounded like the fast engine of the car Charles proudly drove everywhere possible. I had always loved these tiny, swift birds.

Someone once told me how during times of migration these

brilliant winged creatures lodge themselves behind the wings of their bigger cousins, geese especially, and ride to warmer climates. I so wanted the bird to talk to me and tell me if this was true and I so wished that I could roll out the window and lift myself through the clouds and into a place of sweet happiness that I was sure they must live in night and day. The bird fluttered away before I could even get out of bed and I knew then I must hurry. Margaret was scheduled to arrive after church, which I had conveniently begged off of for weeks now, due to my prolonged recovery.

I decided to dress in all black, for I was surely a woman bathed and living in grief. My hands trembled as I fastened the thirty-eight buttons of my dress, struggled to hook the edges of my petticoats and skirt, and lacing up my boots was an exercise in utter patience. I dared not put even a dab of red on my lips. When Margaret came into the house, for she never did knock, I was breathless from dressing and from anticipation.

"Hello, Julia," she said, and I was happy to see her also dressed in black and curiously almost as glad to see her.

"I'm ready."

"One is never really ready, Julia, but we must go. The driver is waiting."

We rode in utter silence save for the clop, clop, clop of the horses' feet on the brick roadway. It was a glorious spring day, the sun was blazing, and the world had turned from gray to green during the past month. We went for miles and miles and suddenly a patch of green grass opened up into a larger field and I realized we were at the Park Lawn Cemetery. Margaret let the horses continue and then yelled out, "Halt," when we approached a large white statue that must have been of some saint or angel I did not recognize. The carriage stopped and she told me to get out, and we lifted up our heavy skirts and touched the ground and I knew to follow her, silently, of course.

We weaved our way through grave marker after grave marker and then Margaret started to slow her walk and I felt as if someone had set an entire cooking stove on top of my chest. I wanted to run and escape, yet I kept moving forward, one foot and then another, until she stopped, pushed my arm, and then pointed to a row of tiny white markers.

There were five snow-white marble markers, barely a foot high and wide, all in a row. Every single one of them said Baby Briton. I turned to her, absolutely incredulous and unable to speak.

"The first two are mine. One was a boy. One was a girl. The third and last baby I had was Charles."

There was a long pause and while she said, "The other three are yours," I was already on the ground, lying with my face in the grass, my arms spread to touch all three of the markers, not realizing that the sobs piercing the air were my own.

I have no idea how long I lay there and it does not matter because now I knew where to go. Now I knew where my babies were buried. Now I could come and talk to them and tell them stories and trim the grass around the edges of their markers and sing them all the songs I had memorized just for them. Baby Briton one, two, and three were not just markers to me, but living signs of love, if only for a moment, that had been inside of me and that would live within my heart forever.

My sorrow, the depth of my loss, the sight of those markers was seeping inside of me and into a place that only a mother who has suffered such a tragedy can understand, and it was only the muffled sound of Margaret sobbing that brought me to my feet. I pulled myself up from the grass, taking care to grab a handful and stuff it into my pocket, and then moved back to stand next to Margaret, who was struggling to compose herself.

I was beginning to realize that life can be painful and absolutely remarkable at the same time. I had lost three precious souls and yet I now knew where my babies were. Then, in the next second, when Margaret slipped her hand inside of mine and pulled it tight against her chest, next to her heart, I realized too that love and acceptance do not always meet at the same moment.

Margaret held my hand until we stepped back into the carriage and from that moment on, she was not just my mother-in-law, but also my friend.

The Namesake Kelly Girl
Spins Back in Time

It took me three seconds to decide that I was never going to have sex, fall in love, acquire a mother-in-law, date, or talk back to my own mother again. I never kept one of those promises, but at the time, it seemed like all of those things were perfectly reasonable life options. When the tape clicked off and I dried my eyes, I tiptoed over to the bedroom window and looked out to make certain Julia was still bird watching.

She had fallen asleep in the chair with her head tipped to one side, the binoculars dangling from her hand, the bird book lying just out of arm's reach at her feet. It looked as if she were the most helpless, fragile woman in the world and that none of the brave and daring adventures she had already undertaken could have actually happened. Then it struck me that perhaps she had not fallen asleep, but died, right there, while I was snooping through her drawers and listening to something she obviously was not ready to share with me.

I quickly put the recorder back in the box and ran downstairs so fast that she nearly fell off the chair when I bounced down the steps and landed at her feet.

"Dear girl, what is wrong?"

"I just wanted to make sure you are okay, that something hadn't happened."

"Oh my! Don't worry about that, Kelly. Once you get past eighty you will need a nap now and then too. I'm still healthy as a big old horse and there's some miles left in me, some things I still have to do."

"But you've already done so much, Grandma. What could be left?"

She was quiet for a moment and then asked me to get her a glass of water, but before I could turn to get it, she grabbed my arm to stop me. Something remarkable happened to me then. It was as if the whole world had stopped and Julia and I were the only two in it. I had the same strange but lovely feeling I had that day on the porch years before when I had been able to see what she looked like as a young woman. This time I saw her lying on the grass at the cemetery, the first time she visited the graves of her lost babies, and there was no way I could stop the tears that started to cascade down my face.

"You are having a tough summer, Kelly. Do you want to talk some more?"

I nodded, she smiled at me, and when I came back with her drink, she asked if we could walk down by the river and sit on the bench that was so close to the water you could dangle your feet in it when the tide was in.

I would never know or get a chance to ask her if she knew I had discovered her secret taping project, but she was so perceptive it's possible she could see right through me. The changing tides of life would come fast and furious after this day, which they always do, but when you are fifteen, life seems endless.

"You know that no one ever really knows a person," she began, startling me with a very real truth. "Even in our most intimate relationships there are things we don't share, personal things that we all need to hold on to in order to keep breathing. Does that make sense to you?"

"Yes. Sometimes it's just not the best thing to say something out loud."

"Sometimes too, Kelly, it takes a lifetime to know what to hold on to and what to share and give away, and sometimes when you love someone, like I love you, you will do anything, share anything, say anything to make someone feel better."

I swallowed and let my feet dip into the water before I turned to look at her. I had no idea what I wanted to hear from her, and I was surely not yet emotionally mature enough to ask her about the tapes or her own locked-away emotional treasures of the heart. Beyond the sadness of all that loss she had experienced I was also wondering about my real lineage. Had she adopted a baby, my own grandmother, if the doctor told her she may never have another child? How had she really gotten from the poor side of town to the rich side? I couldn't remember if she had even told me how she had met the man, Charles Briton, who I presumed had been my great-grandfather because she had always been so focused on discussing just one year. My own family life was in total disarray, and I wanted desperately to know that something was secure.

"Can you tell me more about the time before your year started? You never say much about that. It was a long time ago, but I know you were fifteen once, too."

As if on cue, a snowy egret waltzed in front of us, bobbing its head up and down, cautiously putting one foot in front of the other. I knew that Julia had a special connection to this bird, and it wouldn't have surprised me if she had a secret way of communicating with it as well. The stately white bird with its long black beak, matching dark eyes, and strands of beautiful, soft feathers always looked like a moving work of art to me as well. The bird stopped in front of us and remained there the entire time Julia talked to me, opening up some of her sacred treasures as she shared even more of her life.

And for those few hours, I was transported back to Dorchester while she shared what it was like during the few remaining years of her almost carefree days as a young girl, her gigantic leap into a new world, and the moment she fell in love. And even though I was naive, selfish, and confused, I remember thinking the entire time she talked not only how different our lives had been, but about how she had only been three years older than me when she knew who she was going to marry.

There was a swirl of years, mostly wild hugs good-bye from the brothers who left, her sister who found the man who would kiss her lips for the rest of her terribly sad life, and Julia growing faster than her mother's arthritic hands could sew the dresses needed to fit her. Her mother's world was narrowing, and Julia's was growing larger. She was allowed to stay in school because her brothers were sending home money, her sister had married, and there was finally only one extra mouth to feed and care for. One day her mother dared to whisper the word "college" and showed Julia stories from the magazines her father brought her.

"Look," Julia's mother said, smoothing out the pages of *The Brown*

Book of Boston on the kitchen table, "these women who write in this magazine have been to college. Katherine La Farge Norton, Rachel Emerson, Clara Atwood. Do you think it would be hard? Would it cost a lot of money to go to college?"

At first, Julia recalled thinking that her mother wanted to go to college, and she could not respond. Had this been a long held dream? Her mother loved to read, and when her father returned from his nightly walks, he would always leave her a magazine, a book, or a newspaper on the table as a sign of love, and perhaps, apology as well. Her mother laughed when Julia asked her if she wanted to go to college. Julia may as well have been asking her if she thought men would one day land on the moon. She pointed at Julia and said, "You, Julia, are my hope for everything." The Britons had never discussed college or what Julia would do in the next year when her studies would end. Julia was an average student and she told me that her circle of life was so limited that she assumed she would simply take a position, perhaps in the very office of the ironworks where two of her brothers had worked. College had never been something my great-grandmother thought possible. Then something remarkable happened.

Julia's mother brazenly wrote a letter to the Richards Publishing Company on Broad Street in downtown Boston addressed to "All of the Women Writers" and asked how her daughter, "A brilliant young scholar," might learn about magazine writing for the Brown Book before entering college. Julia was, of course, absolutely embarrassed, as any seventeen-year-old might be to learn of this, but her mother had a plan. She wanted Julia to work at the magazine, learn what she could, enroll in college, and "be someone." What she did was so astounding to Julia that she couldn't say no when the magazine's secretary wrote back and offered her a simple filing job upon graduation. Julia's mother kept the letter they sent her next to her bed until the day she died, and her stunning plan might have worked.

The very first day of work something so amazing happened to Julia that she maintained for the rest of her life it was some kind of magical event that opened the door to her remarkable year. She was absolutely trembling when she stepped from the streetcar and started looking around for the publishing office. Julia told me she must have looked as frightened as she felt because suddenly a man approached and asked if she needed help. This was not just any man—it was William Randolph Hearst, the great newspaperman. Julia knew who he was because her father had given her mother a copy of the newspaper he had just started in Boston called, The American, and she recognized him immediately.

"Excuse me, miss, but can I help you find your way? You look as if you need a bit of assistance."

Mr. Hearst was a very handsome man, even at the age of forty-one, and Julia blushed when she told me this part of her life story. His dark hair was parted in the middle, his eyes were very beautiful, and he was wearing a suit that was made of the finest wool. It would be safe to say Julia Briton of Victoria Street had never met or seen anyone like him before. She boldly looked right into his eyes, and he smiled.

"Yes, I could use a little assistance," Julia admitted, quickly looking down. "I'm to start work today at Richards Publishing and I fear I am not certain where to go."

He laughed then, which she found terribly disarming. "Ah! A writer I assume. I know the publishing company well. It will be a good start. Allow me to introduce myself and walk you to the door. I am William Hearst, and if things don't work out, you must come see me, Miss...?"

"Julia..." she stammered. "Julia Kelly." Julia didn't falter when she remembered these precise conversations, and who wouldn't remember something so absolutely amazing?

He looked her right in the eye again, directed her with his hand, walked her to the front door, and then handed her his business card. "Please feel free to call on me if you need anything. I suspect a woman with your beauty who has landed a job at such an age will do just fine, but I would always be glad to assist."

He tipped his hat and then left Julia standing breathless, almost unable to move, and wondering if every day would be this exciting. She put his card in her purse, slipped it inside a wooden cigar keepsake box when she arrived home, and pulled it out occasionally year after year to remember how her life started accelerating from that day forward.

After that, Julia could have followed the plan sweet Grace MacGowan Cook worked out for her when she sat behind her in the oak-paneled publishing office, sharpened her pencils, and watched her compose the short story, "The Troubles of the Tollivers," for the magazine. Grace was a proud Wellesley College graduate and she thought with a bit of *guidance, tutoring, and her financial donations, Julia might get a place-ment at her alma mater. "Thank goodness Grace never told my mother about this," Julia shared with a rather large sigh. "She was beyond thrilled that I was even in the same room as the men and women whose names she saw in the magazine, and for the brief period of time I worked there that was enough, even though her plan was close to perfect."*

And the plan might have worked. Julia took to the magazine and writing world as if she had been thinking about it her entire life. She read and listened and read some more. Grace took Julia to tea and slowly showed her a glimpse of a world beyond her own that she said often left her mesmerized, eager, and absolutely stunned. Grace called Julia her mouse because she was so quiet, mostly terrified, she would tell Grace and finally me, years later. But before she could get her bear-ings, before she could realize what she might have had and who she might have been, she decided to walk outside one afternoon, a mere three months after the day she met Mr. Hearst, instead of eating the cold meat sandwich her mother had packed for her.

It was a Tuesday afternoon in the summer of 1901. My great-grandmother was wearing an ankle-length brown skirt, a white blouse buttoned to the throat with sleeves that were long enough to cover her wrists, simple brown shoes that were worn so thin she said she could feel the early summer heat rising into her toes, and her hair was combed back fashionably high and swept off her face. She stopped for a moment before sitting on a bench because a cardinal was singing in the pine tree in front of the office, and Julia was desperate to see the beautiful bird's red feathers.

That is where Charles Britton saw her the first time. He stepped from his carriage, lifted his head, and looked directly at Julia as if they had planned on meeting. "The second this happened my stomach rose past my heart, I stopped breathing, and in an instant I fell in love," she recalled as if this had all just happened an hour ago.

When she told me about meeting Charles for the first time, I knew I wanted the same kind of magic that she felt, the same rush of warmness that surged through her body, the same kind of dashing man to look me in the eye and smile. But as her story unfolded and she shared what her life was really like after that meeting, I wasn't so sure love at first sight was the best thing in the world. I kept reminding myself that I was never going to fall in love and have sex. Julia recounted the next chapter of her life in a much quieter voice, and for good reason. This phase of her life was stunning, but it still pales in comparison to what happened during "The Year." However, there was an exhausting few years to go through first, and as a child of the '60's, I found this part of her life story unforgettable, confusing, and sad. Times, and the definitions of love and romance, have definitely changed.

Julia told me that once when she was sixteen she had walked around the block with Harry Chamberlin. He was a year older and he lived across the street from her. And until the day he asked her father if they could take a short walk, she hadn't really thought much about the possibility of love, romance, or courtship. Harry was, as she put it so simply, "a gangly young man who had yet to grow into his feet or learn how to properly shave his five whiskers and wash in all areas of the body." How or why he had become smitten with Julia Briton, the neighbor girl, was beyond her back then. Julia admitted that she was a slow bloomer in the romance department, quickly mentioning that probably happened because her family had babied her. And because she thought it more interesting to read or daydream about heading west to discover her own gold. She also dreamed about doing something brave and satisfying like Clara Barton, who had become her heroine and the inspiration for almost every movement in her then terribly small life.

Clara's special place in her life was a gift from her oldest brother, John. One day, three years prior to her walk with young Harry, John strolled into the kitchen, rocked back and forth from toe to heel with his arms behind his back, and said, "I have something very special for you, little sister." Julia was hoping for ribbons, a new magazine, or something sweet, but he leaned forward and handed her a letter.

"Open it."

"What could it possibly be, John?"

"I had the most remarkable opportunity today. The Red Cross came to the ironworks to seek pledges and Clara Barton talked to me."

"No!" Her pulse was racing to even imagine such a thing. "Miss Barton!" Julia screamed like I did the first time I heard Fleetwood Mac.

What Julia remembered clearly about her heroine was not that she was decorated and lauded by foreign countries, or that she had worked in slums, saved hundred of lives, and had indeed convinced President

Chester Arthur that the Red Cross could help people all of the time and not just during a war. She was bedazzled by the fact that once, while working near the front lines during the Civil War, a bullet had ripped through Barton's dress without so much as leaving a mark on her skin. The bullet had killed the man she was nursing. Julia grabbed the note from John, held it in her hands, and slowly read it out loud, savoring every word.

> Dear Miss Kelly,
> Never fear danger, and if someone tells you that you must do something because that is the way it has always been done, please, turn away and follow your heart.
> Sincerely,
> Clara Barton
> American Red Cross

It is entirely possible that, while poor Harry Chamberlin was trying to figure out how to touch her hand, my own heroine, Julia, was trying to figure out what her father would say if she ran off to help with a disaster in Spain, Turkey, or even around the corner. On Victoria Street, something as simple as a letter from a famous person was apparently not just exciting; it was everything. Julia said life was most often a routine and nothing more. They worked, ate, slept, went to church, and then started all over again. The letter was paraded around the neighborhood for weeks as if it were a huge diamond ring. It was her letter, but it quickly became the golden egg that everyone wanted to touch and feel. It gave her hardworking brother, who already limped from a serious accident at the ironworks, a brief moment of notoriety that he talked about until the day he died.

Clara Barton and William Jennings Bryant? I had only thought of them as ancient and important historical figures until Julia shared this part of her life with me. I had never thought of her this way, even though her stories of The Year were riddled with the names of other famous people. Somehow this new information was better. As Julia continued talking, I could not take my eyes off of her.

So it was Clara and the innocent daydreamings of a young girl that captured young Julia and not the sweaty hand of a boy. It wasn't the quick *glances from men and other boys on the street or at church or when she accompanied her mother downtown when her mother dropped off her sewing. Even though Julia still looked at herself in her sister's mirror, she didn't see what other people saw. The day that Charles spotted her, she had no idea that she was beautiful. She had never kissed a boy or man, been on so much as a date or another walk, and even if she may have occasionally wondered about marriage and falling in love, it was not yet something that she bothered to focus on. Three of her school friends already had serious marriage proposals and were too besotted to speak with her. Her sister had all but disappeared into the arms of a relationship that quickly turned cruel and devastating. Julia's sister's first blush of love cascaded into the unfortunate common reality of the working class. Her husband was a drinker and had inherited his father's, and his grandfather's, horrific temper. Her beloved sister quietly disappeared, and Julia was left with Clara and the uncertainty of her new life in the publishing industry.*

Then Charles appeared.

People speak of love at first sight all of the time and Julia told me that it's absolutely possible and true. When Charles lifted his head and looked at her, time froze, she was certain that her heart stopped beating, and every other thought, sight, and sound disappeared. She remembered vividly that Charles was dressed in a crisp white high-collared shirt, black tie, and gray pin-stripped suit with tails. His blond hair was parted on the side and a thin, well-trimmed moustache followed the line of his perfect lips. He carried a soft, felt, gray Homburg hat in his right hand and a walking cane in his left. They were perhaps twenty-five feet apart, but his sky-blue eyes seemed as bright and close to her as if they were standing face to face. When he smiled at her, she closed her eyes and quickly became dizzy and thought she might faint. Charles ran to grab her by the waist before she could fall.

"Hold on, Miss," he said, sweeping her back to her feet and holding her steady. When she opened her eyes, his face was so close to hers that she could smell his sweet breath, see the perfect lines in his face, and his white teeth made even Mr. Hearst seem unattractive. The man holding her in his arms was absolutely stunning.

Julia recounted that she could not speak but simply stared at him and he did not move. Finally, she heard a man clear his throat. Charles

39

kept smiling at her, brought her to her feet, and said, "Allow me to introduce myself. Charles Briton, at your service!" Then he laughed, took a step back, and nodded to the driver who had cleared his throat.

She took in a breath, composed herself, and managed a small nod of the head, and then what came out of her mouth next was as much a surprise to her, she said with a bold laugh, as it must have been to Charles.

"Well, Mr. Briton, you may have to accompany me everywhere for the rest of my life just in case I need a steady hand."

He laughed again. A long, hearty, forcefully sincere laugh that made him tip back his head, so the sound bounced off the buildings and swirled around them. "And who might I be accompanying?"

"Julia Kelly, Mr. Charles. A very grateful Julia, I might add."

The driver cleared his throat again. Charles did not respond or bother to give the man so much as a sideways glance. Instead, he dipped his hand into his pocket, pulled out his calling card, handed it to Julia, and said, "Please call if you need assistance. It has been a pleasure to catch you today!"

Then he did something that she said she would never forget. He waved on his driver, took her ungloved hand in his, kissed it, and when the driver had turned away, he bent in to whisper, "You are beautiful, my sweet Julia, and I shall see you again. You can count on it."

Julia trembled for the remainder of the day. She dropped an inkwell, threw away the wrong manuscript, and tripped while walking up the steps. She thought she might faint again and rested her head on her desk until the copyboy came by to shake her and ask if she had died. Julia Kelly had died. The old Julia Kelly no longer existed. She had evaporated on the sidewalk, and a new Julia had been born. The new Julia's heart beat faster, her skin felt as if it had been miraculously replaced with a kind of hot fabric that burned ever so lightly, her knees were wobbly, her eyes took on a dreamy, faraway look, and her appetite for anything besides water, and the chocolates that were about to appear almost daily, vanished. The world and everything and everyone in it suddenly became new, fresh, alive, and so very exciting.

How Charles found her the next day is a well-kept secret of the rich, she said, but he did find her and the world quickly became a much bigger blur. And even though she was in love, which leaves one without much control, she quickly lost command of almost everything. Charles

Arthur Briton was twenty-nine years old when they met and Julia was eighteen. She discovered that he was not just a well-dressed man passing on the sidewalk, but heir to the Briton Manufacturing Company, where he served as vice president and supervised dozens of millinery shops throughout Boston as part of his prestigious position. The millinery trade, the design and manufacture of hats, was a huge industry and, as she was about to discover, his world of hats was about to change her world and eventually ricochet down into mine, in so many, many ways.

It wasn't just the millinery trade that made the Britons one of the elite families in Boston either. They were well-educated, had inherited land and money, and were enjoying a surge in income from their myriad businesses and from a country that would not see federal income taxes again until 1913. Julia would never learn about the source of all the wealth, and it really never did matter to her, but the differences in their backgrounds was monumental. Her father earned $250 a year as a brick mason, they did not have a bathtub, she had never been to a doctor, ridden in a car, or owned more than two dresses and three skirts. Her life was simply plotted out within a six-block radius of their rented four-room house.

Charles lived on the other side of town in up-and-coming Brookline with his parents. Streets, houses, the back bay of the Charles River, and railroad tracks separated their familial homes, but they could have lived continents apart for all of the differences. On the other side of the tracks there were servants, more than one indoor bathroom, a stable, a garage for one of the first cars ever to parade through the streets of Boston, a kitchen the size of Julia's entire house, food she had never before seen or eaten—"roast duck and cream of mushroom soup, for heaven's sake," to mention but a few—and a life that she was going to be molded to fit inside of, no matter the cost.

Charles had fallen in love too, and after years of dutifully following orders from his father, George, and mother, Margaret, their only child was determined to marry Julia, no matter what his love might cost him or, as it turns out, his new wife. It would be years before Julia learned what a steep price he paid for his determination. His parents were beyond aghast when they discovered the woman he loved was nothing more than a beautiful working-class girl whose mother had taught her

41

father to read. In their minds, Julia was beneath them, and they often had a hard time remembering Julia was their daughter-in-law and not an extra maid who dared to sit down and join them for dinner.

It was hard for me to understand what Julia revealed to me next, but there was nothing but truth in what she told me. It was a much different time. She always said, "You must remember what even you might do for love." It was also, in a strange and interesting way, preparing her for her incredible year, a year that she never could have foreseen when she was blinded by love and those blue eyes that became all things to her.

During the following year, Julia was tutored daily in the ways of the wealthy. She and Charles were not yet engaged. That would happen six months in after she had proven herself, to his mother especially, with her new manners, dress, and style of speaking. Julia always told me that she imagined if her mother-in-law had known that her well-planned-out social and educational program would send her own life spiraling in embarrassment, Margaret would have done something, anything, to prohibit Charles from marrying her. Eight years later, when Julia first read condensed news reports about George Bernard Shaw's newest play, Pygmalion, debuting in England, she said she was certain someone had written to him about her and her life. Eliza Doolittle and Professor Harry Higgins were literary characters acting out a portion of her life, or so she thought, and she would have given anything to see an early performance of this play.

Once Julia agreed to the plan Charles and Margaret had devised and her father and mother had nodded their consent, everything changed. She immediately resigned from her position at Richards Publishing and began an arduous series of physical, social, and mental transformations. There were dress fittings, her hair was straightened, there were trips with Margaret to the fashionable shops, tea houses, and restaurants, lessons on everything from flower arranging to how to organize an elaborate dinner party. The most wonderful part of it all for Julia was unlimited access to books, newspapers, and magazines.

Margaret and Charles insisted that Julia spend her afternoons in Margaret's sitting area, learning about the world beyond Dorchester, and that became the rudder for the launch of her life beyond even Boston. The world opened up to her during those afternoons when she discovered that the very fabric of her isolated life, and the lives of her family—the old one and the new one—was moving forward at a very rapid pace. *There were labor movements, women's movements, concerns about the welfare of poor children and numerous other causes that women of a certain economic and social level were initiating, and it all felt magical and surreal until she stepped inside of it all herself. But first Julia had to pass inspection, which she did with flying colors, and there was a diamond ring on her left hand and a wedding date. There were also the stunned looks of her friends and of every single man, woman, and child on Victoria Street who watched Miss Julia Kelly become the first person not just in the neighborhood, but in most of Boston, to be dropped off in front of her shabby house by a motor car with a uniformed driver.*

The wedding was grand and elaborate. However, the event itself remained a blur to Julia in spite of the photographs and letters and the huge article in The Boston Globe the week following the wedding that she said were buried somewhere in the library. I eventually found the article and agreed that she looked a bit off center. Her eyes were staring to the left of the photographer, her smile frozen in place, a pearl-beaded wedding gown draped around her then-small frame that must have weighed half as much as she did. And there was dapper Charles in a top hat, tails, and standing tall next to her with a look of utter joy on his face.

How could any of them have known that in less than a handful of years she would have disappeared from his arm, from the life that had been so carefully designed for her, from everything that she was embracing with a mix of expectant confusion and happiness on her wedding day? She did tell me that she remembered walking down the marble steps of the Christ Church in the North End, the very same church where a lantern was hung to alert Paul Revere that the British were coming. Then she disappeared into the waiting and elaborately decorated carriage that would take her to their honeymoon cottage.

The real blur, she admitted, began after that as days and months and then years disappeared like drops of water in the backyard pond of the house Charles had built for them. All of those times became all but lost inside of her, almost as lost as she said she became in her new world and her life as a socialite wife and a would-be mother. She told me the details of those years would slip out and remind her during The Year, the most important year, of who she had become and who she was truly becoming, and of everything and everyone she had left behind.

When Julia finally finished, I wasn't sure at first if her revelations had helped me or hurt me. She must have been able to tell that I was confused by the stunned look on my face and my inability to speak.

"It's a lot to find out, I know," she finally said, patting my leg as the faithful egret flew away. "It's not that what I have just shared was a secret, sweetheart. It's just that now was the time to tell you."

When I found my voice, I made it clear that it would take a while for it all to settle in. "It's just a lot and I know times were different, but it sounds like a movie or something. You were one person, you had one kind of life, and you were molded to fit inside of another."

Julia was quiet for a moment. I suppose she was trying to think of something perfect that would reassure me. "Just take your time. Think about it. I can guarantee that it was all real and it all had meaning and its place in my life. In the long run, the most important thing was The Year. Think of that if it's easier."

I wish now that I had understood more, because something unforeseeable was about to happen that would forever change everything for me, and especially for Julia. But first I was able to listen to several more of the tapes where Julia transported me, yet again, to a world and a time that temporarily replaced a part of my year with a part of hers.

Tape Three

The Doctor's Prescription Changes Everything
Boston—May 29, 1904

It is hard to fathom how a month could have disappeared so quickly. Four weeks evaporated, but the ache that seemed to have permanently wedged itself around my heart did not. Many things changed after the day Margaret took my hand in the cemetery and many things did not. But what this month taught me more than anything is that life can bring unexpected changes, challenges, and choices and not all of those things are necessarily bad or good. I also knew that the innocent young woman who had been swept off her feet by a pair of dazzling blue eyes, and the sweet scents and sighs of love, was ever so slowly disappearing. A new woman, one who may have only been a fraction of an inch more certain, was beginning to appear, and as uncomfortable as that may have been, there was no choice in the matter. I had already made all my life choices, or so I thought, and I must now learn how to survive.

Margaret did not immediately allow me to call her Maggie. We did not giggle on the porch, sneak glasses of whiskey when the men were out, or flip through the magazines to look at the latest fashions during the afternoon when the rest of the world was working all around us. Sometime in the middle of my day, I would stop and try to imagine what I might be doing if I still worked at the publishing company or married someone like the boy across the street. Those images or dreams, if you will, were almost as hard to grasp as the one that had become a reality. My old world and my new world seemed to get further and further apart every day. Although Margaret and I were not yet friends in the sense that women can share and laugh and talk with one another, we had grown closer by our shared tragedies, tragedies that were so very common among almost all married women. The infant mortality rate remained staggering, and most women still gave birth at home. I was smart enough to realize Dr. Langdon had been hinting about birth control, but not smart enough to figure out how to do it, where to get it, or what it might even be. Surprisingly, it would be Margaret, who was very, very slowly inching her way into a real friendship with me, who would eventually show me where and how to find anything and everything I wanted.

Charles reappeared three days after my first visit to the cemetery and our first conversation was tentative and almost frightening. He had sent a note advising me when to expect him and included a sweet declaration of his concern and love. The day he came home, I decided to dress and have the house clean and a meal cooking. I paced in the front hall most of the late afternoon, waiting for his arrival, and when I heard his car drive up, I felt the same rush of expectant emotion that I had experienced during the first year of our marriage. My heart raced, my stomach turned in circles, and I felt a flush move over me as if a fever had decided to dance slowly through my body.

Our reunion was sweet and more wonderful than I expected. He dropped his bag and hat by the door, rushed into my arms, and kissed me for a very long time.

"You are looking well, sweet Julia!"

"Oh! I've missed you Charles! Why did you go away?"

"It was business, and Margaret told me that I must leave you alone, that you needed time all by yourself."

"But what I needed was you, Charles!"

He hesitated and then pulled away from me. "What could I have done? You were ill, we lost another baby, and my mother said this was for the best."

I was torn. One part of me wanted to lash out and tell him he was in charge of me and my life, our lives, and not his mother, but I was unsure and did not want to do anything to push him away, so I lied.

"I understand, Charles. Everything is fine now."

"Not really," he said, stiffening a bit. "Not at all."

And suddenly, our brief reconciliation was over. It was impossible for me to talk about the unspoken physical aspects of our life and apparently impossible for him as well. When I closed my eyes and pulled him close, so desperately wanting things to be the way they had been, it was as if I could feel an invisible wall come between us. Part of Charles of the Heart was in hiding and would remain there for longer than I could imagine. But even though I was not a mother, in the sense that there were living children to tend to and raise, a mother's instinct as fierce and grand as a howling winter wind was beginning to take hold. That very night I took one, of what would be many, bold steps to protect what was mine.

Charles busied himself the remainder of the day with paperwork in his small office off the living room and following dinner, he went to sit on the front porch and smoke a cigar. He had been very quiet, as had I, and when I could see that he was close to being finished, I quickly ran up the stairs and busied myself in the bedroom. I had no idea if he would come up to the bedroom or wander through the house or perhaps sleep on the long, hard, horsehair sofa in the living room. I was aching to lie in his arms, to feel his breath roll over me, and I was determined to make that happen. I waited and waited and when a good hour had passed and he did not appear, I opened the door and called for him. It took a while, but soon I heard him walking up the steps, and he appeared in the bedroom, just as I had hoped and planned.

"Is everything okay, Julia?" he asked, pushing through the door in half darkness.

"It will be soon," I said, lifting myself up from the under the covers where I had been waiting.

He looked at me as if he had never seen me before. Then he turned his head to see that I had lit all of the candles, closed the drapes, and was beckoning for him to join me.

"But... Julia, the doctor..." he stammered and then stumbled as he moved forward.

"Come hold me, Charles of the Heart," I said softly. "Please."

Needless to say, my bold plan was a resounding success and during the next few days, we managed to recapture bits and pieces of our marriage. Charles was whistling in the morning and left with instructions for me to "Walk, walk, and walk some more." We had not yet seriously addressed the loss of the last baby, or the others for that matter, but I felt confident that would come and I pushed aside any bad thoughts or notions that my life would get any harder, that a miracle might not happen, that we would never have the child we both desired.

A steady and fairly happy routine then began. Margaret would come by and drop off books and magazines, which were starting to overtake the shelves in the sitting room, and chat with me a bit about household questions and duties. She also promised me that my girls, Ella and Ruby, would stay on indefinitely. We danced around serious topics, such as sex and what might happen if what the doctor said was true and I could never have a child, and how I might fill hour after hour, day after day, year after year of my time. I was glad for a time to simply be able to walk and be alone and to lose myself in a world that I had never really had a chance to explore.

Margaret, of course, instructed me in what to wear on my walks, lest someone in her circle of friends passed by and see Mrs. Julia Briton out strolling unaccompanied and dressed like a young woman from Dorchester and not Brookline. Fashion had only become important to me when I married, and funds for the dresses, hats, skirts, and shoes that were popular were readily available to me. I must say the prospects of new dresses prior to each season had become a regular and welcome habit. And even though I was instructed to wear a dark walking skirt, a soft white cotton jacket, a small, non-ornamental hat to block the sun and strangers' eyes, and to carry an umbrella to further block the sun, it only mattered that I could be outside and alone.

It was terribly exciting for me to step outside, close the door behind me, and know that I could walk for as long and as far as I wanted without restrictions and sets of watchful eyes. My trips started out small. I was not certain of my strength, and to be honest, my monthly period had not yet returned, and I was far from back to my old self. My body seemed to be in a confused state of hibernation, and I was certain the doctor was hoping brisk walks would help everything move back into place. I was counting on it like I had never counted on anything before in my life, and I took to walking with such vibrancy that my daily routine can only be described as passionate. One day I would turn left outside of the house and explore the blossoming neighborhoods that were beginning to fill up the long, winding streets in Brookline. The next day I would head right, toward the heart of Boston, its business and shipping center, and where a world existed that seemed to grow larger and more exciting with each walk.

I walked every day and quickly began to see it as my job. Didn't the doctor order me to walk and didn't both Charles and Margaret think it was a good idea? Ella and Ruby were running the household and were also more than servants to me, which was perhaps a gift almost as great as the walking. I trusted them and they trusted me, and I was beginning to realize how important it was to build a family that was above and beyond the people who shared your last name.

Ella and Ruby were my confidants, and while I loved and cherished Charles and was beginning to love and appreciate the role Margaret played in my life, these two women were the ropes that held me in place. I would walk for hours and hours while Charles was gone to work, doing who knows what, and when I would arrive back home, dusty and full of stories, they were the ones who listened with eager anticipation and encouraged me to do more because I could do things they could not. Sometimes our conversations about my walking adventures could not even last until I had removed my mud-stained shoes. They would be waiting for me and all but run down the walkway to greet me as I limped onto the front porch and fell into their arms.

"Tell us," one of them would beg as they helped me up the steps. "What did you see today? Who did you see today? What happened?"

There was always something to tell. The world was changing so fast. There were more and more cars every day. Women's hats were all the rage and seriously extravagant, which Charles must have loved as it was the heart of his business. I know for certain that the terribly popular baseball player, Cy Young, winked at me one day. He had recently thrown the very first ever perfect game of baseball while pitching for the Boston Americans and he was walking past me and about to get in a carriage. He stopped, tipped his hat, and blew me a kiss.

"No!" Ruby giggled with delight as she helped me unlace my shoes one late afternoon. "How do you know it was him?

"Photographers were everywhere and who doesn't know him? He was big, his barrel chest seemed as if it were half full of rainwater, yet his smile was dazzling. There were young boys all around him and he was wearing his team shirt. I was near a school and he must have been there for a special program."

That was not necessarily the best thing to tell the star-struck girls as they ran to the sitting room, riffled through the newspapers, most of which I was woefully behind in reading because of my obsessive walking, and they quickly found his picture and brought it to me.

"Him? It was him?"

I nodded and laughed as they ignored my muddy feet and me and then dropped to the floor to examine the newspaper and the story about his accomplishments. And so it went. I told them about new buildings and how I kept seeing more and more women out and about unescorted, which was very exciting because not so long ago it was considered improper for a woman, especially one that wasn't married, to be out alone. I also shared with them how the streets were some-times congested with carriages, horses, carts, and bicycles going so fast that there were often accidents. The closer I got to the heart of the city, the more intense and exciting everything appeared. It seemed as if every day I went a bit further and every day something more wonderful and interesting happened. Ruby started to pack me a small lunch, some cheese, an apple, a leftover roll from the night before, that I tucked into my small handbag so I could stop, eat, and then rest before going on or returning home.

I often stopped at a lovely park off of Beacon Street that I had seen numerous times while passing in a carriage. There were only a hand-ful of benches, but further back, perhaps two blocks into the park, there was a very sheltered and lovely pond. It was surrounded by thick bushes and beautiful oak trees, each one bigger than the next, that fanned out from the pond and made a kind of canopy that made me feel as if I was safe and sheltered. I never saw another person back there and I claimed the spot as my own. Some days I would simply walk to this park and spend hours thinking and observing life around the pond. I also did something very special here that I did not share with the girls at home, Charles, or Margaret, or even my own mother. I named each one of my babies.

I know that my walking was not just a way to gain physical strength, but mental strength as well, and I could not get over the fact that the little babies had not just been taken away from me by God—if such a being existed—but also by Margaret and Charles. It did not seem fair to not let me have a say in any of this. I had things I wanted to tell them, feelings that needed sorting through, and a ride through the caverns of grief that I must do by myself. The girls I named Sarah and Catherine and the little boy, who surely must also be an angel and with his sisters, I named Gabriel. And I especially loved talking to them by the pond, which I called Heart's Haven because this is where my heart really did begin to heal.

I surely was not crazy to do this, I thought it a natural thing to want to unburden my heart this way and it was making me feel better. There were rabbits racing through the bushes and squirrels flinging themselves from one tree to the next. Once I thought I saw the white flash of a deer's tail on the far side of the pond, and the trees were littered with birds' nests, which particularly interested me. It was as if I were sitting in a little piece of heaven myself, and I like to think the babies were with me, their spirits rising and falling on the wings of all the beautiful birds.

The birds and how they could lift their wings and fly absolutely fascinated me. I had the sweet memory of my father's love for birds and also the inexplicable appearance of those birds outside my bedroom, which I was starting to think was some kind of sign that pointed me toward Heart's Haven. And Charles had come home one night thrilled to tell me that he had spoken to Orville Wright, a young man from Ohio, who claimed to have built and flown a flying machine with his brother down the shore in North Carolina. He said Mr. Wright came to speak at a business meeting and shared that the future of the world was linked to the sky. Charles, to my great surprise, was very taken with this notion and kept in contact with Mr. Wright and his brother. I remembered reading about the flight from one of Margaret's old December 1903 newspapers and the entire idea made sense to me. I spent hours watching the birds resting on nothing but air, using their wings for balance, tilting, and executing turns and soft landings that made me think the flying machine business must certainly not be a hoax. Charles became obsessed with the Wrights and the notion of flying, and this would end up being a very good thing. His father did not agree with Charles on this matter, and later their falling out about this, and I suppose about me also, would be a gift to me like no other.

There were many gifts to come before that, however, and one such gift arrived at Heart's Haven on the last Sunday in May. The girls never worked on Sunday, and Charles and I had gotten in the habit of having lunch after church at his parents' house. We would then return home and spend the rest of the day reading, or in my case, working on needlepoint or cross stitch, which by the way I was horrid at and seriously disliked. But on the twenty-ninth, Charles said he needed to stay at his parents' and talk over several business matters with his father. Margaret did not feel well and excused herself. Charles sent me home in the carriage and I immediately set out on a walk to my favorite park.

It was a beautiful spring day, and I was not surprised to enter the park and discover picnickers scattered here and there and not surprised either that farther back by my favorite spot, it was quiet and peaceful as usual. I decided to unlace my shoes and slip them off my feet, unroll my stockings, and push my toes through the warm grass. Sometimes the skirts and corsets and petticoats and layers of clothing we wore made me long for the days back in Dorchester when we ran through the fields near the water without shoes, without worrying about what someone might think, without all the other restrictions that I had accepted the day I married. I was pushing my toes through the grass and smiling, because I was wondering what Margaret might think to see me with my skirt pulled up, my ankles and legs exposed in broad daylight in a public park.

I saw the first three women before they saw me and I was so shocked I did not think to lower my skirt and put on my shoes. I sat there while three women, with their skirts pulled much higher than mine, were wading into the water and searching in the trees for who knows what. A few seconds later, two men and several more women popped out of the trees so silently that I was startled. What in the world was going on?

One of the women turned suddenly and saw me. Mistaking me for part of the group, she wordlessly beckoned for me to hurry, and for some reason, I did just that. I left my shoes on the bench, dropped my skirt, and quickly tiptoed through the grass to the edge of the water where the three women were standing a few feet from shore.

"Come in," the woman whispered. "Hurry, you will miss it."

I thought it unwise to refuse and my budding curiosity was not about to let me walk away. I raised my skirts, entered the cold water, and shuffled past a few rocks until I was next to them. Then I looked up and I had to put a hand over my own mouth, while half my skirt plummeted into the water, to keep from shouting in absolute delight and amazement.

Perched in a grove of trees hanging over the pond was one of the most unusual and beautiful birds I had ever seen. It looked as if it were wearing some kind of lovely crested iridescent purple and green hat that was partially outlined in a pure white strip of soft feathers. The bird had a red breast, its tail feathers were dotted in shades of blue, red, and green, its chest was sprinkled with white specks, as if an artist had painted them just so, and its white neck and red eyes were a blazing contrast of pure color.

Something akin to joy bounced inside of me, and I might still be standing there if the woman next to me hadn't leaned in and said, "It's a wood duck, you know. We haven't seen many. Isn't it spectacular?"

I could only nod in agreement, and then I pulled her back to me and boldly asked, "Who are you people?"

The woman smiled and whispered into my ear, "We are with the Massachusetts Audubon Society, my dear, and you may want to do something with your hat before anyone else notices."

The Audubon Society? My hat?

I quickly backed out of the water, ran to my bench, and pulled my hat off my head before I bothered to lace up my shoes. I had many, many hats and this seemingly simple yellow straw hat that shaded my entire face was one of several that Charles brought home from work for me. It had a wide, pale-blue ribbon wound around its middle, and as I spun it in my hand, I quickly realized what the woman had been trying to tell me. Stuck inside of the ribbon, in a decorative pattern that I had thought lovely when Charles brought it home, were at least eight beautiful snow-white feathers.

Feathers from beautiful birds who must now surely be dead.

In a moment of pure panic, I could only think but to sit on my hat, lace up my shoes, and wait for the bird watchers to leave. When they left, I got up, held the hat against me, so that if anyone from the group remained in the park they would not see it, and I walked toward home, faster than I had ever walked in my life.

Back home, I took the hat up to my room, removed the feathers one by one, and gently laid them in the bottom of my dresser drawer under all of my undergarments. Then I stood with my hands laced against my chest in front of the bedroom window, wondering, not just about the small miracles of life that often point us in the right direction if we are open and paying even the slightest bit of attention, but also how in the world I was going to find out about the interesting Audubon people. Beyond that, what was I going to do about the growing feeling inside of me that my life of needlepoint, giggling on my bed with the girls, smiling through long, wretched dinners, and worrying about taking off my shoes in public was simply not going to be enough to sustain me?

Tape Four

A Shocking Revelation
and a Spy is Born
Boston—Through the End of June, 1904

Sometimes the answers we are looking for are so close to us it's a wonder we do not stumble over them when we are moving about the practiced seconds, minutes, and hours of our lives. I fully felt like a fool when I realized that I had been so preoccupied with my walking and strolling about the house waiting—for what I wasn't sure—that I hadn't really kept up with the world, or Boston, or anything of much importance beyond my tiny sphere of life.

Charles and I surely talked the few hours a day he was home with me, but we still had not frankly discussed my inability to produce an heir to the Briton kingdom, or really anything of serious consequence. He rarely shared anything of his business dealings with me and I had only been to his factory once, and then only to sit in the carriage outside while he slipped inside for a few moments. I knew he had leased a variety of buildings throughout the city for use as millinery shops and when he travelled it was often to buy materials and goods for his stores.

That's the way it had been and was supposed to remain, especially if one no longer lived in Dorchester, but on a lovely tree-lined street in Brookline. In my birth family, the role of the women was just as clear, but in a different way. We would tend to the house, work in the homes of the wealthy, or maybe be employed at a shop if marriage was out of the question. If we came from a family where the father had died or was ill and everyone must work to keep everyone else from starving, we would also find employment outside the home. I am ashamed to say that I never thought much about all of that after I married. I am equally as ashamed to say that I was so swept away by my good fortune, my blinding love, the dresses and food, and everything from a grand new house to servants, that I never wondered what someone like Margaret and myself might do all day—especially if there were no children to raise. One can only walk for so long, the stitchery was not working out very well, and the truth is that Ella and Ruby were running the house, Charles was directing it, and I was observing it all from the haze of loss, lingering depression, and simple ignorance and indifference.

I could not sleep the night after I had the encounter with the Audubon women in my special park. I feigned restlessness, left Charles alone in our bedroom, and made my way downstairs. Our house had electric lights, thanks to Thomas Edison who was, according to Charles, scouting around Boston with his assistant, Edwin Porter, looking for a location where he could capture movement on his motion picture camera. I had no idea what Charles was talking about, but that was my own fault, and I was about to do something about it.

The electric lights were wonderful, I have to agree it did make life easier, but there was something more wonderful to me about the oil lamps we still kept and even the candles that I refused to move from the bedroom. In a fit of compulsive cleaning, Ella had taken all the newspapers and magazines I had not yet read and set them inside of the small office at the front of the house that was for Charles. I rarely stepped into the room; it wasn't as if Charles had forbidden me to enter, but it was clearly his room, his office, his world, and his work.

It was already closing in on midnight when I walked into his office, turned to bend and light the lamp near the door, and then turned off the light switch. My husband's office smelled just like him and I could not help but smile. There was a musky, sweet odor that hung in the air, a tinge of cigar smoke, the pungent smell of leather and his favorite hair tonic. Papers were scattered about his beautiful, dark roll-top oak desk that was pushed against the far wall. For a brief moment, I thought of sitting in his chair so I could turn, like he must have, to look out the front window and onto the street. I decided instead to sit close to the door on a small loveseat. I was going to read every single thing Ella had piled up, even if it took all night.

Once I started to read, and the world leapt into the very office where I was sitting, a month could have passed without me noticing. The world, and indeed Boston, was ablaze with change and activity. I turned page after page and was quickly transported from our tree-lined street, and I lost all track of time. I was surely not naive enough to not know some of the major events that had happened during the past four months, because of conversations with the girls and Charles and also Margaret who always seemed to be well versed in what was happening everywhere. I knew there had been a horrible coal mine explosion in Pennsylvania, that Japan and Russia were battling each other, a huge fire had destroyed almost all of downtown Toronto, the Louisiana Purchase Exposition World's Fair had recently opened in St. Louis, and there were huge lines for something called an ice cream cone. I was reading very quickly and passed over many articles that had to do with events I was already familiar with. By the time I had read through the first three newspapers, it was clear to me that the world was shifting in a way that I might never have imagined just a few years ago.

It appeared as if women were literally and figuratively taking their shoes off without thought for former rules and walking throughout Boston, and everywhere else for that matter, with serious intention and carrying so many banners of change that I could barely keep track of them all. Women were out fighting for everything—the vote, better wages and working conditions, more educational opportunities, political positions, medical care, and the right to own and prosper in their own businesses. The names and causes of the women started to flood over me as I turned page after page and became familiar with who they were. Emily Greene Balch was fighting for peace and justice; Alice Stone Blackwell was carrying on her mother, Lucy Stone's, work to try and gain the vote for women; Mary Baker Eddy was holding lectures at the Massachusetts Metaphysical College that she had founded; Marie Zakrzewska was advertising for women physicians to help at her women-patients-only hospital, The New England Hospital for Women and Children; dozens of upper society women were helping at the Denison House; and a woman-run settlement house on Tyler Street, the Women's Educational and Industrial Union, had just marched downtown to gain attention for its job training programs and need of reform for female workers.

I read and read and slowly, instead of getting sleepy, it felt as if someone were shaking me awake with each page I turned. I stood up to stretch and walk around the office before continuing. By three a.m., I had read through more than half of the newspapers and I was determined to finish them all before sunrise. I walked across the room and stood by the window. It was a bright night and there were stars dancing everywhere I looked. I wanted to feel the night air, and the moment I lifted the window I heard an owl. Its sweet hoot from the huge oak tree on the left side of the house made me smile, and then it was as if the bird were speaking to me and saying, "Audubon Society, Audubon Society, Audubon Society," with each new sound. I was still looking for news of the society the women I met in the park had mentioned, and the owl was apparently trying to remind me to keep going. I pushed open the window as far as I could and the relentless bird kept calling. I walked quickly back to the papers and started to look for any news about the Audubon.

It did not take me long to find what I was looking for. Small bits and pieces of information that must have been floating unattached through my mind started to come into place. John James Audubon was an artist who had travelled throughout America, drawing birds and eventually producing a book, *Birds of America*. I believe my father saw the book once when he dropped off our monthly house rental money and our landlord showed him a copy of it. He talked about how Audubon had painted the birds "exactly how they are" and how when viewing the paintings, it was as if they were right in the room with him. "Birds are free," he would often tell me during the few moments he was able to spend with me. "God painted them with all those beautiful colors so when we want to look down in moments of loss and sadness, we can look up instead and see something beautiful, something lovely, something to lift us up."

I began to believe that my father and the birds themselves were trying to tell me something, and moments later I discovered an article that made my hands shake so violently that it was almost impossible to read. The headline read, "*Boston Audubon Society Meets to Address Millinery Disputes.*" I closed my eyes for a moment to steady myself and read on. "*The home of popular novelist Margaret Deland was the setting last Friday for the Massachusetts Audubon Society's monthly meeting and the gathering was as much a call to action against the needless slaughter of birds for use in the fashion industry as it was a parade of this city's high-society women and gentlemen. In attendance were notable civic and society members including naturalists, Outram Bangs, Charles S. Minot, Mrs. Augustus Hemenway, and her cousin, Minna Hall, who have been tireless in their work against the use of feathers in the fashion industry. Notable ornithological supporters also in attendance included Mrs. Margaret Briton...*"

The world, my breath, my entire being, paused. Margaret? My Margaret? How did I not know this? How could all of these pieces of life have escaped me? What must this mean to Charles and his father and the very business that had put this roof over my head? I started to pace in the office, back and forth, my mind swirling with questions, possibilities, and a sensation of lightness, unease, and expectation that was pushing from my stomach, through my heart, and into my throat. Even an uneducated woman such as me is able to realize when something is amiss, when something needs to be done or changed, when too many secrets have been kept under lock and key. What if Margaret had been bringing me those papers and magazines all along, hoping I would discover she was more than a just a domineering mother-in-law who covered her emotions with a swift tongue and the occasional manner of seemingly rude dismissal?

I went back to the window, leaning against the top unopened pane, and felt the cool glass against my heated forehead. I had never before thought of knowledge as power, but the notion was rippling through me as if a small dam had burst. I was also feeling a bit stronger in body because my health was coming back, most likely from the vigorous walking, fresh air, and from my relatively newfound ability to embrace my three children as once real, not just a piece of me that had been removed and shuttled away under cover of darkness.

It was a tremendous amount of weight to suddenly be carrying around, and I wasn't certain what I was going to do next. The thought of lunging ahead without a plan seemed like it would just create an unforgiveable disaster. I couldn't run up the steps, shake Charles awake, and demand to know what he knew about the Audubon and hats and his mother's activities no more than I could rush down the street and ask her the same questions. A carriage passed and I wondered who might be out at this hour of the day, perhaps a doctor on call, or a delivery cart, or maybe one of the women I had just read about performing a mission of mercy. I pushed away from the window, placed my hands on the frame, and leaned back. There was a hint of light starting to slide in across the far side of the trees. I closed my eyes for but a moment, and when I opened them, the birds started to sing their morning welcoming songs.

A predetermined course of events, an irresistible power, is called fate or destiny, and mine seemed to be flying toward me with sweet songs and wings of beauty. The birds were singing and I was imagining them as secret messengers who did not yet know that I wasn't speaking their language. Their whistles, melodies, and songs gathered speed. Soon there was a chorus out there in the trees, directed by an unseen force that was creating a vocal parade. It was absolutely mesmerizing, and until the light gathered speed, I stood there and I could almost feel my own heart singing along.

I finally turned to face Charles's desk and before I could stop myself, I sat in his fine leather chair, placed my hands on the edge of the desk, and wondered what it might be like to be in charge—in charge of anything. All of the women I had just read about were living boldly and with what appeared to be great intent and passion. Women owned businesses and ran hospitals and were working feverishly to obtain the right to vote. I had not even bothered to think of such things. It occurred to me that just as I had changed and moved into this Brookline life from my Dorchester life, it would be possible to change again and again as I grew and had new experiences. I must find a way to speak to Margaret, to discover more of what was happening in the world so I could become a part of it all—no matter the risk. This thought was so compelling, I felt for a moment as if some kind of supernatural force had moved inside of me. I had given up on religion and almost given up any notion that there was a loving God too, since the loss of the babies, but this surge inside of me was surely something akin to a spiritual moment.

Charles had stacks of papers all over his desk. There was an ink-well posed to the left, some type of ledger where rows of figures had been recorded, a few rolled-up balls of paper, and a small pad where he had drawn lines back and forth. I imagined he scribbled while he was thinking about his own troubles, troubles that he never cared to share with me. I was about to get up when I noticed something rolled into a ball at the very back of the desk. I reached in, unrolled it slowly, unable to tell if it had been in a magazine or newspaper, but it obviously had been crumpled many, many times. I was careful so it would not tear and I leaned in close to read it.

Woman's Heartlessness
by Celia Thaxter, Boston, Mass., Dec 26, 1886.

When the Audubon Society was first organized, it seemed a comparatively simple thing to awaken in the minds of all bird-wearing women a sense of what their "decoration" involved. We flattered ourselves that the tender and compassionate heart of woman would at once respond to the appeal for mercy, but after many months of effort, we are obliged to acknowledge ourselves mistaken in our estimate of that universal compassion, that tender heart in which we believed.

I was immediately taken by this woman's writing and had to slow my reading in order to comprehend what she was saying. Farther down she wrote: *One lady said to me, "I think there is a great deal of sentiment wasted on the birds. There are so many of them they will never be missed any more than mosquitoes. I shall put birds on my new bonnet." This was a fond and devoted mother, a cultivated and accomplished woman. It seemed a desperate case, indeed, but still I strove with it. "Why do you give yourself so much trouble?" she asked. "They will soon go out of fashion, and there will be an end of it." That may be," I replied, "but fashion next year may order them back again, and how many women will have human feeling enough to refuse to wear them?"*

I quickly realized she was talking about hats and fashion and I knew why Charles must have taken the paper in his hands and rolled it into a ball, more than once.

I read on, even as I felt foolish for not knowing about this, for not realizing that if there were feathers in my hat, then surely they must have come from a bird that was killed to get them. Although I occasionally shopped, it was also true that Margaret brought me hats and dresses, and we had fittings at her house. It was a wonder I had been let out of the house alone to walk. I kept reading as this Celia woman wrote about how refreshing it was to see bird-less bonnets and how heaven would bless women who turned their backs on fashion so as to save birds. She shared how silly it was for women to follow each other like sheep, all in the name of fashion, and I must say that because of all my pregnancies and lost babies, I was woefully behind in fashion trends. I do remember that my mother once showed me magazines with women who were wearing huge ornamental hats, but I had only been wearing what Charles and Margaret brought me, and no birds, thank heavens, had arrived as of yet.

But when she wrote, *To-day I saw a mat of woven warblers' heads, spiked all over its surface with sharp beaks, set up on a bonnet and borne aloft by its possessor in pride! Twenty murders in one! and the face beneath bland and satisfied, for are not, "Birds to be worn more than ever?"* I was struck with an idea, a plan that was further enhanced by how she ended her article. She talked of heartless women and how all the dead birds would no longer come home to their waiting mothers, and it was then, absolutely then, that I knew I must do something. I had to do something.

The girls found me first. Charles was not even awake yet when I heard Ella and Ruby come into the kitchen and begin to set up for breakfast with their usual giggles and talking of what had occurred the night before. I startled them when I came around the corner dressed in my bedclothes, acting as if I had just walked down the steps and into the kitchen.

"Good morning," Ruby said, turning from the counter.

"Hello, girls," I said cheerfully. "It's lovely to see your smiling faces."

"Just up, then, are you, misses?"

I took in a breath, stepped forward, and lied. "Yes, just up. The birds are very loud this morning."

"Yes," Ella said quickly, "but they are so beautiful. They bring me to work every morning and I feel as if I have hundreds of friends flying all around me."

I smiled, so wishing I could tell the truth, run to them with news of everything that I had just discovered and find out what they knew, for they were the sweetest busybodies I had ever known. But I stood there instead, watching them pull out eggs, cut off thick slices of bacon, and prepare tea for me and coffee for Charles. By the time the table had been set and Charles, oblivious to the fact that I had not even been in bed with him, walked into the dining room, I was already prepared for my second, third, and fourth lies of the young day.

"You didn't dress, dear?"

"Not yet, Charles. I was terribly hungry and wanted to eat right away."

"Good! That's a good sign. Back to health! The walking must be working. How wonderful!"

"Yes, I feel so much better. I was wondering if I might use the carriage to visit my mother and maybe your mother later this week instead of walking? I'll give my legs a bit of a rest."

Charles looked very happy. He sat down, grabbed both my hands into his, and kissed my fingers while the girls looked on with huge smiles, obviously thrilled by his sudden burst of affection in front of them.

"Yes, what a splendid idea. I'll be more than glad to take the car and you can have the carriage. Do you want me to secure a driver? Are you strong enough?"

"I'm fine," I said, lying for the fourth time. "It will do me good to be out and to see both mothers."

Little did my loving husband or the unsuspecting girls realize that I was about to become a spy. That is surely not something you share with anyone, even if you may end up needing his or her help to do it.

Tape Five

A Month of Amazing Feats and Encounters
Boston—Most of July, 1904

B ecoming someone new does not have to mean that you erase all of the existing features of your life and personality. I started to think about how I had become someone new when I left school and started working for the publishing company, when I married Charles, when I was pregnant, when I lost the babies, and when I started to listen to the songs being played in my own heart that were growing louder and louder by the day. I was surely not the same girl who had been star struck by Clara Barton just a few years ago, but when I turned to look at myself in the mirror that hung next to my dressing area, I still recognized myself.

I had lost a great deal of weight, enough so that my face had narrowed and all of my skirts and dresses had to be taken in, but when I looked into my own eyes, I could still see all the pieces of myself—the good and the bad—and even if I didn't know who I was becoming, I knew who I was. A wife and mother for sure, and I did consider myself to be a mother because had not a baby come out of me? I sometimes still faltered on days when I felt an ache that was like a dull pain deep inside of my chest when I thought of them. There was also a new sureness in my gaze, as well as a new crease that was forming between my eyebrows. I called it, The Liar's Brow, because that was also who I was becoming. And for some odd reason, I was not ashamed. I started to run my fingers back and forth across the bottom of my forehead, right across my eyebrows, every time I was about to do or say something that might not be quite true. It was a wonder I had any skin left up there.

My plan seemed simple enough. I was going to find all those women parading around who were wearing dead birds on their heads. It wasn't as if I hadn't yet seen any of them, because I had. There were fashionable women on the streets when I walked and I saw more than a few strolling through the parks. But I had not taken notice. I simply saw hats, and I needed to see these dead birds stacked on brims for myself. I suppose there was a small part of me that needed to see it to really believe it, yet I knew the stories in the paper must be true as must be the wrath and anger inside of Charles and his father George. Talk of unions and saving birds and feathers must surely be affecting his business, and did he not know his own mother was part of this Audubon movement? If my Liar's Brow did not give me away, I was also thinking of approaching Margaret. Our friendship had surely turned more cordial and her spontaneous moments of affection, a touch of the hand, an occasional hug, a bright smile, were so much more than she had ever offered before our day in the cemetery. And I also needed to go find out what was happening at the millinery shops owned by Charles and what was happening at his warehouse. This, of course, meant driving the carriage past his businesses and maybe even slipping inside. I was not certain I was yet brave enough to follow through with this part of the plan, but then, just like the call of a wild bird that propels you to find its nest, I started to take action.

My first trip took me to a section of downtown Boston just a bit east of the Boston Common off of Tremont Street. Leaving my home had been extremely easy because of my gentle lies, and Charles always had the carriage ready and the girls, preoccupied with their duties, didn't even come to wave good-bye when I left. It was all very natural, the good wife heading out for a little drive, with all the necessary permissions in place. It was a hot, sultry day, a good day one might say for wearing a large hat to cover as much of one's face as possible. A series of short streets run between Tremont and Washington Streets and both sides of every street in this area are lined with millinery and dress making shops. I had only been to one such establishment, a small yet beautiful shop owned by a woman named Miss Delacorte, a robust and very bold woman, who greeted Margaret and me the day we visited with an embrace, as if she had known us forever. She quickly picked out several dresses that fit me perfectly. It seemed so natural to have a woman doing that, and not a man, but I wasn't thinking about things like that way back then. I was new now in many ways.

I found a stable boy in one of the back alleys to tend to my carriage, grabbed my umbrella-like parasol, and started to stroll up and down the streets. I wore a simple, solid-white straw hat with a very small, thin, white cotton band, a high-collared, off-white dress that left so little of my body covered I was drenched in sweat within fifteen minutes of my walking and spying adventure. But this was the style. We all wore corsets and tight-waisted dresses and skirts with a belt to show the world how thin we were. Puffed blouses were very popular also, and it did not escape me as I started walking that I looked like a bird myself. I was a pigeon with its fluffed-up breast preceding me as I strutted down the sidewalk, head rotating with each step, always wondering who might see me, what they might say, what I might see next.

And I saw plenty.

The streets were not very long, and they were much more crowded than I expected, but I picked up a rhythm of walking and looking very quickly. I kept the parasol low enough that my face would be mostly covered but high enough that I could at the very least catch a quick glimpse of approaching women. I also kept to the outside of the walk so if I had to escape—who knew if Margaret or a neighbor might appear?—I could rush across the street. It was difficult from the very beginning to keep from falling on my face because every other woman was, indeed, wearing a bird or a portion of a bird on her hat. How this had escaped me was now simply a part of my past and did not really matter.

There were hats with bird wings pushed up on both sides; hats with dozens and dozens of colored feathers wrapped round and round so it looked as if the hat and the woman wearing it might take off into air at any moment; hats with bird heads looped through pieces of fine fabric so the birds looked poised to speak at any moment, sweet beaks open, neck feathers spread wide; hats with entire birds resting on top and on the sides that must have weighed enough to break off the very necks of the silly women wearing them; hats with colorful wing sets and red breasts and feathers the colors of the rainbow. Soon I was guessing at the birds that might have once been winging through the air and whose beautiful body parts were now sewn into place on human bobbing heads. Terns, blue jays, one entire hummingbird, many egret plumes, sparrow heads, some type of hen, one owl that made me turn away in utter disgust, and, thank heavens, not one wood duck.

Not everyone wore a feathered or bird-bodied hat. During three other trips, I saw many other women who wore simpler hats and some wearing no hats. Once I stood in disbelief when one woman, who wore no hat, stopped a woman who, in spite of the heat, was wearing a hat that appeared to be made of satin and decorated with the most beautiful plumage I had ever seen. I boldly stepped close enough to hear, turned my back, and listened in awe, and disbelief, as the women began to argue.

"Do you have any idea what you are wearing on your head?"

"A hat, of course, and what business is it of yours?"

"It is not just a hat, but a hat fashioned with feathers from a bird of paradise, which may become extinct because you are wearing one of them on your head."

"How dare you!"

"How dare I? Do you realize that simply because of fashion, a beautiful bird has given its life, and perhaps, out there in the wilderness, a baby is crying for a mother who will never come home!"

"There are always more birds!"

"How can you know that? And why not, then, put a donkey head or a dead kitten up there?"

"That is disgusting!"

"And a beautiful dead bird is not? I am asking you to think about it, to remove your hat, to not be so swayed by fashion trends, and to think for yourself, madam, that is all."

My heart was pounding. I so wanted to turn and see who was berating the woman with the hat. I did turn in time to see the woman who was wearing the hat whip her skirts around as she fled so they flipped against the woman who was speaking, just hard enough that the other woman almost fell. I was about to move and help her when she regained her balance, lifted her head, and caught my eye. She was a tall woman with a broad face, dark hair, and a look of sincerity and kindness that seemed at odds with the conversation I had just heard. She was dressed in very fine clothes, a light-blue blouse, and a brown skirt that was pulled up in back in a way I had never seen before, so she could walk quickly. She looked directly at me and smiled. Then I did something that I would soon come to realize can cripple you. I hesitated. Instead of walking closer and asking her who she was and a dozen other questions that were still unanswered, I looked down to gather my thoughts, and when I looked up, she was already halfway down the block, chasing after another woman, and I had lost the moment.

After this encounter, I did grow bolder, partly because I was embarrassed at my own ignorance and inability to act like the woman I had seen on the street, and also because of the pitiful face of the dead owl. I also continued to walk on the days when I dared not risk driving the carriage into the city. Even a woman with fading brows can only lie so much. I also missed the absolute quiet and beauty of Heart's Haven and my talks with the babies. One day I even went back into the water to see if I could find the wood duck, but I never saw it again. And every time I went back to spy on women and their hats, I would pray that a wood duck would not appear as a new ornament.

I did stop and see my mother once in order to cover for myself. Two times when I tried to see Margaret, she was not home and no one could tell me where she had gone, which was interesting, but I had my own ideas about her absence. It seemed as if each trip in the carriage and each walk made me a bit bolder, and one day in the middle of the month, I decided it was time to walk into one of the shops and ask some questions.

I could not go into Miss Delacorte's shop because someone may have recognized me, so I walked one street over in mid-afternoon, took in a breath, and pulled open the door to Madam Stankos' Dress Parlor. Many immigrants were moving into Boston every single day and this particular shop was run by a large, big-busted, extremely tall, Russian woman who looked as if she could run the world. She commanded her shop as if she were the Czar himself, and I could have watched her moving about all day. There were female customers buzzing about, and I quickly walked to the area where hats were displayed and bravely took one into my hands that was garnished with the entire wing of an unidentifiable gray bird. One of the assistants came to me immediately. We bantered back and forth for a bit before I took courage and leaned in to whisper to her so no one else could hear.

"Who makes these hats and where do the birds come from, if I might ask?"

The woman looked somewhat startled and hesitated, but I did not move to dispel her uneasiness.

"Well," she stuttered. "We have a milliner who sometimes comes in and designs special orders for us, but most of our hats are from the bigger millinery factories over in the South End, you know?"

I nodded politely and smiled so she would feel a bit more at ease. "Yes, I am familiar with the factories there. But the birds? Where do they get all of the birds?"

The woman looked down and when she raised her eyes to meet mine, they were wide with fright. "Please, ma'am, I need this job so very much and Madam Stankos forbids us to talk of the birds. So many of those others, those bird lovers, come in and frighten us with questions like yours, and it's been so bad for business…"

I stepped in so we were almost hugging, touched her arm, and told her I was just curious and was not out to cause any harm, cost her job, or trouble anyone. There was a hat, as plain and simple as the very woman standing in front of me, just out of arm's reach. I leaned over, picked it up, and told her I would buy it if only she would tell me anything she knew about the birds.

"The Audubon people know everything, and once at the factory, when I went to pick up orders, I saw boxes and boxes of birds lined up, so surely they must bring them in on ships and trains, and the birds, they must be shot, do you agree?"

"Yes," I said so softly I was not certain she heard me.

"So many there were," she finished, shaking her head. "So many."

I thanked her, let go of her arm, and escaped before I risked anything else, slipping out the door with my hat, a new symbol of the daring life I had apparently embraced. But as I hurried down the street, I also could not stop thinking about that woman at the shop. I could have landed next to her, spending hours each day shifting from one foot to another, smiling at the women of means who came in to fondle hats, dresses, and fancy gloves while they tried not to make eye contact or treat me as an equal. I had only been saved by my physical beauty, by a chance meeting, by a single moment of boldness, by instances so small and seemingly inconsequential that I knew, absolutely, that it could easily be me greeting a woman who dared to ask about birds. I had a sudden urge to rush back into the store, ask the woman what her name was, where she lived, did she have children, a husband, a small house maybe in Dorchester, or anything to connect us in a way that might make me feel better about the life that had been handed to me.

These thoughts plagued me for a very long time and for days I was quiet, did not even bother to walk, abandoned my plan, and was very close to slipping backward into the depression and sorrow that had gripped me in May. The girls kept telling me this was normal, but they did not know everything, and left with no one to talk with, my world became a bit dark. Charles left again and said he was going on a quick buying trip down the coast with his father, and I did wonder if he was gathering feathers for the fall hats. I was not brave enough to ask him. I did do something, however, the day he left that very quickly helped me move forward. I sent Margaret, who had been a rare sight the past few weeks, a note.

> Margaret,
> The men are gone and this seems like a fine time for a ride in the carriage. It also seems like a fine time to talk about birds. I suspect you might have a lot to say about this subject.
> Sincerely,
> Julia, who has now caught up on her reading

The truth is I missed her. I longed for someone to share at least part of my plan with, even as I wondered if I really had any idea who she was, what she really thought, or why she had treated me so harshly when Charles and I had married. So imagine my complete and utter surprise when a note came back the very next day.

My Dearest Julia,

If it is birds you want, then it is birds you will get. I will arrive tomorrow to gather you at one o'clock. Your timing is perfect.

Your Mother-in-Law,
Margaret Briton

I was ready by noon, pacing in the front hall, after I had dismissed a very thankful Ruby and Ella, who really didn't have much to do anyway. Charles obviously had the money to pay them, and they had become more than just employees, but I was also beginning to wonder if we were all going to grow old together while the world spun forward and we peeled potatoes and dusted lamps.

Margaret greeted me warmly and instantly handed the reins to me as if they were hot coals and started talking about how she was going to learn how to drive the Model A Ford that was sitting behind her house before she died, no matter what the rest of the world thought about female drivers. I was taken aback, smiled, and urged the horses on, although I had no idea where we were going. Margaret settled back and for a while talked on as if I wasn't even there. She pointed when it was time to turn, went on about the heat and how she hated to admit it but loved it when Charles and his father left town because she felt so free. I almost ran the carriage into the trees after that statement. Finally, I could take it no longer and asked her where we were going.

"Off to Maggie Deland's for an Audubon meeting, my dear," she said nonchalantly, almost as if she had already told me. "I love that Maggie and I have the same first name."

"Oh," I muttered, almost too astounded to speak.

"Left here, Julia. We're headed to Mount Vernon Street, just the other side of the Common, almost directly across from all those shops you have been walking past."

My heart felt as if it had left my body. "How did you know?" I gasped.

"Oh, my dear," she said, laughing. "Oh, my dear, dear, dear. You will see soon enough."

I all but floated into the lovely Deland house with Margaret laced through my left arm as we walked into a swirl of women, a sprinkling of men, and an atmosphere of pure friendliness and intent. Margaret Deland was a popular novelist and I was in awe simply to be in her home. I also knew that she lived the way she wrote, boldly and with great determination. She wrote about women being able to have freedom of action and I also knew her upstairs bedrooms were filled with unwed mothers who she had taken into her home. She cared for them with great tenderness and with the true belief that if they kept their babies and loved them, their lives would all flourish. Standing in the front hall, as Margaret started her introductions, I became weak in the knees for just a moment thinking of those lucky mothers, and I had to resist an urge to run up the steps, grab one of the babies, and hold him or her to my chest.

Margaret must have sensed my brief moment of unease because she held me tighter and leaned in to say, "Just be yourself, dear," as she walked me into a brand new world. There was so much to take in that I was dizzy with delight and unwarranted intimidation. At first I was dazzled by those in attendance.

The meeting was a Who's Who of the Boston elite and I recognized many of them from the newspaper articles I had been reading. Louise Chandler Moulton, another author who was well traveled and influential, and whose stories had passed over my desk during my brief stint in publishing; Judith Winsor Smith, an active member of the New England Women's Club and a society matron in the East Boston community, who was also a determined suffragette and abolitionist; Emily Greene Balch, a practicing socialist and one of the founders of the newly formed Women's Trade Union League, an organization that was a fascinating blend of the rich and poor—wealthy women working to get better wages and working conditions for the women who might even be working in the factories and at businesses their husbands owned. There were politicians from the Boston Common Council, I noticed at least two ministers, and Margaret seemed to know everyone.

Margaret was quietly introducing me to as many people as possible before the meeting started and explaining who they were, and it was all I could do to hold the questions that were filling my head. Everyone was kind and no one treated me as if I was a foolish girl from Dorchester who had stepped into the wrong meeting. A small podium had been set up at the front of the great room we were standing in and a man asked us to take our seats so the meeting could begin. Just before I sat down, there was a tap on my shoulder and I turned to face the woman I had seen berating the woman outside the shop the day I had been spying.

"So wonderful to see you again, Julia," she said warmly, extending both of her hands.

I must have looked startled because she didn't wait for me to answer. She introduced herself and there I was holding the hands of Harriet Hemenway. She was the woman who, in 1898, along with her cousin, Minna Hall, had marked off the names of influential women gathered from *The Boston Blue Book* and invited them to form a society for the protection of birds.

"It's a pleasure," I said.

"I don't normally stop women on the street who are wearing those horrid hats, but sometimes I just can't help myself," she said with a smile. "I recognized you from the wedding photograph I saw on your mother-in-law's table. I'm glad Margaret brought you along."

She winked at Margaret, the two women embraced, and then she turned back to me and invited me to come visit her Canton farm and summer home the very next week. I quickly looked at Margaret and realized these two women were not just close friends, but had most likely planned this invitation together.

"I'm not sure," I said, not certain if it was even proper for me to travel alone.

"Nonsense!" Margaret responded as if this conversation had been rehearsed. "I've also been invited, too, and it's just what the doctor ordered. You can walk all day and never see another person. Charles won't mind and it will give us hours to talk, my dear, and Harriet tells me there are more birds down there than you can even imagine. We will hike and watch birds until we all drop."

And just like that, I was going on my first ever trip out of greater Boston. I had never been anywhere except the neighborhoods where I lived or shopped, although, like every young girl, I had grown up dreaming about heading west, maybe taking the train all the way to California with a stop off to meet cowboys somewhere in between, taking the steamer to England or France, or traveling to New York City to stroll on the busy streets and look for handsome actors emerging from their late-night shows. Travel for the sake of just that, traveling, was something reserved for the rich, and it was still hard for me to think I was part of that category. But I was, even if I had no idea how much money was in the bank accounts, and I was still asking Charles for spending money.

When we sat down as the meeting was about to begin, I felt as if I were being swept up into a flock of daring, aggressive, and very smart women who had swooped down from sky, spotted me, and plucked me from right where I was standing. I quickly looked around the room—there must have been thirty or forty men and women in attendance—and I wondered if the birds had called to them as they had been calling to me. Margaret, sitting next to me, was poised on the end of her seat and, flushed with the excitement of simply being there, I spontaneously reached over, touched her hand, and said, "Thank you for this."

She patted my hand gently, smiled, and said something I didn't quite understand. "You are my second chance, Julia."

The meeting was a two-hour presentation that could have lasted forever as far as I was concerned. First an Audubon officer got up to remind everyone that the organization's purpose was "to discourage the buying or wearing, for ornamental purposes, of the feathers of any wild birds and to further the protection of native birds." There was a membership update, and I was impressed that there were now close to 3,000 Audubon members in Boston alone and that schools were starting special programs to educate students about the importance of birds and why breaking eggs and tearing apart nests was not acceptable. Several ornithologists spoke about specific declining bird populations and a zoology professor from Harvard discussed spring nesting habits of birds one might find in city locations. When the final speaker rose to begin, the entire audience began clapping and jumped to its feet.

"It's William Dutcher," Margaret told me. "He jokes that he's just an insurance salesman, but really he's an amateur ornithologist and the chairman of the National Committee of the Audubon Societies of America."

The magnitude of what happened next would take time to settle within me. One does not sit and listen to a man talk about how the millinery industry must step forward and change how it is exploiting both birds and women and then rush home to discuss this with a man who is in the millinery business. One especially does not start talking about this if the man in question, my husband, thinks daily walking and stitchery is a fine occupation for a woman. Mr. Dutcher was well spoken, sincere, and urged us all to do our part, to boycott if we must shops that sold feather hats and the very factories where they were made.

Margaret did not address me again until we were in the carriage and on the way home. I was overwhelmed, not just by being in the same room with men and women who were so wise and powerful, but also by a tightness in my chest, fostered by the thought that surely Charles of the Heart could not have boxes of dead birds lined up in his warehouse. Surely he would cooperate with someone like Mr. Dutcher or an esteemed zoology professor or a prominent ornithologist.

So many questions were buried under my tongue that it was a relief when Margaret started talking. She told me she had spent most of her adult life following the norm and worrying about what people thought, and especially allowing for her husband to manage the finances, keep her out of all his business dealings and most every part of his life. I was astonished by her openness, but what came next left me unable to speak at all.

"I have never loved your father-in-law," she admitted with more than a hint of anger in her voice, her gaze fixed off into the distance. "Ours was an arranged society marriage and I had hoped that over the years I would grow to love him, but that is impossible. Ten years ago he took a mistress and my heart turned to stone. I found out accidentally and held it inside for a long time. Then I met a group of very progressive women, many who you met today, and they taught me how to use the mistress to my advantage. I am a free woman in many ways now and I do what I please."

I could have rolled right off the carriage with shock, but she was not yet done talking. Next, she apologized.

"I am sorry for the harsh way I treated you in the past, but the solid truth is that I was jealous."

"Jealous!" I was stunned yet again.

"Yes, jealous, Julia. Jealous because Charles clearly loves you and you clearly love him and yours is a match that I can never have. I am ashamed to say that I made a bet with my son that you could not fit the mold he needs you to fit, that you would never learn what unfortunately are still some necessary rules that people like us must follow, and that he had made a huge mistake."

"Oh, Margaret! I'm so sorry, too. I thought you hated me and that I would never be good enough in your eyes."

Margaret moved her head back and forth. I think she may have been crying a bit, and I let the weight of her words settle in as we rode on in silence. We turned the last corner and I stopped the carriage in front of my house and remained at a loss for what to say next. She took the reins from me as I gathered my skirts to step down.

"We will talk more of this next week on our trip, but you must make me a promise that no matter what happens, you will not discuss any of this bird or feather business with Charles or his father."

"But surely they must know you attend the meetings? I saw your name in the newspaper."

Her hand was gripping my arm and I turned to meet her eyes and something passed between us that made me trust her in a way that I could not trust my own husband, who had not been able to tell me the truth about the wager with his own mother.

"Of course, but they do not know the extent of my work, and George would dare not try to stop me because of what I know. It's one thing to attend a meeting and another to undermine the very business that supports you."

"I promise."

Margaret broke into a small smile, told me she would send packing directions for the trip the following day, and then rode off toward home. I stood on my porch for a long time, watching her disappear down the street, running my fingers across my brow, and it took me a few seconds to realize that when I had said, "I promise," my fingers had not been anywhere near The Liar's Brow.

Resurrecting The Liar's Brow, Kidnapping, and Joni Mitchell

Imagine my confusion when I listened to these tapes and tried to figure out who in the world Julia was talking about. The version of the year I was now hearing from her own voice was definitely unabridged and not what I remembered hearing at all up until that point. Prior to my discovery of the tapes, discussion of The Year was never overly intense or greatly emotional, and certainly did not include intimate details of her marriage, spying, or her obviously increasing realization that the world was a much bigger place than Greater Boston.

I was also captivated by Julia's growing realization of issues like women's liberation, feminism, and equal rights. Being a fifteen-year-old know-it-all, I was certain I was old enough and mature enough to run off and handle my own problems and the problems of the world, which I did soon enough, like the foolish child I was. Julia might have felt like a babe in the woods back then too, but she was so far ahead of me it wasn't even funny.

In the past when Julia had shared stories of the most amazing year in her life, not that every day of her life had not been amazing from what I was hearing, she had left out her deepest personal thoughts and emotions. She simply talked with great excitement about where she went and what she did as if we were listening to a travelogue. The marital and family discretions she shared in the tapes also made me wonder if this was what I was in for with my own adult relationships—lying,

77

cheating, sneaking around, unhappiness, secrecy. Gosh, there was so much to look forward to!

I started to make note cards about her life, jotting down details as if I were researching a term paper, which it turns out is exactly what I was doing. It was as if I were piecing together the unconnected dots of her life and solving a puzzle. Simply writing down the names of the famous people she had met or that her family had associations with seemed, well, crazy and almost unbelievable to me. Clara Barton, William Jennings Bryant, Thomas Edison, Harriet Hemenway, Ty Cobb were just some of the famous people she had met, and there were more tapes stacked up in her drawer. I was guessing there were more historic figures, herself included, to meet. I felt as if I were living inside of a glorious time capsule.

I didn't realize it then, but the note cards and the tapes, and my growing realization about the importance of history and how intercon-nected we all are in spite of our many differences, would become the eventual launching pad for my own career. I started to look at things differently. Even simple objects like Julia's antique hairbrush, the combs she used to pin up her hair, the old books next to her bed, and all her silver jewelry took on new meaning for me. Those things were old and real and a part of Julia's life when she was a young woman launching her own life. I wanted to touch them and think about what it must have been like to hear horses outside the window, to bathe only once a week, and to wear long skirts every day. I sorted through her closet when she was at appointments with her doctor, looking for more clues to the past, and I spent a great deal of time at the library, researching historic details she had mentioned and the people she had known.

Unfortunately, two things happened that disrupted my newfound life and love of history and all things Julia. First of all, my father showed up one day, unannounced, and asked if I would spend a few days with him. I hated everyone that year, even my mother—who as it ends up was so wronged by him that I spent years thinking of ways to have him killed—so I flippantly, and very spontaneously, said yes. I told Julia where I was going before she could rise off her chair to stop me, neglected to ask permission from my mother, and the moment I got in the car and saw the back end piled with suitcases and boxes, I realized something was amiss.

"Dad, why is the car full of your stuff?"

"Oh, I thought we'd take a little trip."

"I thought I was just spending a few days with you at your apartment."

"Well, honey, I really wasn't in an apartment, but I was staying with someone and now that's over and your mother doesn't want me back."

I wasn't stupid, but by the time I realized he was sort of kidnapping me, we were on the freeway and I had one of those "holy shit" feelings growing in my stomach that made me feel lightheaded, slightly terrified, and just a little bit pissed off. This sensation would become my constant companion during the next three decades.

"Dad, you know I'm not a little kid and you can't just put me in a car and take me away like this. I have a life." I tried to reason at first.

"But I just did take you away."

Something wasn't right with him and I suddenly had never longed for my mother, a boring summer, or Julia as much as at that moment. My life flashed before my eyes and I saw myself eating Pop-Tarts at a sleazy hotel in Alabama, then potato chips in Louisiana, candy bars in Texas, and a stale pizza in Utah. There were no cell phones back in those days, I didn't even have fifty cents in my pocket, and the few clothes I had were literally sitting in a paper bag in the back seat. I really didn't think my father would physically hurt me, but it was clear he had stepped over some kind of invisible mental stability line and was absolutely off his rocker and using me as a divorce pawn.

The first day, we drove north and then west through most of Florida. When we stopped for gas, he locked me in the car and stood guard. When I had to use the bathroom, he stood outside the door. I asked him where we were going and he mumbled something about a cousin in California. Well, what fifteen-year-old in 1974 did not want to go to California? I decided I would escape from him once I saw the ocean and maybe run into Crosby, Stills, Nash, or the lovely Mr. Young. I also had my youthful mind set on hanging out with Joni Mitchell, whose music was embedded in my heart and soul. I had played the album Blue so many times I could probably be her double at a concert. I knew where she lived, who she hung out with, and pretty much even what she ate for dinner. Yes, my hair was long and dishwater blond from my days in the Florida sun, and I was going to learn how to play the guitar and sing the moment I was safe. Thus, I focused on Joni as a means of surviving my kidnapping.

My father and I did talk now and then, which helped me realize he was a fruitcake, and besides not letting me call home and telling me what a bitch my mother was even as he admitted his myriad infidelities, he didn't harm me physically. The psychological scars would manifest themselves during the next ten, twenty, and thirty years as I tried to reconcile my obvious disdain for controlling, manipulative, and co-dependent men. I did this by choosing a series of relationships that were so absolutely destructive it's a wonder I am alive now to write this. During the very long two weeks it took us to drive us to California, zigzagging across the country, I had absolutely no idea that my wonderful mother and Julia had pulled out all of the stops.

The police were about as helpful as dead rats. They said because I was with my father, a crime had not been committed and they refused to put out police bulletins to help locate me. Later I figured out that I had been standing at the edge of the Grand Canyon, wishing my father would tumble over the edge, the day Julia hired a private detective to try and locate me. I had read enough mystery and detective books to know that if my father trusted me, I could eventually save myself—but only once I made it to California please, so I could see Joni and maybe even run into Carly Simon while I was at it. By agreeing with him, badmouthing my mother, and listening to his ramblings day after day, I had been able to write a letter, steal a stamp, and mail it to Julia. I told her I was scared but okay and that we were headed to San Francisco. I also mentioned what day we might arrive and where I was going to ask him to stay before we met his cousin, who really did not exist. Fortunately for me, I had also used the words "kidnapped, forced, and can't escape" in the letter, and this finally got the police excited.

Somehow my passion for the tapes, and the parallel life I was starting to live with Julia as I started my own Year, did not enter my mind during those few weeks. I saw myself as the victim of a crazy father and a bitter divorce and mostly I thought about how maybe life at Julia's wasn't so bad after all. Years later I would recreate the drive, day by day, and remember it so precisely that I knew the experience had been a lot more profound than I had ever dared to admit.

My life took such an amazing turn once we got to California that my heart still skips a beat when I remember it all. There's nothing like pulling into San Francisco the first time, especially if you have been a

Florida girl who longed for the big city and then the fading glow of the sixties. The lights, the bridge, the water, the boats, the everything. We drove and drove, because that's what we did, and then we ended up, without my father realizing it exactly, where I wanted to be. Because I followed all things Joni, I knew she was on tour and that she had two days off in between her Universal City and Saratoga Springs concerts, and it was likely she would show up at a small club she loved in downtown San Francisco.

By this time my father, who was later diagnosed as being manic-depressive—we now call it bipolar affective disorder—was in what I called the yee-ha stage and ready for a bit of fun in the city. I had devised a plan to get to the club where Joni might show up, slip her a note asking for help, and then ditch my father. And that's exactly what happened.

We parked the car near Buena Vista Park, under the guise of simply looking around, and he was bodyguarding me down the sidewalk when I sidestepped into the Velvet Hook Lounge, which was on Downey Street, parallel to Ashbury and a blink away from Haight. I was so excited that I almost wet my pants and my father, thank heavens, was clueless. I'm certain he didn't have a plan, a place to go, a pot to pee in, or a window to throw it out of, as Julia would say, but was only seeking revenge for mother's normalcy, which I would soon come to worship. I had no idea we were being followed and that I was about to be on the front page of the San Francisco Chronicle.

And about to spend the night with Joni Mitchell.

I was obviously underage, even if I didn't think so, and when my father slithered in behind me, he immediately ordered a drink and gave the bartender a huge tip so he wouldn't kick me out, and I surveyed the room. Joni was there and even now, remembering that night, I get a bit weak in the knees. She was at a back table with Glenn Frey of the Eagles. Honest to God. They were sitting just off the stage, drinking what looked like whiskey in small glasses, their hands entwined across the table, and I could have died right then and been a happy almost-woman. I had written a note explaining who I was and what had happened and somehow I had the presence of mind to give it to a half-naked waitress after adding to the note, "I'm the girl in the blue shirt sitting at the bar with a man who looks crazy." Here's exactly what happened next.

The waitress took over the note. Joni read the note. She made eye contact with me, smiled, and Glenn Frey excused himself, presumably to call the cops. When my dad turned his head, Joni motioned for me to come over. I obeyed.

"Sit down, honey. Are you okay?"

Unable to speak, I nodded.

"I've got you now. No one will hurt you. Don't worry. Are you hungry?"

"No. I'm okay."

"Hey. Do you sing?"

"A little."

She took my hand, held it tight, ran her hand across my cheek. Smiled. She was absolutely beautiful and kind, and I had no idea that when she looked at me she was thinking of the daughter she gave away so long ago. She leaned in to whisper that yes, the policemen were coming, and she was going to get on stage and sing and wanted me to come up with her.

"Your father won't bother you if you're on stage. Just wave to him and smile as we get up. What songs of mine do you know?"

"All of them," I confessed.

She smiled and whispered, "Join in when you can, hum. I have a feeling you know what to do no matter what stage you are on."

When she wasn't looking, I drank Glenn's whiskey and then the world went a bit blank as Joni took my hand and started playing with me right next to her. I did sing, "Blue and My Old Man," which seemed an appropriate title for what was happening, and apparently I wasn't half bad because I vaguely remember people clapping. If I knew then what I know now, I would have realized that I was having my first of what would be many Clara Barton moments. Joni was my hero and that night my savior as well.

The police and the private detective who had spotted us came, took my father away, and for a brief moment, I actually felt sorry for him. Then to my utter amazement, Joni asked them if I could spend the night with her. Who could say no to Joni Mitchell? By then the reporters had arrived, our photo was taken, and Joni whisked me off for a night that I should have used as a stepping-stone into adulthood. But I was still fifteen and had a lot to learn.

She took me out to eat and Glenn Frey came along. She let me order a glass of wine and then took me to a late-night store and bought me some clothes because I was a bit ragged by then. We talked about James Taylor, Stephen Stills, and Carole King. Joni knew who Julia was and asked me if I would tell her how much she admired her. I spent the night wide-awake, in the double bed next to hers, watching her sleep and thanking God that my father had abducted me.

I'm sure I let Joni down during the harsh, hard, and selfish years that followed, but she had taken a while to figure out her life, too. She handed me off to a police matron in the morning, with a pocket full of autographs and her personal phone number. Then I had to get back home where another disaster that did not have such a happy ending was brewing.

My mother convinced me not to press any charges against my father, who was promptly sent to some kind of facility where they pumped him full of drugs and let him explain away years of ill behavior. My mother, being the good Briton girl that she was, took him back, for a while anyway, and I refused to move back home. Needless to say, there were more than a few shouting matches and then Julia intervened on my behalf and said it was a reasonable request considering what I had been through. What I didn't realize is how much of a toll the kidnapping had on Julia, or how much our relationship really meant to her.

My Joni Mitchell encounter, the father-daughter road trip, and my brief and terribly exciting fame in several newspapers made me even more self-absorbed than I had been before we left. I barely thought about the tapes, or Julia, as my friends paraded in and out of her house, begging to touch the clothes Joni had bought me. My sisters and brother were mostly living with my mother, and all three of them were getting ready to go back to college in a few weeks. My grandmother and mother were at the house almost every day to check on both of us. I should definitely have been paying attention to Julia's behavior. She was sleeping more and more every day, had grown terribly thin, and her focus was way off. One day, just a few weeks after I had gotten back, she called to me from her bedroom and when I went to her, I could tell she wasn't well.

"You'd better call your mother, dear," she said, calmly perched on the side of her bed as if she were asking for a glass of water. "I believe I may be having a stroke or some kind of heart problem."

Julia was having a stroke, not a bad one, but it was enough to change

83

her life, and mine, in ways that I continue to measure even today. The stroke did affect her speech, which meant that communicating at first was not as easy as it had once been. She was in the hospital for almost a week, and the first time I visited her, I was shocked by how much she had deteriorated.

I went to her, took her hand; she clasped me tightly and pulled me into the bed with her.

"Rem...ember?" She was slurring and I could tell she was trying to say more.

"Of course I remember. How I loved it when you told me stories!"

She nodded and it looked as if she were struggling to try and say something, and I had a profound emotional feeling that brought a swell of tears to my eyes. What if Julia died? What if there were no more stories, lies or not, from The Year and beyond? What if I could never listen to her voice on the tapes or look out and see her patiently waiting for the next flock of birds? No one had ever died that I had known, or loved, and it was at that moment that I realized how much I did love her. Had I even bothered to tell her? I felt such an overwhelming feeling of sorrow that I clutched her, perhaps a bit too tightly, and she let out a little squeak.

"No cry, no cry." She was trying hard to talk.

"I'm sorry. I don't want to lose you, Grandma. I didn't mean to hurt you."

"You ca...never hur...me."

It was such an effort for her to talk that I put my finger to her lips and said, "It's okay. I know. I love you too."

She closed her eyes then and fell asleep. I felt if I let her go, or got out of bed, that she might slip away from me.

Loss is very hard to measure when you are still partially a child, but I remember lying there and thinking about Joni again and her Big Yellow Taxi song... "Don't it always seem to go that you don't know what you've got 'til it's gone?" Julia wasn't gone yet, but it was apparent that it might not be long, and I had no idea what to do about that but decided to hang on and try to make amends for my self-centered past.

And I did okay for a little while. That very afternoon I went back to her house, a place I now also called home, and was relieved to find the tape recorder in the same drawer, and it looked as if she had been *making more tapes. No one else was there, but I stayed in Julia's room, kneeling again on the floor at the foot of her empty bed, watching as the reels went round and round and Julia's voice filled the room.*

There was absolutely no way to know, that late August afternoon, that it would be the last tape I would hear for many, many years.

Tape Six

Feathers in the Sky and a Moment Unlike Any Other
Canton, Massachusetts—July 27-31, 1904

It's hard to imagine owning a thousand acres of land, and even harder to imagine that someone who does can be lovely, open, charming, and as my mother used to say, "Stitched with the fibers of realness." Harriet Hemenway was all of that and so much more. She must have sensed my nervousness about the visit, because two days following her invitation, a lovely note arrived informing me that she looked forward to our visit, and I should expect a grand, healthful, enlightened break from the sights and the sounds of the city.

The truth is the city is all I had ever really known. Streets and the sound of horses clopping night and day, children yelling, and the comings and goings and often loud noises of neighbors were the normal sounds of my life, even after I married. Growing up, we ran through the empty fields and pastures down by the water, and I was always the girl standing alone, looking out to sea or across the fields, totally absorbed by all the emptiness and the beauty of the natural landscape. I was terribly excited about the trip, and I spent days trying to imagine what it would be like and what other secrets Margaret might reveal.

Charles did not think it odd that I wanted to "take a visit" with Margaret, and he seemed more preoccupied than ever with work and worry. His usual nighttime chats with me were diminishing and he abruptly retreated into his office right after dinner to do whatever it was he did in there. I must confess that when he returned from his business trip and I hugged him for the first time, knowing about his wager with Margaret, I felt a bit off. It may have been the combination of my own set of lies as well, but I felt a distance between us that had not been there before. I suppose it was natural for this to happen, given everything that I had been through, everything that I was involved with, and my burgeoning enlightenment about worldly objects, causes, and emotions.

I hate to admit it, but the day I left, there was a small sense of relief that for a short time I could think only of the moment and not of what was behind me or in front of me. Margaret came in an open-air carriage, much to my great delight, but she had also enlisted the help of a driver, which meant we were unable to talk about anything personal. Several quiet hours passed as the houses grew farther and farther apart and then it seemed as if the world opened up. Suddenly there were rolling hills and farm fields and soon we were all alone on a gravel-lined road that I imagined could take us all the way down to Florida. I immediately felt calm and peaceful looking out across the tops of trees and seeing nothing but summer blue sky and all the shades of green. I had to force myself to stay in the carriage because I had an odd desire to jump down, hike up my skirts, and run forever through the fields of clover that were planted alongside the road.

When Margaret and I crested a small hill several miles from the Hemenway summer farm and she asked the driver to pull over the carriage, I could not take it any longer. I quickly stepped down and headed to the edge of the field. I bent down to touch the soil. The scent of the clover and the warm earth was absolutely intoxicating, and as I moved my hands into the greenery, three robins, their orange breasts pumping toward the sky, rose and frightened me. I took a step back and promptly fell on my behind. Margaret started to laugh and the sound seemed to bounce off the very sky above us.

"Oh, Julia, you are quite the country girl!"

I turned and saw her with her head tipped back and enjoying herself and I started to laugh, too. "I have been dying to touch the earth since we left the city," I said, still sitting on the ground. "The smells out here are so lovely."

"You are going to have such a wonderful time during this visit if something as simple as touching the earth makes you happy."

"I think it's also all the space," I shared, finally getting up. "There's no one to see you out here. I imagine you can run and walk and do whatever you like without dozens of sets of eyes watching every move."

"That, sweet Julia, is precisely the point. This will be quite an education for you."

Back in the carriage, Margaret swept her arm in front of her as if she were a conductor and told me that everything I could see was natural and would always stay that way. She told me that Harriet, and her beloved husband Augustus, knew it was important to protect the land, nesting grounds for the birds, animals, and the very air they all breathed.

"We cannot keep taking things, building things, and emptying our garbage into the rivers and lakes," she explained as she motioned to the driver to move on. "Everything is connected, you see, and we must take care not to destroy one thing, for it may depend on the next. Life is a circle, really, if you think about it. We must all do our part."

I had never thought of things like this before. I suppose if one can say a heart changes and grows, just as a young boy or girl also grows, then a mind can grow and expand also. I was seeing and doing things that I had never before dreamed possible or thought I might experience. Riding in a lovely carriage with a hired driver to a woman's retreat with the mother-in-law I thought hated me was as much of a miracle as were these open and thoughtful discussions. I almost felt as if I could fly myself, and we hadn't even gotten to the house yet.

Less than an hour later, the road turned off to the right. We took a left branch and the road immediately narrowed considerably. Margaret pointed out that we were now riding parallel to a small river, and as we drove on, the river widened and it looked so inviting, as the heat of the day had risen up to cover all three of us. Finally, we came to the end of the road, and I was delighted to see several large barns, a stable, and a long white wooden and stone house that was almost engulfed in beautiful flower gardens. Harriet came out to greet us immediately and the surprises were apparently just beginning.

She was not dressed formally at all—in fact, I had never before seen a woman dressed the way she was. She wore a basic black skirt

that was inches above her ankles and did not appear to be supported
by the layers of petticoats that added extra weight to every woman's
body. It looked as if she was wearing her husband's white dress shirt,
and it was not tucked in so she could move about freely, and she was
barefoot. She looked so comfortable and free as she moved toward
us! I know my mouth dropped open at the sight of her running to the
carriage.

"Welcome to paradise, dears!" she said, extending a hand to me.

"It's beautiful here," I said, already feeling overdressed and inar-
ticulate. "I suppose this must be what heaven looks like."

"It is heaven, dear. Heaven is right here, where we live. We must
create it or go out and find it, and here you are!"

The driver disappeared and would return in five days, if by magic,
when it was time to leave. In a matter of seconds, I was not-so-quietly
swept into yet another new world, and it was one that I would hate to
leave and try to recreate the rest of my life.

The next surprise was the fact that the three of us would be alone
in the house and that we could do, be, and say whatever we wanted.
Augustus was at one of their other properties—there were three
more—and Harriet had dismissed her cook, housekeeper, gardener—
everyone but the stable and farm workers—so we could "be ourselves
without the eyes of the world." I was delighted when I went to my room
to unpack and found a lovely simple skirt and short-sleeved blouse sitting on the bed. I was hesitant at first to put on the clothes, and I kept
looking out the window in hopes of seeing Margaret dressed equally
as informally. When I padded down the steps, gloriously barefoot, and
headed back into the kitchen, I could not believe my eyes. Margaret
was sitting on the counter, dressed the same way, her own bare feet
dangling, and she was eating an apple.

Before I entered the kitchen, I stood there quietly for a short while,
wondering how all those sweet moments of my own barefooted youth
could have been swept away so quickly. Five years before this moment,
I had been but a child myself, and just before that I had been running
through the streets with the neighbors, not caring what I looked like
or who saw me. How my life had changed and it wasn't necessarily, as
Margaret and Harriet were proving to me, all for the better. Where
had all these rules about behavior come from? I let out a big sigh and

walked into the kitchen and into five days of adventure that would set my sails in an entirely new direction.

Margaret and her best friend had a plan for me. This was not going to be a simple, sitting on the counter respite, but a full-on course in freethinking and accountability. My education began over tea and warm bread as Harriet told me about her family's wealth, her husband's wealth, and the duties one must accept that go along with the gifts of money. She talked about her own family background in the cotton and mercantile industry and how her relatives had all been active in the anti-slavery movement, social issues, and always helping others less fortunate. Her husband's money came from South American nitrate and silver mines, and Augustus was also a politician who had donated money to build the Hemenway Gymnasium at Harvard. The arts, theater, the suffrage moment—she went on and on about everything they were involved with and how important it was for not just the men, but also the women to step forward and make a difference in the world.

"I want to show you some things during your visit, Julia, things of great beauty, and I want you to think about your life in a way that perhaps you have never thought of it before," she said, grasping my hands across the table. "I know you have suffered a great loss, as have both Margaret and I, and you must think of that loss and use it to gain strength. "

I was very touched by her openness yet also confused. I had no idea about money, how much we had, how wealthy Charles was, and I had especially never thought of his money as mine. The world from my point of view was still very divided, with men on one side of the street and women on the other. Dare I risk sharing these thoughts?

Margaret stepped in to ease my mind. "It's not as easy for us as it is for Harriet, Julia. Augustus was raised by strong, open women who were always a part of business and domestic dealings, and our men are different, and I must confess part of that is my fault and I'm sorry."

"Oh! Margaret! Don't say that!"

"It's true. Until I met Harriet and the other women in the Audubon, I all but encouraged George and Charles to dominate me, and you, as well. You must consider both of us as friends and sisters. There is so much work to do! So much that we can change. It is so very exciting to know what I know now and to see the world in such a new way."

"I don't know anything about money or even what businesses Charles and George are all involved in," I finally said. "I feel foolish, yet I can't stop thinking about the meeting you took me to and the birds and those hats. It's so sad!"

Margaret and Harriet both smiled at the same time, and I correctly guessed that the birds and the hats and the Audubon were the causes closest to the center of their hearts. I was about to learn so much about life and men and my own husband that my head would spin for days and days after I got back to Boston. But first I had to do something that I thought only young schoolgirls did during recess. Margaret and Harriet made me put my right hand on the table and they put their right hands on top of mine.

"You must promise to say whatever it is you want to say and to keep what happens this weekend in a safe place inside of you," Harriet said, looking me directly in the eye. "We will never hurt you and we know you will never hurt us."

"I promise," I said with every fiber of my being and with such a feeling of safeness and tenderness that I had to fight back tears.

These feelings of great joy and love around women were new to me, but I realized how much I needed their support and care, and I only hoped that I could give them something in return. I did love Charles with all of my heart, but the feelings for these women, my new sisters, was beyond the closeness I had once even felt with my own sister. I fell into their arms and their kindness those few days, and just as I thought my marriage and falling in love was life-changing, I learned that many things could change a life.

We laughed and cooked our meals together in the kitchen. Harriet took us for a ride in an old wagon around the edge of the river, driving us herself—with great skill, I might add—while we talked nonstop, and I learned so very much. I discovered that I was terribly wealthy because the day I married Charles I had become part of the Briton family and its financial dynasty. Margaret taught me how to add my name to the bank accounts if it was not already added, and she told me where Charles kept a bit of cash—bottom desk drawer, behind his Bible, of all things—and from the first night on, we concluded every day on the back side of the house by drinking sherry and talking about everything, especially about the Audubon.

Kris Radish

The first night, I realize now, was in preparation for what they were about to show me the following night after a record-breaking three glasses of delicious wine. I had not picked up on the subtle nuances between these two best friends who could have an entire conversation with a nod of the head, a blink of an eye, or a sweet smile. So the first night, we sipped our drinks, watched the fireflies descend and light up the horizon, and listened to the birds saying goodnight to each other as the sun slipped behind the far side of the river. But the following night, after my first glass of wine and a day that had been spent exploring and wading through the water, they were ready to show me something I would never forget the rest of my life.

It was another beautiful summer evening with the heat receding and the frogs chirping and the birds finding their nests after a hard day of hunting. Harriet had cooked us a lovely roast with potatoes and vegetables fresh from the garden, and I was drinking my sherry with such gusto that I did not feel the change that suddenly surrounded me or the exchange that surely must have passed between these two bright and generous women.

Harriet simply rose, took my arm, and without saying a word, walked me into the house and through the kitchen and into the semi-formal dining room. We had been eating all of our meals informally in the kitchen, and I had not even bothered to look around the house because it was the outdoors that really interested me.

She walked me to the far side of the table with Margaret on her heels, stopped, and then turned me and held me with both her hands.

"We need you," she said so very seriously, and I had absolutely no idea what she was about to say. "I'm going to show you something, something horrible, but something that can be stopped. Now, take your glass and drink it all down and then come to the other side of the table."

I did what she told me to do and felt the wine rush into my system and embolden me with a surge of energy and power. Then I walked to the other end of the table and looked down.

Harriet had assembled dozens of photographs of dead birds. I leaned over the table to get as close as possible and to make certain that what I was seeing was real. I braced myself with both hands as my eyes went from one photograph to the other. Beautiful dead birds hanging from clotheslines. Beautiful dead birds lined up on a beach with smiling gunmen standing next to them. Beautiful dead birds lined up in crates for shipment to who knows where. Beautiful dead birds lined up on a porch with the guns that shot them visible in the background. Beautiful dead birds lined up with their broken necks pointing toward their lovely winged feet.

I didn't say anything for a long time because I could not speak. I picked up each photograph and held it close to my eyes, and I was overcome with a sense of loss that surely did not equal the loss of my three babies but, nonetheless, was a surge of devastating grief. Even without being able to hold a baby in my hands, I was thinking like a mother because I was a mother. I thought about how these once-free birds had been simply skimming along the base of the sky when they had been shot in midair. I thought about how there was a baby, or a mate, waiting back at the nest or on some tree branch, calling, calling, calling for one of these dead birds that would never return. I thought about the sacred nesting spots of birds and how they must have taken great care in building their lives, just as I was taking great care of mine, and then I knew how ridiculous it was to put fashion in front of something as important as the life of a bird that was a living thing. I also knew that there was a great difference between hunting for food and hunting for fun and to please the whims of fashionable women.

Margaret and Harriet were looking at the photographs also, but standing back a bit and letting me form my own thoughts and feelings, which made me love them even more. It's never easy to pause for a moment like I did and see things that others might deem as obvious but that have passed unnoticed right by your own eyes. My birth family never really told me what to think, but the expectations of life, of what they had known, and what they thought I might attain were as obvious as the nose on my own face. It was time for me to think for myself, and as easy as that might seem, it would not be a simple task. During the coming months, I would challenge every single notion that the world thought proper and every expectation society had on a woman named Mrs. Briton.

My conversation following the viewing of the dead birds with these two women took more than a few hours and thankfully, more than three glasses of wine, which was something I had never done before—only men were allowed to drink and enjoy themselves the way we were those precious, lovely days. We ended up back outside, because I was quickly discovering that's where I felt most at home, after the photographs had been packed away and they had needlessly reassured me that the photos had been taken from Maine to Florida and that we must work harder.

"It is getting worse instead of better," Harriet said, moving to the very end of her chair on the porch. "Our biggest concern now is in Florida. The legislature there has passed the Audubon Model Law outlawing plume hunting, but enforcing is very hard, and as you know, women still want birds on their hats."

"And our husbands are making the hats," Margaret chimed in.

"I had no idea there were laws about these things," I said. "How can they still be shooting birds for feathers if there is a law?"

"Enforcement is difficult when you only have one game warden for the entire state and it's been a very lucrative way for many men to make a living," Harriet said. "Education is key, but no one is stepping up to handle Florida, and believe it or not, many people still do not see this as a problem or important at all."

"What needs to be done?" I was eager but still felt like a schoolgirl who's missed every important lesson on test day.

"We are trying to get someone interested in going to Florida to set up an Audubon office, to let the hunters and their families know that the slaughter of all these birds is wrong, and to work with politicians," Harriet explained. "And of course there's also the overwhelming task of convincing the men and women who make the hats and sell them to stop it. When you check your bank book, dear, you will see how lucrative it is."

"Of course," I said, looking at Margaret, and then boldly added, "Margaret and I have our work cut out for us, and I'm sure someone will explain to me exactly how this is all going to happen."

Both women laughed and said that's what the meetings back in Boston were for and that was also why I was being recruited.

The wine was a great tonic as we all spoke our minds so freely, not that it had been much of a problem before this, but some things are spoken much easier with a bit of help. It was true, they both agreed, that the key to keeping birds alive was to work with the milliners and importers, men like Charles and George, and this was the part they especially wanted kept secret. I had no idea how that was going to happen, and I decided to let my questions rest as I thought about all those birds and then began imagining them lined up in boxes in one of the stores that Charles owned or at his own factory. The thought, and what I had just seen in the house, made me shudder.

"Are you okay, dear?" Margaret asked as she leaned over to put her hand on my knee.

"Yes, but it's so much to take in," I said, trying to imagine what in the world I could do to change what seemed like a very serious problem. "It's so needless and I've never bothered to think of such things before."

"You are thinking now, Julia, and that is all that matters. Some women never even get this far, but as you can now see, the world is spinning faster every day, every single day," Margaret said with great tenderness.

"Well, enough of this serious talk for tonight, then," Harriet said, rising to her feet. "Tomorrow will be a day filled with nothing but joy so you'd better rest up. I'm going to show you both something that will astound you, and then, if you are feeling daring, we will finish the day off with yet another adventure."

That night, as I did every night there, I slept with both of my windows pulled open and listened to the night sounds that eventually narrowed off into a lovely near silence so all I could hear was the sweet rushing of the river, water moving against the rocks, and the light wind pushing waves into the shoreline. I fell asleep imagining I was lying with my hand dangling in the river and immediately had a sweet dream about all those dead birds. Margaret, Harriet, and I had become miracle workers, and we were traveling up and down the coast from Florida to Maine, resurrecting all of the dead birds. There were rows and rows of them everywhere we went, and we took turns touching their wings and every single one of them came back to life, rose slowly into the air, circled us, and then dipped away and disappeared in the clouds.

In some ways this dream, which I had many, many times following that night, would become almost a reality. But that night, when I drifted off to sleep, I was only thinking about the next day's adventures, which were remarkable to say the least.

It was still dark outside when I felt someone gently pushing on my arm. Harriet was standing by the bed with an oil lamp in her hand and wearing a very large grin.

"The day is starting early and it's going to be hot later so wear as little clothing as possible," she advised. "Shoes for sure though, and come down when you are ready. We'll have a very quick breakfast in the kitchen and be on our way."

What in the world? I quickly hopped out of bed and put on the light clothes, the short skirt, and blouse that had been waiting for me in my room. When I laced up my shoes, I laughed out loud, imagining what the high fashion women in downtown Boston would think of my strange outfit. It would become even stranger very quickly.

The three of us ate a slice of bread and drank a glass of milk, and I could see a small sliver of light breaking through the night's darkness outside the kitchen window. When I could not stand the suspense any longer, I asked what we were doing, and Harriet smiled and handed me a long piece of thin rope.

"First we are going to tie up our skirts so we can walk very fast, and then we are going to go bird watching and see something that very few people have ever seen."

"What?" I said with a bit of uncertainty and excitement. "This is all such a mystery."

"We are going to walk through the fields and we must walk quickly to get into place, and well, here, dear, watch me."

Harriet took the rope, looped it around her waist, and then brought it between her legs and pulled up her skirt so it looked as if she were wearing a pair of men's trousers. It looked silly to me at first, but the moment we headed out the door and I could walk with such ease and quickness, my skirt moving with me and not against me, I felt as if I could run all the way back to Boston. There was barely enough light to see, but Harriet walked first, carrying a long spyglass and a small basket that had jars of water, bread, and fresh berries she had picked the day before. We walked very fast to the river and across a wooden bridge, with just enough light so we did not stumble. We walked for close to an hour through a long field and then down a hill where she stopped to tell us that we must now walk as quietly as possible. There were towering oaks and maples and then we were inside a pine forest and suddenly there was a huge lake in front of us. Harriet put her finger to her lips and we continued to follow her around the edge of the lake for just a few minutes until we came upon a shelter that had been made with downed pine branches.

The shelter was three-sided so we could look out onto the lake and the small island that was directly in front of us, and it didn't take me long to discover why we were there. The entire area was an oasis for birds. We sat in a row on the pine boughs—legs crossed, thank heavens for our makeshift trousers—and simply looked.

There were dozens and dozens of ducks and geese padding in circles everywhere, and yellow, green, and red hummingbirds swirled around the flowers so close that I could have reached out and touched them. There was a nest of blue birds off to the side where Margaret was sitting, and a group of birds that I could not identify were circling above the island. I had never seen so many different species of birds in one spot, but it made sense because of the fresh water, foliage and food, and because there were no men with shotguns waiting in the bushes.

During the next few hours, I saw my first common merganser, a glossy green-headed, red-billed, regal-looking duck that had ruffled feathers, and its female mate which had a gorgeous gray bushy head. Harriet leaned in occasionally to say things like, "It's rare to see a merganser this far south in summer," or, "The sparrow hawks just moved into that dead tree last month." When we took to using the telescope to watch a bald eagle feed its young, I thought for sure that would be the highlight of the adventure, for I had never seen anything so beautiful and amazing. The nest was in the highest tree on the island and the birds were striking, not just because of their bold black and white coloring, but also because of their stately magnificence, and when I watched one skim the water, pluck out a fish, and then tilt back its head in a moment of utter triumph, I felt my heart stop. Margaret said she had seen eagle feathers in hats, and I could not fathom shooting such a majestic creature. The eagle swirled joyously for a few moments, then circled and landed back in its nest where the mouths of the babies were open and eager for the bits of fish they were about to receive.

We sat in the small structure for hours and moved just enough to keep the blood flowing in our legs. I was certain the eagle was the highlight of the day when Harriet suddenly grabbed my arm, took in a very large breath, and simply pointed her head directly to my left. I learned later that we were watching a pair of fork-tailed flycatchers, an absolute rarity in a place like Canton, or really, anywhere this far north. James Audubon had painted one in New Jersey, but that was considered an amazing oddity as the birds lived in the West Indies and Mexico. The blue-gray bird had a dot of orange on the top of its head, but what made it truly remarkable was its tail, the longest of any bird in relation to its size, in the world. The birds we watched had tails that were at least three feet long and bodies that appeared to be only several inches in length. To say it was mesmerizing is not saying enough. I could not take my eyes off of these exquisite creatures and their grace and beauty made me seem small somehow, and then something else rose up inside of me.

I felt an emotional wave rush through me, and it felt as if someone or something had gotten inside of me and was running a paintbrush inside of me and changing who I was, what I looked like, the very direction of my entire life. The world around me grew hazy—for a time even Margaret and Harriet disappeared—and the beautiful mysteries of nature and the birds that I had witnessed felt like a sacred and lasting revelation to me.

I sat in awe for a very long time until Margaret and Harriet got up, and when I joined them, it is safe to say that I was no longer the same woman that I had been. It may sound strange, but ever since that day, it felt as if one of those birds had flown inside of me and I had become one with them and they with me. Everything had changed.

We walked quietly back toward the river, no one said a word, and then we sat on the bridge and ate the food that was in the basket. I could not get my mind or heart to stop swirling, and then, on a day that was already remarkable, one more thing happened.

In the heat of the day—even with our skirts still roped up high it was terribly hot—when I swirled to look behind me and then turned back, Margaret and Harriet were disrobing and giggling like naughty schoolgirls.

"Join us," Harriet screamed in delight as she walked off the bridge and jumped into the water.

There was no turning back for me. I slipped off my skirt and blouse, and even my undergarments, and joined them in the cool, glorious water. I floated and laughed and felt as if I had been re-baptized and that life was once again starting anew.

The Sadness of Loss and Forgotten Passions

I was so moved by the tape I named The Defining Moment of Julia's Life that I did something terrible. I stole it. And it's a good thing I did because what was about to happen dealt both of us a terrible blow that even now makes my hands shake, my eyes fill up, and my heart surge with an avalanche of sadness.

Julia came home from the hospital but was really never the same again. My grandmother moved in to help with her care, which meant my mother was around all of the time too, and I was not very fond of my mother because I felt she had chosen my father over me. I also blamed him, and her too, for Julia's stroke. How can you not know your husband is nuts? I obviously had a lot to learn, but I was still fifteen, even if I had sipped whiskey with Joni Mitchell and seen half the country. There was much more to come, but hindsight is a wonderful tool for navigating the future and not the past. I wish I could go back and recapture what I lost and missed, but that is, of course, impossible.

Instead, I turned sixteen, my brother taught me how to drive, and while Julia was undergoing speech therapy and slowly trying to regain her strength, I was not-so-subtly learning how to be even more of a jackass than I already had been. My father was in and out of several institutions and my mother was, of course, in and out of denial. I manipulated Julia into letting me use her car, a green 1962 Chevy Impala that I would give my eyeteeth to own right now, and I tried to be gone as much as possible.

News of her decline circulated around the globe like wildfire, and letters and cards filled up the mailbox. My grandmother talked to reporters, updated the necessary friends, and put notices of her progress in The Briton Birding Journal, which was one of Julia's projects that my grandmother had taken over when Julia became ill. I still have some of the newspaper articles from back then and sometimes when I get full of myself, I pull them out and bump my big ego back to humble status by looking at the sullen, unattractive girl sitting with her hands on her chin in the background. What a shame I was, what a shame.

It wasn't that I had forgotten about the tapes, especially the one I kept under my padded bra in my dresser, but it was impossible to get into her room because someone was always in there with her, and my newfound kidnapping notoriety had brought me my first boyfriend. Think about it. I was semi-attractive, no one paid me much attention, and I had twenty-four-hour access to a vehicle. It was a near deadly combination and I embraced it all with great gusto.

I drank and made out with old what's-his-name and started to smoke tons of weed behind the house. School had started and my grades dropped and no one seemed to notice, which of course was a shame, but it wasn't as if I were still a little girl. I did get lost in the shuffle of my parents' messed-up lives, Julia's demise, the absence of all three of my college-attending siblings, and a world that had been dropkicked into liberal orbit by the revolution of the '60s. I was going to make a lot of mistakes, learn so many things the hard way, and stretch out my own "year" way too long.

Julia and I did have a few moments of closeness here and there during the next year, which passed so quickly I was astounded when I realized I was a senior in high school. She never did regain all of her speech abilities and when I went to sit by her, it was mostly to watch her sleep and dream, and I always thought she was reliving her life all over again. She would toss her head back and forth and mumble words that I guessed at: Charles, mother, Sarah, Catherine, Gabriel—the names of her lost babies—various bird names, and a variety of other names that I would eventually discover in the remainder of the tapes.

I realize now that I was already grieving, and no one ever really teaches you how to do that, do they? I held her hand those last few times, letting the warmth and remaining energy of her body seep into me, and when I knew no one was going to interrupt us, I climbed into bed with her and pushed my face against hers so I could always, always remember what she smelled and felt like.

Julia had another stroke less than a year after her first one and could no longer be cared for at home. I knew she was going to die, but nothing prepares you for that moment, even if you know it's coming. It's like being struck with a fast-moving semi-truck that has literally dropped from the sky. Unfortunately, I was not home when the phone call came, summoning me to the facility where she was being cared for and that fact—me not being able to say a real good-bye—only took me thirty years to get over. When I arrived home, I found half the world sobbing in Julia's kitchen and I knew without anyone saying a word, ran from the house, and did not come back for almost an entire day. But I really didn't go far.

I sat down by her bench, tucked into the bushes, and looked out across the river. I watched her beloved birds dip and circle and salute what they surely must have known was the passing of one of the greatest women who had ever lived. I felt hollow and ashamed of myself. There was such a feeling of general emptiness that I wondered if I would ever get over her death. The funeral was so large they had to move it to my high school gym, and for once, my immediate family pulled themselves together to handle an event that is still talked about in Vero Landing. It was attended by a Who's-Who of the environmental, ornithological, political, and Hollywood famous: Katharine Hepburn, Jacques Cousteau, Robert Redford, Maya Angelou, and First Lady Rosalynn Carter, to name a few. In lieu of flowers, donations totaled just over a million dollars, all of which went directly into a specific Audubon fund that had been designated in Julia's will. The fund was used to buy and protect six thousand acres of wetlands in Central Florida, three thousand acres of nesting grounds in Iowa, and a small island off the coast of North Carolina that Julia had spotted on her voyage to Florida in 1904.

It was so overwhelming, like her life and that Year, and then we were all left to try and go on without her. It took me so long to realize that she was always with me and around me, but this is really her story. When Julia died, I was seventeen, about to graduate from high school, about to enter a university she had once wanted to attend herself, and wondering how I was going to survive such a devastating loss.

One afternoon, my mother came into my room and said she had something to give me that Julia had left with her. My mother, and my sometimes-jealous two sisters, were well aware of my special bond with Julia, and they were very kind to me following her death. My mother was crying, and for a long time we held each other and had one of those fabulous get-it-out, purging, sobbing cries that are a necessary part of the grieving process. It also brought my mother and me an inch or two closer and I know Julia would have loved that.

When we finished, she stood up, handed me an envelope, brushed the side of my face with her soft hand, and said, "She loved you very much. We are so lucky. So damn lucky, aren't we, sweetheart?"

When she left, I opened the envelope with trembling hands and then pulled out a very old photograph. It was her. Julia Briton. My trembling immediately escalated because the woman in the photograph was the same woman I had seen all those years ago when I was a girl, on the porch, listening to her tell her story. Although the photograph was not in color, it was the same woman I had seen in my mind's eye—the skirt and boots and blouse were there, and so was the unmistakable gaze of strength that had warmed me until the day she died. I had seen other photographs from her life, but never this one, the exact image that had faded into the great-grandmother I had known as a young girl.

There was also a small note inside the envelope. I touched each letter with my fingertips, trying to resurrect yet another image of her writing the note from her oak desk while she watched one of her last beloved sunsets.

My Kelly,

This young woman has always been inside of me, just as the young woman you have become will always be inside of you as you continue to grow, and now it is your turn. Carry on, my sweet girl. Just as you saw me, you will see what to do tomorrow and the day after. Live boldly, without regret, share my year if you think it may help, and when you look to the sky, every bird winging past in glorious delight will be carrying with it a sweet song from my own heart—just for you.

Love,

Your Julia

I treasured the note and her memory as I spun forward in my own life, mostly randomly and out of control. However, once Julia died, I truly felt abandoned and alone, and even the note wasn't much help. My siblings were gone and it would take my mother another ten years to realize she could not save my father. My grandmother moved into Julia's house, and eventually my mother did too, and once I left I stayed away a very long time. I dropped out of college twice, lived with a succession of men who never treated me very well, lived in Spain for another year, wrote hate letters to lots of people when I should have been undergoing therapy, married a man from Mexico who needed a green card, divorced him, developed a bit of a drinking problem... Well, I could go on, but what's really important is what happened when I went back home in 1994 when I was thirty-four years old and my grandmother died unexpectedly.

I hadn't bothered to try and figure out why I had been inexplicably drawn to history. I eventually graduated from Wellesley College, where Julia's mother had hoped she would attend school, with two degrees, one in Women's Studies—where Julia and her legacy was part of the coursework—and another in Twentieth Century History. I also had a master's degree in History but kept dropping out of the Ph.D. program. I was a bit lost again in 1994, out of a job, living with a friend, and then I came home for my grandmother's funeral.

Life, as most of us know, has a way of running over us and occasionally burying things that were once important and terribly meaningful. Julia's stories had been buried inside of me my entire life, and I still had the one precious but forgotten tape. But when I came back to face yet more grief and loss, it was as if she had been resurrected, and I remembered the emotional force of what I had heard on those tapes. Where were they now?

My mother was dealing with the loss of her mother, and being a bit older and somewhat wiser, I had almost come to understand why she had done some of the things she had. The tapes, as it happened, would bring us full circle. I approached her two days after the funeral when Julia's house was empty again and it was just the two of us walking around in a fog with a box of tissues in each hand.

"Mom, I have something to tell you and ask you."

She looked at me as if she were going to go look for a weapon, and

I can't say as I blamed her considering what I had put her through the past thirty-four years.

"I'm afraid to ask what it might be this time, oh wild child."

I took in a rather large dose of air and smiled, which threw her off a bit. "A long time ago during that summer when you were having a nervous breakdown, I found something in Julia's bedroom. "

"Do I need to get a strong beverage now?"

"Maybe later we will both need one, now that I am a responsible drinker, but for now, Mom, just listen."

I told her about the tapes and how they were not anything like what Julia had shared with us about "The Year." I said there were tons of details and experiences and emotional revelations that she had never shared with us. And I told her I had taken one of the tapes.

"What are you talking about? Have you already been drinking?"

"No! I found an old tape recorder and when Julia was busy, I started to listen to the tapes, and I kept one." I was almost shouting with excitement and shock. "You don't know about this?"

"Hell no, I do not know about this." My mother looked as if she'd seen her own mother's ghost just pass through the kitchen."

"You've never seen the tape recorder or the tapes?"

"Absolutely not! Where was it the last time you saw it?"

"In the bottom drawer of Julia's dresser."

"Well, Grandma moved up there and this house has not been cleaned thoroughly in forty years. I was never one to snoop anyway, not like someone else I know."

"Oh, Mom! I was fifteen and you were living on antidepressants and I had just been kidnapped for crying out loud."

"I thought we were over all of that."

My mother said this to the back of my head because I was racing up the steps and running toward Julia's bedroom. I ran to the dresser and politely waited for my mother to catch up before I pulled open the bottom drawer, and in an instant, I was a teenager again, reaching in to get the secret treasure.

"Oh my God!" my mother screamed as she saw the recorder and realized, this time anyway, I had not been lying. I swear the tape recorder was exactly how I had placed it nineteen years before. There was a thin layer of dust on it and all the tapes were lined up just as they had been

the last time I used it. I pulled it out and placed it on the bed, just as I had done all those years ago, and I looked up at my mother.

She was standing with her hands covering her face, and it was the first time that I bothered to notice how much she looked like Julia. She had not let her hair go gray, had the same high cheekbones and lovely eyes, and the lines that descended from her eyes and the corners of her mouth only made her appear more beautiful, natural, and real. I could only hope to hold my age that well. In a burst of sweet emotion, I grabbed her to my chest and just held her there.

"Let's listen to every single tape," I suggested.

"Where's the missing one?" she asked without letting go of me, her face snuggled against mine.

"In my jewelry box back home. I'd forgotten all about it until I came back, and I'm sorry it took me so long."

"Julia would have something to say about that, you jackass. I've missed you."

That was enough emotion for me and I pushed away and went to see if the recorder would work. It was the first recorder that was really portable, but it needed batteries after all those years. My mother not so much ran as flew down the stairs and came back with penlight batteries. After I clicked them into place, I asked her if she was ready.

"What could there possibly be on those tapes that we don't already know?"

"Oh, Mom, it's... well, amazing, and are you sure you want to do this?"

I think she was about ready to slap me when she said, "Yes. Please turn it on."

The tapes were numbered and before I clicked on the first one, I pulled over a chair for my mother because I thought she might faint when she heard Julia's voice. It's a good thing I did because when I turned it on, I needed something to lean on, too. My mother cried so hard, hearing Julia's voice and the beginnings of her true story, that I had to stop the tapes several times. We didn't exchange one word, even when I got up to change the tapes, but it was obvious we were both struggling and overcome with the weight of it all. When I got to Tape Six, the one I had taken, I simply told her, as best as I could, how it was a transforming adventure that I was certain had totally changed Julia's life.

"I'm just astounded, you know. How could we not have known all these things? Why didn't she tell us the real story? What does it all mean?" My mother's lip was quivering and it was the first time in my life that I wanted to protect her, take care of her, be the mother myself.

"I suppose there's a reason for this and for her editing out what we are hearing about now," I said, simply thinking out loud. "I'm different now in many ways than the first time I heard these tapes, but it's so overwhelming and touching."

My mother was staring at the machine and I was standing next to her. It must have looked like we were crazy, and for those minutes and the hours that were about to come, we were not just crazy looking, but totally transported. My mother turned to look at me and I knew we were going to listen to every tape, one after another, even if it took all night, which is exactly what we did.

I put in Tape Seven, sat down next to her with my hand on top of hers, and it was suddenly August of 1904 and we were back in Brookline about to help Julia move into the fifth month of her most amazing year.

The Arrival of the New Mrs. Julia Briton

Boston—First Two Weeks of August, 1904

O ne afternoon when I was a little girl, my father took me aside and handed me a small bag of hard candy. The candy may as well have dropped from the sky because treats like this were a rarity in our house. My father knew I had a large sweet tooth. I was always the first one at our house to grab for a piece of cake or a cookie on the days my mother baked.

"Don't tell anyone about this," he whispered, bending down to push his lips against my ear.

"Oh Daddy, I won't!" I promised and then proceeded to eat every piece of candy in the bag during the next hour, and of course, I also became violently ill about an hour later. During the next few years, until I turned into a teenager, he brought me a special bag of candy at least once a month and I never told a soul.

My return to Charles and the girls and Brookline made me feel as if I were once again taking candy and couldn't say a word, only this time, the bag of candy was the weight of what I now knew, not just about myself, but of the world around me. The world of Charles and fathers and money and all those beautiful birds and my new and blossoming thoughts about women and what they can and must accomplish. There was no one I could talk to about this besides Margaret, and the weight of it all quickly made me feel as if I had once again eaten an entire bag of candy. I felt a bit sick, and I'm certain those around me thought it was a bit of a regression from the last pregnancy.

Margaret warned me that coming back into the world I had left so innocently was not going to be easy. We talked about it the last night before we left. I was so very emotional because one part of me wanted to stay with Harriet and Margaret and spend the rest of my life walking through fields, watching birds, and drinking whiskey and wine on the back porch. Who wouldn't? Reality does not hold hands with frivolity and ease, and I knew there were many things to face back in Boston. I surely did underestimate how difficult it was going to be.

Charles had not been his usual self before I left and only seemed more withdrawn when I returned, which may have been a bit of a blessing. I was astonished that my feelings for him had turned so sour and hurtful. Knowledge can do that, I know, but the strength of my doubt about my place in his world was almost too much for me to bear, and I had to bite my tongue almost every second I was in the same room with him. A few times it was all I could do not to blurt out questions like, "Are there dead birds in your factory?" and, "Why do you not share your business dealings with me?" But I was always able to control myself and step away. I was spending a great deal of time perfecting The Liar's Brow, which would come in very handy during the next few months.

I started to walk again, to visit the birds in the park and talk with the babies, but my mind was now clouded with thoughts of winged creatures and the Audubon and what must be done to save their precious lives. I did not feel guilty that I was thinking of the birds more than of the children, but I had this strange feeling, a kind of quiet sureness, that the birds that had appeared outside of my window were winged messages of love from me to the hearts of their sweet spirits. I was restless and it was more difficult for me to simply sit on the bench and stare off into the trees. It was worse at home because there simply wasn't much to do.

Ella and Ruby had polished, shined, cleaned, and sparkled every inch of the house, and Charles had put on a bit of weight from their new recipes as Ella, unfortunately, had decided to hone her baking skills in hopes of one day owning her own bakery. I decided to catch up again on my reading, which was fine for a few hours, but after that, a try at needlework, pacing on the porch, and walking still left me hours and hours every day.

One afternoon several days after my return, I not so much asked, but ordered the girls to come with me outside and I did something that shocked them. I made them sit and rock on the big front porch chairs as I mixed up some sweet tea and I waited on them. It was as if we were having a grown-up's tea party and they giggled and we talked and I so wished I could share with them everything, but I could not. I did ask them about their lives and dreams and I felt a pull at my heart and the growing realization that it was only money and status that kept people apart. I felt great tenderness for these two women in the exact same way I did for Margaret and Harriet.

"Oh, I think we all have the same dreams," Ella shared. "This here is one of my dreams for sure! Just to sit and rock and have a cold drink and know that no one is going to yell at me or make me do something horrible. This, misses, this is part of a dream."

"Well, you are so sweet to us," Ruby added. "I don't believe anyone I've ever worked for has been nicer or bothered to even ask what I think or feel. I have to stop and think for a minute now. Dreams, well, my mum would say that dreams are for the foolish, and I am foolish so dreams are okay, then."

"What are the dreams?" I asked, thinking to myself that mine had been totally rearranged the past few months.

Both women were quiet for a moment and then turned to look at each other. In that moment, I realized they most surely must be best friends and confidants. They traveled to work each day on foot from the same neighborhood, spent more time with me and my house than in their own homes, and they had hours to talk while they worked. A very small part of me was jealous for a moment and then very quickly I was ashamed, let it all go, and wondered what it was like where they lived. Before I could ask about that, Ruby began to speak.

"We would like a house like this and a stable behind the house and all these fine things you and Mr. Briton have, everyone would want this, but when I really think about it, I would love to be on a farm and out of the city and to live just simply with the man I loved, and now don't take this wrong, but I would love to never have to work for someone again."

"I take no offense," I said, touching Ruby lightly on the hand.

Ella just smiled and nodded in agreement, and then I asked if and when they had children, what then would they want for them?

They both stopped rocking at the same moment and turned to look at me. I reassured them that I was fine but simply curious about the dreams they might have as mothers.

Ella nodded to Ruby and it was apparent they had already discussed the answer. Ruby spoke softly and with sureness.

"I would want my children to have what I do not have and may not ever have and that would be a choice. They could go to a university if they wanted, buy a house on this street, travel the world, and perhaps do something wonderful that changes the world or maybe discover something to help people. But really, that's all, just a choice. That is something I have never had and neither has Ruby."

This conversation would weigh on me for a very long time and I would never let go of Ruby and Ella, and they would help me in ways that they could never have imagined. I like to think I helped them too, and after that day, I set up new house rules that meant there were no rules at all—except when Charles was around. I even went so far as to drink sherry with them on the back steps and I told them I had swum naked in Canton and witnessed the most magnificent slice of wilderness I had ever seen. But when Charles came home, we all had to play at being what he thought we were, and that was a terrible burden to carry with me. Margaret had warned me about this and I was trying to be true to my word. I said I would be careful and take my time and think before I did anything that might jeopardize my marriage or my status as a Briton.

I was clearly not the same woman I had been when we married, yet I was frightened to share any parts of my new self with Charles. I tried several times during the first week when he asked about the trip, but it felt as if the time away was mine and mine alone, and I had absolutely no idea how to launch into some of my concerns and openly discuss something as simple as what I was supposed to do for the rest of my life if we could not have children and there were not even any windows to dust. Fortunately, something occurred to bring at least one

111

important issue out in the open. And it ended up being the beginning of a very rapid chain of events.

I had been tempted almost every day to sneak into Charles's office and look for his secret stash of money behind his Bible and to go over the books he kept. I was trying hard to honor our relationship and the boundaries that had been drawn to keep us, well, I suppose, each in our own place, which was making less and less sense to me. The second Friday after my return, when I thought I might go out of my mind if I did not do something, I sat down in the living room—a lovely room I might add with a full view of the street, solid maple and oak furniture, and the most lovely deep green velvet couch—to read the paper and drink tea.

It did not take me long to discover a story about a man I did not know even existed but who would end up playing a rather large role in my life. His name was Guy Bradley and the Audubon had hired him as their first game warden down at the very bottom of Florida, and he was definitely having a very hard time. My tea went cold as I read every word of the story with trembling hands.

Mr. Bradley was once himself a plume hunter and is thus well aware of the ways in which hunters are illegally killing thousands of nesting birds for their plumes so that they may decorate women's hats. "I've seen three men kill hundreds of birds in one afternoon," Mr. Bradley explained. 'The birds most favored now are the roseate spoonbills and ibises. They are a beauty to behold in the wild, and I know with all certainty if it were not the fashion and these men were not paid so handsomely by the milliners, that the birds would live and flourish."

Needless to say, my heart landed in my throat as I read about his hardships, how he feared for his life on a daily basis, and how in the wilds of South Florida, beauty, survival, and adventure were wound as tightly as the vines meshed on the tree outside my window. That night I could not help myself and perhaps that was a good thing. A woman, or even a man, cannot keep emotions and thoughts and longings bottled up for too long.

The girls had prepared a lovely dinner, and I could barely swallow a bite. I was nervous and knew that I had to say something to Charles, yet I also knew I had to pick the correct moment. I dismissed the girls after dinner as Charles retreated to his office for his cigar and brandy.

I waited until I thought he may have been enjoying his second drink and then I knocked.

"It's me, Julia. May I come in?" I asked tentatively, as I had never before approached him while he was in his private world.

"Yes," he said with surprise in his voice, pulling open the door almost instantly. "This is a surprise, Julia. Is everything okay?"

"Yes, dear, yes, it is. I thought we might just have a chat."

"Sit, please."

"May I also have some brandy?"

Charles was so startled that he didn't know what to say, so I got up and poured myself a glass and sat back down as his wide eyes followed me. The first sip gave me courage and so did the second and third. We talked for a short while about household affairs and the girls, and I was thinking how lovely it would be to do this every evening. I so wanted a glimpse of his world and I knew I would never get it unless I pushed, and finally, after the fourth sip, I started in with questions about his work.

"Tell what is going on at the factories and the shops, Charles. I'd like to know."

He looked even more startled. I was grateful that I had waited for him to start on his second glass of brandy because he then launched into a tirade of revelations that is just what I wanted to hear.

"There is talk of unionizing all of the factories, and I have to tell you, Julia, that these bird lovers, your own mother-in-law included if you do not know, are going to ruin us! They are watching the ships deliver goods and working to enact laws that will prohibit us from getting what we need for our business, and so many of our sources are being affected. It's terrible, just absolutely terrible!"

I felt a line of anger rising inside of me that I struggled to push aside, and I nodded as he went on about rules and laws and how just yesterday women suffragettes accosted him on the street and asked to help with their cause. I could no longer stop myself.

"Would that be so wrong, Charles? Women have brains and we own businesses. I support suffrage. I would love to take the vote."

"Have you gone mad?" Charles was not quite shouting, but his voice was nowhere near the normal conversational tone we had been enjoying.

"Not at all. Why should one sex have the upper hand? Explain that to me if you will."

"That is just the way it's always been! Men are stronger. We are more educated. We all have our roles in this world, Julia, and the vote is for men and men alone."

"I disagree."

He went pale and I decided it was time to slice open the entire bee-hive. First, I had my fifth and last sip of brandy, and then I very gently put the newspaper I had been reading and had picked up before entering his office on his lap and opened to the page about Guy Bradley.

"What is this nonsense?"

He took a moment to read and I was tempted to get up and pour myself another glass of brandy, but I did not yet have quite enough courage. I simply sat and looked at him, trying very hard to conjure up Charles of the Heart and every ounce of love, admiration, and gratefulness I had for my husband. He was still very handsome, even with the new worry lines that were beginning to form on his forehead, and a very large part of me wanted him to get up, take me in his arms, and discuss everything that came to mind. But that was not to be.

"What of this?" he didn't so much say as snarl.

"Do you use feathers from these birds, these beautiful protected birds, in your millinery business?"

He threw down the paper, got on his feet, and took a step toward me. Fear rose inside of me, but I fought that too, got to my feet, and met his gaze.

"My business is my business."

"But technically it is also my business because we are now married."

"What would you know about running a business, making ends meet, balancing the books, managing employees, and walking amongst the giants in this world, Julia?"

I wanted to throw my glass in his face, slap him, hurl his desk out the window, but I knew I must outwit him to get what I needed. I desperately fought the urge to behave as he was behaving.

"Surely you did not fall in love with me and marry me only because I was beautiful, Charles? I am well read, smart, and I am bored sitting in this house all day long. The world is calling and the world is changing and you must hop on the train. Please answer my question. The birds, Charles. I want to know about the birds."

There are moments throughout all of our lives when time seems to stop, when the world that is spinning around us is suspended, and all motion except the beating of our own hearts has been put on hold. It's almost as if the world itself is undergoing a period of transformation and change and needs a second to realign its bearings. This was such a moment between Charles and myself. His beautiful blue eyes were dancing with anger and I was struck by the parallel between that, the softness and light inside of him that I knew existed and the harsh, bigoted, closed-off mind that was desperately trying to overpower me. Something inside of me surrendered then, but it was not to Charles and his old beliefs, but to the new world I had already stepped inside of and was about to embrace in ways that must have brought Charles to his knees.

This pause seemed endless, but I imagine it lasted less than ten seconds. I refused to move and held his gaze while his face reddened and he finally took a step back, set down his glass, and let out a breath so long and large I felt it brush across my face.

"The birds are none of your damned business, woman!"

Charles brushed past me, being careful not to touch me or look at me again. He grabbed his hat off the chair, picked up his light topcoat, and slammed the front door as he left the house. He did not come home that night and I did not sleep at all. I thought of my father, leaving every night, not as nosily as Charles had left, but leaving none-theless, and once the panic inside of me subsided, I held firm to my new convictions of a woman's place and my right to ask simple ques-tions and get answers. I was terribly worried about him and hoped he was not out wandering. Maybe he had gone to Margaret's house, or… where? Where does a man who might realize that his wife is changing in ways that he never dreamed possible go? What does a man do when he realizes that he can no longer control the woman he married? I had no idea. And I sat through the night thinking of not just Charles, but also of the unanswered question.

The morning birds caught me dozing in the bedroom chair just after dawn, as I had gotten into the habit of sleeping with the window open. It sounded as if they were lined up on the window and singing only for me, which may have been true. By the time I heard the girls laughing in the kitchen, I knew with all certainty that Charles had been very, very wrong when he said the birds were not my business.

The birds would soon not just become my business, but also the focus of my splendid and extraordinary life.

Tape Eight

The Most Frightening Day as Truth is Revealed

Boston—August 18, 1904

Charles unwittingly helped me decide what to do and where to go next when he left me a note two days after, not just our first fight as a married couple, but the first real yelling fight I had ever been a part of up until that point in my life. I had witnessed many arguments between my own parents, and my older siblings, but had always been protected from the emotional outbursts that others view as an ordinary part of life. I am certain this is because I was feeling things I had never felt before and because some of that feeling was for a man whom I thought was slipping away. Or perhaps it was I who was slipping away.

It was very awkward around out house the following day and the day after as I was very quiet—even the girls noticed—and Charles slipped in and out of the house and the bed the second night without so much as a word or a gesture that might have at the very least acknowledged my existence. I was about to send a note to Margaret, asking for help, when I came downstairs for breakfast that second morning to find a note from Charles tucked under my plate.

Julia,

I am sure you will see how necessary it is as my wife, as a Briton, to continue to function as we always have. Please think about this during my absence, and about how much you have to lose if you continue to think the kinds of thoughts you expressed in my office. I do love you very much and it is not simply because you are the most beautiful woman I have ever known. However, it is 1904 and not 1994. God knows what that will be like if women have their way. I am off to the Outer Banks with my father for an extended business trip. I trust when I return that things will be back to normal.

Your Loving Husband,

Charles Briton

This was a week of firsts because the moment I finished reading the letter, I picked up my plate and threw it across the entire length of the dining room with such force that the plate left a small dent in the wall. I also let out a bit of a scream, which I only found out about because the girls came running when they heard me.

"Julia, what is it? ... I mean, Missus," Ruby stammered, fearing I would scold her for calling me by my first name.

"From now on you both should call me Julia," I shouted as if I were mad at her for being so familiar and not the opposite.

"Yes, Julia, but are you okay?"

"I am very angry at my husband, ladies. I think you might say I am pissed at the bugger."

They both simultaneously put their hands to their mouths, and I could see they were trying to conceal a laugh, which is just what I needed. I smiled also, and they both started laughing so hard that they had to sit down, and I walked over to pick up the plate and the eggs, and I stood up and put my finger on the dent in the wall.

"Let this be remembered as the day Mrs. Julia Briton stood up, threw a plate, and said tradition be damned! It is 1904 and not 1804 and women have a right not only to vote, but to speak their minds and do more than sit and cross stitch!"

I was so empowered by my own words that I could have flown like one of my precious birds. I stood with the plate in one hand and the other hand on my hip, and the girls were not sure if they should laugh or applaud. I waited because I had suspected for quite some time that they were like-minded and most likely knew even more than I did about the changing world.

"Bravo! Bravo!" they exclaimed, and that is exactly what I was hoping to hear.

Emboldened by my wild morning, I talked to them in the kitchen, while I helped with dishes, about the exciting changes in the world without giving away the exact details of my confrontation with Charles or my growing inability to live the life that had been designed by someone else. I was very careful what I told them for several reasons. I did trust them, but I also knew they needed their jobs and I did not want to harm them in any way. I also wasn't sure what I was going to do next. We finished the dishes and they went about their household duties, and I came to stand in front of the office where this whole mess had started.

I decided not to go in but pushed the door open and noticed immediately that the desk had been cleaned off, the shelves on the back bookcase straightened, and the brandy bottle that usually sat on the front end had disappeared. I chuckled at that but then wondered how long Charles was planning to be away. What had been on his desk? What could he possibly be doing in the Outer Banks except scouting for more plume hunters?

It took me but a second to grow furious again, and I walked into the stables and was glad to see that the man who tended the horses was still there. I asked him to please hook up a carriage for me, and then I went back into the house and prepared myself for a journey into Boston that I hoped would answer the one question Charles had not been able to, or more likely, refused to answer.

I really didn't have much of a plan, but this would become my way of life during the next few months and as I headed toward the South End and toward the main factory where Charles did business. I only focused on the journey and not what might happen when I reached my destination. It was a Thursday, and one of a succession of lovely mid-summer days that called people to the streets and parks for a day they would remember come December, when the snow covered the ground and it was a chore to walk a simple block without wishing it was the hottest day of the year.

I had always relished summer and heat, and even when the most beautiful snowflakes had landed on my fingertips and I had danced on the frozen river with my new skates, I always wished for the sun and green grass and the flowers and trees that seemed to bask in the light. When I was a girl, I always thought the trees, shrubs, and flowers had died. The bare limbs and spindly stalks made me pine for blossoms, the sweet smell of summer, heat rising from the cobblestone streets. The summer of 1904 was hot and intense and just the way I liked it, and it seemed to get hotter the closer I got to the heart of the city and the busy streets and buildings that housed businesses and factories.

Margaret had told me during our Canton visit that Charles and George operated all of their millinery businesses out of one main factory and that is where I was headed. I turned right onto Summer Street in order to get there and then connected to Winter Street. The irony of this was not lost on me. I passed a suspender factory, a button factory, two blacksmith shops, and numerous small businesses and factories with names like S.C. Williams and Sons or John Hadley and Sons and was not at all surprised not to see something like B.K. Smith and Daughters. I'm certain that, if I had uttered this thought out loud—due to the fact that it looked as if I was the only female within a five-mile radius of Winter Street—I may never have gotten out of there alive.

It's safe to say a woman of my age, driving a carriage alone down the street, caused a bit of a commotion and it's also safe to say I enjoyed every moment of it. I waved as if I were in the midst of my own parade, shouted hello as if this was something I did every other day, and laughed when two men standing on the street asked if they could marry me. It's true I had no idea what I was going to do or say next, but I certainly did enjoy the ride!

And suddenly there it was, George Briton and Son, a brick building. Thank heavens for that, considering all the fires in Boston's wooden frame buildings. I stopped the carriage at the front door and realized that unless there was a miracle, the sign would never say Charles Briton and Son, or daughter for that matter. What in the world was I doing? I had no plan, no idea what to say, not one notion of what I was going to do.

It's common to want to retreat the moment before a battle or confrontation. Humans, after all, are animals, and I suspect those of us who are smart would rather go sip tea, or brandy, than have an unruly encounter. I was a bit torn as the horse snorted, because I was thinking about Charles and his honor and place in the world and also of the birds at the same time. Considering I was right there in front of a business that I technically owned a part of, I decided to draw around to the back and was glad to see there was a place to tie up the carriage, water the horse, and gather myself for a moment. Sometimes there is really nothing you can do to prepare yourself for what will come next. I thought for a moment, ran my fingers across my brow, and if by magic, I knew what I was going to do.

I grabbed my hat, featherless I might add, pulled it down over my eyes, and decided it made sense to enter through the back door, kind of a surprise entrance so to speak, and it was not only a surprise to me, but to the three men who were standing just beyond the door as well. The door was unlocked, and I walked right into some kind of heated discussion that stopped short the moment one of them, a small, bald man with a dark complexion and wearing tiny eyeglasses, saw me.

"What are you doing, Miss?"

"I came to have a look around."

"A look around, are you daft? This is a private business. You can't just wander in here."

"Allow me to introduce myself. I'm Mrs. Nellie Lewis," I lied.

"What?"

"Mrs. Lewis, and I was directed here to take a look around as I am opening a new millinery shop and I will be doing business with you."

The poor man was sputtering and his two comrades went slack-jawed as the short man came over and extended his hand. "I'm so sorry. I'm Jacob Duseman, the foreman here. Mr. Briton is out of the area and must have forgotten to let me know you were arriving. Our guests usually come through the front door. "

"I left my carriage back there. I was scouting new locations as we have big, big plans for several shops associated with Mr. Briton. I happened upon your offices by chance, I'm afraid. Is this appropriate?" The lies were pouring from me as if a faucet had been turned on inside of my lively brain.

"A look around…" The poor man was as red as a beet and had no idea what to do. The other two fellows had simply stepped back and disappeared. I took a step forward, put my hand on his arm, and said, "I just want to see what goes on here. It's so important to know all the ins and outs of a business. Don't you agree? May I call you by your first name?"

I believe I was flirting and he was so short I actually had to bend down and look him in the eye as I said it. I wasn't certain if Charles had ever shown them a photograph of me, and so I initially kept my hand across part of my face until I could tell there was no recognition. And yes, The Liar's Brow was definitely in high gear.

"That's fine, Mrs. Lewis," he stammered again. "Let me get you some water and wash my hands and I will show you around, but there ain't much to see. Just the things we divvy up to take to the shops and an office and lots of storage spaces."

"That's fine, Jacob. I'm just curious. The Britons are very reputable business people. I'm certain they will be glad you took care of me so well. Thank you for your attention."

I stood where I was for a moment and looked around. Next to the door I had entered there were two very large wooden doors that could be lifted, I assume, to bring in freight. The floor room was paved with bricks and there were boxes and crates packed tightly against the far wall. I already knew I must look inside the boxes, but I decided to let Jacob at least think he was in charge for a short while.

He came back with the water and looked as if he had wiped off his face and freshened up.

"May I call you Jacob?"

"Of course, Mrs. Lewis."

"Please call me Nellie."

He nodded, surprise clearly evident on his face, and he escorted me through a door and into the front of the building, which was a shock to me. I expected a casual, if not rustic area, but it was a lovely, oak-paneled entryway where a receptionist sat at a desk, filing through papers and making notes in a ledger. The receptionist was not a woman, but a man, dressed in a vest, white shirt, and a tie. A gold watch dangled from his vest pocket and he stood up immediately.

Jacob introduced us and told me the man was a recent college graduate who was learning the business. His name was John Lesing. I gave him my congratulations, secretly jealous that he had been to the university, and I asked him what his goal in life was.

"Well, Mrs. Lewis, I want to learn this business from the bottom up so I can run it one day. I have a lot to learn, that's for sure."

I struggled to stay composed. What in the world? My mind whirled and I asked him how he had come to work for the Britons, and the answer would have dropped me to my knees if I had been anywhere else.

"My mother and the elder Mr. Briton are very close friends and George recommended me, seeing as how, well..." He began to stammer and looked away.

"Please finish," I said with the most generous fake smile I had ever produced in my life.

"There are no heirs at this time and business is very good and we wish to expand."

"I see." I surely did see. This young man was the son of my father-in-law's mistress, and I felt even more betrayed. How dare they! "I wish you well in your career, Mr. Lesing."

He tried to shake my hand, but I could not bear it and nodded to Jacob and we moved into the next room. All I could think of was Margaret, and my heart was so very heavy with what she must have to bear. I wondered if she even knew about Mr. Gold Watch Lesing. My anger was stirring up inside of me again, and I pushed back my shoulders and entered the office that Charles and George shared.

I was immediately struck by the smell, the same mix of tobacco, lotions, and wool that filled up his office at home, and I had to fight a pang of sweet emotion. I was really not in the mood to be gentle, loving, and think thoughts of youthful love. The room itself was nothing special. There was a desk on either side of the room and in front of each desk there were two fine leather chairs. There were papers stacked on each desk and it almost looked as if whoever was working had gotten up suddenly and left. There were no pictures or decorations of any kind in the room. It was clearly a space to work and, perhaps, hold meetings.

"Jacob, who sits in this efficient space?"

He pointed to the first desk, the one with the most papers, and said that was where Charles Briton sat, and the other desk was where his father worked. I thought quickly and turned to him and asked a favor.

"Would you mind leaving me alone in here for about fifteen minutes while I freshen up a bit? I just need a few private moments, oh… you know." I tried my best to blush and look away.

"Oh! Of course! Please take your time, Nellie. This is about as private of a space as we have here. I'll knock before I come back to show you the rest of the business."

He closed the door and I immediately went to Charles's desk, sat down, and started looking through the papers. There were several ledger books, various newspapers, and I quickly determined that the stacks of papers lined at the front of the desk were for each one of the millinery shops that the Britons operated throughout the city. I saw notes about importing textiles and real estate, and it appeared as if the business was moving into other cities as well. It was a bit much to take in during a short fifteen minutes, but I kept looking, not certain what I was truly looking for. Then I found one group of papers, neatly written and clipped together with a silver metal clip. I read through as many pages as I could with a clenched jaw and a heart that was about to grow very hard.

Willow Glenn, Maine—James McNaughton—Three
containers of plumes—4/10/04—$75.00—PAID
Outer Banks—Laughlin Brothers—Four containers assorted
feathers—5/8/04—$125.34—PAID
North Shore, New Jersey—P.D. Smith—One box—Shore bird
feathers—5/10/04—$13.50 - PAID
Florida—East Coast—Charles William Pierce—Six Crates—
Numerous species, plumage, all sizes—6/7/04—$350.00

I could read no farther, and I rested my head on the desk for a moment to compose myself and to regain my strength for what I knew I was about to see. I was tempted to leave a note for Charles on the desk, but I knew that would be the end of me and us and maybe everything, and then what? Instead, I lifted my head, quickly thumbed through the stack I was looking at, and randomly picked out two pages. I folded the papers until they were very small, tucked them into my bosom, and then rose and waited for Jacob's knock.

I greeted him with a warm smile. The Liar's Brow was growing so fast it was beginning to cover my entire face, and I thanked him for a few moments of privacy. He ushered me into a few more rooms, explaining things that I really wasn't listening to because I wanted to go look in the boxes and crates in the large storage room where I had entered the building. We came back through the way we had gone and there was the disgusting little Lesing man, no fault of his own I know, acting busy and pushing papers around his desk. I ignored him and finally we were in *that room*.

I am not certain what came over me, but I was able to tell Jacob that I was concerned about the quality of feathers and plumes. I made up a ridiculous story about seeing other suppliers and storage areas and told him I would like to be able to see what was in the crates and boxes. Jacob, the poor man, appeared to be shaking and I wasn't certain if it was out of fear or if my newly developed talent for flirting had him overly wrought, but he did not hesitate. He went to the crates and boxes that were sitting closest to the wide doors and, using a hammer, he grabbed off the top box and began opening them. I correctly assumed they were recent deliveries waiting to be taken to the milliners and turned into ridiculous adornments. Jacob was doing as I instructed and he probably regretted it the rest of his life.

Sometimes it's impossible to prepare yourself for what you know is coming. I had seen the photographs in Harriet's living room of all the dead birds lined up on shores and beaches all up and down the coast. I had read the newspaper stories and thought about what it might be like to kill a bird for its feathers and not simply to shoot one to feed a hungry family. But nothing prepared me for what I was about to see. I steeled myself as best as possible when Jacob finished opening several containers and invited me to inspect the contents.

"These were just delivered from Florida," he said proudly. "The birds down there are absolutely beautiful and these feathers command a high price, and you can see why."

I stepped forward and once again everything changed.

The boxes were filled with the most beautiful array of feathers I had ever seen in my life. The little wings and plumes, and some entire breastbones, were lined up in rows in the crates and boxes. I thought my heart would break right there in that terrible room. I took a step closer, the strong smell of preservatives, some type of chemical, flooding my senses, and lifted a plume of pink and white feathers from the first crate. I ran my fingers up and down the feathers and could not help but wonder where this bird had been flying when it was shot out of the sky.

"These are perfect," I managed to say, fighting back my rising stomach and a sea of tears.

"Keep looking," he said. "I believe this crate even has some flamingo wings. They are highly prized and we get them from someone who knows the area down there better than anyone."

The wings looked like the first moment of a soft summer sunset, light pink with radiating streaks of white, and I wanted my resurrecting dream to work at that very moment. I wanted to touch every wing, every feather, every breastbone and have all the birds they once belonged to come to life, fill up the room, and then fly out the wooden doors and away as fast as possible.

Somehow I managed to look at another box and another crate, and I kept my back to Jacob the entire time lest he see that I was fighting back not just emotion, but the entire contents of my stomach. I finally stood back up, took in a breath, turned around, and said thank you with a jagged half smile.

"These are extraordinary specimens, Jacob. Thank you for taking the time to show me them and the building as well. I'm certain we will be meeting again."

"You are so welcome, Nellie. It's been my pleasure, I assure you," he said with a slight blush creeping across his face.

I wanted to run out the door, but I kept my composure and waited until I was well down the street before I pulled the carriage over and became ill in the gutter. For days and days, my dreams would be filled with wings and feathers and the terrible stench that seemed to have penetrated the very skin on my own body.

There was no turning back for me after that trip into Boston. My identity as Mrs. Charles Briton would all but disappear during the coming weeks, as I slowly turned into Nellie Lewis and became even bolder, wiser, and more ready for what would soon be the hardest decision of my life.

Tape Nine

Yet More Loss and Confusion
Boston—Through the end of August
and to September 22, 1904

In the real world, which often does not include the places of the heart or the newfound passions of a young woman, time and circumstances march forward. Before I had a chance to contact Margaret and let her know what I had done, and to try and manage the information I had gathered on my trip into the city, I received word that my mother was ill and could I please come as fast and as soon as possible. The minute I heard this news my entire body felt as if it had been run over by a very large carriage.

The thought of another loss in my life almost paralyzed me. In one way, my growing passion for the Audubon and my love of birds had kept me from clinging to my own grief over the loss of my babies for an extended period of time. It's surely not that I didn't think about them, because there were rare moments when I did not. I still talked to them, managed to walk to the park to sit in the quiet, imagine them, and visit the nesting birds. They were so much a part of me that I often celebrated them, and somehow I knew I would see them again, for I had seen them and held them, if only in my mind's eye. It's safe to say that yes, I was distracted from my grief, but it's also safe to say that all my new realizations were saving me from one type of life and leading me into another.

I was totally thrown off from everything by the summons from my father, which came just days after my adventure in Boston at Charles's office. I had the girls quickly pack me a bag and I asked that they notify Margaret. Charles had already sent word that he and his father had decided to extend their trip, and I left a terse note in case he returned before I did. But I really had no idea how long I would be gone or how long he would be gone, as well. This would end up being a very good thing in some ways and horrible in many others.

My parents were mostly alone during those years after my marriage, and my sister shared with me that my father was not out wandering any longer and a quiet peace had settled on them. I saw them occasionally, but as is the case when there is a marriage and a daughter moves, the ties to that first family become less and less needed, or so I thought.

My father greeted me at the door and for a moment I thought he was the one who was ill. His eyes were sunken back inside of his head and rimmed with dark circles. He had lost weight and it was the first time I considered that he might be old. I hugged him and he felt like a bag of bones, all jagged and hard, and when I pulled back, he had tears in his eyes.

"Prepare yourself, Julia. Your mama is very sick."

"What is it? Why didn't anyone tell me?"

"It happened fast," he explained, pulling me inside and out of the midday heat. "She went down but two days ago. The doctor came and it's not good, Julia."

"What is it?" I was dreading that it might be pneumonia or tuberculosis, two of the main causes of death.

"It's her heart, I'm afraid. It's just worn out. The doctor said there's nothing he can do. Keep her comfortable, he said. Give her food and water. Do not let her move about. I called for you because, well, the others have children and they can't help now, but will you stay and help, Julia? Will you?"

My father had never asked for anything, that I could remember, in his entire life, and I knew then that this was terribly serious. I set down my bag and pushed through the door of my mother's room. Instead of her, I found a much smaller and much, much older version of the woman she had once been. In just a few months since I had last seen her, she had aged at least twenty years. When she opened her eyes and tried with great effort to smile at me, I knew there was not going to be much time left.

One never imagines at first when you are going through something hard that there is any meaning or use for it, but I was learning that each loss, each heartache, and every painful experience makes you stronger and hopefully wiser. If I had not struggled through the pain of childbirth, lost those babies, discovered what I knew about Charles and his family and the Audubon, I'm not certain I could have done what I did for the next seven days.

I took over her feeding and care and also the feeding and care of my father. There was no time to stop or send off notes or do anything but tend to my parents and, on the fourth day, my mother grew markedly worse. After that, I rarely left her side. I slept sitting next to her with my head resting on the bed, and I whispered over and over again what a wonderful mother she had been. And it was true, for I had always felt loved and cherished and well cared for, and that is a remarkable gift.

On the seventh night, I somehow knew the time was near. Her breathing had gone deep and raspy, she was calling out words that made no sense, and she had spiked another fever. It had been three days since she'd had water and the oddest thing seemed to be happening. The lines in her face slackened and she seemed to be looking younger, and why I knew this meant her time was close is beyond me. My mother looked happy, free, and totally as if she were already gone to the sweet heaven she believed in. I know now, because I have since seen this many times since then, that my mother was surrendering.

Before I summoned my father, I wanted to hold her one more time, feel her breath on my face, and tell that I loved her and would always love her. I also had something else I needed to say. I pulled back the covers, quickly untied and slipped off my shoes, and then crawled into bed next to her. She was so light that it was easy for me to lift her and roll her into my arms. I knew it wouldn't matter if I cried and told her I loved her over and over as I kissed her soft face. Then I only had one more thing to ask her.

"Mama, please see to my babies when you get to heaven. Hold them and love them like you always held and loved me and tell them I will see them one day. Please, Mama, and send me a sign, send me something so I know you are all safe. I love you so much."

My father must have heard me crying because moments later, he pulled open the door and ran to the side of the bed.

"Get in, Daddy," I said, moving off the bed and helping him get into it. "It's time. She's leaving us now."

I left them alone and stayed out in the kitchen. It was well into the heart of the night before I heard my father wailing, and I knew that my mother had died and that her spirit was floating away from us.

During the next week, as we passed through the period of mourning and prepared for the funeral, there was a new well of strength that opened up inside of me. I organized and took care of everything and everyone. I can only think that it was my instinct for survival that was carrying me, though, because there is absolutely nothing in the world like the loss of a beloved mother. My siblings were grief-stricken, as was my father, and the world might have totally fallen apart if I had not forged on and steeled myself to the tasks that needed to be done. My turn to slide backward and fall into yet another great loss would have to wait until after the funeral.

It was clear from the moment of her death that my mother was the center and the heart of the family. My brothers and sister bemoaned the fact that they had not told her how much they loved her enough times. My father had his own demons to address and I thought it was necessary for him to do that alone, and I vowed the day of the funeral never to let a feeling of love go unspoken. I also wanted to fall apart and walk through her bedroom, endlessly crying, but someone had to feed all of these people and comfort them.

I didn't have time to stop and look at myself in the hallway mirror and compare the woman running the show to the timid young bride-to-be who'd lived in the same house just a few years ago. There would be no time then to answer the question, "Who am I?" and as the days and months and years of my life not so much sailed as sped forward, I would eventually come to realize that the answer would change over and over again anyway. The question must always be, "Who am I becoming?"

It was Margaret who came to whisk me away and care for me as only another mother could the week following the funeral. By the time she walked up the stairs and into my parents' home, I'm certain I didn't look much better than my father had when I had seen him less than three weeks before. She took one look at me, opened her arms, and I fell into her, and then she took over. It was my turn to grieve, yet again.

My father's sister came and I left. Margaret took me to her house and it was there that I realized my husband had missed yet another life event that should have been shared. I had been alone through the grieving process for the babies and now the same thing had happened with my mother. Margaret was gentle with me, set up the guest room, and informed me that Charles and George had been sent word of the death, but it was likely that news had not reached them.

"How could that possibly be?" I had hoped that he had left word at our home, but the girls, who both attended my mother's funeral, had not brought any messages or mail.

"They have gone south to Charleston and were headed to Savannah when a storm rolled in and they have been waiting to continue now for almost two weeks."

I was astounded that news like this had not reached me, although I understood the circumstances and considered that I had been attending to my family. But Charles was my family, even if he did not seem to act like it, and had regulated me to a specific role that was getting less and less comfortable with each passing day.

"I don't understand why men and only men go on business trips, and I also don't understand the secrecy behind the Briton businesses. I would love to have a husband who was part of my life and not apart from it!"

It was obvious I was upset, and instead of trying to explain it away, she got up and came back with two glasses and a decanter filled with brandy. She filled our glasses and asked me if I still loved Charles.

"Yes, I love him," I answered without hesitation. "But how can a relationship flourish like this when one of the partners is never around? This is not what I imagined."

"What did you imagine?"

"Love and laughter and someone maybe like Harriet's husband. Someone to walk through the fields with me and someone to treat me as an equal."

Margaret took a rather large sip of her drink and spoke with the hint of a laugh, which I found disconcerting.

"You did not think about that when you married Charles! It was only later when you began to change and he did not. You loved his blue eyes and the look of love he had for you and you knew exactly what kind of man he was the day you married him."

She was mostly correct, of course, but that did not lessen the feelings I had. I was very confused because this new part of me, which appeared to be almost all of me from what I was feeling, was terribly angry and unhappy. Yet when Margaret reminded me of my initial love for Charles, I knew she was right. How to reconcile these two things was eluding me, and I knew it could not simply be because of the death of my mother.

"How do women do this?" I asked, almost as if I were begging her. "How do they mingle their lives with men who do not listen to them, consider their deep thoughts, and honor their intelligence?"

"That is what other women are for."

I thought about that for a moment and it was true that in many ways my relationships with the three most important women in my life, Margaret, Ella, and Ruby, were intimate, lovely, and the most rewarding I had ever had. Surely there had been closeness with my own sister when I was a girl, but I was now a woman and the joy, safeness, and sureness I felt in these female relationships was something I deeply treasured. Yet, in my naivety, I had also assumed I could have not just a physically intimate relationship with my husband, but an emotional one as well. I was not simply confused, but a bit heartbroken to think this must be how it would always remain.

"So this is it? But if I can change and grow, then why can't he? Must I just accept that he will always have the last say, be in charge, dismiss my questions, and storm out of the house?"

I had forgotten that Margaret did not yet know about our spat and my adventure into the city, but it was too late to take back my words, so I followed her advice, and as she was a woman, and my friend, I told her everything. I explained about the confrontation in Charles's office, his leaving, the note, and my adventure into the city where I turned into Nellie Lewis. Then I hesitated and tried to decide if I should tell her about the man our husbands were grooming to take over the business. Margaret looked aghast before I could decide.

"What have you done?"

"I had to see the business. I had to know about the birds," I explained as Margaret jumped to her feet and began pacing. "I did nothing wrong, except perhaps lie about my identity. Oh, Margaret! You should have seen it! It was one of the most horrible things… to see those dead birds and to imagine how beautiful they had been when they were soaring toward the clouds and gently feeding their babies."

"You are young and foolish, Julia! You have risked a great deal to snoop about the business, and I am not in agreement with this spying or whatever it is you are doing! We have channels to go through and ways to work that do no include changing your name and asserting yourself in such a way."

I was now even more confused. I stood up to stop her pacing, put my arm out, and made her stand still. "I have no idea what those channels are, Margaret. All I know is that there are dead birds piled up and that Charles and George are looking for more plume hunters right this moment. I am young, that fact is true, but I am not stupid and I will not sit by when I may be in a position to help."

A look of sadness crossed over her face, and she suddenly sat on the edge of my bed and lowered her head for a moment, as one might do if they were about to say a prayer. I waited while she composed her thoughts, still trying to decide if I should tell her about the man who might one day run the family business.

"Julia, dare I say that one part of me is jealous of you again," she started out quietly. "You are young and beautiful and I think you will live to see the world change in ways that some of us will not. I am also torn. I love my son so very much, yet he is like so many other men who are influenced by what has been and not by what could be. He is also readily influenced by his father, who, pardon me, is a bit of a jackass!"

Margaret continued to surprise me every single time I was with her and this day was no exception. I usually saw her as a strong, tough, and intelligent woman who also had a bed of softness and generosity that was a lovely life balance. It's so easy when you are caught up in your own life, its pains and sorrows as well as its sweetness, to become selfish in thinking that you are alone and no one else has ever felt the way that you do. My feelings for her had changed drastically since our first meeting, and standing there, looking at her in a moment of what I took as sadness, I realized she did really not have the same choices as I did. In many ways, her life path had been sealed long ago, yet she struggled and worked for change and all the time she had to fight many other things that I did not. Margaret did not have a Margaret like I did, and the moment I took this all in is the same moment I knew I would make her proud and glad that she had trusted me.

But first there would be so many hardships to come, and for a while she would be the one to pay the price.

I knelt in front of her, took her hands into mine, and told her that I loved her, was grateful for everything, and that I would always love Charles and try to honor our marriage in ways that would not harm her.

"I would never hurt you on purpose," I said. "This is all so very hard for me, so very hard because you have shown me a new world and I'm not certain I can go back."

Margaret grasped my hands very hard. "Never go back! Never! But you must be cautious and careful."

I nodded, but I also did something else. I ran my hand across The Liar's Brow and it felt almost as if someone else was lifting my hand to do it, but I had been empowered by everything that I had done. It is true that each new daring deed, success, or attempt at change makes one stronger, because even though I was yet again pawing through the fog of grief and loss, I knew the fog would lift and I would go on. There really was no choice. I had no idea what I was going to do next— Margaret would soon enough help me with that—but I had another week of settling to do. I could not bear to tell her about John Lesing that night and for the next week, while she so generously took care of me and we had our own remembrance of my mother.

Margaret's house was much larger and grander than mine and Charles's, but we spent most of our time that week outside in her lavish and well-cared-for gardens. I was surprised to see that she tended a vegetable garden all by herself and even more surprised when she talked about her own mother and shared loving and very tender stories about losing someone she loved when she was but a young girl herself. We drank tea, and plenty of wine and whiskey, in those seven days, and the companionship and strength that I drew from her was a tonic that I hoped I could one day pass on to another woman who might also need the loving support of a true friend.

We steered clear of bird talk and feathers, and, thank heavens, men too. I relished the time to simply remember my mother, tenderly and throughout my life and not just those last hard and terribly sad days. I shared the little things that made her so special and loving to me. I told Margaret how my mother spoiled me and loved to whisper in my ear and how she also loved to tell me the story of the day of my birth. I realized, more than ever, what a gift of life a healthy child must have been to her after so many of her own losses, and I shared with Margaret that mother kept my father from her bed and how hard that had been for both of them.

I did not tell her how much I missed sleeping with Charles, and I do not mean simply lying in bed and falling asleep. There were nights when my body ached to be near him, and even though we had been careful after the loss of my last baby, we had still managed to have more, much more, than a bit of joy under the covers. There are some things a mother-in-law simply does not need to hear, and in the end, I could still not tell her about John Lesing. I was certain she didn't know, and I needed to find the right moment and it was not yet appropriate as my time of mourning was precious to me. I knew these days with Margaret, when I did not have to be working or cooking or really doing anything, were also a gift that Charles had given me and there was an obligation, not just to him, but also to the vows we had taken as man and wife. I was certain that another man would never settle into my heart like Charles had, but that was just one of many, many things I would eventually be wrong about.

Life could only be put on hold so long, and I knew that I must return to my own house, my own life, and it was on the last breath of September, Friday, the 30th day of the month, when I saw the trees were beginning to lose their bright colors and the sun was setting lower. The smell of returning fall was in the air, but I was already missing the heart of summer and, to be honest, the familiarity of my own home and Charles, who I was beginning to wonder if I would ever see again.

The day I left, Margaret walked me through the gardens and then out through the back gate, where a driver was waiting in a car nonetheless, to take me back home. She held me close and then kissed both my cheeks and said she would come to pick me up in three days time to "meet some most important changers," as she called them. I had no idea what she was talking about, but I nodded and smiled.

"Thank you for this week, Margaret. I'll never forget it, and one day I hope I can be and do for you as you have been and done for me." I was holding her hands in front of the car as the driver looked away and she gazed at me for a very long time.

There was a moment of total silence and an unruly blackbird, that people dislike immensely simply because of its menacing color, swooped in front of us and we both turned to watch it fly across the top of the house. It was a nimble bird that knew where it was going, what it had to do, and I wished to be in the same position—sure and true and following a path that had no sudden turns or unexpected gusts of wind that I could not overcome.

Margaret and I turned at the exact same moment, and I smiled and let go of a small chuckle. "A messenger from the sky, Margaret." I laughed.

"Indeed," she added, returning my smile.

I was about to get into the car when she stopped me by pulling me close for one last hug. I was delighted, but not prepared for what happened next.

"Please, dear, please call me Maggie," she said.

I was touched by this gesture of tenderness and kindness and felt a new sureness and strength as I got in the car, threw her a kiss, and headed toward home.

But nothing, absolutely nothing, could prepare me for what waited and for the hard and life-changing decisions that were just weeks away from that very lovely moment.

Tape Ten

Some Most Important Changers Claim Nellie
Boston—October 3, 1904

True to her word, Margaret showed up three days later at the same moment I had just started reading a very long letter that had finally arrived from Charles. I had taken to sitting in his office since my return because even though we'd had a nasty argument there, it was a place I felt close to him and I missed him, truly missed him. I had been thinking about what Margaret said about the basis for my love. It was true that I loved him the way he was when we first met, and there was truth to the fact that there was also an obligation because of that fact. I often woke in the night—my dreams were an equal mix of delight and demons—and my first impulse was always to reach for him. This paradox of love would, unfortunately, never get much easier for me.

When I heard Margaret enter the kitchen, I quickly shut the door because I wanted a moment of privacy while I read his news. The letter was not what I expected and I read it with trembling hands.

My Dearest Julia,
I am so sorry to be away so long, but we have had many unforeseeable incidents. Before I launch into that, I must first offer my sincere condolences at the loss of your mother. I know

that you loved her and I found her to be a true and lovely woman. She raised a wonderful daughter and that says much about the kind of person she was. I will never forgive myself for not being by your side during this time, and I hope that as the months and years pass you can forgive me. I'm certain that my mother was a great comfort to you and I trust that you will continue to turn to her in your time of need. I know that in the beginning you and Margaret had a rocky start and I'm not sure what happened to change that, but it has made me happy to know you have become closer and, dare I say, perhaps even friends.

There is no easy way to say what is coming next. I know you are recovering from the shock of death right now, but I must share this so you can prepare yourself to be a support for my mother as she has been to you. Please do not tell her what I am about to share. You must promise me! My father does not want her to know until he arrives, that is if he arrives at all. I know I have already asked much of you, but this is also a request from my father.

George is gravely ill and I fear it is pneumonia and that he may never recover. We have been traveling down the coast, all in the name of business, and were driven inland when severe storms came out of nowhere and caught us unaware. By the time we found shelter, the temperatures had dropped, and as George is not the most vigorous man, he was noticeably affected by the cold immediately. We stayed at an inn near Charleston for almost two weeks, and he seemed to get better and so we continued on our journey, but his cough persisted, and we again rested near Savannah. It quickly became clear to me that his condition would not get better and I had to make a decision that I hope you will also forgive me for.

George is on his way back home and I have gone on and now am in Florida. This trip is crucial to the continuation of the Briton business, and even after I pleaded with my father to let me go with him, he all but demanded that I go on. I cannot express to you, although you must know, what it was like to say good-bye to my father, knowing I may never see him again.

*I know there are things in his life that not all agree with, but he
has been a good father to me and that is all that matters.*

*I am writing this now from a small village on the East Coast
and I am wishing with all my heart that I were there with you,
my dearest love. Thinking of you on this journey, and knowing that you are well cared for and secure, has helped me go
on. Now, as my father returns home, I must ask you to make
certain my mother has what she needs as well.*

*Had I known I would be gone this long, I would have also
made financial arrangements for the household and your
needs before I left. Please, if funds run short, go to the Second
National Bank near the commons and ask for Mr. William
Bradley. He will assist you in a professional manner.*

*There really is no way for you to contact me, as I will be
moving about, but I will send word as soon as I know I am
coming back to you, my wife and my heart.*

Lovingly,

Charles

*P.S. It is blazingly hot here and the bugs and way of living
are something I have never before encountered. Thanks to the
good Lord we are Bostonians!*

I set the letter on the desk and promptly put my head on top of
it. Is this what life was going to be like? One tragedy and loss after
another? Would there be five and ten and twenty years of letters and
regret and secrets and wondering and compromise? Would there ever
be more than a few days or a week when there was peace and joy?
The letter from Charles had spun me around for several reasons. Of
course I was sad about George and how I was now going to have to
cover with yet another lie, and I was angry because I knew exactly
why he was in Florida, and those two emotions were colliding with
great force throughout my entire body. It took me a moment to realize
that I had also been given a great gift. Charles was trusting me with
intimate details—his father's declining health, the banker's name, a
sweet expression of love for me—and that brought me up a bit.

But there was also the reality of what was to come. I was absolutely torn about Margaret and preparing her for what seemed a close reality, but I also knew, and maybe Charles did not, that she was no longer in love with George. I imagined he must also know about the mistress and the fool they had chosen to take over their business. I also knew that Margaret had harvested a kind of devoted acceptance of whom Charles was and what she must maintain to keep the parts that she wanted to keep on with her life. What I didn't know is how she would carry that out if he returned ill and weak, or worse—in a coffin.

I turned, my heart a turbulent circle of uncertainty, and faced the window. I willed myself away from everything and everyone and to a place where there was silence, albeit for the wind in the trees, the sweet sound of it rippling through the wings of birds that were flying overhead, and the distant call of a mate on a lake, river, or stream calling for the one it loved. My comfort was in the sweet memory of the time at Harriet's and in the lovely way the beauty and the birds collided to give me peace. If the smallest of birds could fly thousands of miles, could not I then handle whatever obstacles were placed in front of me?

I wasn't sure, but not trying would be impossible. Whatever came to me was out of my control, but I knew what I did with it was in my control, and considering what others had gone through before me, there was nothing I could not face. This is what I was trying to convince myself of anyway as I heard Margaret call my name while she walked up the stairs to the second floor, looking for me. I had exactly one minute to enlarge The Liar's Brow and pretend I had been in the living room and that life was wonderful and I did not yet have another secret to fill my rising chest of confusion.

"Here I am," I called just after I had tucked the letter into the first drawer of Charles's desk to hide it, slipped out of his office, and started to climb the stairs to greet her.

"Are you ready?"

I found this question funny, considering what I had just read and the swirl of uncertainty inside of me, and I started to laugh.

"What is so funny, dear?" Margaret asked as she approached me halfway down the stairs.

"Is one ever ready, Maggie, especially a woman? Just think about it. There is love, loss, tragedy, and the weight of the world on our shoulders all of the time. Who knows what might drop from the sky or land on the porch during the next three minutes? The last time you took me away like this, I was gone for days and my entire life changed."

"Well, you should be prepared for today, then, because it's about to happen again!"

I kept on laughing as we said good-bye to the girls and Margaret ushered me out to the waiting carriage and into a day that had already started out with a sudden jolt and that would end up with so very much more.

I suppose you could say that what happened next was the equivalent to a coming out ball, which I, of course, had never had during my days on the other side of town. The mere thought of such an extravagant affair, with dancing, food, and introductions to the city's finest as a new blossom ready to be plucked and inserted into one of the royal Bostonian families, would have brought everyone in my house to their knees in laughter. One afternoon not long before I started at the magazine, my mother had been reading out loud a story in the newspaper about the latest debutantes. Even though a small part of me was jealous, I grabbed an old dishtowel off the counter, placed a bowl on my head, and jumped on top of a kitchen chair.

"Ladies and gentlemen, here for your pleasure, but not until you marry her, is our lovely daughter, Miss Julia Kelly. Her brothers are drunks, her sister has run off to marry a fool, her father is delightful but doesn't speak much, and her saving grace, besides her great wit and obvious beauty, is without a doubt her wonderful mother!"

"Julia!" my mother screeched, half in delight and half in shock, and I kept going.

"This fine young woman can be had for a small pittance! Please step up and begin the bidding. She can wash dishes, clean your house, bear you many fine children, bake and cook your favorite dish, and service you until it's time for her to bring in the cows and milk them again! In fact, she can do all of these things at the same time!"

"Oh my, oh my dear! Where did you learn such things?"

I hopped down, threw off my crown, and ran to my laughing

mother. "From the drunken brothers," I said, laughing with her and then scooping her up so that we had our own debutant dance around the kitchen.

When we finished, we sat and my mother confessed how she had once dreamed of such a thing for me. I held her hands and listened to her tell me about the dreams of mothers for their daughters.

"Oh, Julia, I am laughing, but it's every mother's wish to give her daughter what she could never have. I wish for you to never have to work as hard as I do, to have a bigger house, and to sit and sip tea with all those girls in the paper. Life is hard enough, and the truth is, I wish you had been at the ball and danced all night and met every rich person in town. It's money, you know, and nothing else that separates us from them. I want you to remember that every day of your life. You can go places, sweet Julia. You can and you must!"

What I would give to have my mother back again and chatting for hours in the kitchen! Thoughts of her, and her great love for me, were with me throughout the day, even as we pulled away from the house, and Margaret, who was driving the carriage as if that were her chosen profession, was a wonderful substitute for the mother I missed so much. I had to force myself to push thoughts of Charles's letter from my mind as we headed at a slow pace down the street and toward this latest adventure.

Margaret was quiet, and I was glad for that at first, but I suspect she was on to me. It didn't take her too long to ask me if everything was okay.

"Thinking of my mother and missing Charles a bit," I said, this time running my hand over my brow. "Have you heard anything?"

"Not since the last letter, but no worries, dear. I am sure they are fine and going about their business, and we can just go about our business while they are gone."

I had to speak up, as there were parts of me that felt as if they might burst. Even the best liar has her limits.

"Margaret, I mean, Maggie, I know what they are doing down there. They are searching for more plume hunters and that is hard for me, so very hard, as you know how we both feel about the birds and the Audubon."

"We will address some of that today, and I am not certain that is what they are doing, but I suspect you may be correct. It is almost as if we are all on a seesaw and what they do, we try to erase and what we do, they try to erase, but there are more and more laws every day and there are ways, believe me, there are ways to put a stop to all of this."

"I hope so, Maggie, because I have to say I might choose the birds over Charles if it ever came to that."

Margaret did not miss a beat as she turned to meet my gaze and, without expression, wordlessly urged on the horse. I wished she would have said something, as I was testing her, and myself too, for it was the first time I had dared to admit the truth. But Charles, even at his worst, was always her son and her only child. There could be no choice in who she would choose or which side she might pick in a fight, or so I thought. She did not speak again until we stopped the first time, and I felt strongly that I had to say something.

"We both love Charles, Maggie. That is very clear and I meant no offense when I said I would choose the birds, but I also know it is not that simple," I offered, my hand on her arm. "Passion and love can be directed in many ways. I am learning about that, and I know that you have already risked a great deal in sharing with me. I am grateful for that and for you in my life. I meant no harm, none at all, but there is a power inside of me, growing steadily, I might add, and sometimes even I am afraid of it."

Margaret looped the horse reins around the edge of the seat and swiveled to face me. She had a tender look in her eyes, and she told me not to worry.

"It will all settle out, Julia. I do not know what will happen with me or you or the birds or even Charles or George. I do know that quite a while ago I surrendered to fate and to what I might try and control in my little corner of the world, and as it turns out, that is a lot more than I thought it would be. I do know that the world now, more than ever, needs women like us. We are strong and capable and I have seen you grow a bit every day. Today I am going to show you some remarkable places, and you are going to meet some women who were once in your same position, a bit frightened and unsure. But wait until you see what they have done. Anything, dear Julia, anything is possible."

With that she jumped from the carriage, as if she were a young girl, and motioned for me to follow her. We were on Berkeley Street and in front of a red brick building that I recognized immediately. It was the Young Women's Christian Association, the YWCA, gymnasium and classrooms. I knew about this organization because several of my school friends had stayed in its rooming house, and I remember thinking if it were not for Charles, I might have been living there also. It was a safe, clean, boarding home for girls who were working in the city, but beyond that, I didn't know much about it. I was about to find out plenty.

I followed Margaret inside and we stepped into a tile-covered vestibule that was in front of a large gymnasium. I could hear balls bouncing and girls yelling, and we stepped into the gym and it was as if we were stepping into a wild and very wonderful new world. Girls were running back and forth with wooden swords in their hands and they were fencing! I was mesmerized for a moment and then had to fight the impulse to jump in and join them. They were all wearing long, dark stockings, skirts that were cut off at the knee, and matching blouses that gave them plenty of room to run. They looked as if they were having the time of their lives.

An elderly woman came dashing across the floor, and Margaret moved forward to greet her and did so with an embrace. I watched them with delight, as they were clearly friends who liked each other very much.

"Come meet my daughter-in-law," she said, leading the woman over to me.

"Julia, I want you to meet Mrs. Durant, Pauline Durant. She is one of the founders of the YWCA and one of the finest women I know. Her work here, and throughout the city, has changed so many lives and helped so many women. I have wanted you to meet for a long time, and today is the day!"

"Julia! How glad I am to have this chance to show you our work and to hear about your life, too! Let us refresh in my office for a moment, where we can talk, and then I will show you around."

Her office was not grand, but a simple small room filled with boxes and files and notes and everything from stacks of those dark uniforms the girls were wearing to bags of what appeared to be used clothing. During the next hour, I heard a story that was going to be repeated by several other women the remainder of the day. No woman has ever had such a remarkable society debut as did I.

Pauline Durant, who wore a simple dark skirt and brown shirt, was a small woman with gray hair and so much energy it was a wonder she could sit in her chair long enough to talk to us. She was seventy-two years old, and I hoped if I lived that long to be as vigorous and real. Pauline was a widow who had spent her life helping others when she surely did not need to. She had been married to a terribly wealthy man, Henry F. Durant, who had made a fortune and then some as an attorney, but one day he abruptly quit his practice and became a preacher.

I was not just perplexed by this, but curious and even a bit shocked. Who would give up a law practice, apparently one of the must lucrative and successful in all of Boston, to preach? I asked this question, boldly leaning forward from the waist and putting my hand on her desk in a gesture that I hoped she would take as sincerity.

"Oh dear, I think from what Maggie has told me that you will understand why when I tell you that we lost our son, our only son, suddenly and at that moment everything changed, absolutely everything. He was a splendid, lovely, bright boy and it made both of us stop and ponder what is really important."

"I am so sorry. So very sorry." I was also slightly embarrassed for having asked the question, but she did not seem to mind and continued on.

"It's been said that I am a woman of high character with extreme principles who had a great deal of influence over her husband," she said with a wink and a smile. "Men want to think they are in charge, but your mother-in-law and I both know the truth, and it is a very important truth to behold!"

Margaret was smiling at her friend, and it would take me the rest of the day to realize this was the heart of every woman's message during my very interesting society debut.

I thought Pauline's revelation was what she wanted to tell me, but I was sorely mistaken. She went on, with Margaret's help, to tell me that she and her husband had founded Wellesley College, numerous charities, and the very YWCA that was I sitting inside of while we were talking.

"You are that Durant?" I said with a slight stammer, as if I were a young schoolgirl who had met a famous stage actor.

"Yes, dear," Pauline said with a hearty laugh. "I am that Durant.

My husband and I were quite a team. His death has not changed the direction of my life."

"It is an honor to meet you. I would have loved to have gone to Wellesley. It was my mother's dream for me too, and I think it is wonderful what you and your husband did for women and for education. To think that someone thought women needed the same education and opportunities as men, well, that is so wonderful!"

"It's never too late for anything," she said. "There is much work to be done and there are many women, and dare I say men too, who need the strength and will that only a woman can bring to society. We are important and very much needed and you must never forget that."

I would not forget that or the tour I had later of the YWCA facilities that was conducted by the founder of Wellesley College and one of the founders of the YWCA movement in the United States of America. Pauline talked with great and intense passion about the importance of her work and how working women needed a safe place to stay so they could chose to work at a decent job and not walk the streets like so many women had to do before it was acknowledged that single women should have a choice. Pauline led us through classrooms where women were taught penmanship, sewing, secretarial skills, bookkeeping, and everything from botany to astronomy.

She told me how every addition to the programs had almost always been a battle because so many believed that women were weak and could not support themselves or handle intellectual stimulation or challenges. The teaching of sports and physical classes, she shared, was especially hard for many people to adjust to, but she said there was no turning back and the need remained endless.

"It would seem simple, would it not?" she said as we were walking back to where we had started. "Safe housing, vocational training, exercise, life enrichment, and preparing for a career seem to make sense to me, but I have also found in this world that the pace of acceptance does not always equal the giant leaps I want to take."

I felt insignificant and small next to this great woman who kissed Margaret on the lips and hugged me as if I were her own daughter as we thanked her and prepared to leave, but she wasn't quite done impressing me.

"My dear, please remember that you do not have to start a college to make a difference, but also know that women have great influence over men. We are all, and this includes you, much, much stronger and wiser than we have ever been given credit for. Think of something absolutely amazing and very important and then go do it."

By the time we got back out to the carriage, I felt as if I could fly to the next destination all by myself. Her inspiring life and her words of encouragement were a tonic rich in truth and sincerity. What a woman she was! Margaret must have sensed my excitement, and as we started up again, she told me how she had met Pauline at a social meeting years ago and how they have maintained a friendship and often met to discuss which of the many social causes was the most needy that particular month. Margaret, it was beginning to seem, knew everyone in the entire world and was a much deeper and involved woman than even I had thought.

We were far from done that day, but truth be told, the first debut introduction would have been enough to keep me inspired for an entire lifetime. Our next stop, less than a thirty-minute ride away, was to a private home. Margaret went right on through the back gate—obviously she had been here before—pulled into the stable, and asked the stable man to water and feed the horse while we had lunch. I was about to spend two delightful hours with Alice Stone Blackwell that I would not forget and would boast about for a very long time.

There were few women who did not know who Alice was and that she was a crusader for women and the rights she so firmly believed they deserved. Her mother, Lucy Stone, was the first woman in Massachusetts to receive a college degree and keep her maiden name when she married! Imagine! Lucy had also started the *Women's Journal*, a weekly newspaper focusing on women's rights and other issues of importance, and she was an abolitionist, an amazing orator, and the most convincing writer and voice for women. It must have been something for Alice to have been raised in such a way as to be free and open and to have touched on all of those issues since she had been a little girl. Alice had prepared a simple lunch for us and we sat and talked around the table, and again, here was a woman of greatness and importance that Margaret knew intimately. Alice was a serious woman, with bold features, her long hair tied up in back, as wisps of loose hair danced about her head like spiders' legs while she talked with us.

147

"When mother died eleven years ago, there was no question that I would continue on as editor of the magazine and keep the flame of her causes burning bright and forever, if that is what it takes," Alice shared. "I believe we all have a duty, a deep obligation, to help others no matter the cost, for that is the real reason we even exist. One of us is no better than the rest. We—every race, nationality, and gender—we are all the same under the very beautiful skies where the birds you love so well should fly free."

I was impressed with her dedication to the causes her mother had fought and worked so hard for, and I had a sudden yearning for a daughter, a daughter who would one day grow and challenge and work to better the world. The causes of my life were beginning to come into focus, and as I listened to Lucy, I decided that if it was true I might never have a child, then I must work even harder to do my part.

When we finished with lunch, Alice took us into the sitting room for a few moments to show us the portrait she had received in May from a group of over two hundred friends who wanted to honor her important work. She was very involved with helping the Armenians, and I could hardly believe she had time for yet one more cause! Did this woman ever sleep? She talked about poetry and some of the people she had helped and how a country and its people as well off as ours must help other countries and situations of evil, too. She said something that I thought was extremely important about the boundaries of love and difference.

"Until the world learns that the word equality falls on everyone and can erase hatred and open up channels of love and sameness, we will always have work to do, Ms. Julia. The world needs us. It truly does."

We were about to finish and depart when there was a knock at the door and Alice excused herself to answer it. I stood looking at Margaret with my eyes as wide as saucers, and words could not even form in my mind. What happened next made my sudden inability to speak even worse. Alice walked into the sitting room with a man and a woman, and when she introduced them, I thought I might faint.

"Ladies, allow me to introduce two very special friends of mine. Margaret and Julia Briton, this is Julia Ward Howe and this is Mr. Samuel Clemens."

I somehow managed to smile at the woman who was famous for

writing the "Battle Hymn of the Republic" as well as for her work in a variety of causes and her poetry. Samuel Clemens was Mark Twain, one of the most famous and brilliant writers and someone I admired greatly for the way he had transported me with such lovely joy along with the adventures of Tom Sawyer and Huckleberry Finn. I touched both their hands and can say that they were both genuine, friendly, and their eyes twinkled with delight and who knew what adventures they were about to create with Alice!

We left immediately and the moment we got into the carriage and pulled away, Margaret let out a belly laugh and admitted that even she had been startled and amazed by the surprise meeting of those two remarkable people. I was in a kind of a daze as we trotted away. I turned to look at the home we had just left and kissed my hand and then threw it back toward all three of those people. I almost said, "I can't wait to tell my mother!" and then realized that could never happen. My feelings were suddenly a combination of excitement and awe and sadness. The ups and downs of life were an amazement to me, and I wondered if I would ever adjust to their ever-changing parade inside of me.

I was hoping we were done for the day. It was midafternoon and my head was also swimming with inspiration and fresh thoughts. There was one final stop to make, and it was not like the one-on-one debut meetings we had just finished, but more like meeting a small army of determination that never seemed to settle down for one second. Margaret was taking me to the Denison House on Tyler Street, and I again marveled at her connections, the way she moved easily from one side of the city to the next, and the interesting array of friends, acquaintances, and experiences she had amassed. This could not have happened overnight, and I began to wonder if she and George had ever had a moment of happiness, or if she had galloped away as often and quickly as possible from the day they were first married.

I let those thoughts slip away as we once again tethered the horses in a back alley and jumped from the carriage. This is one destination that I did know about, and I was excited to see this experimental and highly successful compound with my own eyes. It was a collective of sorts, three buildings directly across the street from Quincy School that housed so many activities and opportunities it was a wonder our visit only lasted a few hours. I know that a group of college-educated women living in a neighborhood that was inhabited by a variety of nationalities, and was not considered a place where any respectable woman should live, must have been a huge challenge and undertaking. But the women who founded Denison wanted to honor the Lebanese, Syrian, and Italian immigrant women who were their neighbors, some who lived with them.

Somewhat experimental at its beginnings, Denison became a model for other like organizations, and I know it had been written up in papers and journals around the world because it was definitely progressive. During the next few hours, I saw women learning English while their babies romped in a clean, grass-filled yard. I watched as they worked on baskets and beautiful tapestries that were reminiscent of their homeland. I walked through a very modern medical clinic and I had short conversations with two social workers who were working with the women to get better wages.

In many ways, it was as if I had stepped into a new, modern, and seemingly perfect world. When we left, I turned to see this lovely sea of women helping women and making such a difference in the world. "Imagine," I said to Margaret, "what a loss it would have been had not the first woman stepped forward to do something like this. They have touched so many lives and given so many other women hope."

The all-knowing Margaret simply smiled as if I had passed a test by reciting the correct answer. When we got to my house, she came in for a short while, and I found Charles's brandy in the kitchen cupboard and poured us each a much-needed glass. We talked briefly about the day and about how women of means have more of an obligation than anyone else. I could not stop going on about the Audubon, and she said it was clear to her that I had already chosen my path. "Now let's see what you do with this new direction, dear."

When she left and I went to sit in Charles's office, I felt a pang of guilt knowing what awaited her, and I wondered if I had done the right thing by keeping my promise to Charles. It was impossible to know then what we both were about to face. Life had its own plans for us, and as is often the case, there isn't one thing you can do to turn the direction of fate.

Tape Eleven

Speaking to the Moon as the Heart Takes a Leap
Boston—The Remainder of October, 1904

Time seemed to move like the swift passing fall clouds that were heralding the arrival of yet another dreaded winter. The days were actually still quite warm, and I tried to take advantage of each one of them by walking as much as possible, while I not so patiently waited for Charles. I felt very strong, and when I took my weekly bath, I was surprised to notice that my legs were firm and well shaped. I had also lost all of the weight I had gained with the baby, and I felt vibrant and, if such a word even makes sense, *possible*.

I had heard nothing more from Charles, and as I waited for more bad news about the arrival of George, I leaned into the words and wisdom from the women Margaret had introduced me to, and without realizing it at first, I was moving forward on my own. Everything, and I mean everything, was going to start accelerating as I felt a pressing restlessness. I was not content to walk the floors in my house, sit and read, chat with the girls, or simply talk. I had to do something, and it was Ella who started me moving.

"Julia, we need money to buy groceries and to pay the stable man," she told me several days after I'd had my latest adventure with Margaret. "I'm not sure what to do now. Mr. Briton has been away a very long time and there are things that need attending to."

I all but jumped to my feet when she approached me. "I will take care of everything," I said as if I knew exactly what to do. "Make me a list of expenditures and I will go to the bank and we will be just fine. What else needs to be done?"

Ella lowered her head. "Well, we have not been paid for two weeks either. The horses also need shoeing, and Mr. Briton usually starts the car once a week if he is not going to drive it. The gardener needs some direction and we need to address the winter needs of the house. I will think about what else he usually does, but now it is mostly the need of money."

I felt like a simple fool! What had I been thinking? I took charge very quickly and went to sit in Charles's office. I located his paper and made a list of expenditures. How hard could this be? It turns out not so very hard at all. Men had apparently been lying to women all these years so we would feel helpless and as if running a household was complicated and required hours of hard work. It actually required less than two days of work.

I designed a ledger, like I had been taught in school, and with Ella and Ruby's help, we made a listing of expenditures and costs. They sat in the office with me and they could not stop smiling as we discussed the cost of food, arranging for the shoeing, sealing up the windows, and bringing in the gardener to prepare the yard for the first frost. They were excited to be a part of everything and I do believe it was the first time they had ever been allowed to sit in a "man's office."

The following day I hitched up the horse by myself—well, actually the girls helped a little—and I headed to the bank with a note listing the funds I needed and the name of Mr. William Bradley on my mind. I noticed on my ride that so many of my beloved birds had already left for warmer climates. I thought how ironic that they might have passed over Charles on their way to their sandy tide pools and tropic air and how he might see them and think about hats while I simply thought about saving their lives.

Mr. Bradley was a pleasant man and all business and did not seem at all surprised to see me. I identified myself and he seemed to know who I was. While I waited for him to prepare, I looked around the bank, and much to my surprise, at least a fourth of the customers were women. They were simply going about their business, and I was almost embarrassed to think that I had never before been to a bank or even thought about such an endeavor. I watched one woman, dressed in the simple costume of a working woman, talk with a bank teller, exchange money, and then stand and fill out some papers, and something moved through me, a surge of power that made my entire body tingle, and I knew I was going to do something very bold.

When Mr. Bradley took me into his office, instead of asking for the forty dollars I was going to ask for, I asked instead to see the deposit and withdrawal records and the balance sheets. He didn't look startled but said, "Of course, Mrs. Briton," and then left again. This was a good thing because I was trembling so badly I needed time for some deep breaths to settle myself. I was also pleased that Charles had already listed me as a joint partner with the accounts. When he came back and handed me the books, I asked to be left alone for a few moments so I might go over them. Again, he said, "Of course, Mrs. Briton," nodded politely, and left.

I opened the books slowly and had to fight with every ounce of my self-control to contain myself. The balance at the top of the records sheet said, "Combined balance of all accounts equals $589,765." I looked at it for several minutes, wondering if my eyesight was bad or if the lettering had been entered incorrectly, but each time I looked it was the same. We were rich. I was rich. My father had supported all of us on $375 a year. The dead bird business, and whatever else Charles was involved with, must be terribly lucrative. The sum in the account with my name on it was staggering to me, yet I had to maintain control. I bent over the books and read though them quickly, remembering easily how to read records such as this and remembering also how my teachers were always amazed at how quickly I could grasp anything having to do with arithmetic.

The deposits and withdrawals did not seem out of the ordinary, and I could see where the money for the house upkeep and regular expenses was deducted. In my twenty-minute perusal, I found nothing out of the ordinary, except at the very bottom of the last page a reference to another bank. I was in Second National Bank and there was a reference to Hornblower and Weeks, an investment banking and brokerage firm, and it looked as if the accounts might be linked somehow. This meant there was probably even more money! Sweat was pouring off my face. I dabbed it off and then closed the books, which was a signal for Mr. Bradley to return.

"Everything satisfactory, madam?"

"Yes. Thank you so much."

"You would need a withdrawal slip, yes?

"Yes."

"Here you are," he said, pulling one out of the drawer.

I did not hesitate and filled it out for five hundred dollars, as if this was something I did every day. I handed it to him and asked that he give me a mix of small and large bills, but nothing larger than a ten-dollar bill.

"Of course."

He came back quickly, counted out the money, smiled, and asked if there was anything else.

"Not today. Thank you so much for your help," I said, carefully placing the money inside of my handbag and then rising. At the last moment, I thrust out my hand like a man would, and I could see that he was startled, but he took it anyway and his smile widened.

On the way home, I thought about what I had just done. There was no reason for me to take all of that money, and it was a large sum of money, exceptionally large, and when I thought about it, it was almost as if someone else had taken it or something had taken over me and urged me to withdraw more than I needed. I was shaking so badly that it's a wonder the horse followed my commands. What in the world was I doing? The large sum of money that was in the account was another thing. Charles must have added my name to the account after we married, but I had absolutely no idea we were that wealthy and it was possible that even more funds were in other accounts. This struck me as hilarious, and I started to laugh so hard I had to stop the carriage for a moment lest we go off into the ditch and roll over into one of the ponds we were passing. Rich! Rich! Rich!

By the time I arrived home, I knew that I would pay the bills and put the extra money upstairs in my special drawer next to the feathers I was keeping as my special treasure. I reasoned the money was mine to use for expenses and if there were an emergency, well, it would be right there and save me a trip to the bank.

It took but two days for me to tackle the household chores, pay everyone, and make certain there was nothing else that needed tending. The girls and I checked everything in the house and they wanted to know if we could install a telephone while Charles was away. Charles had been promising to do just that, but I thought that might be a bit much and I promised them I would work on it when he returned. Telephones were being installed up and down our street, and I had already thought how wonderful it would be to hear anything at all from Charles. If he could stop and borrow a phone and tell me he was okay, oh, what an ease of worry that would be! Florida was so very far away, and what if he never came back? What if he fell ill like his father? I had to chase these thoughts away and then, with all the work done, I was back to where I had been before Ella had shaken me awake.

The following day, my restlessness back in full bloom, I walked to Heart's Haven, which was deserted, and settled in on my bench to think. The summer greens were slowly being replaced by a hundred shades of brown and so many birds had disappeared I feared for a moment that plume hunters may have invaded my sanctuary. I knew it was the migration and the coming winter weather, yet I felt an ache for missing them, not unlike the missing of my own babies. I know I was trying to find courage and direction and I knew, too, that I couldn't count on Margaret to be my guide for the rest of my life. She had all but handed me a map of where to go next and there I was sitting on a bench and acting like a rich matron. I closed my eyes and said what I'm certain many would say was a prayer.

"Help me find the way. Help me find the way."

I said this over and over and there was no great miracle when I opened my eyes. Like everyone else who is searching and has done a bit of work, I knew what I was supposed to do, where I must go next, and what was calling me, but we are human and sometimes weak and often afraid and unsure. I was learning how that was not wrong, but part of the process.

Julia Briton was going to go to the library and feast on facts and then to an Audubon meeting. But then, halfway through the park, as I was swinging my arms back and forth and thinking about Charles's obsession with flight and airplanes and how surely those Wright brothers must be bird lovers, there was a tiny miracle that appeared from the branches of the pine tree I was passing. It was a gorgeous red cardinal,

the most colorful bird of the north, to me anyway. It swooped in front
of me, its brilliant red color a glorious sign of strength and vitality,
and from that point on, I ran home because I had wasted enough precious time.

The next day I was up very early and out of the house before the girls
even arrived. I left each of them a ten-dollar bonus on the kitchen
counter after I decided Charles had probably never done that in the
time they had been employed by him. I deduced this was part of the
reason we had so much money in the bank, and I was thinking of ways
to spend it every second I was awake, and I was amazed at how much
pleasure this gave me.

My plan was twofold. I was going to do some library research
about laws and the Audubon and then I was going to go to the next
meeting, which was the following day, and volunteer for a position
that only a woman of means, means meaning money and time, could
afford. I had both and on top of all of that, a passion for the birds that
made feel as if I had a pair of wings waiting to sprout from my own
ribcage at any moment.

The library was, of course, toward the center of town and it's a
wonder I even had to direct the horse, as it seemed that was where I was
always headed. It was a large, beautiful, stone and concrete building in
Back Bay right on Copley Square, a very important and well-traveled
corner where Boylston and Dartmouth Streets met. Richardson's
Trinity Church was across the street and I passed the Boston Museum
of Fine Arts as I drew near as well. The building was absolutely grand,
in renaissance style, yet I was not about to be intimidated by a building, considering everything I had already been through. I had never
been in this library, but I certainly knew how to use one because in
my former life, owning a book was a luxury and the library was, as my
mother said, "The garden of free knowledge."

Oh what a grand place it was! There were rows of books and
newspapers and marble tables and lovely oak chairs. It was a place
one could get lost inside of and stay for a very long time, pondering
the past and great works of the men and women who had the gift of

words. I was determined and beginning to realize that every moment was important and there was no more time to waste thinking or sitting on park benches. I moved quickly to a table and then approached one of the librarians and asked for help to speed up my research. I wanted newspapers and pamphlets and anything I could find about the Audubon, ornithology, and laws that had been enacted to protect the birds.

The librarian jotted down some notes and I settled in and she returned very quickly with stacks of newspapers, pamphlets, and *The Audubon Magazine*, which I did not even know existed. I was very quickly lost in a world of birds and legislation and, unfortunately, mass slaughter and possible extinction all in the name of fashion. My hands weaved in and out of paper after paper and my mind worked feverishly to keep up with all of the information. There was so much to learn and I tried to absorb as much as possible.

What excited me was the fact that the Audubon Society was growing and there were already over forty chapters spread throughout the country. I was not the only person who had been captured by our companions with wings. Women, men, children all over were doing everything from building birdhouses to working with legislators and trying to design laws that would protect birds from not just plume hunters, but also the ignorant citizens of the world who often took delight in killing creatures just to kill them. The Lacey Act had been passed by Congress in 1900 to prohibit the interstate trade of both plants and animals that had been illegally transported, taken, or sold. The problem with the law, as I could see, was that only a few states cared about birds and animals and protecting them with laws so the Lacey Act, while wonderful, needed more help from those of us who knew the importance of protecting birds.

This also meant that there was a good chance Charles and his father had been illegally transporting plumes and feathers to support their businesses and to keep their bank balances so high. When this realization struck me, I did not even realize that I said, "Oh no!" very loudly and then set my head down on the table with a rather loud thud.

I sat like that for several minutes and it must have looked as if I had fainted because I felt a hand on my shoulder and the soft voice of a woman asking, "Are you okay?"

She leaned her head down and when I looked up, there was a woman who looked vaguely familiar to me.

"I'm fine," I whispered. "I'm researching and sometimes when you do that, you find things that are overwhelming, I'm afraid."

"I believe we have met," she said, turning the chair next to me and sitting down. "Emily Greene Balch, and you are Julia Briton. We met at the Audubon meeting."

"Of course!" I now remembered her and as we launched into a discussion, I remained in awe that she was taking the time to sit and talk with me. Emily was a renowned economics professor at Wellesley and a national and international expert on immigration and trade unions for women, and she was a tireless supporter of peace at all costs. She was also researching, and for the next hour, we sat with our heads together and talked about the Audubon, plume hunters, and how the next few years were going to be critical not only for legislation, but education as well.

"I am feeling compelled to do something," I shared. "I have the means and the time and I have a great passion for the protection of these animals. I fear there is much at stake here."

Emily was quiet for a moment. She was a serious but open woman who wore round glasses pulled taut against her head. Her hair was pulled straight back and tied tightly and although she was dressed in a lovely long dress, circled by a stylish leather belt, it was clear that her life focus was on helping others and not tending to fashion, style, and society rules.

She leaned as close as possible and put her mouth to my ear. "You have a lot to lose, considering the millinery business is in your family and what your husband does on his business trips. But the Audubon needs a woman like you and your influence is needed. We desperately need help in Florida. Please remember that all daring includes great risk, but a woman cannot fight the passion in her own heart and soul or she will surely live a lonely and very sad life."

I was breathless, and when she got up to leave, I grabbed her, hugged her, and said, "Thank you so very much."

Inspiration was an unlikely gift that was prodding me to move forward and do something about the swirling mass of indecision inside of me that was making my chest a bit heavier each day. How could I ignore all the signs the world kept giving me? What were the chances I would run into a woman such as Emily Greene Balch when I had seen her name in many of the various newspapers I had been reading just moments before she placed her hand on my shoulder? My direction could not have been obvious, and the moment I realized this, although there were still a few giant steps to take, I felt a kind of calm come over me.

I read for two more hours and it seemed as if every article was about Florida and the wide stretch of swamp-like wilderness that stretched across the entire bottom of the state called the Everglades and nesting birds and how the economy and lack of leadership was making it possible for plume hunters to flourish. I was not a totally uneducated woman. I had read many, many books, and unlike many women of my age, I had graduated from high school, and thanks to my mother, I had a great curiosity about all kinds of publications. Even with all of that, I was astounded that I had missed something that I found remarkable, compelling, and exciting when I found a huge article in the *New York Times* about the first wildlife refuge in the United States. I had no idea such a designation or place existed and I unconsciously let out another inappropriate gasp.

A mere year before, in 1903, President Theodore Roosevelt had signed into a law a bill that had created the first Federal Bird Reservation. Roosevelt was a great lover of the outdoors and I knew he had a vision for protection and care of the lands and wilderness in our country. I could not read the article fast enough.

The designated and protected reservation, a tiny three-acre speck of an island, was called Pelican Island and it was in the Intracoastal Waterway, which included part of St. Johns River, just off the Atlantic coast in east Florida. The island needed protection because it was a crucial nesting ground for egrets, herons, brown pelicans, and other birds that were being slaughtered by the thousands by plume hunters. My heart was beating so fast I became lightheaded. Pelican Island was put under the jurisdiction of the Division of Biological Survey and the American Ornithological Union Bird Protection Fund was paying a man, Paul Kroegel, one dollar a month to act as a game warden. The final sentence of the article however wiped the smile off my face. "In spite of this new Reservation designation, members of the Audubon and the Ornithological Union say plume hunting and the obliteration of numerous species of birds remains a grave and serious problem."

If I could have been transported magically to Pelican Island, I would have done so immediately. I sat in my chair and looked out the window, trying to imagine what it might be like to be there, what I could do, where I might go next. Then Emily flashed past me, brushed my shoulder lightly, dropped a note in front of me, and disappeared out the front door.

I picked up the note and read my directions. *"Mr. Thomas Briggs will be waiting for you tomorrow in the back room of this very library. There is a 2 p.m. Audubon meeting. Sit with him. Listen. If you agree, he will escort you to another meeting. These are all upstanding people that I hold in the highest regard. Remember to risk is to live. Your friend, Emily."*

That night, I sat in the dark on the back porch, rocking in a chair I had purchased when I thought I might be rocking my first baby to sleep, and watched the moon rise slowly across the tops of the trees until I felt as if had paused and it was waiting for me to say something. So I did.

"What do I do? Should I go? Am I brave enough?"

A huge cloud passed in front of the moon and the wind picked up suddenly, and of course, I took this as some kind of meaningful exchange because that is what the mind does in circumstances such as this. I had a light woolen shawl around my shoulders and I pulled it in tighter, wrapping myself in my own arms. I was alone and, yes, lonely and had begun to realize that my life might always be like this. I had already made up several conversations about birds and plume hunters in my mind that I might have when, and if, Charles returned. I could never end these make-believe conversations happily, as I realized Charles most likely would never listen to me and I would be dismissed. He would come and go and I would be there, on the porch, always waiting unless I decided not to wait, unless I decided to do what Emily had suggested, and risk. But what if I was wrong and Charles did listen? What if he returned full of remorse and loathing for what he had seen and in fact encouraged by the continued purchase of plumes and portions of dead birds? That was part of the risk also, yet I found it hard to believe he could change and it was impossible for me to erase our last exchange from my mind.

The clouds moved away and it was time for more questions. "Will he hate me? Will I lose everything? What could the Audubon possibly want from me?"

The moon was not full, but beautiful, nonetheless, as is every planet and wonder of the world to me. It was sliding sideways a bit and it looked like tiny clouds were pushing it along, much like fate was pushing me forward as well. There was no loud response from the moon as I sat and rocked, but I knew this was the same moon that would be flickering over Pelican Island and all of those unsuspecting birds that wanted the simplest of things: survival.

It was then that I realized I did not simply want to survive, but to live with great passion and to do something that made a difference in the world. I already knew that life, as I had come to know it since the loss of the last baby, was not going to be enough. Margaret had opened up a door to a new world, while she kept her feet on the other side, but I knew I could not do that.

I was not Margaret—I was Julia. I was young and strong and smart and there was a nest inside of me that had room for thousands of birds.

The moon stopped for a sweet moment, hanging from the dark night sky, as if it too were trying to make a decision. I jumped to my feet, spread my arms wide, and let the cool breeze wrap itself around me as I swayed back and forth. My arms became wings and I felt a kind of calm surety come over me. I would go to the meeting tomorrow and see Thomas Briggs. I would bury what fear I had and step off into the unknown, a bird dipping by chance, off a cliff with only the wind and the sweet instincts of passion to show me the way.

Tape Twelve

A Moment or Two
of Resurrection
Boston—November 1, 1904

It was the coldest morning of the season, and when my feet touched
the floor, I knew that it would not be long before snow would begin
to fall and I would have to start sleeping with the window closed again.
It had been a fitful night for me in spite of my new resolve to step
forward and fly wherever the winds of life might take me. My dreams,
vague scenes filled with a variety of troublesome events, had me rolling from one end of my bed to the other so when I finally woke, I felt
as if I had not slept at all.

The day was ominous. The clouds had rolled in to fill up the sky
and were hanging so low that it looked as if someone had dropped a
dark veil over the entire world. I shook off my tiredness, my resolve for
making the day the start of all things new and wonderful pounding
through me as I dressed, and went to join the girls. I was unusually
quiet and they made mention of it. I said I was tired, distracted by my
dreams, and would be attending a meeting in the afternoon.

It is interesting how we might think we know what is approaching in our lives, but it is impossible to predict the rush of reality that
awaits us. The girls had no idea what I was up to, and I trusted them
but thought it best to keep them clear of my intentions. I also had
no idea what awaited me, and when it's all said and done, would we

really want to know what we are walking into? I think not. Most of us would turn and run and then the world would stop spinning and everything would stay the same and life would be a dull reminder of what we could have had, what might have been, and who we could have become.

By the time I left to go back to the library, a slight drizzle had begun, and I decided to walk down and ride the street trolley, as the carriage did not have a cover. I occasionally took the trolley, but there was something lovely about using the carriage and slowly watching the world pass by and being in command of my own pace as well as my personal surroundings. The trolley was nearly full when I got on, and I immediately thought about all of the noise there was riding with other people and how, even though we lived close to the city, it was very quiet at the house. Quiet was apparently something I was realizing I was very fond of.

The trolley was quicker than I remembered and I was a bit early for the meeting. I was also anxious to see what Thomas Briggs looked like and even more eager to hear what he had to say to me. I looked at the daily newspaper for fifteen minutes. I was delighted to read that the Wright brothers were up and flying again and their airplane had stayed aloft long enough to complete a circle. I was also astonished to see that a subway had opened in New York City! Surely if men could fly and travel great distances under ground, they could also come to understand that the needless slaughter of birds must stop!

Thomas Briggs was waiting for me at the entrance to the room and I was immediately taken aback. He was young, very well dressed, and very handsome. He was close to six feet tall, wore a thick but neatly trimmed moustache, and when I introduced myself, he flashed a smile that revealed perfectly straight and very beautiful teeth.

"It's a pleasure to meet you, Mrs. Briton."

"Call me Julia, please."

"And you must call me Thomas! Emily said very wonderful things about you and I think you may have come to our rescue at just the right time, but we must not talk of that now. Please let's sit through the meeting. Then we will leave separately and I will be waiting for you on the far side of the building."

I nodded in agreement. He was very charming, but I was taken aback by the secrecy. What could all of this be about?

We sat down and he leaned in and said we should simply listen to the presentation, then shake hands politely, and depart as planned.

The meeting was not really a meeting at all, but a presentation about the mating habits of birds from the Amazon. I was so nervous about what would happen after the meeting that it was impossible for me to focus on parrots, rare tiny yellow birds, and the lovely photographs that a jungle researcher was discussing in front of a rather small audience. Thomas didn't turn to look at me once we sat down. He was either terribly interested in Amazonia birds or a very good actor. By the end of the hour-long presentation, I was so tense my back was aching. Thomas turned and said, "It was nice to meet you, Mrs. Briton." He bowed and then left the room.

There was no one else at the meeting I knew. I sat and studied my hands for a few moments, quietly turned and left the room, and then exited the library.

Thomas was waiting for me on the side of the building and he smiled at me when I approached, his dazzling teeth like a beam of light in the dim daylight. He was standing by the car and motioned for me to get inside, and without hesitation, because Emily said he was trustworthy, I slid into the passenger seat and waited for him to say something. This was not only a bit strange, but I have to admit it was also very exciting. The minute the car started and we drove around the library, all thoughts of needlepointing, reading on the porch, waiting for Charles to arrive, or anything but the moment I was in all but disappeared. I felt like someone new, and as he started to talk, I could only think that Nellie Lewis had been resurrected. I would soon discover that truer feelings had never before entered my mind.

"I hope you enjoyed the lecture," he said, turning for a moment to look at me.

"I have to admit that I wasn't really focusing. It's not every day I get into a car with a man I don't know and drive off to some undisclosed destination."

He chuckled and headed the car back the way I had come on the streetcar. "I can't say as I blame you. I was told you were brave and

I can assure you not only am I a gentleman, but I come from a fine family, and you and I have the same goal in mind."

"How could anyone know how brave I am?" I was starting to wonder if someone had been spying on me.

"I know Emily—I believe you talked with her yesterday in the library—and I work closely with Harriet Hemenway on many projects, especially this one."

That was enough reassurance for me, and before long, we had driven past the street I lived on and were headed west and closer to the area where Margaret lived. The houses were larger, and although I had driven past many of the homes, I had only been inside Margaret's house. He turned into a paved entrance that seemed to go on forever and the house we were approaching was totally hidden by large trees and a very beautiful garden that must be exquisite in full bloom.

He opened my car door for me and I quietly followed him inside. The house was not really a house; it was a mansion. We entered through a huge iron gate and then there was another door, and finally we walked into a large marble foyer. Thomas could see that my mouth was hanging open and he laughed so loudly there was an echo that bounced off the floor and soared to the ceiling, which had to have been thirty feet high.

"It's ridiculous, isn't it?" he said, continuing to laugh.

"You could drive your car in here," I said with my head tipped backward.

"I actually tried that once, but my great aunt stopped me at the door."

This time I laughed, and he kept walking and walking until we came to the back of the house. Then we were outside in a huge yard that stretched so far I couldn't even see where it ended. There was a swimming pool, what I assumed was a guesthouse, a stable, and who knows what else? It was a bit much. We finally came around the left side and there was a table set up and a woman was sitting at it, drinking something, surrounded by stacks of papers. She must have heard us coming because she turned, and my jaw dropped again. She was smoking a long, brown cigar.

"There you are, Julia! " she shrieked and jumped up to embrace me.

"Hello," I mumbled, trapped in her embrace.

"Julia, meet my aunt, Bertille Forbes Briggs, cigar-smoking philan-thropist to the birds and whatever else strikes her fancy. Her friends call her Bertie."

"The cigars are a terrible habit, I fear, but I love to do everything I'm not supposed to do, and I have the money to do it!"

It was impossible not to like this wild, brash woman who made me feel welcome and as if I had known her my entire life after the first five seconds of our meeting. She was dressed in a man's button-down shirt and she also wore a man's tie, and unlike every other woman in Boston, her hair was not tied up, but hanging loose around her face. It wasn't really warm enough to sit outside for a long period of time, but she seemed to be generating enough heat to keep all of us warm. There was a kind of pale-yellowish glow to her skin that made me wonder if she had applied some kind of makeup to her face, but her dark eyes all but danced, and she seemed feisty and somewhat vigorous for a woman who appeared to be in her mid-fifties.

I felt like a fool, but I said, "I love how you're dressed," anyway.

"Oh! This will be all the rage here in a few years. You just wait and see. Someday, women will wear trousers and whatever they want all day long, too. Have you ever tried to hike or ride a horse in one of these skirts? It's ridiculous."

I looked at Thomas and he had his hands in his pockets and his teeth were showing again. He was enjoying the show.

"Actually, I have tried to hike in a skirt and I ended up turning it into trousers with a rope. It was like a miracle."

Bertie threw back her head and all but barked into the still-dark afternoon sky. "Oh! Thomas! She's wonderful! Now we must convince her. Let's go in. Would you like a puff?"

She held out the cigar and there was absolutely no reason not to try it. I held it, turned it around with my thumb and forefinger as if I'd done it before, smelled it, and then took a puff. Then I coughed. But I liked it and so I took another puff.

"Don't inhale," she advised. "This is fine tobacco. Simply having the tip in your mouth, and the smoke right behind it for a moment, is all you need."

She was correct. The cigar, on the third puff, mind you, tasted like a caramel that had been dipped in a lovely piece of toasted bread. Then

I became lightheaded and must have swooned a bit. Bertie grabbed the cigar out of my hand, threw it into the dying grass, and clapped her hands.

"Let's get on with the business before this tobacco virgin asks for brandy," she said, already ahead of us and halfway back to the house.

Thomas scooped up her papers and I followed her into the house, back the way we had come, and into a small room on the far right side of the house that looked like an office. There really wasn't a desk, per se, but wooden boxes set end to end and Asian tapestries on the walls and thick carpets, unlike any I had ever seen, on the floor. It was delightful and warm and welcoming and I so liked this woman, who seemed to be exactly as I had always thought a generous and loving queen might be if I were to meet one. She was absolutely certain of who she was, gracious, kind, attractive, fun, and eager to make certain those around her were not uncomfortable in her presence. It was hard to imagine a person or situation that a woman like Bertie could not handle or control.

I took off my overcoat and before I could set it on a chair, Thomas stepped in and took it. Bertie motioned for me to sit down and asked if I really did want a brandy.

"Well, maybe after you tell me why I am here I might need one," I said in all seriousness.

"Thomas, bring us two very large glasses of the best brandy we have and then go busy yourself until you either hear Julia laughing or running quickly out the door."

Both Thomas and I laughed, and then once the brandy had arrived we moved to a small sitting area by the window that had a lovely view of the trees I had seen when I arrived. Bertie clearly loved the outdoors and probably would have preferred to stay in the backyard, but I was glad to be indoors and dared not think of the coming winter months lest I start to cry. She kept looking out the window, either longing to be back out there or trying to summon up the courage to tell me whatever it was she was going to tell me. I noticed when she sat down, she did so very slowly, being careful to ease back in the low chair. Perhaps her lifestyle was beginning to take its toll.

"I want to thank you for coming and I knew once Harriet told me about you and your family and your growing fondness for the Audubon that you might be able to step in and help." She began. "Please sit back and you may as well start sipping the brandy. I will tell you a bit about myself and what I am so hoping you will be brave enough to do for not just those of us alive today, but those coming after us as well."

I took her advice, picked up my glass, took a very large drink, and for the next hour listened to a story and a request that made me very glad that I was drinking a beverage that was laced with spirits.

Bertie explained that she was a Forbes heiress and that her family had made "tons and tons" of money in transportation and trade. She apologized for the extravagant house and told me she had inherited it and used it mainly for charity events and as a home base when she was not out traveling the world and discovering what cause or country might next benefit from her generosity.

She said she had married young and that her husband had died tragically in a fall from his horse just a month after they had been married. I held my breath, trying hard to imagine what that must have been like.

"My grief crippled me for two entire years. My husband, a doctor, was the love of my life, a remarkable man who was operating a free clinic for the poor here in Boston. He was gentle and kind and his heart had immeasurable capacity for love. I thought I might die of a broken heart, and I moved into the family summer estate in Maine. No one could help me, and I was left to wander the trails on the property and pity myself and I became very good at that. Then one day, as I walked the shoreline and was seriously thinking of throwing myself into the crashing waves, I witnessed the massive slaughter of hundreds of shorebirds who were simply standing on the beach."

Bertie said this was her "moment of resurrection." She ran down the hill she was standing on, screaming and shouting at the hunters to stop. They thought a mad woman had dropped out of the sky and they quickly retreated and left her standing almost to her knees in dead birds.

"I spent the next three days burying them, and with each bird that I buried, it was as if I were getting a small piece of myself and my life back," she said. "That was a long time ago and the beginning of this life, the one I have now, and the one that has led me to some amazing places."

She stopped for a moment to take a sip of her brandy and I could see she had tears in her eyes. I reached out and put my hand on her arm. I felt inadequate and small and could only imagine what she had done and where she had been. "I'm so sorry," I managed to say, knowing myself that grief can rise up at any moment to remind us what we have lost over and over again.

"Well, one must move on and you know about that too, don't you?"

"Yes. There are some who don't understand how you can grieve the loss of a baby that you never held or touched, but they were inside of me, right next to my heart, and they were very real to me."

"We forge on. That is what women do, and I challenge any man to bear a child, work the way a woman does, and carry the burden of so many losses. It drives me half mad sometimes, but what I have that so many of them do not is money! And, Julia, I am going to spend it all on whatever I want and what I want right now is to save the birds."

"Me too!" I all but yelled, carried away by her impassioned speech.

"I hope so, my dear. I truly hope so."

She got up slowly then and paced a bit. It was the first time I had seen her look uncertain.

"What is it?" I stood up, held out my hands to stop her, and she then walked over to the desk made of crates and picked up a small envelope. She looked at the envelope and looked at me three times before she told me to sit down and passed it to me. Then she sat down and I stood there looking at the envelope, and it struck me that this had been one of the strangest and most interesting days of my life. What did I have to lose at this point? I sat down and opened up the envelope.

It was a blue ticket for passage on the steamship *Queen of the Sea* sailing on November 2, 1904, from the South Boston dock to Jacksonville, Florida, with one stop for a two-day service and transfer in Savannah, Georgia. I looked at the ticket for a very long time and had absolutely no idea why it was in my hand or what Bertie was going to say next. Boarding was the following day at half past six in the evening.

She got up, went to the door, and yelled, "Thomas, fetch us the brandy bottle please!" walked back, and sat down. Thomas appeared very quickly, this time without his smile or the overcoat, and his sleeves were rolled up. He wordlessly set the bottle down on the floor next to Bertie, turned, and walked out.

She filled both our glasses, then took a sip, advised me to do the same, and then pushed back in her chair.

I had not moved or blinked but sensed something beyond unusual was coming. There was no way to guess what she might say or ask of me, but I remained eager and finally I could stand it no longer.

"Why did you give this to me? It's a one-way ticket for passage on a ship that leaves tomorrow. Why am I holding it?"

"We want you to go."

"What?

"Well, we is mostly Thomas and me, with a bit of help from Emily and Harriet and even Margaret, although Margaret does not know of this meeting and what I am asking of you. Thomas is my right-hand man and will inherit everything you see one day. He also has my brave and wild heart. It's a wonder he was even born to my dusty sister, who, by the way, buys her damned hats with bird feathers from one of your husband's stores!"

My reaction shocked not just me, but I think Bertie, too. I did not jump up and leave. I did not throw the ticket in her face or laugh and drink the entire bottle of brandy. I looked down at the ticket and saw that the passenger's name was empty. That is what I asked about first.

"That's what you want to know?" I was happy to see that she looked more surprised than I did.

"I'm in a bit of a daze over here, but you are a very smart woman and the women you have mentioned, well, I think highly of them. I have been recruited for something and the ticket is blank, and I think this would be the time to tell me what in the world this is about."

The story of the ticket and Julia Briton took a very long time to tell, and once I thought how I should rush home and then I realized the girls would be gone and no one would miss me anyway. Charles was in the swamps somewhere, Margaret didn't know it, but she was waiting for George, and I was sitting in a mansion, holding a ticket to Jacksonville and sipping brandy with one of the wealthiest women in America. It only made a difference to me that I was not home and would miss dinner and that it would soon get dark. No one knew where I was, and I was beginning to wonder if anyone really cared.

Unbeknownst to me, Thomas was in the kitchen, cooking dinner, while we talked. But it was really Bertie who talked from this point onward and it was quite a story and quite a request. I held the ticket in one hand and the glass in the other, and I listened.

Everything was about the birds and Bertie's distressing but grand Moment of Resurrection was not just the beginning of her new life, but also of her involvement with local, state, and national ornithological societies. She didn't just donate money, but she studied and learned and met with important people. She had attended some of the earliest Audubon meetings and was one of the first to realize that plume hunting was the root of a huge problem and that Maine, Florida, and Virginia were the three states most affected by the massive slaughter of birds.

I knew much of what she was telling me from my own research, but it took on new meaning to be able to sit with someone who had been there from the very beginning of the movement. Bertie also knew that the millinery trade and the very women who feed fashion must also be part of the solution. She also had relatives in the millinery business and she knew plume hunters and she was taking them all to task.

"It's amazing what money and no fear will do to further a cause," she told me. "I've been to the jungles and I've met with the President and I've seen baby birds literally starve to death while waiting for their dead mothers to return. It's not easy to get the world to project into the future. How can there be an endless supply of birds, and are we not all linked and dependent on one another? A bird drops a seed that grows a tree that covers the earth that drops food and stabilizes the soil… Well, life is a circle and we are all connected. Call me a free thinker or a crazy rich woman, I care not, but we must take care of the things around us. We must, Julia!"

I let her go on without question because she was speaking my exact thoughts. She said the most urgent need remained Florida where the most beautiful and the most prized birds nested. This is when I could no longer stop myself from speaking.

"I believe Charles is there right now, searching for plumes and more hunters," I said, embarrassed for the first time to acknowledge that my husband was part of the problem.

"I know that, Julia, and so is my brother and so is Margaret's husband. It's up to us to create a balance. It's up to us to do something!"

Kris Radish

"What is the 'something' someone like me holding a ticket like this can do, Bertie? I thought there was a warden there now, Pelican Island is being protected, and I've read there may be more protected areas in the future."

"Of course! Most of the money to pay for the warden came from me, and I donate handsomely, but the truth is that Florida needs a strong woman right now to organize and lead. It is not a wealthy state and the plume hunters are not easily going to stop when it is often the only means they have of feeding themselves and their families."

I started to be concerned. Florida? Organize? Me? Plume hunters?

"There's more," she said, pushing back her head and closing her eyes so it looked as if she were trying to decide if she should even speak again. "We need a new set of eyes. Someone respected, someone who can travel and see things, write about them, and befriend the people who live there. We know the warden's job is very difficult and if you saw what he was up against, you would understand."

I finally looked away and my thoughts sped forward. Charles arriving home just as I passed the Port of Charleston. Charles discovering where I had gone and why I had left. Margaret standing alone at her husband's funeral. The girls in the kitchen reduced once again to their quiet roles of domesticity. My father weeping when he discovered I had abandoned my husband and a life that everyone envied. There was nothing simple or easy about any of this, yet I could not let go of the ticket.

"Bertie, why is the passenger name on the ticket blank?"

She grew quiet and then stood up so slowly I was about to rise and help her to her feet. "It was my ticket to be filled in at boarding, but, Julia, it is not to be. I have cancer. It is in my bones and I cannot tell you how much brandy I am drinking these days! The journey would take me down faster and there's much I can do from this oversized and absolutely hideous mansion. I chose you. You are young and strong and you have the passion. The truth is that I have been fighting the urge to scream for a good hour. Thomas has made us a dinner and he has an injection ready for me. We can talk while you eat and then, well, no one knows better than I, but time is of the essence. There isn't much left for me or for the sweet birds we both love so much."

Dinner was not memorable and eating was close to impossible.

Thomas and I sat alone for most of it after he had injected Bertie with what I assumed was a dose of heroin for her pain. He told me she was a brave soul and that whatever I decided she would abide by. It was clear that he had great affection and devotion for his aunt and he assured me that he would prepare me as best as he could if I decided to go.

"There's a bit of danger," he also said. "We have people who help us, and that information will all be prepared for you, but as you are aware, not everyone is in agreement with our cause. And I'm afraid you must decide before I escort you home in an hour. She must know and she would not want me to tell you this, but the time she has spent with you has been nothing short of a parade of bravery. She is in terrible pain."

I looked at his lovely face and the pink apron he had tied around his waist that he had forgotten to take off before we sat down. I looked at my own hands and then the wall and then out into the dark night. Then I looked at the nameless ticket that was sitting in the center of the table as if it were a much-cherished centerpiece.

When he left to bring back Bertie, I picked up the ticket and then I got up from the table and went back into the room where I had been drinking brandy and learning about why I had been summoned. I found a fountain pen on her desk and took it into my right hand and set the ticket on the desk. I bent to write on it, but when I paused for moment to look outside again, I saw that it had started to snow. The streetlights way up to the front of the lawn had been lit and I thought of the large cold house that awaited me and the empty bed and how the night would stretch, silent and long, until the morning light began to melt whatever snow had survived. I felt an ache and a yearning and a thirst that made me feel as if I were empty.

I bent down again, pen in hand, and wrote.

When I went back to the kitchen to meet ashen-faced Bertie, I handed her the ticket. She looked at it and then back up at me.

"That's who I really am," I said, pointing to the name I had written. "I'm Nellie Lewis and I must get home and pack."

Tape Thirteen

Maintenance and Restoration for the Daring Wife
Boston Harbor—November 2, 1904

I t was not the kind of day one would hope for when one world is about to disappear and there is nothing but uncharted territory lying ahead. Boston Harbor was locked in a kind of misty early winter haze, and the snow from the previous night had decided to stay so the world looked like a sprinkle of brown and white. It had snowed about two inches during the night, and while most of it had melted, it was apparent that winter had arrived just as I was about to leave.

It was three in the afternoon and Thomas had gone off to find me a basket of food, newspapers, and who knows what else this thoughtful young man might think of to keep me company during my travels. He was not just an attractive man, but his heart was generous like his aunt's, and he was perceptive enough to know that my own heart and head were reeling with the decision I had made to carry through with Bertie's wishes.

I was bundled against the cold and sitting on a bench outside the Merchants and Miners Transportation Company. My steamer, the *Suwannee*, was docked on the wooden dock off to my right and I could hear the ship bumping and grinding as the seas rocked her back and forth. There was a considerable lack of other passengers. Thomas had finally confessed and told me this was mostly going to be a cargo-laden ship with a major stop in Savannah to unload supplies and load cotton for a drop off in Jacksonville. There were not many steamers scheduled during the next few months because the cold was settling in and passage would become most difficult, as winter storms were imminent.

The brochure about Merchants and Miners ships was in my hands and I read it with a smile on my face because I doubted this would be my experience.

The North, South, East, or West will find the Queen of the Sea Routes the ideal way of journeying. Here may be enjoyed the true elements of luxury at a minimum expenditure, combining therewith the opportunity for pleasure, recreation, and recuperation of health in the pure and bracing salt-sea air, one of nature's greatest tonics. It is a somewhat curious fact that to the average American, an "Ocean Voyage" means a Trans-Atlantic trip. He seems unaware that it is possible to take an enjoyable ocean voyage coastwise on a luxuriously appointed steamer at a comparatively slight expenditure of both time and money. To those seeking a short and delightful voyage for a vacation or those making a journey southward or northward for business, the Queen of the Seas Routes offers a most delightful way of traveling. The exercise in the bracing salt-sea air, change of scenery, and sense of rest, secure from interruption, worry and excitement, more or less incident to life on the rail, combine to create a most beneficial influence. It is impossible to overestimate the value of a short sea trip for the maintenance or restoration of health.

I was fairly certain this literature was not designed for a woman who was running away from everything she knew, and owned, to rescue birds in the wilds of Florida. I tucked the brochure into the bottom of my thick bag and sat watching the smoke billow from the boilers of the ship. The last eighteen hours seemed to have flown past me as if I had been standing still, and I did feel like I had been caught in some wild wind that had captured not just my body, but my soul as well.

Thomas had driven me home and presented me with a list they had already prepared with names of men and women to contact during my journey who would help me. There would be a hotel for me to stay in once I reached Jacksonville and then a ride had been arranged south to Vero Landing and the area near Pelican Island. Bertie suggested what to pack, what to leave behind, what I might say in the letters she thought necessary I write to Margaret and Charles. She gave me one hundred dollars and said she would be with me in spirit and that when she passed, she had decided to return as a feisty egret.

"I will fly over you always, my brave, lovely Julia," she said as we hugged one last time. "I will be your guide and protector and I know you will have a life of richness, great, great richness."

When Thomas pulled out of the yard and we stopped for a moment to check for traffic, I turned and saw her standing in the shadows of the darkened house. The snow had stopped for a moment and she was a black shadow standing against the white brick house. For an instance, it seemed as if there were a glow around her, not unlike what humans believed angels might look like if indeed there were such creatures. I waved to her and it came to me that she would not live much longer and that I would never see her again.

"Thomas, oh Thomas! She's going to die very soon, isn't she?"

He was crying when I turned to receive his answer, giant tears cascading down his face, and he could not speak, but his head nodded up and down, and I took great courage from the moment. The courage, however, would falter a great deal during the coming hours, days, and months.

It was close to ten when I arrived back home and discovered a precious note from the girls who had left me a cold supper and wanted to remind me that the following day they were scheduled not to work. This both eased my worry and made it worse. I had no idea how I would say good-bye to them and now I didn't have to. But I might also never see them again! The results of my decision were already falling into place and even though I knew I had time to back out, I felt as if I would not. Bertie's angel-like form was haunting and the nest inside of me was growing larger every day.

The next two hours were nothing short of frantic as I threw myself into packing and deciding what might stay and what might go. Thomas had advised me to travel as light as possible, as I might be going by car, horse, foot, and probably a small boat or two during the course of my travels. I decided to limit myself to one trunk and a bag that I would carry with me that included essentials if I should get stranded. This goal was not easy to accomplish.

It was embarrassing to discover how my simple pre-marriage wardrobe had grown. There were dresses and skirts and blouses and hats and belts and sleepwear, and I was appalled to realize I now owned eight pairs of shoes! I thought of what Charles had said in his letter about living conditions and quickly eliminated heavy winter clothing, anything fancy, and all but two featherless and very practical hats. I had no idea what to take and what to leave. I had never been on a ship, or out of Boston, except that brief trip to the country, and it was hard to know what a plume hunter observer and bird crusader might need hundreds of miles away from home.

Home.

The word struck me as I hurried about a bedroom I had taken to calling "mine" and not "ours." Where would home be after this? Would Charles come after me? Would Margaret turn away from me? Would I have second, third, and fourth thoughts about what I was doing? Would I ever return? It was clear to me that once I closed the door and headed to the harbor, there would be no going back and that this serious decision would once again change my life in ways that might not allow me to ever return.

There really wasn't time to linger, and as the packing continued and my resolve occasionally weakened, I knew keeping busy was a good thing. Behind all the uncertainty, I did feel this was what I must do, but even the most strong-hearted person might have doubts. It would be unwise to always move forward without introspection and I knew there would be lots of time for that during my travels. I kept moving and soon there was little room left in my trunk.

It was close to midnight when I looked around the room and picked the wedding photograph of Charles and me off the dresser and slipped it between the dresses in my trunk. I took several books, which I know would add to the weight, but I had to know they were there, and I remembered the feathers I had placed in the drawer the day I had taken them out of my hat at Heart's Haven. Perhaps that's when this journey had started, and the feathers would remind me of that day and my babies and the magical moment when I saw the wood duck resting in the tree. When I picked up the feathers, I also remembered that I had a small treasure box in the same drawer. I picked it up and walked over to the bed to sit down. When I pulled open the wooden lid, I smiled to see the Clara Barton letter, the business card from William Randolph Hearst, a copy of our wedding announcement, and notes and letters and other special mementos that I had always kept in the box. I put the lid back on, held the box close to my heart, closed my eyes, and had to force myself to keep moving. There were so many memories in the little box, yet I knew the memories were also inside of me and that I would carry them with me forever. I could not stand to leave the box there so I put in the trunk and then hurried downstairs. I had a long night ahead of me.

I drew myself a bath first, wondering how long it would be before that simple luxury was available to me again. I put on my nightclothes when I finished, foolishly thinking I might actually sleep, and then I went into Charles's office to compose a series of letters. It would be close to daylight before I left.

The first letter was the easiest. I told the girls how much I cared for them and they had become like sisters to me and that I would always consider them family. I was not entirely specific about what I was doing but only told them I was involved with the Audubon and had been assigned a position that was taking me away for an indeterminate amount of time. I told them I would write them when I had an address and that if they needed anything at all until Charles or I returned, they should contact Margaret. I also told them to be gentle with Charles if he came home and I was not there and to not take offense if he was angry or rude to them. Before I finished the letter, I went upstairs and took the money Bertie had given me and put it in the envelope, which I then set on the kitchen table by their workspace.

My heart could not have been heavier when I left the kitchen and walked back into the office. I did love those girls so very much and they had shown me the true face of friendship and caring. During the hard days ahead, I would miss them so very much, yet I knew they would care for the house and Charles, if need be, with great concern.

My next letter was to Margaret and after much thought and struggle, I decided to make it short and to the point, almost like Margaret herself.

My Dearest Maggie, I am first asking your forgiveness for what I am about to do, but I do so with the knowledge that women such as us must risk and live the way our heart tells us to live. I learned that from you, as well as many other wonderful, loving things, and if I thought you might not forgive me or might disagree with what I am about to do, I might not be able to go forward. By the time you receive this, I will be on a steamer headed to plume hunting territory. Please contact Bertille for information about where I am going and what I have done. Charles may never forgive me for this, and if that happens, I am begging you to please stay in my life. Rest assured I will send news and an address as soon as I am settled. Ella and Ruby may need some assistance. They are very dear to me and it would be a great favor if you would make certain they are taken care of in my absence. With great affection, Julia.

I sealed and addressed her letter and then got up to look out the window for a moment. The world was asleep and I was wide-awake—my emotions a wild mix of excitement, dread, and misgiving. When I went back to the desk, I remembered that Margaret had said there was money inside of the Bible Charles kept in his desk drawer. I quickly located it, opened it up, and found five twenty-dollar bills. I set them down next to me as I tried to decide if I should take them. It felt like stealing, but I convinced myself that the money was also mine and Charles would want me to have it. Who knows where I might be living or when I would have access to money again? I would have six hundred dollars, which still seemed like a small fortune to me.

My letter to Charles took hours to write. I told him everything, sparing only the great education I had received from his mother, and I decided to mention Bertie and Thomas because I knew they could hold their own against him if he became angry and tried to talk with them. One part of me hoped and prayed that Charles of the Heart would rise up and accept my leaving and mission as something grand and acceptable and another part could not help but remember how Charles and I had parted. I wanted him to know that I loved him, but I also felt it was important he know I could not be dominated and that I now saw marriage as a partnership.

I know this is not what you bargained for that day you saw an innocent young woman standing on the street corner. I have grown and I have changed, and I must say the loss of the three babies turned me upside down and inside out. You may not think it fair for me to change, but I think that is the purpose of this life. There is much to learn and experience and to cut one's self off from that, to live the same day in and day out, is not really a life or living at all, but simply existing. I have missed you, Charles, so very, very much, and the days and nights without you have left a void and an ache inside of me. The truth is that we are on opposite ends of the world right now in so many ways. I am opposed to the plume hunting and I urge you now, with all my being, to please reconsider this part of the business. It is a new time and also time to be brave and realize that the world, and all of its creatures, is more fragile than you might imagine. I know my departure may harm you personally and professionally, but I urge you to consider what I have said before you make any decisions. You will always be my Charles of the Heart and I remain your loving wife. Forever yours, Julia.

I sealed the letter and then kissed it and set it on his desk. I found it difficult to leave his office because it had been the one room where I felt the closest to him when he was gone. This feeling, the sights, and smells I would also have to seal in my heart so I could remember them. I slowly closed the door when I left, as I wasn't certain if I could bear to look inside tomorrow when it was time to go.

The remainder of the night I tossed and turned in bed, but it was impossible to sleep with my mind swirling so fast that I felt dizzy. When it was just starting to get light, I got out of bed, dressed in the most comfortable skirt, blouse, and shoes that I owned, and went down to eat a light breakfast. Thomas was arriving around one o'clock to take me to the boat and that left me part of the day to go through the list they had given me and to make certain I was as prepared as one might be on such an occasion. I eventually added a few articles of clothing, subtracted a few, tucked the money into the bag I was going to carry, and then decided it might be wise to split up the money, so I put some in the pocket of one of my dresses. I had no idea how long I would be gone or if I would even be allowed to come back after my tasks were completed.

There were two things I needed to do before I left. I wanted to say good-bye to the babies and I wanted to say good-bye to the house. I didn't have time to ride to the cemetery so I put on my coat and braced for the November air and headed toward the park and Heart's Haven. I felt very close to my children there, and it was also where the birds really swept me off my feet and flew into my heart for the first time. I was alone in the park, because most wise people were huddled in their kitchens, drinking warm beverages and praying for an early spring. The air was crisp and almost like a constant slap in the face as I went directly to my favorite bench.

The trees were bare and my green paradise had been replaced by dozens of shades of brown. The birds, if any were brave enough to still be in Boston, were huddled in their nests and deep into the thick bushes. The sky was not going to open up and let the sun through at all, and I tried not to imagine what this would mean for a ship heading partway out to sea. I touched the cold bench and remembered what great comfort I had taken from being in this quiet spot during the grieving over the loss of my babies.

What was strange was the feeling that I was saying good-bye, and not just temporarily, but for a very long time, maybe forever. It was almost as if I knew I would not be coming back and that made no sense to me, but I looked at everything—trees, pond, ground, sky—for a very long time so if I wanted to, I could close my eyes and remember this sacred and meaningful spot. I had come to say good-bye to my babies, but another strange feeling came over me, and I realized that I could carry my thoughts of them with me and that maybe this is where I came to bury my grief. It wasn't as if I had forgotten them, because not a day went by when I did not love them and think of their lives as angels, but it was true that my work with the birds had helped me move forward and my grief was not as prominent.

This walk cheered me and I hurried back home and ate a late lunch, carried my small bag downstairs, and then spent the next two hours walking through the rooms of the house. I laughed remembering the first time Margaret had taken me into the bedroom and instructed her son on how to behave, and I smiled remembering the first time Charles and I had made love there. There were, indeed, many things to miss by leaving. I walked in and out of every room, except the office, because I had already said my good-byes there. I lingered in the kitchen where I had had so many lovely and fun conversations with the girls and I decided to take Ella's favorite mixing spoon and put it in my small bag. It was a silly thing to do, as I didn't think I was quite that sentimental, but when I picked up the long wooden spoon she kept on the counter, I thought if I kept it, then every time I looked at it I would remember the kitchen, and them, with a pinch of tenderness. I sat on the back porch in my favorite rocking chair and for the next two hours tried very hard to talk myself out of leaving.

It did not work.

Thomas arrived a bit early and before he came up to the bedroom to carry down my trunk, we stood in the entrance and talked for a moment. It became clear very quickly that Bertie had asked him to make certain I knew what I was in for and he did a great job.

"You know voyage at this time of the year can be rough."

"Of course."

"You know that Charles will most likely be very unhappy about this."

"Of course."

"You know there will be, how should I say this, interesting characters on the steamboat."

"I hope so."

"You know there will be a layover at the Port of Savannah and you may have to disembark and stay for a night or so at a lodge that may be, well, not what you are accustomed to."

"I can hardly wait for the new experience."

"You know when you arrive in Florida it will be hot and bug infested and that Florida is still, for the most, all but pioneer territory."

"Of course."

"You know that you may face grave and great danger because some people are opposed to the protection of birds and other species of wildlife that they feel they are entitled to hunt, shoot, and kill?"

"I am aware."

"You know that travel, and accommodations, in some of the areas where you will be going are considered unacceptable by women of your social status?"

That was enough for me. I held up my hand and stopped him.

"Thomas, do you know that I was raised in Dorchester and that there were some evenings when there was barely enough for all of us to eat?"

Thomas tried to say something, but I would not let him. I was not yet done.

"My father worked like a dog and never made more than a few hundred dollars a year, and my mother worked so hard that her heart gave out not so long ago. I am a woman who has been graced with the love and kindness of the wealthy, and I never have cared much for the social appropriateness of this new world where I am accepted but adopted nonetheless. I am young and strong and I have lost three babies and am mostly alone in a house that is big enough to sleep twenty people. "

I stopped to take a breath, Thomas shuffled his feet, and this time he put up his hands.

"Oh, Julia! I had to ask one more time and not just because Bertie told me too. You are remarkable and beautiful and if Charles throws you off, I'll be down to fetch you as soon as possible!"

I assumed he was trying to make light of this big day and decision and that he wasn't serious about running off with an older woman. I smiled, and so did he, flashing those sweet snow-white teeth and then, without looking back, I locked the door, tucked the key into my undergarments, and got into his car.

I could hear Thomas approaching before he arrived as he was mumbling, and when I turned there he was, his arms full of packages, and I hoped they were not all for me.

"I think I may have gotten carried away," he said, dropping them on the bench. "Bertie gave me orders and I got you some extra things as well."

He presented me with a lovely leather-bound notebook that I was instructed to use for note-taking on the journey. There were stamped envelopes for mailing reports and a packet of instructions on what to look for and other details that he said I could peruse when I was on the ship. There were newspapers, a small bird book, a novel, fresh fruit, candy, and a box he said I should open when I was in my stateroom.

Before I could respond, the steamship whistle blew four times and I saw several people come from the office building behind me and make their way to the ship. I looked at Thomas and he looked at me.

"It's time," he said.

My stomach was chasing itself in circles and I stuffed his packages into my bag, stood up, and realized tears were seaming down my face.

"Oh, Julia…"

"I'm fine," I lied as I turned to leave, but he stopped me, pulled me close, tipped back my head, and kissed me right on the lips.

"No one should leave without a proper good-bye," he said, pulling away and giving me one last beautiful smile.

With that I turned and walked away, daring not to look back, and boarded a ship that should really have been named *Julia's Destiny*.

Tape Fourteen

Queen of the Sea and a Blossoming Heart
Sailing South, Atlantic Ocean—
November 3-7, 1904

It didn't take me long to realize that the brochure I had been holding before embarking was designed for the ship before it had been
stripped for the winter and prepared to haul cargo, and not graceful
ladies seeking to freshen their lungs with the very healthful salty sea
air. The *Suwannee* was a beautiful boat and seaworthy and medium-
sized, but without most of its furniture, with a crew who did not know
how to cook or console passengers when the waves were coming over
the side, and the lovely stench of some kind of animals that were
being transported, it was less a lovely cruise and more like a bit of
unplanned torture.

Part of me had hoped it would be a slow and graceful cruise all the
way to Savannah. I was anxious to be gone and to try and push all the
doubts that had built up inside of me away. I had imagined strolling
along the deck, and watching for the birds would be just the way to do
it. There was, however, way too much else to worry about.

My cabin was adequate and actually quite lovely. It included two
small beds, a dresser, my own lavatory, a small porthole to look out of,
and a sitting chair. What it did not include was my trunk. The little

man—and by little I mean that the top of his head was not even close to the top of my head, and to be precise he was looking straight at my bosom when he greeted me. I was not offended, the poor man—Chester was his name—probably had a hard enough time because of his height, and as he showed me to my stateroom, he talked about the ship, the pigs that were in the cargo area, apparently "the largest herd of swine ever transported by the Queen of Sea" line, and the other five passengers.

"There's a strange lady from New York who came on board in an evening gown, the farmer who wanted ta meet and escort his pigs, two brothers who claim ta be Boston businessmen who are headed ta Florida ta do somethin' with oranges, and you."

I could hardly wait to meet them all, but first Chester had a bit of bad news for me. He said it was impossible to get my trunk because it had accidentally been loaded down by the pigs and they were not about to let anyone down there until they were off-loaded. "Them pigs are mean! I saw one eat a man's leg once," he shared.

"Well, Chester, I suppose I will have to make do, then, won't I? I suspect you are quite fond of your legs."

Chester laughed, told me I was a good sport and that the captain wanted me to know he had some extra clothes from his wife and personal items that I was welcome to use if I needed anything.

That was the auspicious beginning of my trip before the ship had even left the port. It got only worse, or better depending on how one looks at these things, from there on. Thankfully, I had packed a few items in the bag I carried with me, and I realized that from here on everything that happened would just prepare me for what was coming next.

This is a bit of wisdom that would grow inside of me every single day. Once you have done something that you thought hard, it opens the way for something harder and then harder after that. I knew that every loss and challenge I had overcome during the past few years had changed me and made me realize that my life could not be commanded or designed by anyone but myself. Charles had chosen me, but I had also chosen him, and even though I was doing something I was certain he might not agree with in many ways, it was almost as if I had no choice.

I had decided not to go back on the deck and watch as the ship pulled out of the harbor, but I thought about Thomas, standing on the dock, waving to me and wondering if I had already fallen overboard. Boston was my home, my life, my everything, and waving good-bye would not be easy. But alas, it would make me stronger.

The ship's horn blasted for a very long time and startled me as I was walking to the deck, and there was Thomas jumping and waving and throwing me kisses. I would have been a fool to miss the show! I threw him a kiss back and wondered if I would ever see him again. He was yelling something to me, but the ship was loud, and in a matter of minutes we were surging forward and into a white mist, and then Thomas was gone and so was I.

During the next several hours, I explored the ship, much like a young girl or boy would do on his or her first voyage. Charles had suggested a honeymoon trip to Europe on the *R.M.S. Lucania*, a gorgeous Cunard ship, but I wanted something simple and he agreed to a weekend stay at the Parker House Hotel, which was the beginning of many firsts for me. My first marriage, first ever stay at a hotel and in a luxurious suite, and the first time I realized why my father had gone walking and why my mother cried behind her closed door.

The ship I was on was actually quite lovely even though most of the furniture and the people who might use it were missing. The wooden floors and rails had been polished and there were at least half a dozen rooms for sitting, reading, music, and what I thought must have been a dining hall. Lord knows where we were going to eat, but as I wandered here and there, I decided that traveling by ship, with or without passengers, could be the wonderful experience described in the brochure. However, that was before the waves started coming over the side of the ship.

I noticed the vessel rocking a bit as I was looking around and I was glad it did not affect my stomach. I walked through the dining hall to the other side of the ship, opened the door, stepped out, and it looked as if we were riding through a waterfall. I thought it too interesting and lovely to be afraid, until Chester came up behind and told me to shut the door and, "Get the bloody hell back inside!"

"We've slowed to a crawl," he told me once we were safely back inside with what I presumed was a Irish accent. "We knew there was a storm a comin' and we're used ta dis kinda weather. You ain't seasick, missus?"

"No, I'm fine."

"Well, the other lady, she's a needin' some help. She's somthin' else that one. Could ya help?"

"Of course," I said, hardly knowing what I was getting into.

Chester led me through a small maze of rooms until we went up some steps and we were on the upper level of the boat. He knocked on a door, announced our arrival, pushed open the door, and told me he would be in the kitchen if I needed anything. Then he all but ran from the room.

There was a woman huddled on the bed, her face coved by a washbasin, and she was retching. When she came up the second time, I went to her, and before I knew who she was, I wished with all my heart that I was back in Boston doing needlepoint.

"Thank almighty God that little midget has left me!" The woman rolled over onto her back and I searched for some towels and got to work.

She was indeed dressed in an evening gown and she had on very heavy makeup that came off when I tried to wipe her face. I quickly discovered I was administering to Clara Bloodgood, an infamous socialite and stage actress, who had a story that bested mine. During the course of the next day, when she was recovering, she told me she had performed in *The Gentleman from India* the previous night and had fought with her husband, her stage director, and apparently everyone else in sight. Then she had retreated to her hotel room where she had enjoyed two bottles of French wine. When her husband came back, they fought again, and she told him she was going to catch the next steamship out of Boston, which is exactly what she did.

Her story was exciting as were the remainder of the stories she shared as we spent that entire day and night together, as I fell asleep next to her in her bed. Chester brought us tea and food, and I, much to her chagrin, was famished and ate everything. I heard about her men and marriages (she was on her third!) and dancing on the stage and all the ins and outs of a world one usually just reads about.

This all happened before I had the pleasure of meeting the pig farmer and the two jovial, and very naive, brothers from Boston who were very eager to spend their inheritance.

When Clara recovered and the seas calmed a bit, we walked about and met the captain, a burly man who constantly smoked a pipe and smelled like coal, and then we dined with the other three passengers. Dine is a polite word, for Chester, the chief and only steward, was also the cook on the interesting voyage and his food reminded me of the one time my oldest brother tried to cook a meal and we could not swallow a bite. Thank heavens for bread and fruit, and thank heavens for Clara who kept us entertained and demanded that we have access to the captain's supply of liquor.

The second night, when we had our first meal together, I was almost tempted to introduce myself as Nellie Lewis but thought better of it—but I did invoke The Liar's Brow when they asked me why I was traveling to Florida. I said it was to take care of some family business, which was in a way a half-truth, and then I distracted everyone by asking about the pigs.

The pig farmer was a charming man who dressed for dinner in a fashionable suit and told us stories about animal breeding, slaughtering, and farm life in such a humorous way that Clara thought he might make it on stage. The two brothers were college educated and from a wealthy Boston family, and thankfully they did not know Charles or George. They had a plan to purchase a large tract of land inland and a bit south from Jacksonville. They had been studying about farming and citrus for quite some time and informed us that there had been a great freeze in North Florida a few years before that had wiped out all of the other orange and grapefruit crops. Thus, they were headed south, not far from where I was going, to make their fortunes.

"And work off your arses," the pig farmer yelped.

"There won't be much left of you when you are done swatting the bugs, dear lads," Clara added. "I heard some of the creatures actually carry off dogs and small children down there."

I was laughing during this conversation, but both men had gone white. The pig farmer did not let up.

"Those nice shirts you all have on will come in handy, too," he said, looking absolutely serious. "When the bushes rip your face and legs and arms open or you get a snake bite, you can rip them up and you will be ready to go."

It was true the brothers were greenhorns, but it's amazing what

189

you can do once you make up your mind. They took it all in stride and the following two days were very much fun. I did manage to spend a little time in my room where I remembered to open the gift Thomas had given me and was astonished to see that he had written me a sweet note. Truth be told, it was a bit of a love note. He said he had been charmed by my bravery and by my eagerness to sacrifice and to strike out and that he was serious about coming to find me if Charles should not want me. I must admit that I thought about his kiss more than once and how it felt to be close to him. I decided I had done nothing wrong but be myself and that if the opportunity arose again, I would make it clear we were friends. He had also purchased a very lovely bottle of perfume and at the bottom was a beautiful gold bracelet!

I still wore my wedding ring and Charles had never purchased me anything besides a strand of pearls he presented to me on our wedding day. Would it be wrong to wear the bracelet? It was half an inch thick and there were strands of silver weaving in and out of it. I was astonished when I held it up and saw that the word *Courage* had been engraved on the inside. No wonder he had been gone for so long! I thought it harmless and slipped it on my right wrist, and it would remain there for a very long time.

The package from Bertie included details about known plume hunters, the address of the new warden, as well as listings of known breeding grounds that might be in danger. Either Bertie or Thomas, or Margaret for all I knew, had circled birds that were popular with the hunters and with the milliners. There were a great many details and many things I must learn.

It was interesting to me how, when I kept busy or looked at the materials, thoughts of Boston and all I had left behind seemed to fade. It was one thing to be there and to think about leaving, but once I was gone it was not as difficult. I wrote a letter to my father one afternoon, trying as best as I could to explain what I was doing, and also a letter to my sister. I wrote also to Bertie and Thomas, making certain I kept the letter about the trip, the interesting characters I had met, and how I was studying the books and the materials when I was not listening to wild stories or watching Clara perform a scene from one of her plays.

The night before we were to dock in Charleston was a night, I daresay, none of us would ever forget. It's a good thing I had already had three puffs of a cigar and developed a love of brandy and spirits because a party ensued following our last horrid meal that I never knew could even happen. The captain passed out cigars and ordered all of the mates, except the assistant who was steering the boat, to join us. Chester gave Clara some competition on the dance floor, and I laughed so hard when they were waltzing from one end of the empty dining hall to the other that I almost fell off my chair. She was bent over almost in half and he had his arms stretched up as far as they would go to hold on.

I danced with everyone, even Clara, while the Victrola played endlessly and one of the deckhands joined in with a fiddle. The brothers were adept at dancing and the pig farmer was the smoothest dancer who had ever escorted me around the dance floor. He was also a bit forward and leaned in to tell me he thought I was beautiful and if I was lonely in the night to please feel free and come to his room. I must say I was speechless when I heard his proposal! I simply ignored it and kept on dancing and from that moment on, I thought it best not to finish any of my drinks as my head was already swimming.

At one point every single one of us was smoking a cigar. I looked around the table we were sharing and I could not help but feel as if time had been suspended. How funny we all looked, but how wonderful to be so open and embrace frivolity like this! I thought it was exciting and lovely at the same time that complete strangers could come together with such openness and help one another, and I was hoping this would keep up throughout my trip. One does not always get what she wishes for, but it never hurts to try.

It was well into the next day when we began staggering off to our separate headquarters, all except Clara and Chester that is. I saw Clara go into her room and leave the door ajar as I was turning the corner and I stepped into the hall, but I heard footsteps behind me. It was Chester! I had to suppress a laugh as I remembered them dancing and the awkward position, but my heart also felt light, and I thought it a wonder that people could act so quickly on their emotions. I spent the night thinking about that, about happenstance and living in the moment and taking a chance or an opportunity that might never come again. I also spent a great deal of time twirling my new bracelet and that night, as the ship and the wine rocked me to sleep, my dreams were a wild mix of adventures.

And the man in my dreams was not Charles, but Thomas, and what happened in the dreams is something that cannot be shared, but I did wake up smiling and naively convinced that Savannah, and everything else, was going to be a perfectly wonderful and very safe adventure.

Tape Fifteen

Southern Charm and
a Hint of Charles
Charleston Harbor—November 7-9, 1904

There's nothing quite like the unloading of several hundred pigs at a dock in hot and terribly humid Savannah, Georgia, to make one realize that the world is indeed a mix of the interesting and unexpected.

We arrived in port midafternoon, and I must say that we all looked as if we'd been dragged behind the ship and not ridden on top of it. I was to learn later that we were all experiencing a hangover, the name applied to what one feels like the day after drinking too much alcohol. We staggered about the ship when we heard the horn blow, signaling our imminent arrival at port, and were advised by Chester to try and get something into our stomachs. Chester was the only one who seemed chipper and happy and it doesn't take much guessing to figure out why.

Clara and the pig farmer were departing and, of course, so were the pigs. The pigs had to leave first and we gathered along the railing to watch as the pig farmer, dressed in high rubber boots, carrying a whip, and wearing a large straw hat, jumped into the hold and started whistling. It didn't take long for the sound of squealing pigs to greet our ears and the moment Chester dropped the gangplank, there was a small herd of pink bodies running toward earth. It looked as if they were supposed to be herded into a pen and then loaded onto waiting wagons, but something went amiss.

One very large pig pushed against the fence, as if it knew just what to do, and after the third shove, the fence came down and there was an avalanche of pigs running and squealing all over the dock.

"Help!" the pig farmer yelled.

Chester went running, and much to my amazement, so did the two brothers, and I instinctively started to run, too, but Chester yelled for me to stay back. It was difficult for me not to be involved and there was a natural impulse for me to do so. I realized that is why I was standing on a ship in Savannah, watching pigs run all over the dock. Thank heavens I also realized there was a difference between working to stop the slaughter of birds and chasing after runaway pigs.

It took quite a while, but the pigs were eventually captured, much to the visible relief of the pig farmer. He re-boarded the ship to gather up his bag and approached me as I was turning to ask the captain about lodging for the next two nights. He had asked us to leave the ship so that the loading of the cotton might be handled without interruption.

The pig farmer tapped me on the shoulder and I turned to face him. He was very pungent at this point, as the pigs had let loose of their bowels in all of the excitement, but he still managed to look like a gentleman.

"Julia, it has been a pleasure to share this lovely voyage with you. I wish you all the best of luck on the remainder of your trip and I would like to leave you with my card. If you ever have need of anything, please do not hesitate to contact me."

"Thank you so very much. It was a most enjoyable adventure, wasn't it?"

His eyes sparkled and he bowed and took my hand into his, raised it to his lips, and kissed it. My heart was beating and I was touched and taken aback.

"The adventure was only enjoyable because you were part of it," he said, backing away and handing me his calling card. "I have an abundance of resources, land, and money if you ever need anything, and of course, bacon and ham!"

How could I not laugh? I waved good-bye and then looked at the card he had handed me. *Senator Milton Bullock—Eaton Plantation and Financial Holdings—Savannah, Georgia.* The pig farmer, which is what he had asked us to call him, was a wealthy senator. I watched him all but skip back down the plank and thought it interesting that men did not care if women were married. Had it always been like this or was it because I was traveling alone? I imagined sitting in my own kitchen and telling the girls about the senator and Thomas. How they would love those stories!

By now they had read my letters, Charles may even be home, and Margaret would have also been privy to my adventures. I'm not certain I would share with her how many men seemed to be willing to carry me off into the sunset—and of course, Charles, what would I tell him?

There was no time to think of that, as the brothers were in line to approach me next. I was almost afraid to talk to them, considering what the pig farmer had said, but they said they had secured lodging at the back side of the wharf and had taken the liberty of reserving a room for me. I knew they were going on to Jacksonville, and frankly, it was nice to be tended to a bit and to not feel alone. This feeling was accentuated when we started walking across the dock and almost as many rats as pigs were running back and forth. I tried not to scream when I first saw them scurrying about, but I couldn't stop myself. The men jumped and so did the rats and we all but danced across the wooden dock, dodging their tails and heads, and I was terrified that one might get caught up in my long skirts and come up my leg.

The rats were apparently greeting me as part of my welcome to the South, as their brothers and sisters and cousins would become a serious and continuous part of the landscape and my life as I continued to Florida. The brothers, obviously city men through and through, were as happy as I was to get off the dock. Although that hardly alleviated the rats. They were everywhere but in lesser degrees. Their furry bodies should have prepared us for what was to come next when we reached Florida.

The brothers, Phillip and Barton Williams, had secured lodging through one of the deckhands and when we found it, well, my heavens! I had never before been to an establishment where women were prostitutes and all three of us were taken aback when we entered the tiny lobby of the Hotel Miranda and there was Miranda herself—a painted lady with the largest breasts, mostly exposed, that I had ever seen in my entire life. There was a bar doing a lively business in the next room and room keys hanging behind the counter directly below a sign that read: *Rooms Rented by the Hour.* All three of us stopped, our eyes grew wide, and Miranda started laughing and moved from behind the counter to approach us.

"I'm guessing someone from one of the ships sent you our way," she said, standing in front of us with her hands on her hips, and even I could not seem to take my eyes off of her breasts; they seemed to have a life of their own. "I can handle the two men, but I'm not hiring right now, sweetheart. Although I daresay you would fetch a pretty penny. You are a looker!"

The brothers were speechless and it was up to me to talk us out of this situation. I smiled and thanked her for the compliment. "Obviously we took a wrong turn someplace. If you could direct us to more suitable lodging, I think we'd all be most grateful, wouldn't we, boys?"

Miranda started to laugh again, as it was apparent the men had been struck dumb. The brothers were not bad-looking men. They were both of average height and one might think they were twins, but I knew that Barton was two years older. They had longish black hair, dark eyes, and neatly trimmed beards and moustaches, and they were wearing beige suits made of lightweight cotton. I'm certain they would have made fine customers and that's what I said next to get them moving.

"Oh no! No! I'm sorry. Yes..." Barton was stuttering and so Phillip jumped in to save him.

"We are so sorry to have bothered you. Would you be so kind as to direct us to more appropriate lodging?"

Miranda suggested the DeSoto Hotel, which she described as "the right place for folks like you," and before we turned to leave, I couldn't help myself. I winked at her, linked arms with the men, and we walked back out onto the street. What had happened to me?

The company of strangers, the good times aboard the ship, and the air of great adventure that seemed to be my constant companion emboldened me, and the brothers were, thankfully, also laughing by the time we made it back outside and they hailed a ride to the hotel.

The DeSoto was indeed lovely and also costly, but under the circumstances I felt as if I had no choice. We took adjoining rooms and planned to meet for dinner in several hours. This gave me time to try and freshen up my clothes and to bathe, and to write Charles a letter. I started to write but then stopped as I thought how ridiculous it might be for him to get a letter that said something like this: *I danced all night, smoked a cigar, drank too much, had my first hangover, watched a midget slip into a famous woman's bedroom, had a pig farmer kiss my hand and tell me he would do anything for me, entered a house of ill repute and was offered a job, and am now having dinner with two brothers from Boston who are delightful traveling companions and eager to spend the family fortunes.*

It sounded as if I had lost my mind, yet it was all true, and if Charles read a letter like that he would divorce me in three seconds, and who could blame him? I paced about the room while my clothes were drying and wondered where he was and what he was doing at that very moment. I also wondered what adventures he must be having on his travels. In one way, it didn't seem fair that he was allowed to go about his business and the world at large unexplained, yet I felt as if I had to detail and explain every movement. Who had ordered the world this way? My marriage had given me much to think about beyond the simple notions of love and pleasure. Brave and bold women like Harriet and Bertie had opened up new worlds of thought and action to me, yet my heart was a tangle of confusion when it came to Charles and his expectations. I know he expected me to be there when he got home, to support him in all things without question, and to suppress any feelings of deep emotion that might upset him or disregard the path he thought we should be traveling.

I owed Charles so very much! His love for me had changed my life and opened up a world to me that I could barely glimpse from the other side of town where I grew up. It was very difficult for me to think that I had hurt him and that he may have gotten something he did not want when he married such an innocent girl. But I was no longer innocent, and what was left of that trait seemed to be escaping from me at a very rapid pace.

Parading naked back and forth in my room, with the shades drawn, I imagined what my life would be like if I went backward instead of forward, if I ran to the train and headed straight back to Boston, if I wrote Bertie and told her I could not go on, if I could suppress my passion for the birds and the Audubon. There was a long mirror next to the dresser and I stopped to look at myself—all of myself from head to toe. I was still a fairly young woman and my walking had firmed up almost all of my body, all expect for the area around my stomach that had been stretched with the babies. It felt as if they were traveling with me, too, because even in the midst of the frivolity, I had thought of them, and in an odd way it as if they were on the same voyage as their mother.

I ran my hands down my entire body from the top of my head, across my breasts, to my stomach, and all the way down my legs, until I was touching my toes. When I stood up, the blood took a few seconds to catch up and I felt lightheaded and leaned against the wall and closed my eyes. How long would it be before Charles touched me again and kissed me in the slow gentle way that I had come to love when he was Charles of the Heart? How long before I woke up in his arms and felt his heart beating against mine and watched as his beautiful blue eyes slowly opened and I told him that looking at his eyes was like looking into the bluest sky in the world?

The strangest notion hit me then. What if he was in Savannah at this very moment on his way back home? I grabbed the bed covering off the bed, wrapped it around myself, and went to the window with the ridiculous idea that I might see him walk past or ride by in a car or carriage. It was late afternoon and I pulled open the window and felt a rush of heat pour over me almost as if it were a bucket of hot water. The hotel overlooked Madison Square and it was a terribly busy place. The chance that I would see Charles was a silly notion that I soon realized was simply created so I might feel better about what I was doing. But I stood there for quite a while, watching men and women walking and riding to known destinations. And there I was wrapped in a sheet of cloth, thinking I could dream up my husband and have him arrive on the spot!

I moved away from the window, sat down, and wrote him a simple note. I told him I had arrived in Savannah unharmed and exhilarated by the voyage and that I had met an interesting group of characters. I kept the note short, told him I loved him, and planned to write the moment I was in Jacksonville.

The brothers met me in the hotel dining room three hours later and we had a wonderful dinner, which they insisted on paying for, but I refused to have any wine or spirits. The hangover was still very fresh in my mind, and I must say it was a delight to get to know them better. They were both shy men who admitted they could never strike out on their own. Their father had recently passed away, and their mother before him, and so they decided to do something they had talked about for a very long time, thus the dream of citrus farming.

We were finishing an extraordinary piece of chocolate cake for dessert when Phillip asked me why I kept turning around. I hadn't realized that was what I was doing, but it was true. I pulled the letter from my purse and told them I had been overcome by an interesting feeling while in the room that had started upstairs.

"I suppose I am looking for my husband," I said.

"Is your husband in Savannah?" Phillip asked. "I thought he was away on business and that you are also away on business."

"The last I heard he was in Florida and I left before word came of his return. I had the strangest sensation he was here somewhere. It's just a very odd feeling and I've been learning not to avoid those feelings."

"That's what I always say!" Barton exclaimed, almost jumping from the chair. "Go with the feeling! Have you looked around?"

I laughed and realized these were sensitive men who might never make it past the first season of farming, but they had generous hearts and were so very sweet and open.

Barton proceeded to talk about the seventh sense, which he called "the ability to see and know things before others," and he had once been a magician's assistant and loved going to séances and always felt that he had a gift for being able to predict the future.

"Julia, I have had a strong sense about you from the first moment I saw you," he said, leaning across the table, and I prayed he did not want to kiss my hand or run off with me to Paris. "You have been hedging about what you are doing and we both understand completely that your business is your business, but I know, and when I say know I mean with all certainty, that you are going to do something remarkable. I see feathers and birds around you and, I'm afraid to say, a bit of hardship as well."

I immediately dropped my fork onto the china dessert plate and it sounded as if a window had cracked in half. The entire dining room turned to look at me, and I grabbed for my water glass so I might regain my composure.

"Oh dear!" Phillip said, rising to pick up my fork. "Are you okay? Barton should keep these thoughts to himself. I am so sorry, but he can't seem to help himself."

"You are a very, very perceptive man, Barton," I said, looking directly into his eyes. "I believe some of us have gifts for the seventh sense and other things as well. In my case, you are correct about the birds, but I hope you are off a bit when it comes to the hardship. I have already had enough of that, but it seems to be part of life, does it not?"

Barton looked absolutely relieved and as if he had just won a grand prize of some sort. Phillip looked a bit relieved also, and I suppose his brother had been incorrect with his seventh sense more than a few times. I said I was not at liberty to discuss what I was doing but told them I already considered them friends and that I had my own feeling we would always stay friends and maybe see each other again in Florida.

We adjourned after dinner to a sitting area off the lobby where the men enjoyed a brandy and a cigar and where I was tutored in all things citrus. The brothers were not as naive as I thought and had already done much work and study to prepare for their new venture. They even promised they would discard their more formal attire for work shirts and work boots when they arrived at the acreage they had purchased in Indian River country. They asked me if I would like to accompany them the following day on a tour of the area. They were lovers of history and had studied various battles and encampments of the Civil War, as well, and I did not hesitate to agree. I was learning fast that you must grab an opportunity when it presents itself.

I dropped off my letter to Charles at the front desk, where I almost asked the clerk if a Mr. Charles Briton was a guest or had been recently, and when I hesitated, she looked at me and asked if I needed something else. I said no and hurried off to my room, where I must admit I was glad to sleep in a bed that was not swaying. I slept soundly, and it was a good thing because the citrus farmers had quite a day planned for us and I was eager to see what they had scheduled.

We started at the hotel with a special tour by the manager who told us the hotel had been built on the very site where British General James Oglethorpe had placed his barracks. I was rather fond of Oglethorpe, as he had the bright idea that keeping debtors in British prisons was a bit foolish because they had no money anyway. He wanted to bring them to Georgia, and he did and let them help build a new colony. Some of the British descendants were no doubt passing me in the lobby. He was also opposed to slavery and religious persecution and, I thought, a man who was ahead of his time. I really did not need to see the hotel kitchen and the back rooms and half of the guest rooms and the steam room and underground wine vault, but I very quickly discovered that the brothers had an insatiable appetite to know even the smallest details about simply everything.

I was tempted to feign a headache and retreat to my room until the ship left, but I didn't want to miss an opportunity to see Savannah, even if it meant listening to the most repetitive and often boring questions. After the first hour, it became very clear to me why both the men were not married and probably never would be. A woman living with either one of them might go mad or commit murder. But I forged on, and in all other ways, they were harmless.

They had done their homework and would not let me pay for the driver and carriage they had hired for the day. It seemed as if we traveled halfway back to Boston, and I must say that what I saw was worth the time and toll on my ears. Savannah was a beautiful city with lovely well-built brick buildings and fountains and an interesting mix of people of all kinds. I was fairly smitten with the city and more so with the damp air that seemed to delight my skin and my senses. Everything seemed a bit more alive in the warm air, and I was also remembering how cold it was the day I left Boston.

Something interesting and telling happened very quickly after we left the hustle and bustle of downtown Savannah and headed toward the country and the plantations and now empty battlefields that the brothers were excited to see. They seemed to know what had occurred in Savannah since the beginning of time, and within minutes of leaving the buildings and people behind, I was with them physically, but not mentally.

I was with the birds.

In the back of my mind, I could hear the brothers going on about cotton and plantations and slavery and this general and that general. And once, we actually stopped for a long period of time and they came back with Confederate uniform buttons and an old bottle. They were so excited I'd thought they'd struck gold. They had discovered a bat-tlefield-dumping site and while they roamed through the still-barren field (and what field would not be barren if it had been blasted with cannon balls?), I went to the bushes to look for birds.

I had not yet memorized or thoroughly studied the materials Bertie had given to me, but I knew enough to identify many species. I saw a yellow-headed blackbird, sparrows, and a summer tanager, so scarlet and beautiful that it took me a very long time to move as the beauty of the bird took my breath away. I wondered what it must have been like for the birds during the war even if there had not been fighting everywhere. The sounds must have driven them deep into the woods and they must have been frightened and absolutely unsure. The birds were here first and then came man, and I could see how the ones with the bigger brains would rule, but must we rule with such harshness and lack of respect for what had come before?

I was sitting on a log with my elbows propped on my knees, think-ing about the softness of feathers, when I heard one of the brothers calling for me. I had lost all track of time and being in the forest and with the birds and in the fresh air had made me feel more excited and happy than any whiskey I had ever tasted. I was drunk on the pure glory of the outdoors!

Barton met me as I was walking at a rapid pace toward him and smiling as if I were the one who had found the gold Confederate button.

"Julia, you look so happy!"

"It's the open air and the birds, Barton. You were correct. I imagine you could guess my cause, for you are a smart man."

"I already know because my seventh sense is in high gear. It's about feathers, is it not? And the trade in plumes?"

"Yes."

"Julia, oh, Julia! What a challenge you have before you, but I know in my heart that you will prevail. Man cannot and should not domi-nate anything weaker or capture or harm anything in the name of beauty. It is wrong."

We walked slowly back to the carriage, talking of birds until we saw Phillip and he shushed me.

"Phillip thinks I am half mad, and he will never leave me, but the truth is that he is not well and the citrus farm is a way to try and keep him alive as long as possible. The doctors said he needs to be in a warm climate and I hope this plan of ours works, and I hope yours does as well, Julia. I must say also, in case I do not get a chance before we part ways, that the hardship will be worth it. You must prevail!"

It was impossible after that conversation to be anything but tender to both of them. Later that day, following a quick dinner back at the hotel, I sat by the window again, looking for Charles. The feeling that he was close remained unmistakable, but I could simply have been missing him. I did know that my life would have been amiss had I not met the two brothers and watched for birds in the Savannah backwoods, and I chose to believe that Barton was correct. I would prevail.

The following morning was bright and glorious as we made our way back to the steamship with a brief stop at the adjacent cotton docks. I had never before seen so much cotton—bales, and stacks, and rows of cotton—all waiting to be loaded onto ships. We stood on the docks for a good hour, watching them load a ship until we saw our captain coming down the sidewalk arm in arm with none other than Miranda!

The brothers and I exchanged quick glances and the moment Miranda came close, she winked at me and acted as if she had never met us before while the captain introduced us.

"This is my sister, Miranda," he said.

"It's a pleasure," Barton said while Phillip tipped his hat.

"Will you be joining us on the ship?" I asked, trying with great difficulty not to spill the beans.

Miranda threw back her head and laughed enough for all of us. "Oh, heavens no! I have way too much work to do!"

She swished her skirts, kissed the captain on the lips, and turned to leave as three men approached from behind. They were surely not businessmen. They were dressed in high boots and carrying a variety of luggage, but what I noticed were the guns protruding from their bags. They came up to us and stopped.

"These men will be joining us," the captain announced. "They are hunters and headed for the wilds of Florida, so they tell me, to make their fortune."

My heart stopped beating for a moment, and I was grateful for Barton, who clamped his hand on my arm in such a way as to let me know I should not give myself away. I had no intention of doing that, but I did suspect that the hard times he had predicted were upon me.

I followed the plume hunters onto the ship and stopped at the last step, looking back to survey the docks one more time for Charles. Barton would tell me soon enough that my feelings of his nearness had been justified, and a veil of absolute sadness came over me as the boat horn sounded and I saw Chester untie the ropes that held us to Savannah.

Jacksonville loomed and so did so many, many, other things.

Tape Sixteen

Sketching Changes on a Sea of Calm
Atlantic Ocean off the Coast of Georgia—
November 9-11, 1904

I didn't have to meet the plume hunters to know they were a poor substitute for a polite pig farmer and a seductive stage actress. I stood on the deck for a short time and watched Savannah disappear, guarded on either side by the brothers, who had apparently adopted me. We were blessed with clear skies and soft waves, unlike our departure from Boston. The three of us stood silent as the docks became smaller, the brick buildings disappeared one by one, as if Barton had deployed his magic, and finally the entire city evaporated and we were out at sea.

Barton kept looking at me as if he wanted to say something, but I was lost in thought and told him I was going to escape for a while to my cabin, as I had to organize for arrival in Jacksonville. The was part of the truth, but I was also weary of the hunters and needed to steady myself, for I was certain I would meet them during dinner, if not before.

My trunk had still not arrived in my room and I was thinking that I may have to burn my clothes when I arrived in Florida. I had prepared for the heat by wearing cotton and the lightest clothes I owned, but I was realizing there is really no way to prepare for the southern heat. My room was stuffy and the air terribly dank. It almost felt as if it could rain, inside, at any moment. As much as I wanted to retreat to a chair on deck where I could catch a breeze, I stayed in my room for several hours, going over the information Bertie and Thomas had prepared for me.

Bertie had apparently hired someone to fetch me from the ship once we docked and take me to lodging in Jacksonville. She had paid for accommodations for two nights so I could recover and "prepare for the somewhat strenuous and challenging tasks ahead." The morning of the third day, a man named Pinky Foster was scheduled to appear and drive me south. Pinky Foster? There was a name one would never forget and I quickly formed an image of him in my mind. He would be tall, thin, unshaven, pink-skinned, of course, and speak with a drawl. He would be married with numerous children who ran about barefoot, and his wife would be a shy young woman, who was also shoeless and terribly backwards. I would be wrong on every assumption, but for the time being, it was impossible not to guess and wonder what would happen as the days passed. Bertie informed me that Pinky was absolutely to be trusted and had been working closely with Paul Kroegel, the Pelican Island warden. Her instructions became much more vague after that.

"*Pinky and his associates will direct you and you will have to find some long-term lodging. I am sorry I cannot arrange that from here, but you must be prepared. I hope I was honest about this, for conditions there are often less than acceptable even for a courageous woman. The moment you arrive in Jacksonville you must start to be aware and watch for plume hunters and any other illegal activities, especially at the docks. Pinky and Paul will have assignments for you and it will be up to you if you want to use your name, Julia Briton, or the name you put on your ticket, Nellie Lewis. You might want to consider that it's possible Charles has done business with plume hunters in the area, and for your safety, Nellie may be the better choice. I am sending you to a sometimes harsh and hard place, and I am certain as you settle in, your duties will become clearer. You are a smart woman. We must document as much abuse as possible. You will know what to do.*"

I finished the note, set aside the bird books and illustrations that she had included, and felt like a fool! There was a chance the captain could be transporting plumes and there was no doubt in my mind that the men who had boarded the ship were plume hunters. I recalled seeing the invoice in Charles's office for the purchase of plumes from Florida and it was likely the plumes had been loaded in Jacksonville. What was I going to do now that everyone knew me as Mrs. Briton? Why had I not been thinking ahead?

In my haste to enlist the help of the brothers to help me with this problem, I all but flew out the door and directly into the path of one of the hunters. I almost fell into his arms but stopped short, even though his arms were outstretched to help me. I instantly disliked him and had to be careful, very careful. He was unshaven, his clothes stained with dirt, and if I didn't known better, I would say that he had been standing in some of the pig remains in the bottom of the ship.

"Whoa! Look at you! There's no place to go. Are you in a hurry?"

"Apparently."

"What's your name, pretty lady?"

"My name? Why don't you just call me pretty lady? And I will call you Mr. Forward."

"Ouch. I'm forgettin' my manners. Excuse me. I'm not useta being around wimmen."

This was not going to be easy for me until I got used to it. I could either walk away or make amends, and making amends, considering my situation, was unfortunately the best thing to do. I told him I understood and his apology was accepted, and then I ran my fingers across my forehead, invoked The Liar's Brow, and told him my name was Nellie. I tried hard to get him to tell me what he was going to hunt in Florida, but he danced around my question enough for me to know that it must be illegal. The moment we parted, I went searching for Barton as quickly as possible.

I told him as much as I dared and asked him to do me a favor and tell the captain and Chester that I was to be called Nellie Lewis for reasons that did not concern them. Barton was eager to help and said he would do his best and meet me in my room if that was appropriate. I couldn't think of another person, expect maybe Bertie, who would be better to help me at this moment.

Much to my utter relief, he returned rather quickly with good news and some valuable information, but there was a small price to pay.

"The captain said he thought you were Nellie all along because that name was on the ticket and he thought that you were simply running away from your husband," he informed me, taking the extra chair next to me. "He said a ship captain is always discreet and that he would call you whatever you wished. Chester said essentially the same thing and asked if he could dance with you now that Clara was gone."

"So no one cares?" I should have guessed this to be true from the start, but I had a lot to learn about my new position in life.

"Chester really wants a dance and I imagine we will have another party the night before we reach Jacksonville, and I also have a favor."

I had a sudden wish that I had been born unattractive, not that I actually considered myself to be even close to attractive, but all of this attention was unnerving. I prayed that his request had nothing to do with physical affection or a marriage proposal.

"Do you trust me, Miss Nellie?"

I looked at the kind, seventh sense wonder of a man sitting in front of me and said, "Yes, I do trust you. "

"You should trust me. I will be as loyal to you as I am to my brother and you must stay in touch and let me know if you need anything, anything at all, Julia... I mean, Nellie! I will leave you with our information when we depart, which will be a sad day for me, as I have grown so very fond of you and your bird mission. So yes? You will keep trusting me and stay in touch?"

"Yes, of course I will. I am so grateful."

"Now, you must excuse me because, as your assistant, I have taken it upon myself to get at least one of those ruffians to talk. Let's use them. They will never know they are confessing to an Audubon assistant!"

I couldn't help but smile, and when he rose to leave, I embraced him and said thank you, and it was a relief to have a man as a friend and not as someone who was hoping for more than that. I spent several hours studying birding notes and writing a quick letter to Bertie to let her know I already had a trusted assistant. I had hoped to suppress my appetite and miss dinner, but I was famished and absolutely flabbergasted when I arrived in the same small dining area and saw

Phillip arm wrestling with one of the hunters while Barton collected wagers.

The captain winked at me and said, "Welcome to dinner, Nellie!"

I winked back and said, "What a pity your sister could not join us!"

"Yes, it is a pity, as I am very, very fond of her."

There was an unspoken moment of camaraderie and absolute delight as the captain pulled out my chair and Chester came out with a huge platter of meat, something I hoped was not a horse or a dog, and made a very huge point of calling me Nellie. And the moment we started to eat, Barton went to work.

The man should have been working for the *New York Times* as a reporter, as he was able to coax more information out of the three hunters in less than an hour than I might have in a week. The three men were indeed plume hunters and headed for a location so secret they had sworn an oath not to repeat it. Barton managed to get them to say it was south and west and that they were going to get off in Jacksonville and travel toward Miami. They said they were after the egret plumes, and when Barton boldly asked them if they knew about the protective laws, they all laughed and said the laws were only good if you got caught.

I should have guessed they would start in on me, which they did, and I was aware of what they wanted me to say. They told me I looked well off and how they could tell that was beyond me, as my clothes were beginning to look as bad as theirs. They suggested I might own hats with decorative plumes.

"Absolutely not," I said with more than a bit of disgust in my voice. "Feathers belong on the birds and not on top of some woman's head. I think you will find that your trip here is a waste of time with the new laws and the decline in interest."

They laughed at that, which angered me, but I held my tongue. The man I had run into on the deck said they had orders for so many plumes they intended to be very rich by the end of the year. He said there were many people still hunting plumes and with only one warden, they expected to have an easy time of it. Barton was staring at me and shaking his head back and forth, and as much as I wanted to rise up and knock some sense into him and his companions, I followed his advice and simply continued eating.

My composure and resolve was a bit shaken by this encounter and I retired to my room directly after dinner to try and get my bearings. I did what Bertie had instructed me to do and wrote down what the men had said. It was the first time I was using the special book she had given me, and the simple act of writing something down restored my resolve. The process of writing, which was to become one of the most important tasks and joys of my life, made me feel powerful and important and, most of all, needed. This was a remarkable feeling that overtook me and made me stop what I was doing. This important feeling had been missing in my life. The only time I had ever felt needed was when my mother was dying. Margaret, the girls, absolutely no one really needed me, and even if I had felt and known love, it was not the same as being useful and an important part of something.

Charles did not really seem to need me either. I got up and began walking about my small room. Could a man like Charles, who was secure and important and seemingly able, learn how to need anyone? Could he admit that it was a mistake to take people for granted and to assign them preconceived positions in a life that might be just fine without them? Was I thinking too much?

A sweet feeling of something like a kind of serenity or peace returned when I went back to my notes and I convinced myself that this was what was truly missing in my life. Surely the babies were missing, but part of the gift they give back to their mothers is unconditional love and the wonderful feeling that in order to survive and flourish, a mother is very much needed. I felt that I might be too hard on Charles with this line of thinking and feeling because of how he had been raised and the expectations that had obviously been placed on him, but I made an important decision. My life, for the time being, was going to be about me and what made me happy, not about Charles or anyone else.

It is odd to say this, but I immediately felt lighter, as if something had flown out of me to make room in my nest for something else. Who knew what that might be, but I had made a serious decision and a new commitment to my beloved birds and I wrote as much as I could remember about the plume hunters on the ship and my feelings, which I tried to keep focused on the facts, and then I went back to reading.

Chester came to my door and asked if I was coming down to have a sip of whiskey, and I feigned tiredness and said I would join them the following night, which would be our last night on the ship before arriving in Jacksonville.

That night I was so engrossed in studying the books on birds and learning about their nesting habits that hours and hours passed without me moving from my chair. I took notes while I read, so I would know what the birds' nests looked like and the differences between male and female birds. I became versed in mating habits and the sounds birds made, and mostly I realized that I could spend a lifetime studying ornithology and only know a fraction of what there was to know. It was fascinating and exciting to me and when my eyes grew tired, something else remarkable happened.

Bertie had included a set of ink pens and pencils in her materials and there were several blank notebooks that I assumed I would be using during my travels and investigations. I know the idea was for me to take notes and get as many details as possible so we could have proof for the authorities and government entities that more laws and protection were needed. Even though I was a horrid liar, and my husband purchased plumes, I was apparently an upstanding young woman. I will never forget what happened next, for it changed my life yet again.

I don't know why I did it, and I suppose Barton would say it's one of the great and lovely mysteries of life, but I picked up a pencil and one of the notebooks and placed one of the books in front of me and opened it to the page that showed an Audubon drawing of a snowy egret. This bird species was in grave danger from the plume hunters because its snowy white plumes were highly prized, and perhaps that's what inspired me. The feathers I was carrying with me were from a snowy egret and I felt a great love for this bird. I started to draw it on my paper and I was able to do it with such accuracy and detail that within thirty minutes, I had made a lovely replica of the very painting drawn by the famous artist James Audubon.

Never before in my life had I felt compelled to draw or become an artist or sit with a pencil or pen or artist's materials in my hands, but there I was, not simply drawing, but falling into it as if I had been doing so my entire life. I could not stop myself and for several hours, way into the early hours of the next day, I drew bird after bird. My

211

renderings were surely not as perfect as the ones in the books, but they were more than passable.

I moved out onto the deck late the following morning, after finally falling asleep with yet another wonder of the world and life gliding through my head because of my newfound ability to sketch. I wanted to see if I could draw a bird that was alive, exactly as I saw it. The great John James Audubon had shot and killed all of the birds he painted, which helped him detail his drawings in ways he might not have been able to if he had done what I was going to try and do. How ironic that all of his dead birds and paintings had brought me to the bow of a ship where I knew a tiny gull with a broken wing had taken refuge.

The slaty-backed gull was resting on a coiled rope and I knew kind-hearted Chester had been feeding it. I pulled over a deck chair, settled in, and was quickly engrossed in my task. I was able to shade in its lovely gray feathers and its checked tail and the black spots on the tip of its beak. The poor bird would probably not make it much past Jacksonville, and I wanted to reach out and caress it, but that's an instinct that is best left for small children and kittens. I could tell from my reading that this was an adult bird, because its pink feet and coloring had replaced the beige colors of young birds. The bird was not moving much, and I managed to do a more than adequate job, and just as I finished, I heard someone come up behind me.

It was polite Barton who wanted to talk but who also didn't want to invade my privacy.

"Look," I said, holding up my drawing. "There's been another miracle and I know how to sketch!"

Barton rushed over, took the drawing, and looked back and forth from it to me several times before exclaiming, "Julia! You are a wonder! Do you know how useful this is going to be?"

"I was just starting to think about it. What are you thinking?"

The sunlight was hitting Barton on one half of his face and it made me realize that he was more attractive than I had originally thought. He sat right down on the deck and excitedly told me that I could send sketches to newspapers and important politicians.

"Sketches such as this will help your cause, especially if you are out in the wilds and it's impossible to bring along a photographer and one of those large cameras," he shared. "This is good, Julia. I'm impressed."

"Barton where did this new talent come from? I had no desire to sketch or draw before. I'm bemused but also a bit, well, startled I guess is the correct word."

He put his hand on my knee, a simple lovely gesture, and told me that my passion and desire to help the birds, combined with my new awareness of the seventh sense, was like opening a door.

"We all have certain powers that we were graced with at birth and some of us can tap into them, and some of us, I daresay, live in fear. The human mind is without question the most powerful force in the world and once you open up your heart and life and soul, if you believe in that sort of thing, to all possibilities, then all truly is possible."

Barton took my breath away, and I placed my hand on his and told him that he was remarkable and that my friendship with him had already turned into one of the most wonderful gifts of my life.

"It's not easy for women and men to be friends in our society," I said. "What a shame that is and what a loss it would have been for me not to have met you."

Barton thought for a moment and then he shared something with me that I know must have been his deepest secret.

"I treasure you as well," he said. "And, Julia, you will always be safe with me as I prefer the company of gentlemen, if you get my meaning."

Another surprise! I told him that I did get his meaning and that I knew the life of a homosexual must not be all that easy. "I would imagine it's going to be worse in Florida," I said.

He just winked and said, "You'd be surprised!"

With that he said he had been busy working on the plume hunters and that he had some information he thought I might like to make use of as soon as possible. I was all ears.

He told me that the night before he had managed to get one of the hunters to tell him their traveling plans after the hunter had consumed a great amount of whiskey. The other two men had already retired and Barton said he had been tossing his own whiskey overboard all night when the men were not looking so they thought he was also as drunk as they were. When the last man and Barton were standing, the man told Barton everything.

The men had thankfully been hired by a milliner from New York, not Boston. One of the men had a cousin who was already in Florida and had sent him notice of a place called Cuthbert Lake deep in the swamps way east of Miami. The men were going to spend several weeks traveling and hoped to arrive the first or second week of December, slaughter as many birds as possible, ship them to New York, and then keep hunting throughout the winter. The hunters were well aware of laws and the magnitude of their actions, but they had also been seduced by a large sum of money.

"Do you think these men are dangerous?"

"Any man with a gun can be dangerous and there is money involved, and that means, yes, they could be dangerous."

"Barton, you are a remarkable assistant! I can't help but think that these men are not alone and that there are plume hunters times twenty out there as we speak."

"This is a big task you have undertaken, Julia, but just as it is with most things in life, every little bit, one step at a time, inch by inch, and all of that. Most people dare to do nothing and look at you! Here you are in the Atlantic Ocean, sketching birds and preparing to take on a small army of men with shotguns!"

"It sounds as if I am brave and very stupid as well."

"Nonsense, my friend! I see an aura around you that will not extinguish for a very long time. I think you are going to outlive everyone on this ship and that you are going to change the world while you are at it!"

Barton looked away for a moment and I saw a hint of sadness cross his face. His features darkened just a bit and then his shoulders slumped.

"What is it, Barton?"

"My brother will most likely not live to see his orange and grapefruit trees grow, and he is my cause now, Julia, but I will be there if you ever need me and I think that I may join you when the time is right. There are no more beautiful and necessary creatures than birds!"

Barton and I lingered on the deck for a very long time, and I would cherish our final conversation until I met him again. I would meet him again, I knew it, and felt it in my heart now that my seventh sense had been awakened from such a deep sleep. We watched the clouds build on the eastern horizon and talked about travel and love and what might await us the following morning when we disembarked into the tropical arms of Florida.

I stretched out next to him after a few hours and then he asked me if it would be okay if he put his arm around me. I was so touched by his request that without answering, I moved against him, placed his arm around my shoulders, and nestled as close as possible, almost as if I had found a new and very familiar nest. Tears fell from his eyes and landed on my arms, and I decided they were simple tears of happiness and I was also very happy with my friend, outside, talking with an open heart and without worry of criticism or any harsh words.

We left the deck before anyone saw us and during dinner, I was careful not to arouse any suspicions. It wasn't as if the hunters bothered to give me a chance to speak. They were boastful about their lives and their many pursuits of manliness and adventure. I tried hard to look at them, really look at them, and wonder about their lives before they were hunters. Hunting for meat to put on the table was much different than slaughtering helpless birds. It was also true that these gruff men had once been little babies who were rocked to sleep in their mothers' arms.

That was an image I decided I must hold on to so I could remember to treat them and other hunters I would surely encounter not so much kindly, as I was already struggling with that, but as human beings who had become victims of circumstance. I must stay centered and be logical and try to keep my own wild emotions in check. Otherwise, I feared I would get nowhere and nothing would change.

There was one last party that night and I was not in the mood to celebrate, but I had one glass of brandy with the captain and had a lovely discussion about Jacksonville and Florida. The men played cards and after a few hours of pure nonsense, Phillip, Barton, and I went to stand out in the moonlight. I stood between them and we were mostly quiet, thinking about what lay ahead and how precious our time together had been.

Phillip and Barton excused themselves to go back to the party and I stood alone for a long time thinking that I could already smell the hot earth of Florida, and I was so excited at the possibility of seeing flamingos and egrets and the roseate spoonbills that I wondered if I would ever sleep.

Much later when I walked back to my stateroom, it did not shock me to see Barton slipping into the room that I knew was occupied by

Chester. I smiled because I had deep affection for Barton and I knew that his path in life must not be easy. I also knew that the need for physical affection was as normal and as important as the very water I was sailing through on my way to yet more adventure.

Tape Seventeen

A New World of Wonder and Worry
Jacksonville—November 11-13, 1904

The coast of Florida was already visible when I walked from my cabin in the morning, and to say that I was awestruck is not saying enough. I walked out into the morning air and was shocked that it was already thick with heat and it was November! I looked left and right and saw a jungle of green and never before had I seen so many shades of the same color. I stood with one hand on the door and the other on the railing, unable to move, and I took in as much as I could, relishing every ounce of the damp, sweet, terribly important moment.

When the ship started to turn, I closed the door and stood alone by the railing as we passed into the St. Johns River. The green closed in on both sides and I saw houses, or more aptly huts, and then the birds started to appear. Seagulls and ducks and egrets and petrels, terns, and a flock of bright green-and-red parrots. I had two sudden urges. One was to run and get my sketchbook, and the other was to fling myself off the deck, wade to shore, and sit in the jungle in hopes that a bird, any bird, would land near me. Thankfully, reason prevailed and I simply stood there until I heard someone approaching and there was Chester, all smiles, with a tray of food.

"We missed ya at our early breakfast, Miss Nellie. I saved you a bit," he said, placing a tray with something that actually smelled good on the chair near the railing. "We have a bit a time before we arrive and Barton told me ya might be watchin' from up here."

"You are so sweet, thank you, Chester." I had to bite my cheek to keep from asking him if he had a restful evening.

"Ya just sit now and watch. It's a pretty run from here, it tis. I will be down in the bow watchin' for small boats if ya want to come and I'll tell ya what we be passin', but eat now. Be alone. Florida is a place ya must take in one look at a time. Ya know? It's not fer everyone, but I think it might be for you, missus."

My appetite had all but disappeared, and I was afraid to look at what he had prepared, but I couldn't refuse his gesture. There was yet another surprise waiting for me under the cloth he had placed over the food. Chester had made fresh pancakes with berries, bacon—probably from one of the pig farmer's animals—and tea, and I have no idea where he got it, but there was a flower in a small vase on the tray as well! It was the best meal I had eaten on board and I ate every bit as I watched the palm trees grow larger and the jungle flatten out the closer we got to Jacksonville.

I eventually joined him at the bow and he talked to me about Indian encampments and fishing and shipwrecks and pirates. Chester was a talking history book and I got lost in his stories. He handed me a rope to hang on to as he watched for logs and small boats and motioned for the captain to turn or slow down as we got closer to the city. He told me about the devastating fire that had all but destroyed Jacksonville three years before and pointed out where buildings had once stood. It was just past noon when I saw a very long wooden dock, Chester signaled for the captain to slow down, and before long we were docked and I was in Florida.

The next hour was a mixture of excitement and sadness. I had made it this far, totally not realizing how far I had yet to go, and I had to say good-bye to Barton and Phillip. I would soon be truly alone, for these men had been my companions and had looked out for me since Boston. They were both my friends, as were the captain and Chester, and parting at the end of the dock was almost as hard as leaving Boston.

The brothers had a carriage waiting and whoever was picking me up was late. Barton and Phillip had quite a drive so they were eager to go, and Phillip hugged me and then it was Barton's turn. I will never forget how he held me so close and told me to take care and then pressed his address into my hand as well as a very special gift. He gave me one of his Confederate buttons and said he was keeping the other to remember the special day when we found it and to commemorate our friendship, which he promised would never end.

I fought back tears when their carriage pulled away and I watched until it went around a corner and disappeared. Men were unloading the cotton and soon my trunk appeared, and I thought to look around and watch in case I saw any plumes or hunters. The dock was fairly quiet and I could see up and down the river and noticed that there were docks everywhere. It would be so easy to slip in and out unnoticed with cargo that was illegal. It didn't take me long to realize how difficult it was going to be to try and stop the export of feathers from Florida. Boats could launch anywhere, and without the proper authorities to watch and guard, anything was possible.

The plume hunters from the ship approached with their bags slung over their shoulders and stopped to say good-bye to me. I was polite and, of course, ran my fingers across my brow when I wished them well. They were excited to see the town and I hoped they would go find someone like Miranda and her associates and delay their travels as long as possible.

Workmen came and went and within an hour, most of the cotton had disappeared. The captain and Chester were staying onboard to ready the ship for the return voyage and they waved to me as they disappeared and went about their duties.

Then I was alone and in Florida and waiting for the next chapter of an adventure that was beginning to seem endless.

The Windsor Hotel was a grand, solid building that I welcomed with open arms when my ride finally arrived a mere three hours late. By the time the elderly carriage driver picked me up, I was a wilted Boston flower and drenched in sweat from sitting in the sun. This was my introduction to Florida and it was an apt and real one at that, for the heat was unrelenting and shade hard to come by. The driver apologized over and over again and I was very happy to stand in front of a lovely electric fan when I checked in, and the boy hoisting my trunk had to all but beg me to follow him.

Before I noticed the letters sitting on the nightstand, I drank four glasses of water and disrobed. I was already wondering how long it would take me to get used to the heat, but in many ways, that was to be the least of my worries, problems, and struggles.

I discovered the letters after my bath, when I had bundled my clothes to be washed properly by the hotel staff. And I must admit that a small part of me was homesick for familiarity and something predictable. A normal bed, washroom, and food on a plate would have to suffice, and soon all but the food on a plate would also disappear.

There was one letter from Margaret and another from Thomas and there was not one bit of good news inside of either envelope. I read Margaret's letter first, and halfway through it, I had to sit down.

Dear Julia,

I hardly know what to say! One part of me is angry that I ever steered you away from your traditional role as a wife and the other is a bit jealous. There are many people who will be affected by your decision to run off and save the birds, but it is mostly Charles whom I worry about. He may never get over this and I have no idea what will become of your marriage. What were you thinking? Was it not enough to be involved in Boston? I am sick with worry, not just about you out there wandering around with plume hunters and whatnot, but also about what my son will do when he arrives home and discovers that his wife has left him to chase birds.

I am very upset, but there is also a part of me that understands. I have no idea how I will reconcile these two feelings, for I have other very horrid news.

George has arrived home on death's doorstep. He has pneumonia and is gravely ill and I must cut this short as I am attending to him night and day. I expect by the time you receive this, he may even have passed on. In spite of everything, he is my husband and I am bound by vows and duty. You may want to think about this.

I trust you are safe and that nothing bad has happened. I
need time to think. My entire world is now upside down.
   Sincerely,
   Margaret

This was not the kind of letter I expected, but that is my own fault.
I opened up the letter from Thomas and my world was suddenly nothing but a disaster and upside down as well.

   My Dearest Julia,
   I trust you have arrived safely and are about to start your
journey south. I have thought of you constantly and prayed
that you would be well and safe and happy with your decision.
I am so sorry that my first letter to you brings nothing but sad
news. Our beloved Bertie died yesterday on the fourth day of
November and I am posting this so you may have this news
before you are unable to receive mail.
   I was at her side the entire time and you must know that you
made her last few days memorable and very happy as it was
so important for her to know that someone would carry on her
work with the Audubon and her beloved birds.
   This will be short, as I have many arrangements to make.
Please carry on and know that as you do, I am thinking of you
with great affection.
   Fondly,
   Thomas

When I finished reading Thomas's letter, I rolled over and let my
tears come. It should not have been such a shock that Bertie died, but
it was a shock. There is no way to ever prepare for the loss of someone
you have great affection for, even if you know it is coming. It is as if a
hole has been dug into your heart and all feeling but sorrow has leaked
out of your body. I had only known Bertie for a short while, but as
Barton would say, my seventh sense allowed me to know her in ways
that a lifetime would not have changed.

There was also my feeling of sadness for what I interpreted as the
loss of my friendship with Margaret. I was surprised at her devotion

to George, but I decided that I had partially misread her intentions. I was sad that I could not be there for her the way she had been there for me, and I wallowed in those feelings for a great deal of time until I fell into a deep slumber. The heat, emotion, and lack of sleep caught up to me and when I woke, hours later, it was dark outside and my mood had not changed at all.

I ate dinner alone and then went outside on the porch to sit and rock and think. Jacksonville was terribly civilized and I watched a stream of carriages and buggies roll past and waited for my resolve to return. It was still so very warm outside and I wished I had my rope handy so I could boldly tie up my skirts like I did with Harriet and Margaret, but that would truly point attention in my direction. I was trying to do anything but think about the lives that had been affected by my departure. Suddenly, a group burst from the hotel dining room area and crowded about the porch so I could not even see the street. They were clearly excited.

"What is the fuss?" I asked a young man standing close to me.

"Henry Ford and Thomas Edison have just gotten off a ship and will be passing by in one of the motor cars!"

"Why are they here?"

"I heard that Mr. Edison is looking for a location in Florida where he can build a studio and a winter home. They are going to ride around the city and then stay at this very hotel!"

I could not let the one-car parade go by without seeing it myself because I was a very huge fan of the electric lights, and very soon the car approached, gliding past with the two smiling men, two women in back, and luggage strapped behind them. They looked like a jolly group and they were clearly enjoying themselves. The women were chuckling, and even though the sight of the couples made me think about Charles, I pushed away the thought.

The crowd began to melt away and I sat down again. It was just getting dark and a few small children played in the street in front of me, and that is when I felt a tug in that old familiar location just below my waist. I was here for the children. All children. Children who might one day, years and years from now, be able to see a snowy egret dancing in the shallow waters of the St. Johns River or in a tidal pool at the edge of the ocean, and there was absolutely nothing wrong with that.

Margaret and Charles would have to be content without me, and I would mourn Bertie and keep going.

I slept soundly that night and the next day, which apparently would be my last day in civilization, and decided that I must get to work. I took my sketchpad and notebook and headed though the city streets and toward the river. It was just as hot as the day before, and I knew I would have to get accustomed to this huge change of climate, and the sooner the better. I loved walking and there was nothing in the city that appealed to me. A building was a building and the stores and people and activity were not attractive to me. I could smell the water and that is what I wanted.

The farther I walked from the city, the lighter and happier I became. There wasn't a thing I could do for Margaret or Thomas or even Charles from this location and with each step I made up my mind that I was done questioning my own decisions. I thought and thought as I walked and there wasn't one thing I could come up with that Charles or Margaret or Thomas or even George needed from me besides my simple and quiet presence at their sides. They could all send me ten letters a day and I would not change my mind.

It took me about two hours to get past the city and soon I was on a dusty road and there was rarely a carriage or buggy or one of the Ford automobiles passing me. I passed several trails and finally, when I sensed it was time to take one, I did. Barton would have loved this explanation and it proved him correct yet again.

I walked about a mile on the trail, smelling the water as I neared the river and noticing more and more birds with each step. The rest of the world slipped away and without realizing it, so did I. When I saw the edge of the river, I stopped because a flock of least terns, their fork-like tails flashing in the sun, were dancing in the sky just above the top of the river and it was absolutely mesmerizing. Their yellow bills and sleek black heads were moving, moving, moving as they skimmed across the surface of the water, searching for tiny fish.

It's hard to know how long I stood there or how long the woman stood there watching me, but suddenly there she was. She was much shorter than even Chester and I guessed older than every bird in the sky with her snow-white hair, wrinkled and sun-stretched face, and tattered dress. Her blue eyes were almost as piercing as Charles's and I caught her eye and smiled.

"Hello. The birds are so lovely and very happy today," I said, moving my gaze back to the sky.

"No one bothers them here. They are still free and if you have come to harm the birds, then you must go before I raise my gun to you."

My heart quickened. I had not seen the gun, but there it was, leaning against her right leg.

"Oh no! I am here because I love the birds," I all but shouted.

"I killed a man once," she said, her fingers lightly touching the barrel.

"He probably deserved it."

And that is how I met Brindel. No last name, no need for it, just Brindel she said, who lived on the river and had for eighteen years ever since the man she killed, her husband, had beat her about the head one last time. She stood quietly and looked at me for a few moments and then asked what was in my hand. I held up the sketch of the lonely gull from the ship and my pencils, and she didn't say a word. She motioned for me to follow her and then turned around and started walking.

The rest of the day was my welcome into the backcountry of Florida and a way of living that is harsh and hard but serene, simple, and all about day-to-day survival. Brindel was a woman of few words, but words were not that necessary. She showed me her small one-room home, not much more than a few boards and tarpaper with a sandy floor, a table and two chairs, and a bed of straw. She was one of the happiest women I had ever met. The rest of the world might think she had nothing, but Brindel did tell me that she had everything she needed and wanted because she was free.

The very idea lit up her face and when she smiled, her broken and blackened teeth could not diminish the glow of her happiness. "No one will ever hurt me again," she told me and then quickly added, "You too. Never let anyone hurt you or tell you what to do."

"Don't worry about that," I said. "I'm not as brave and sure as you are, but I am getting there."

I followed her from her doorless house and a little black dog scurried from under the house and all but leapt into her arms as we headed down a well-worn path that paralleled the river. I had no idea where we were going, but I couldn't imagine Brindel not being able to handle anything that came across the path. We walked for almost thirty minutes and then she put down her dog and it darted under a bush, and so did she and then so did I, crawling on all fours. I'm certain there would be more than a few people back in Boston who would think I had lost my mind, but when we came out of the bushes and I saw where she had taken me, I knew I was right where I should be.

It was a small lake that had formed off of the river and because the bush was so thick, it would be impossible to know it was there unless someone had at one time chased a small dog through the bushes to discover it. Brindel looked at me and put her finger to her lips so that we would be quiet, and then she crawled a few more feet and sat down in a spot that was grassy and where she must have sat many times.

I wanted to tell her about Harriet and Margaret and the day we sat by the pond in the country, and I would later, but not until we had seen at least three hundred white ibis, their bright-red beaks and legs and snow-white feathers parading through the small pond in constant movement. The pond was shallow because it was low tide and the birds were searching for crayfish, crabs, and water insects.

My hand started flying across the sketchpad, and after I had filled several pages, Brindel slowly moved back and we crawled out exactly the same way we had crawled in.

"Beautiful, yes?"

"Oh, yes!"

"Now we are going fishing."

"I've never been fishing."

"That's because you are a city girl. We'll fish. I'll show you how to clean and cook them, and you in exchange will tell me what in the hell you are doing running around sketching birds four miles from the city."

Brindel started to talk after that and she showed me how she caught tiny fish to use for bait and where the biggest fish like to hide out in the deepest holes. She caught three huge fish. I have no idea what they were, but she showed me how to gut them and clean them, and I had to take care of the last fish and prepare it for the fire. It was not how

I planned on spending my day, but it was without a doubt one of the most useful afternoons of my life.

She cooked the fish on an open fire, and just to prove I was not a complete city girl, I helped build the fire and rake the coals so the fish would cook evenly. I don't believe I had ever had a more delicious meal in my life. She pulled out the two chairs from inside of the house and we ate from the same pan that she placed on her leg, and then it was time for me to tell her why I was there. I told her everything while she sucked on a fishbone and then picked off some pieces of meat for her dog.

"You are a brave one, sister. I wouldn't have thought it when I saw you sauntering down the road like you had fallen off a carriage."

"Why did you trust me?"

"When you live like I do, you just know after awhile. You have a kind face and I can tell by your hands that you mean well. Don't ask me how I know; I just do. Plus, it's the birds. I love the birds. They are my family now."

"I understand completely. I do."

She grew quiet then and then told me something that I should have seen coming. It was her real story. Her name was Edna Hugo and she had unwillingly come with her husband to Florida from Pittsburg to seek fortune, but there was no plan on how to do that and Mr. Hugo was a mean, hurtful man who had already battered Edna so much she could never have children. She devised a plan and waited until he had built her the shack and she had learned how to hunt and fish. The day after the man who ran up and down the coast with his homemade whiskey had paid them a visit, and her husband was in a stupor, she killed him in his sleep.

"I tied rocks to his feet and one to his head and then I pushed him into the river," she said matter-of-factly. "No one but the whiskey runner has ever asked where he went, and I have lived a peaceful and clear life ever since."

If I had any notions that my life in Florida was going to be simple or anything like my life in Boston, Edna Hugo helped me erase those notions. She told me that sometimes people left packages of food for her and shells for her gun, but otherwise she was on her own and expected to spend the rest of her days on Earth watching the birds and listening to the river.

I promised her that her story was safe and then I told her about the Audubon and plume hunters and she was so excited I thought she might want to join me. Instead she told me about the numerous hunters who had come through the area and how it was rumored that they were all moving south because so many birds in the area had already been killed. She asked me if I was carrying a weapon and we had a laugh about the wooden spoon I had taken from the kitchen in Boston.

"It's wild where you might be going and the people are even wilder than I am," she said in all seriousness. "Women can be dropped into a river just as easily as men."

I took her warning to heart and hoped that Pinky Foster was the kind of man who could defend two people at one time. Edna told me about the boats running up and down the rivers and lakes and how the hunters were beginning to realize that the big payoffs might be coming to an end, but that made them even more desperate.

It was very late in the day when she told me I had better start walking so I could get back to the city before it was no longer safe. Before I left, I tore out two of the sketches I had made and gave them to her, and I thought she might cry. She told me that our conversation was the longest one she'd had in at least five years and it would hold her now for a long, long time. I hugged her good-bye and then asked her if there was anything in the entire world she wished for.

"I would love a door," she answered without hesitation.

A door. I thought about her answer all the way back to the hotel and I tried to count how many doors were in my Brookline house. Doors and windows and rooms and furniture, and none of it had made me happy. My mind was back in Boston as I walked up the hotel stairs and bumped into Thomas Edison, who was just leaving.

"My, my," he said, laughing at me. "You look as if you've been out fishing and camping in the woods, my dear."

"I have, Mr. Edison, and it's been quite a day. I'm in need of a bath, a good meal, and maybe a glass or two of wine."

"Splendid idea! My wife is quite fond of wine and it makes for some lively after-dinner conversation. Mr. Ford and his wife are with us for just a short period of time, as he's just started a new car company. Please feel free to join us and tell us about your adventures, Miss...?"

Who was I? Julia Kelly Barton or Nellie Lewis? I felt a bit like both

227

of them but also thought at this point it was time to make some kind of decision and get on with it all. Edna Hugo had given me a bit of courage and advice and I decided on the spot to tuck Nellie away and pull her out when I might be in a fix. I told him I was Julia Briton with the Audubon and on a special assignment, and just saying that made me feel as if I could fly myself.

"Oh, that's so wonderful. The bird issue is very serious and I imagine when you wash that streak of mud off of your face, you will look like the ambassador that you are."

I should have been mortified, but instead I took my sleeve and wiped off my face, and Thomas Edison laughed and laughed and said that it looked as if I was more than suited for a life as an ornithologist.

By the time I had bathed and dressed, the Fords and Edisons had already eaten, but I was thrilled when the waiter brought me over not one, but two glasses of red wine with a note from Mr. Edison. "Sorry we missed you, Bird Lady. Cheers and good luck to you!" I treasured the note because I thought he was a genius, and later, I tucked it into my wooden box.

There was also a note waiting for me under my door when I went back to my room after dinner from Pinky Foster, who said he would be around to "fetch me" after breakfast. I had no idea what time a man named Pinky ate breakfast, but I had lots to do before morning.

I wrote letters to Charles, Margaret, Thomas, and Barton. Barton's letter was the longest and filled with the most details, as I knew he would love to hear about Edna and my encounter with Thomas Edison. I made certain my things were in order, laid out my freshly washed cotton clothes for whatever lay ahead of me, and then I had one more task.

I made a shopping list that included the following: lumber and other materials necessary to make one door, two rolls of thick cotton cloth—one in light blue and one in a lively pattern—with thread to match and needles, one sketch book and several boxes of pencils, a box of fresh vegetables, six bottles of wine, a pair of women's walking shoes size six, a box of washing soap, one large floor rug, two cans of white paint and brushes, a variety of seeds for planting a garden and garden tools, a new shotgun and a dozen boxes of shells, and a spyglass. Then I wrote the following letter:

Dear Brindel,

My day with you was a sweet gift that I must repay. Here is your door and a few things that will make you realize it's okay to live like the beautiful woman you are. I want you to watch the birds for me, to take notes, and to use the spyglass as a way to be even closer to the birds we both love. I will see you again and we will compare notes. Consider yourself as a special assistant to me, for that is what you are.

Your Friend,

Julia Briton

P.S. If you see Edna Hugo, please tell her to stay the hell away from the river.

In the morning, I put five twenty-dollar bills into the envelope and went down to the front desk and told them what I wanted. I asked them to send a kind, gentle man on this errand, who might also be able to build a door out of the lumber. I said I wanted Brindel to have any extra money and that I hoped to send more in the future if they would kindly deliver that as well. They knew of Brindel and I tipped them well, had my last civilized meal, and then went to my room to wait for a man named Pinky Foster.

It was 7:15 a.m. when Pinky knocked on my door, and I was beyond ready to go but absolutely not ready at all for the man who stood on the other side.

Tape Eighteen

The Chronicles of a Bird Woman
Sebastian, Florida—
The Remainder of November, 1904

My tiny room at the back of the tiny house had a very tiny window.
I had to bend down and steady myself against the wooden walls
in order to look out and see the jungle that surrounded us, and every
time I did, I wondered why Florida had so many short people living
inside its boundaries. Pinky told me the house had been built by a
German farmer who had been so enamored by his young daughter
that he put the window in very low, forgetting that his baby would one
day grow up and not be able to look out of it either. "He was also short
and a bit of a fool, but then anyone who settles in this rat and insect-
infested land is a bit of a fool," Pinky told me.

I kept telling Pinky that it took one to know one and he would just
look at me with that handsome face of his and say, "Yes, Julia, it does."
The window always gave us a laugh, and considering what we were
doing, a laugh was a good thing.

My journey from Jacksonville to the world Pinky Foster ruled
was a lesson in survival and the woes of assumptions. I had assumed
Pinky would look like his name and be a slovenly recluse who had a
bird fetish. I couldn't have been more wrong. The morning I opened
my door at the Jacksonville hotel and looked up, and I mean way up,
I was looking at one of the most ruggedly handsome men I had ever

seen in my life. Charles was handsome but in a stylish city way, as were Thomas and Barton. My brothers had a similar affect, as they were self-assured, streetwise, and had essentially the same features as me, but they were more filled in, if that even does them justice. Pinky was breathtaking and I was worried that my knees might buckle by simply looking at him.

He was over six feet tall and he had raven-black hair that hung to his shoulders. Pinky had high cheekbones, a dimple in his chin that could hold a gallon of water, and remarkably strong and very white teeth that he later explained to me were kept that way by eating some kind of root an Indian had shared with him. He wore high leather boots, a soft blue cotton shirt, and there was a whip over one shoulder and a gun over the other. As if that wasn't enough, Pinky Foster had the darkest, most astounding big eyes I had ever seen on a man. One look and it was almost, and I say almost with the loss of my breath, impossible not to fall right inside of them.

To make things even worse—or better, depending on one's martial status—Pinky was kind, gentle, smart, and funny. When we were walking through the hotel lobby to leave, he informed me that my trunk would be shipped to his home in Sebastian, and it was a wonder all of the women looking at him did not faint. I didn't know every detail about him at first, but we had several long days on the road and we were not riding in a carriage; we were riding his twin ponies, Gennie and Jones, which gave us plenty of time to discuss life and many other items of importance.

I first realized his keen mind when he was adjusting the saddle for me and I asked him about the names of the horses. He response and the story that followed astounded me and my mouth fell open.

"I saw the most remarkable book when I was in New York years ago, titled *Illustrations of the Nests and Eggs of Birds of Ohio,* by a woman named Gennie Jones," he explained, while I tried not to faint. "This young woman had seen a copy of Audubon's colored engravings from *The Birds of America* at the Centennial International Exhibition in Philadelphia and while she was smitten with his work, she was also mystified that Audubon had not included eggs and nests in his paintings."

There Pinky stood with his hand on the horse's arse, telling me how Gennie decided to make a book of illustrations with nests and eggs of American birds. She had a good start, he said, but fell ill and died, and her family took over the work, but not much ever came if it. Pinky said a few of the books made it to collectors, but he had been so moved by her story and the intricate drawings that he wanted to honor a fellow bird lover and the only thing he could think of was to name his horses after her.

I was beginning to think something magical had happened to me because of all the wonderful men I was meeting. Where did they all come from? Pinky fixed my saddle and then walked around me as if I were also a horse and looked me up and down.

"You are a tiny thing," he said matter-of-factly. "Can you ride?"

"I can ride and I am in excellent and strong health. I've also recently learned how to gut a fish and crawl on my belly through the brush. I'm also fond of an occasional cigar, a bit of whiskey, and riding on the bow of a ship though rough water while holding on to a rope."

Pinky all but dropped to his knees laughing and then stuck out his large hand to shake mine and to let me know that we were going to get along just fine.

During the next five days, Pinky and I traveled south on a long and very hot and dusty dirt road, making our way seemingly inch by inch to the Sebastian area, a small enclave north of Vero Beach and very close to Pelican Island. I'm certain my trunk passed me on the train that ran parallel to the road, and when I asked him why we were not on the train, he said it was important for me to see the country, to learn more about the birds, and to get a feel for what it is like to live in a land where the conditions are often harsh. There were no more hotels or dining rooms for me, either. We camped off the road at night and that was an experience in itself. We stopped to pick up some vegetables from small stores along the way and to water and feed the horses, and to talk with an occasional carriage that slowed to ask us for directions.

My dream to be outside and in the wilderness came true very fast. Pinky had a bedroll for each of us, cooking utensils, and some staples in his pack, such as beans and rice. I was glad I had learned about the fish and even more glad that I liked to eat it because it became the morning and night meal almost every day. There was no noon meal except for a hard piece of bread that I sucked on for a good hour in order to be able to swallow it while we rode on and on.

This was also the beginning of my long and hateful association with the horrid bugs and mosquitoes of Florida. There were flies and beetles and roaches, yet it was the mosquitoes that nearly did me in and made me almost want to run all the way back to the captain and the freezing air of Boston. They were relentless and everywhere, and I mean everywhere, all of the time, and it wasn't as if there were just a few of them. When we passed close to the water or the lower areas near the road, they came after us in swarms. Pinky gave me a neckerchief to tie around my head so a portion of my eyes and my nose were covered. He also gave me a potion, a thick mix of something that he would not share, that I applied to any uncovered areas of skin. When I asked him what it was, he said, "I think it's best if you wait before I tell you. It does work, but if you find out what it is you would never use it and then you'd be eaten raw." I assumed from that moment on that I was applying some type of dung to my body.

We talked mostly of birds during the day and it became clear very quickly that Pinky knew more about them than anyone I had ever known, including Bertie, Harriet, and several of the Audubon people. What was most valuable is that he knew the Florida birds, where they nested and all of their habits, and which birds the plume hunters especially preferred.

It wasn't only the birds that he knew. This man was like a walking textbook of flora and fauna and creatures of all kinds, and I had to wait until our third night out before he shared his own story with me. He had already told me that his name was hatched the day he was born when he came into the world, as his father said, "Looking as if a mother pig had misplaced one of her bright-pink newborns." Pinky told me he felt more like a flamingo from the time he was a little boy, too, but the name Pinky had stuck with him and now he was fond of it.

We sat around a small campfire that third night, which helped reduce the bugs and made me very happy, and he shared his story, which was partly like my own. He was from New York City where his father worked in a factory and his mother worked as a maid for a large hotel. He had six brothers and sisters and only three of them had lived to become adults. His grandfather was the one constant in his life and he also happened to be a lover of birds who shared that love with Pinky.

"I went through the eight grades and then my grandfather died of influenza and then my mother and father as well," he recalled, unable to look at me when he spoke of this great sadness. "I became lost and angry, packed up as many books as I could fit into a bag, and I traveled out West for a time, knocking about, a lost soul for sure, and then I heard about the plume hunting and the money one could make, and I changed directions and came here to Florida."

Pinky had a bit of money from working on the railroad and in the mines as he headed to Florida and purchased the small house where he now lived. He thought he could become a plume hunter, but he was unable to fire a single shot.

"The first time I came upon a rookery and saw what it was like, the beauty of it all, the sweet baby birds calling for their mothers, I could not even raise my gun. I thought of the hours I had spent with my grandfather and I vowed then to become a protector and defender of all the birds. I am now a guide for the wealthy people who come to stay at Summer Haven. I have also discovered that knowledge is the key to everything, and I am a great reader and studier of nature. Life is simple but very meaningful. I have become associated with the Audubon and there is so much work to be done."

Pinky shared more as we continued the next two days and he told me about the wealthy people at Summer Haven, a development of cottages and homes on the ocean where people of means came for rest and to enjoy the sea air. I told him about the plume hunters and Cuthbert Lake and my sketches and how I needed to see Pelican Island and that I hoped to be a new set of eyes that opened up other eyes to the need to stop needlessly killing birds.

It was odd that I never talked about Charles, but the truth is that both Pinky and I focused on the tasks at hand, moving forward, and talking about the best ways for me to do my work. I would have to tell him eventually what Charles did for a living, and I hoped Pinky would not judge me or think me naive to have married him at all.

I was beyond glad to finally get off of my trusty steed, Gennie, the day we reached his house. My poor behind had never sat on a horse for more than a few hours and the word sore is an understatement when

I try to describe what it felt like. There were bruises up and down my legs and my trips into the bush to relieve myself were anything but pleasant. Pinky was quiet when we dismounted and simply dropped the reins and then approached me.

"You'll be meeting Jessup Rose now," he said. "She's been with me now going on five years and we're partners in everything. She knows almost as much as I do about the hunters and birds and she'll be a big help to you when I'm out at Summer Haven."

"Your wife! I'm sure she's a wonderful woman."

"Jessup doesn't believe in marriage. She is my wife as far as I'm concerned, but she's a very modern woman and we live together as a husband and wife without the necessity of legal or religious approval."

What a delightful concept! I nodded my own approval, and as I grabbed my small bag off the horse, I studied the small-frame house and marveled at not only the distance I had come in miles, but also in acceptance of lifestyles, differences of opinion, and life choices. To even imagine five years ago that I would temporarily be moving in with an unmarried man and woman, have a homosexual for a best friend, a younger man who is an ardent admirer, and a husband who does not even know where I am would have been out of the question. But I was realizing more and more that if we were all the same, lived the same, or thought the same, life itself would be as boring as an afternoon in Brookline.

I was raised Catholic, but we were not that serious about it—at least I wasn't—yet there was an air of love and beauty in our house. The Kellys were kind people who yearned to have fun and celebrate, and for most of us that meant a lifetime of hard work in one small area of the world. I would have plenty of time during the coming months to think about how the stars aligned so that my life and understanding of it was so much broader and more different than my family's or many people that I knew. What I did know was that I had a job to do, a calling, and that I had met some of the kindest, most interesting, and generous people imaginable during the past eight months.

Jessup Rose, or Rose as she was called, ended up to be no different and the most interesting, well-educated, insightful woman I had yet to meet. She was college educated, a rather tall, dark-haired, and dark-skinned woman, who laughed easily and had come to Summer Haven with her wealthy family on a summer vacation where she met and instantly fell in love with Pinky, and who could blame her!

She told me her story during the next few days as I settled into my room and began to organize my thoughts and some type of a plan. Pinky was gone to Summer Haven, and as much I liked being with him, or simply looking at him, it was grand to be alone with a woman and discuss life. It was a lovely thing to step into a new friendship with a woman who I determined was absolutely golden from the first moment we met. She embraced me as if we had known each other forever and were long-lost friends, and that was the beginning of a nonstop conversation.

I was open with her and told her about Charles and his plume gathering, and she said she already knew. "The bird world is very close," she said. "We have all be waiting for you to come and explore and give some validation to our cause. I think it's remarkable that you think for yourself, and if Charles is half the man you think he is, your marriage will be secure."

Rose and I fell into a bit of a routine—sharing meals and walking and going over literature. Rose was a teacher at the local school and when she was gone, I worked on composing letters because I was anxious to get my address circulated and start receiving news from home. The first night she came home, I surprised her by having the meal prepared, fish of course, and then I was delighted when she asked if I would like to share some port. I suspect it was the port that gave her the courage to tell me her family had disowned her when she ran off with Pinky. They didn't think he was suitable for a well-educated woman from a wealthy family, and she had not seen them since.

"There's a bit of an ache, you know, but I was fortunate enough to develop my own sense of values and morals, and I see no distinction in classes or education," she told me as we sat at the kitchen table. "What I see is that love is the guiding force of the universe."

I learned much from Jessup Rose as the days passed, and by the time Pinky came galloping home at night, we had even mapped out some important nesting areas. I was anxious to see Pelican Island, but then the rain started and kept on for three days in a row. Rose told me that rain was also something I must get acquainted with and used to because it was a big part of life in Florida. The three of us made good use of the time when we were together, and with their help, I mapped out a course of action.

Pinky was going to take me around the community the following week to make introductions to important residents, other Audubon members, and some of the wives of known plume hunters with whom he had forged relationships. We quickly decided the best way for me to bring more attention to the cause was through the writing of newspaper and magazine articles that they would help me funnel to the proper outlets. They were also honest about the fact that I was married to a man who bought and used plumes in his business, and this, of course, would give me even more credibility. Not only had I married into a wealthy Boston family, but I was also a woman who refused to wear birds on my head, was a supporter of the Audubon, and had decided to devote my life to the cause of stopping plume hunters.

"It also helps that you are attractive and a bit on the brave side," Pinky told me as we were sitting around his kitchen table, surrounded by our notes and his hand-drawn maps. "You, my sweet Julia, are the whole package, and women everywhere will read what you write and hopefully take note and then take off their hats."

That's how one late November afternoon I launched my writing career by penning the first installment of what I suppose you could call "The Chronicles of the Bird Woman." I wrote the first article from my heart and with great honesty, realizing that with each word I might be further distancing myself from my husband, Margaret, and maybe even the Kelly family. I wrote about my love of birds and how I felt when I saw one on a woman's head for the first time, and I spared no details. I hesitated when it came time to reveal what my husband did, but I forged on, confessed to everything, and when I finished the article, I showed it to Rose. When she was done reading, she looked at me and I could see that she had been crying.

"This is remarkably honest and beautiful, Julia," she said with nothing but sincerity. "This is going to help in ways that we might not know now, but it's going to help and I admire you so very much for being so bold and taking such a great risk."

"I try not think about what I might lose but about what I might gain," I said, more worried than ever about my marriage. "I love

Charles, but I want a relationship based on equality and respect, and I hope Charles can meet me halfway on that."

"A woman deserves nothing less, but I know it's not easy for all men and that I'm lucky to have found a man who sees me as an equal."

It was helpful to be around her in the moments when my resolve faltered, and we had many discussions about women and men and the expectations of society. Rose also suggested that I include some of my bird sketches with my article, and then Pinky brought home a photographer from Vero who set up his camera in their kitchen, posed me on a chair, and took a series of photographs so one might be included with my submissions. They wanted me to look serious, and so I turned sideways and thought of those glorious birds I had seen when I was with Edna, and when I saw the finished photograph, I was pleased.

Rose and I made a small ceremony out of the mailing of the first article. We sent it to the Associated Press in New York, where Rose had a friend from college who was also a great Audubon supporter. She was hoping the writing would become syndicated and multiply the numbers of readers we could reach by thousands. We stood at the post office, a wooden one-room building in Sebastian, took turns kissing the envelope, and then embraced and walked out into the street where we instantly saw a flock of parrots squawking as they chased each other across the sky. We took that as a positive sign and we laughed all the way home.

While we waited for a response from New York, there was much to do. Rose had her school and teaching to attend to and Pinky had a break from his guiding duties and took me to meet George Nelson, a botanist, taxidermist, zoologist, and photographer who was employed by the Harvard Museum of Comparative Zoology. I spent a great deal of time looking at his photographs and talking to him about bird habitats, protection of nesting areas, and the importance of Florida for migration of numerous species of birds. I also learned about plants and vegetation, and he allowed me to sketch some of his specimens, which greatly helped my artistic skills improve.

Pinky also arranged a meeting with Mrs. Harriet Vanderpool, who was working to expand the Audubon membership throughout Florida. She lived in Maitland, which was inland from Vero, with her husband, an orange grove pioneer named Isaas, and she took her civic duties very seriously. We met while she was traveling to the East Coast on business and had a delightful lunch where she suggested I also start giving lectures and meeting with women's groups when my time allowed.

I was so busy that I could hardly believe the end of the month was drawing near and I still had not been to Pelican Island or received any letters or news from Boston. But all of that was about to change very rapidly.

Pinky told me that he had received word from Paul Kroegel, the warden who had been hired to protect Pelican Island, that plume hunters were still very active and all but ignoring the huge sign he had erected near the island that said the birds were "wards of the government." He said it might be dangerous to go, but I was compelled and thought I must write an article about the island and visit there.

"You've only met poachers who have changed their lives and understand that slaughtering birds is wrong," Pinky told me. "The others, the ones who make a living at it, will hate you and their families will hate you, and I may not be able to protect you."

"I understand, but I have come this far and it doesn't appear as if I am turning back anytime soon," I told him, convinced that in order to do my job I must see and experience what I wrote about.

"I will take you. I would never try to stop you, but before we go you must learn how to shoot a gun and be prepared for the worst."

"If I must."

The shooting lesson went well mostly because I had near perfect eyesight and also because Pinky was a patient teacher. He told me I should purchase a weapon and I asked him to do it for me, as I wouldn't know what to get. He bought me a lovely Winchester self-loading .22 rimfire caliber with a dark wood stock and beautiful silver plating, and to make it even more special, he carved my name in the stock, *Julia—The Bird Woman*. I can't say as I had ever dreamed of owning a rifle, but for some strange reason I couldn't stop looking at it. Pinky told me to carry it around and get used to having it near and I must say I grew very fond of it quite fast.

The rifle cost me twenty-eight dollars and my money was starting to dwindle. The lodging, food, what I had given to Edna, and some other expenses had been adding up. I had been using my money to help with the purchase of food and other necessities and it never occurred to me that I might run out of money one day, but many things hadn't occurred to me. I still wore the gold bracelet from Thomas and I knew I could sell that, and if need be, perhaps ask him for funds. I also knew I couldn't stay with Rose and Pinky forever, but I pushed those thoughts out of my mind. It seemed to me that life had way of presenting opportunities and other things if you lived the way Barton did and kept your fingers on the pulse of your seventh sense.

The last day of November in 1904 would go down in Julia Briton's world as one of great and lasting importance. It was November 30 and the day Pinky announced that the following day, December 1, we would go to Pelican Island. He said we would rise early, pack a bit of food, view the island, and return home before dark. He left for the day to meet with one of the men from Summer Haven and when he returned, he had a stack of mail for me.

I took the mail from him, which included one package and one very large envelope, and my hands started to shake. Rose was not yet home and Pinky suggested I retreat to my room and read the news in private, and I was not about to argue. I was about to find out I was holding the bitter, the sweet, and the sad all in my hand, and wise Pinky must have guessed as much.

There were letters from three men, Barton, Thomas and Charles, and I found this funny at first. There was also one from my sister and the largest was from the Associated Press. I suppose the order in which I opened them was very telling. I started with the Associated Press and shrieked with joy when I opened the envelope.

They were not just thrilled with my story, but they were going to syndicate my articles throughout the country, possibly overseas, and they had included a mockup of the presentation. They were going to call my column *Fearless For Feathers—One Boston Woman's Quest to Battle Fashion and Save Birds*. They were offering me fifteen dollars a month and expected one major article, as long as I wished, detailing my life in Florida, what I was witnessing, and what progress I had made for the Audubon. They also suggested that in a year or so, the articles would be turned into a book, with a negotiable fee to be determined at a later date.

I held up the proposed column and my heart swelled with pride.

My photograph had turned out nicely and the sketches I sent had reproduced well. Their own artist had included a drawing of me on the bow of the ship just as I had described it in my article, as I was arriving in Jacksonville. I was beyond thrilled and awed and felt a sense of achievement unlike anything I had ever felt before.

I opened my sister's letter next and she told me she had been shocked by my departure and also jealous, as her marriage was in shambles and her husband nothing but a worthless drunk. I had it in my mind to think of a way to help her, and after I read that my father was doing well, as were my brothers, I moved on to the letter from Thomas. He was recovering from Bertie's death and was busy settling her estate and carrying out her wishes.

I think of you often, every day, and imagine you out in the wilds with your beautiful face pressed into the wind. I am sending along the best spyglass money could buy and this should help you to see the birds more clearly. Please write soon and let me know if there is anything at all that you need.

Barton's letter was a pure delight and he said he and Phillip had arrived safely at their farm only to discover that it included a house that was about to fall over. They were now in the process of building a new home, hiring workers for the farm, and wondering what in the bloody hell they were doing. His note was filled with several hilarious stories, news that Phillip seemed to be a bit on the rebound, and sweet thoughts for my well-being. I missed him terribly and hoped that I could visit him before an entire year had passed.

The great joy I felt in reading the last two letters was quickly erased when I opened up the note from Charles.

Julia,

It is a good thing you are not near me right now because I might do something I would regret the remainder of my life. How dare you run off! How dare you take money from the account and go to Florida! You have made me a laughing stock and I am not certain I shall ever be able to forgive you.

My father has died and you are out doing God knows what! In my wildest dreams I never imagined something like this could happen to me.

I have absolutely no idea what else to say to you at this moment.
Charles

I wanted to weep and throw myself on my small bed, but instead I knelt down by the window, pressed my nose against the warm glass, and closed my eyes. Had I done the wrong thing? What would become of me now? My heart and mind were awash in a war of emotional confusion.

I heard the door open sometime later and the heavy footsteps of Pinky behind me. He lifted me up, held me against him, and it was then that I let myself cry and also let myself feel the tender warmth and strong arms of a man who was beginning to be almost as irresistible to me as the birds that were waiting on Pelican Island.

Tape Nineteen

Perilous Pelican Island
Pelican Island—December 1, 1904

It was dark when Pinky knocked on my door the following morning and I threw my legs off the bed, already dressed and eager to let the day unfold. I wanted to do anything but think about Charles and the letter I must eventually write him in response. Pinky and Rose convinced me to celebrate the good news from Associated Press and let the words of Charles simmer in the background for a time. It wasn't hard to imagine what he would think the day he picked up the Boston newspaper and saw his wife on the front page, but I pushed that thought out of my mind as well. I was finally going to see Pelican Island.

We ate a very quick, mostly silent breakfast and then we saddled up the horses, which I had gotten very good at, and Pinky had to remind me to go back in and get my rifle. He had attached a sling for it on my saddle and I was astonished how comforting it was to feel it there against my leg.

We headed south along the dirt highway, single file, and I was enjoying the cool morning air and watching the way the sun glided across the sky one tiny inch at a time and illuminated the treetops. I was already in the habit of wearing a scarf around my neck that I could pull up when the bugs grew thick, and my trusty spyglass was hanging from my neck so I could drop my reins and examine a bird at any moment. It was amazing the clarity that I received from holding up the lens to my eye, and I worked hard to memorize the images that appeared so I could recreate them later when I wrote my article.

Pinky turned occasionally to ask me if I needed anything and I waved him off with a smile. His broad back and wavy hair were a distraction to me that I tried hard to ignore as I thought about the significance of Pelican Island. I had read much about it, but Rose had also filled in some details. The notion to preserve the island, which was a prime nesting ground for the brown pelicans, dated back almost thirty years when the Curator of Ornithology at the American Museum of Natural History, Frank Chapman, first had the idea to purchase the small island as a bird sanctuary. He was afraid that if he didn't do something, men like my husband would steal the island away so they would have a plentiful supply of feathers—as if there was an endless supply of nesting birds! Mr. Chapman seemed to me to be well ahead of his time, and maybe I was also because I had the feeling that all things were interconnected. And thank the heavens for President Theodore Roosevelt who heard about Pelican Island when he was studying at Harvard for his natural history degree.

I thought about Roosevelt, who also seemed like a man who was in tune with his seventh sense and who had watched the brown pelicans from the Tampa Bay area prior to sailing to Cuba during the Spanish-American War. Maybe I would see some of those same pelicans if they had not all been slaughtered. I was almost glad as we trotted along that President William McKinley had been assassinated so Roosevelt could become president and declare the island as the first ever National Wildlife Refugee.

Pelican Island was a small dot of a place, but I knew it was just the beginning because anyone who thought about it, really thought about it, would realize that even as grand as this country was, we would eventually have to save some of it for those who came after us. I thought about wars and people and what we might also run out of when I justified saving land for the birds and maybe even other animals. If we continued to shoot each other in needless wars, would we not also run out of people? How many men were lost in the Civil War? How many in the Spanish-American War? If man could become extinct, then wouldn't it make sense that it could also happen to animals, insects, birds, and everything?

After traveling about two hours, we veered off the main road onto a small dirt path. The moment we were off the highway, I could sense that there were more birds and animals everywhere. I knew Roosevelt had seen huge piles of dead birds from plume hunters when he was in Florida, and I tried to imagine life without the colorful dance of birds flying above me. I had seen those wings and bird bodies in Charles's warehouse, but the thought of the featherless and lifeless bodies piled up made my stomach turn.

Pinky turned now and then to see if I was following and I smiled and nodded as we kept riding. We stopped in late morning and I could smell the water from the St. Johns River and imagined we would be getting close to the island within an hour or so.

"Time to stretch and have some water," Pinky ordered, swinging his legs off his horse. "We have a bit of a ways to go and I haven't seen any sign of hunters."

I lingered in my saddle for a moment and then looked down and saw the largest rattlesnake one could ever imagine coiled in the bushes to the left side of Pinky, its colorful head slowly rising to strike. Some magical instinct took over and I tightened the reins and quickly looped them around my saddle horn, pulled out my rifle, aimed it at the snake, and fired.

My shot struck the snake about an inch below its head and Pinky had the good sense to grab his horse's reins before the poor frightened animal could run down the trail.

"Julia! For the love of God! Thank you!"

My heart was beating so fast I thought it might come right out of my chest, and I looked at the dead snake and at my rifle and then at Pinky, who was staring at me as if he'd seen a ghost.

I started to laugh in an uncontrollable way, a sort of post-shooting release, and Pinky joined in, and I all but rolled off the horse, hit the ground, and walked over to see the snake.

"That was one hell of a shot."

"I just moved fast, Pinky. The snake was about to strike. I was almost certain you weren't ready to die today. We have to get to the island first!"

Pinky kicked the snake just to make sure it was dead and then picked it up. The snake was huge, over six feet long, and Pinky tied it behind his saddle and said we'd be having rattlesnake stew for dinner.

"I'm going to skin this beast when we get home so you can have it as a souvenir," he said. "I bet they don't have afternoon tea parties like this in Boston!"

The rest of the morning, I watched the dead snake sway back and forth on Pinky's horse as we inched closer to the river and to the island. I let my mind drift back to my days in Dorchester when I thought great adventure would be riding in a car or falling in love with a handsome man, and here I was riding a horse into the jungle, shooting snakes, and following a man who reminded me of one of the heroes I read about in books when I was a swooning thirteen-year-old.

I was already composing my next story for the newspaper in my head as the trail narrowed and we dipped into a marshy area that was swarming with mosquitoes. I pulled up my scarf so I could barely see, until we came out of the wet area and a soft breeze started to move down the trail. There were enough trees to shade us so the heat was not unbearable, and I relaxed and started focusing on the landscape and listening for birds that might be nesting or resting in the trees.

The jungles of Florida were so much different than the hardwood forests and fields where I grew up. The scrub oaks, palmettos, and palms were vibrant and so very alive with dozens of shades of green. I loved the way the sun filtered in through the leaves and the damp smell of hot soil that rose constantly from the earth. There was mystery everywhere I looked—new plants and flowers, insects, animals—and of course who knew when a flock of birds might swoop over or a bright-green parrot appear suddenly and yell at us for intruding?

We were getting close to the water and I was excited to see a sign posted along the trail, announcing that Pelican Island was protected and that the shooting of birds was not allowed. Pinky told me that the warden patrolled by foot and boat, but it was impossible to guard the island constantly. He said the thick foliage was good for birds and even better for plume hunters who had secret paths and trails on both sides of the river.

When we got to the river, the trail all but disappeared, and we watered the horses. I stood by the edge of the river and saw that we still had quite a hike ahead of us. We tied both of the horses and I was about to start walking when Pinky reminded me to take the rifle.

"From here on in, if we are at Pelican Island or anyplace where there might be plume hunters, you must carry the rifle," he advised. "It's one thing men seem to respect and that was not the only snake in the jungle."

"How far is it before we can view the island?"

"Less than two miles, but it's hard going and who knows what we'll run into? We'll walk slow and it's a good idea to be quiet. The one good thing about the refuge is that ornithologists and bird lovers are starting to come and there's a small viewing area, but that's on the other side and we happen to be on this side."

"The hard side," I added.

"I like to think of it as the adventurous side," Pinky said.

"A gal can't have too much of that, now can she?"

Pinky flashed his Indian-white smile and we started our hike. We were walking parallel to the river and I saw several small sailing sloops pass, their white sails floating as if a cloud had dropped and was gliding on top of the water. The sky was deep blue and the entire world was stunningly vibrant. I heard chickadees in the trees, and flocks of white ibis and snowy egrets were circling. There were raccoons running everywhere through the bushes and their little footprints ran back and forth across the trail we were following. There were also spider webs hanging from just about every tree and I wanted to tell Pinky I'd trade every last one of them for a snake without hesitation.

We hiked for over an hour until we came to a small clearing where someone had cut through the mangroves to make a small open area, and when I looked up there was Pelican Island.

It was triangle-shaped piece of land that was covered with low green shrubs, and even without my spyglass I could see there were brown pelicans and birds resting everywhere. It was remarkable to me that such a small slice of land could have changed so many lives. I rested my rifle against a tree while Pinky stood behind me and watched as the pelicans, with their long bills and beautiful yellow heads, dove time after time into the water, searching for food. It was one thing to watch the birds, oblivious to the potential perils that simply being alive and sharing the world with humans might bring, and another to stand there and get lost in the wonder of such a beautiful place. I was memorizing every bird and tree and ripple on the water so I might recreate this scene later, in hopes that a woman reading it might see how ridiculous it is to rob a creature of its life and joy so she can appear stylish.

It was not lost on me either that magazines and newspapers had helped promote feathers as fashion with advertisements and stories. Now I was using the same means to show how ridiculous it was to kill something so you might be fashionable.

It was quiet where we stood and I could actually hear the wind ripple through the wings of the birds as they glided past and their bird exchanges as they flew about. Pinky sat down to rest, but I stood, afraid that I might miss one bird if I moved. I was running my spy-glass around the edge of the island when I spotted a small boat coming quickly from our side of the river and moving toward the island. The front of the boat was covered and one man was sitting up there and two were behind them. All three of them were holding guns.

"Pinky! A boat is charging toward the island and they have guns!"

Before Pinky could even get up, there were gunshots and I saw birds falling out of the trees where I had only been looking moments before. There were more shots and birds fell from the sky and Pinky started screaming.

"Stop shooting! Stop shooting! This is a protected wildlife area!"

The men turned toward us and Pinky pushed me to the ground. "Stay down," he screamed.

I did stay down, but I reached for my rifle and crouched into a sitting position. The men kept shooting and finally Pinky fired three shots into the air as a warning.

The men stopped firing at the birds for a moment and then in an apparent attempt to call our bluff, began shooting again. I could see more birds drop, and it looked as if the entire island was about to pick itself up and fly away, because birds were scattering everywhere.

Pinky fired again and then told me to get on my stomach and prepare to fire if the boat came around. "Fire at them?" I asked.

"If they fire at you or me, yes, shoot at them and do not aim for a leg or arm."

Pinky stepped out into the water and lifted his rifle. I could see that he was aiming for their boat and he fired three times and I could hear the bullets hit the wooden vessel as the men screamed.

He threw himself on the ground as they fired at him and three bullets ripped through the trees directly above our heads. Pinky ordered me to fire into the air and I did, even though I wanted to stand up and blast their boat with every bullet in my rifle chamber.

I could see their boat turn and head to the other side of the river and within three minutes, the world was quiet again, except for the horrid cries of wounded birds who lay dying and the anguished screams from their terrified mates.

We both stood up and Pinky touched my arm to make certain I was okay, and I could feel that he was trembling as much as I was.

"Oh, Pinky! How horrible! Is this what it's been like?"

"Worse," he said. "Everyone knows this is protected now, but these men are ruthless, and for what? I am so angry, so angry!"

I had never seen Pinky like this and he turned away from me to calm himself and I had an urge to go to him and take him in my arms like he had done for me. I waited and after awhile, I moved beside him and simply put my hand on his arm and squeezed it.

We were quiet for quite a while and then he apologized and said that if he would have known, we would never have come. I argued with him and told him it was impossible to have known and I would have come anyway.

"Who would protect you from snakes?" I tried to joke.

"Well, there are reptiles and there are men who are snakes, and I am glad you can handle one of them and maybe the other through your mighty pen."

"The world will hear about this, but I'm afraid for all the other islands and birds who will perish before we can convert the rest of the world."

"At least we are trying, Julia. That's what matters now."

I wished we'd had a boat so that we could gather up all the dead birds and dispose of them properly. The screeches and cries from the island did not let up and in a short while, several of the dead birds were pushed our way by the waves. They looked so absolutely pitiful with their contorted, lifeless bodies bobbing up and down. I didn't realize that I had come to rest my head against Pinky's shoulder and quiet tears were rolling down my face. When I realized it, I stayed right there, afraid that if I moved, what we were experiencing might be lost forever.

I know that sharing moments of great importance with someone bonds you in ways that are unexplainable. It's as if something unseen joins you and creates an intimacy that will never go away. Pinky was a wonderful man who shared a cause with me and who had also shared a moment in my life like no other, and I knew that we would always have that.

We rode home mostly in silence, but I also had to let him know that plume hunters and snakes were no match for the likes of Julia Briton.

"This did not deter me, Pinky," I said as we saw the lights shining in his windows and Rose's silhouette moving about in the kitchen.

"I would expect nothing less," he said as we arrived at the house. "You are one of a kind, Julia, and it's a pleasure to know you and share this part of your life."

I wanted to say that I loved him, because I did, but I was getting wiser every day and I knew that some things were better left unsaid. The young woman who had fallen in love with Charles had all but disappeared and the woman who replaced her was growing more and more fearless by the day.

Tape Twenty

A Touch of Fame and Two Many Flames
The Remainder of December,
1904 and to January 10, 1905

The last month of a year is usually given to preparing for celebrations and family gatherings and taking stock of the year gone by, but there was no room in my life for any of those things. It was a rare day when I had a few moments to even try to remember what the rest of the world might be doing. I was by no means unhappy but there were still many things unsettled in my life. The number one item on my list of things to figure out was my husband, or rather my lack of a husband, and number two on the list was where I was going to live.

I'm certain Charles was also wondering about the lack of a wife, yet I remained his wife in all things, even if I was looking way too often at another man, which was one of the reasons I felt I must find new lodging.

Charles had not written to me since the last letter and it took me a week to form my thoughts and write back to him. Unfortunately, my letter was posted the day I received news from Margaret that might have changed what I wrote to Charles.

The day following our return from Pelican Island, Pinky and I had a long discussion, in front of Rose thank heavens, about men and how hard it might be for someone like Charles to change the way he thought. He asked me what I loved about him and I told him about his beautiful eyes and how he trusted me to move into his world and how he promised to take care of me.

When I said those rather innocuous things, Rose got up and poured each one of us a glass of whiskey, not wine, and said those were not attributes of love.

"Take a drink of that, Julia, and listen to me," Rose ordered, straddling a chair and sitting right in front of me. "You close your ears, Pinky. This is for Julia. Pinky is generous and kind and very smart. He accepts me for who I am and lets me live the way I want to. He does not judge people but is accepting of all types and kinds of humans, well, except plume hunters, and I have seen him step over bugs so as not to harm anything. My love for Pinky is a feeling of sweet warmth that floats through me and makes me strong and happier than I would be alone."

Pinky was grinning from ear to ear, and of course, Rose knew he was listening.

I tipped my entire glass into my mouth and told them about Charles of the Heart and how I had seen and felt the gentle insides of what I thought of as the real Charles. But then I hesitated.

"I have been lonely and when he left me after the death of the last baby, well, I think something inside of me closed over the affection I had for him," I admitted, looking out the window and into the dark night. "I think he can change and see that what I need is a partner and not someone to dominate me, but I am beginning to think that might not be possible."

"I changed," Pinky said.

"But you changed for yourself and not because of someone," I said quickly. "Charles is very stubborn and he has never raised a hand to me, but I have been frightened a few times. I know I can't go back there and I know that he must come to me."

"You could divorce him," Rose said.

The thought had entered my mind more than once and I pushed it away as quickly as possible. I told them that I had to give him more time and that I was going to write a straightforward letter to him about the feathers and birds and how he had to stop using plumes if he was ever going to win me back.

"Be gentle," Pinky suggested. "I think your transformation may have been too quick for him and maybe he does need time. You are very beautiful and smart and he will never find anyone even remotely as good and true. He will think about that and I am certain, absolutely certain, that he misses you and hates himself for misjudging who you really are and what you are capable of."

I blushed and then took the opportunity to tell them that I was going to find a new place to live as soon as possible. And yes, I did invoke The Liar's Brow when I said it was to give them the space and time they deserved as a couple, but the truth is that I was more than infatuated with Pinky. I dreamt about him, could hardly wait to see him every morning, and I was a bit jealous of his physical affection with Rose.

They tried hard to dissuade me, but I held firm and told them that the work would go on and that, of course, I needed them but that I thought it was for the best.

I wrote to Charles that night, and thanks to the second glass of whiskey, I was brazenly honest. I told him that I loved him and was still his wife and that in order for us to reconcile he must stop using plumes, and while I stopped short of demanding that he join me in my cause, I more than hinted at it. I wanted to reassure him that nothing I had done was to hurt him and that it would be wonderful if he came to Florida to see what it was like and to witness the importance of what I was doing.

Before I sealed the letter, I picked out one of my sketches—I was now experimenting with colors a bit—and folded it into the envelope after signing my name and writing *With Great Affection* on it. The following morning, I gave it to Rose to mail and when she returned that night, she had a letter from Margaret with her that made my world spin yet again. I had spent the day working on sketches and an article about the shooting on Pelican Island. I sat down at the kitchen table to read the letter, which I had to absorb in three readings.

Dear Julia,
There is much to tell you and much sadness and change to share. I will get right to it, as my life has changed so drastically that it is rare that I have a free minute. I do hope Charles

informed you that George has passed. He did not linger or suffer long and that is a blessing. I must put aside any feelings about his death and our life, as I have decided to take over running the Briton enterprises.

I wanted you to know this because my decision as the major stockholder in the company has turned my own son against me, but that will also have to be sorted out later as I have much to do. George always said he was going to change the will to make Charles the major holder, but he never did, and I am taking advantage of his omission. Charles and I are no longer speaking. He has refused to show up for work or discuss any details of the business with me. This has left me little choice but to move forward and make changes as I see fit.

The first thing I have done is to fire the little bump of a man who was hired by George and who is the son of his mistress. But I understand you already know about this and I will also deal with that later or not at all because some things now matter less to me. The second thing I have done is to suspend all purchases of plumes for the millinery shops that we own and manage. When Charles hears about this, he may throw himself in the Boston Harbor. But it is what it is and he will have to decide which road he will travel.

Charles and I had a huge fight and he showed me his true colors and feelings about women and their place in the world, and I now understand where I have failed and a bit more why you have followed your heart and the cause of the birds. Thomas came to see me and I believe your work is important and that my son, your husband, must discover how the world is changing in his own time. I no longer have room in my life for emotional travails, but there will always be room for you. I ask you, yet again, for forgiveness, considering the last letter I sent was horrid.

The truth is that I was again jealous of you and wish I'd had the courage years and years ago to take charge of my life. I am doing that now. It is important to know that we can all begin again, even if we are a bit older. I believe Charles has most

likely not sent you any funds and I am enclosing a sizeable
check so that you may continue without worry.

Please keep me abreast of your work and understand if I am
too busy for a time to respond. I am running the empire and
the honest truth is that makes me terribly happy.

Fondly,

Maggie

A check floated out from the envelope when I picked it up and it
was written for one thousand dollars. And if Margaret would have
been near, I might have dropped to the floor to kiss her feet. The
money would give me more time and more freedom and maybe even
a place of my own.

I could hardly move when I finished reading the letter for the
last time and once again my emotions were crashing into each other.
Margaret was running the business! Oh my! I could see her with her
skirts trailing behind her and her arms flying about, ordering the
workers and making changes and redesigning and going through the
books with great efficiency and seriousness. I smiled thinking of her
moving into the office and curtailing the plumes and I had to balance
the joy of all of that with what Charles must now be feeling.

What a shock the death must be and then the reading of the will
and then Margaret asserting her right, and all of that on top of his wife
running around with a rifle in the swamps with a man she has fallen
in love with! Poor Charles! I was worried about him, but what could I
do? I thought about the girls and hoped he was not taking out his anger
on them, as it was obvious to me that Charles did have a temper, and I
thought also about what Pinky and Rose had said about love. I had to
do something and the only thing I could do was write another letter.

I wrote it quickly and told him Margaret had written to me, and
I did my best to persuade him to think of this change as something
good.

Charles, I know this must be hard, as you had plans to run the busi-
ness, but now you can run it with Margaret and blend your ideas and
make things even better. I also urge you to take this time to really study
the plume issue and the world and please consider a trip to Florida to
see what it is like, and to visit your wife, who remains true and hopeful.

I was doing a wonderful job of convincing myself that lusting after a man in your mind could also mean that you were still faithful to your husband. I would be absolutely lost without The Liar's Brow! I did hope that Charles would reach out and challenge himself, and I also wished I had thought to get the address of the Ella and Ruby, who I know would give me a honest assessment of what was happening.

It's almost laughable to think that things would get worse, or better, depending on how you looked at it, but on December 15, I received word via a very anxious and excited postmaster that a stack of newspapers had arrived and my photograph and story were on the front page. I stood in the post office, absolutely numb. There I was on half of the front page and the article was just as I had written it. When I turned to the inside pages, three of my sketches and more copy filled up another half page.

It took three days for me to turn into somewhat of a local celebrity, but apparently I was also a national celebrity. Telegrams arrived from Thomas, Barton, and Harriet. Thomas said he would be delighted to field any requests for interviews or publicity. I was certain that if Charles had misgivings about me before the articles, he was now in even more turmoil, but I had made my choice and it would now be impossible to step back or erase what I had done. The newspapers somehow made my work and my choice valuable and real to me, and I would have to settle for whatever path Charles chose to follow.

That night Rose, Pinky, and I celebrated the release of my first article with groceries and wine I had purchased when I was in town. It was bittersweet for me because I had something else to share with them and I knew our dinners and daily meetings and encounters would soon be coming to an end. But first we ate a lovely meal that I prepared and took turns reading sections of my article out loud and discussing the one I had just finished that described the trip to Pelican Island and the encounter with the plume hunters. I had also purchased Rose a new dress, a pair of sturdy boots, and several books that I knew she wanted. I gave Pinky a gold pocket watch and a handmade leather belt that a local man made for me. It was unique in that it had a special holder for a knife and a handgun, and I knew Pinky would wear it when he took his customers into the swamps and backcountry. Then it was time to share the rest of my news.

"I believe I have found a piece of land on the river with a small house," I told them. "Margaret sent me some money and I need to keep moving forward and I haven't heard a word from Charles, so it's time for me to settle in and make my own way."

"Are you certain?" Rose said.

"Yes, I'm very certain and this seems like a place where I can rest my heart and life and be with the birds. It's a birding paradise along the river, as you know."

"It's not easy to be a woman and live alone out here," Pinky said, trying his best to be realistic. "I can't think of more than a handful of women who are doing it now, but you do have a rifle and lots of sketch pads so maybe you will be okay."

We laughed and I asked if he would be willing to go with me to the property the following morning before I made a final decision. "It's twenty acres and fronts the river and it's a bit isolated, but I've come to know that is how I would like to live. The quiet and the birds are paradise to me."

"Of course."

"And I will need help picking out a horse. I'm not sure what to look for in a good steed except one that does not bolt when a rifle is fired," I said, trying to keep the conversation light and wondering if I might be taking on too much.

But really what could be too much, considering everything I had already gone through? How soon one forgets how expanding the soul and heart leaves room for more challenges and how soon one begins to wonder if she has not gone mad and no one has bothered to tell her.

The following morning, with excitement rolling around inside of me as if I had swallowed an anxious mouse, Pinky and I mounted up and headed to a small area known as Vero Landing south from the Sebastian area where Pinky and Rose lived. I had a rough map of the area from the man who was selling the property, a German man whose wife had taken one look at the swarm of mosquitoes, slithering snakes, and the alligator that was fond of chasing little dogs and hopped on the next train back to Philadelphia. He had also mentioned something about "the inappropriate house" and without a doubt he proved to be correct about that.

The property was easy to locate because the farmer had cleared a long and open roadway into it and had also erected a huge sign with his name on it. The land looked untouched on either side of the entry road and it was thick and green and I imagined full of creatures and critters of all kinds. I told Pinky about Edna Hugo as we rode side by side and how she lived so simply and yet was at total peace because she could be who she wanted to be and do what she wanted to do.

Pinky started to laugh when I talked about peace and quiet and I asked him what was so funny.

"Julia, you are going to need this location to keep your followers and admirers from finding you. I don't think you realize what an impact your series of articles and the risks you have taken are already having on people all over the world."

"Oh, nonsense!"

"It's not nonsense and I'm so very proud of you, and I think Charles is a damned fool!"

My heart started beating a bit faster and when I turned to look at him, the smile was gone and he had something akin to a look of love on his face, which is the same look I had been wearing myself for more than a few weeks. I had to let it pass. I adored Rose and would not come between them, but oh how I wished that everything was different and that Pinky and I were the ones looking for a new home, our new home, but that was not to be. Instead of throwing myself off the horse and pulling him into the bushes, I thanked him and said that I had high hopes that Charles would come to his senses at any moment.

I had gotten so very good at lying that Pinky flashed me his smile and kicked his horse and dared me to catch up, and I fear he may have been crying when he turned to see if I was following.

"Damn! Damn! Damn!" I shouted when I knew he was far enough ahead not to hear, and I rode hard to catch up.

I could hear the soft roar of the river almost immediately when I caught up to him. We dismounted and without looking at each other, we tied the horses to a post near what I guessed was supposed to be a house.

Pinky put his hands on his hips and then turned back to look at me, and I was standing the exact same way. It was not a house, but more like a hut that I'm certain even Edna might not approve of. Pinky kept looking at the wooden structure and back at me and then asked if I also wanted to go to Pittsburg, and that made me laugh again.

"Heavens no, Mr. Foster. There are no flamingos in Pittsburg, and what would I do there?"

The house was one large room about twenty feet wide and forty feet long. There were two windows in the front, no indoor plumbing or electricity, a scattering of furniture, and a dirt floor. I almost had second thoughts about Pittsburg, or anywhere for that matter, but Pinky had an idea.

"I think we should go down to the river and see what that's like, and then I have some ideas."

Pinky! Pinky! Pinky!

I would have hated myself if I had not followed him out of the house and to the river where I was so absolutely moved by what I saw that I had to reach over and support myself on a very tall pine tree. The riverfront was an absolute oasis for birds and they were everywhere. There was a tiny island about fifty yards off the river bank, a speck of waving green, where I could see nesting white birds, but without my spyglass, I couldn't pick out details. There was a tropical hardwood hammock stretching to my left that appeared to curve to the end of what I had decided with my first glance at the river would be my acreage. I knew that dozens of bird species already must call it home and I could hear other creatures moving about as we stood and looked around.

The German pioneer had done one marvelous thing—he had built a long pier that stretched out into the river where I knew I could fish, possibly have a small boat for bird watching, and sit to watch the sun and moon and stars. The tide was out when we walked out onto the pier and there was a natural sandy beach beneath us that I would be able to use as my bathtub.

Pinky sat down on the edge of the pier and I told him the land and the so-called house would cost me four hundred dollars. I already knew that I would consider selling my soul to the devil in order to live there, but he grew quiet and I could tell he was thinking. He asked me how much money I had, and I told him, and he said that erased the possibility of building a new home and that we would have to think about fixing up the "frame hut" so I could be comfortable until more funds were available.

I hated thinking about money, but I was no longer above asking for it from Thomas or anyone and I knew how much money was in the bank account back in Boston. Pinky told me that a new house would cost about $5,000, maybe more because of the distance materials would have to be transported, and who knew how long it might be before electricity would extend this far? He said for a couple hundred dollars, he knew some men who could put in a wooden floor, paint, install some cabinets, and make it look like home. I agreed that was the best way to go. Then we sat there on the pier, dangling our feet like an old married couple, until we both started getting to our feet at the same time and then laughed about that all the way back to the horses.

The next few weeks were a flurry of activity in every avenue of my life. Pinky was correct when he said my articles would make a difference and there were dozens of letters from Audubon supporters, milliners who said they would no longer use plumes, young boys and girls, and the most exciting letter came from President Theodore Roosevelt, who wanted to come meet me and "…sit and watch the browns dip and dive." The letter I was looking for was from Charles Briton, but it never arrived.

I knew answering all the mail was important and after my article about Pelican Island and new sketches were complete, I set to the task of writing each and every person who had spent time writing to me about my work and how important it was. I had moments when I could not believe this was all happening to me, but I also had little time to ponder anything because it seemed as if fifty things were happening at once.

Pinky hired the men to work on the house the day I signed the papers and became the owner of twenty acres of land in Vero Landing, Florida. I held the pieces of paper in my hands that gave me title to the land so long that my fingers were stiff. I thought about Margaret as I walked away from the lawyer's office in Vero where I signed all the paper work and sent her off a telegram with the news. I think she would have been proud and happy for me and I also wished that I could have shared the news with my mother. I knew my mother would also weep with joy if she saw my story on the front page of the newspaper. One afternoon when I rode out on my new horse—that I promptly named Bertie—to inspect the progress of the house, I also thought of my lost children and how it would have been grand and exciting for them to grow up in a wild place where they could fish and run without shoes.

I thought of them often but never discussed my loss with anyone, even as I imagined what they would have looked like, how they would be growing, and how I would have taught them to read and write before they even started first grade. I knew I would always think of them like this and that if they were alive, I would want their children and their grandchildren to be able to come and stand on the shores of St. Johns River and watch the birds hovering over Pelican Island.

I also wondered if I would ever be in a position again to physically be with a man so that I might try having another baby. I had worked hard to push away thoughts of the physical and emotional pain I had gone through during and after childbirth, but my instincts for wanting to be a mother had not died as easily. It was much easier to throw myself to the cause of the birds and the Audubon than it was to think about lying with a man and having another child. But every woman alive has physical longings and I longed to be held and touched and loved.

The rides back and forth to town, and to my home, gave me plenty of time to think about such things, but once I arrived at any destination, it was usually nonstop work. I was eager to see the progress on my little house and the two men who were working on it were locals who had been very busy. It was the week before Christmas and they were taking a break when I arrived.

The simple plank floor was already finished and the windows sealed and they had finished off the four walls with cedar planks that made the interior smell lovely. They were now building a kind of half wall to make me a sleeping area and one of the men, Joseph, was a wonderful craftsman. I had also asked him to build me a desk where I could work. I was excited to see the tiny house looking so wonderful, and I stood in the center with my hands on my hips and knew with a woman's touch—curtains, candles, the smell of something baking, and a lovely covering for the bed—that this would indeed be the most perfect spot to work and study the birds. I had a thought as I was standing there to ask them to make one window larger so I could see out to the water and they said it could be done but would require a bit more money. I also thought a porch that extended from the entrance at least ten or more feet would be a wonderful place to sit and sketch, and maybe even cook, if I could get one of them to build an outdoor fireplace. They were eager for the work and I finally asked them what they had done before this type of work, and they both lowered their heads and mumbled, "Hunting for the plumes." I thanked them for stopping and then I had a sudden idea.

"Joseph, do you have a family?"

"Yes, I have a wife and three children."

"Can I ask what prompted you to stop the hunting?"

"Well, it was mostly because of my wife but also because Rose teaches my children in school and she talked to us about how the birds suffer, and well, I had to stop after that."

"Was it a hardship to stop?"

"Oh yes! I made a lot of money from the plumes. I am now embarrassed to say, but two years ago when I stood over by the ocean and saw that the birds had declined, I knew it was wrong. I work at the lumber mill now and build furniture, and Pinky helps those of us who have quit hunting to find work like this quite often."

Pinky was not just handsome and invincible, but more active than I thought. I was going to miss him, but this change was for the best in many ways.

"Joseph, you know I am writing for the newspapers and that I'm all about protecting the birds."

"Yes. We are honored to be working for you."

"I'm the one who is honored because you are both wonderful workers, but I was wondering if you could ask your wife and if I could ask you if I might visit and talk to you about the plumes and write about your lives in one of my articles?"

Joseph's eyes grew very wide. "Put us in the papers?"

"Yes."

"I would be so proud! But let me ask my wife and I will tell you tomorrow. Will you come tomorrow?"

I did come back the following day and was astonished to see the new window already in place and bricks already delivered for the fire-place. Joseph also told me that his wife had said yes to my proposal, and would I like to come on Christmas Eve and have dinner with them? I was taken aback but accepted the sweet invitation, which was ten days away.

Time seemed to move faster each day after that. I wrote and sketched and answered letters and went to Vero to find things for my house. It seemed as if the more I did the more I wanted to do, and I talked with Rose about organizing an Audubon meeting after the Christmas holi-day to try and get more members. I also wrote to Thomas and asked him to send printed birding materials that I could use, and I already had the idea that I might hold meetings and talks about ornithology at my new home and allow people to learn and study.

Pinky also had the idea of expanding his work at Summer Haven and offering escorted birding ventures up the river with a stop at my home where I could greet people and they would have a chance to meet me. Apparently my fame was growing. But I wasn't certain people would actually travel to see the brave bird woman who had left behind a beautiful life in Boston.

The week of Christmas I spent much time writing letters and one was to Edna Hugo. I sent her twenty dollars and suggested she come visit if she wanted a change of water scenery, and I told her that I had found my slice of birding paradise too. I struggled with what to say and do with Charles, but I sent him another letter telling him, as if he even cared, what I was doing and that I hoped to move into my new house very soon. I hoped this might stop him from thinking I was going to drop everything and come home because he had been silent.

Two days before Christmas, the best present ever arrived when I looked up from the banks of the river where I was sitting and there was Barton, standing under a tree, with his hands in his pockets. I dropped my sketchpad and ran to him and he picked me up as if I was nothing but one of my beloved feathers, held me close, and immedi-ately started to cry.

"Phillip has died, Julia, and I am beside myself with grief!"

"Oh, Barton, I am so sorry! When did he die? What happened?"

"It was two weeks ago and so sudden, but I should have known. He had grown weaker, but we have been working so hard on the land and the house and everything that I just thought he was tired. I went to wake him and he was gone. I expected it some day, but you never are really ready, are you, Julia?"

I could write a book on loss and never being ready. I would not let go of my dear friend and I told him that he was lucky to have had such a wonderful friend and brother and that we would find a way to remember him.

"Barton, let the grief take you away for as long as it must. Don't fight it and let it flow through you because if you stop it, then it will just come back until it has run its course. It gets better, but in many ways it never gets easier."

Joseph and his assistant were watching us and I'm sure they thought from our shared affection that Barton must be Charles. I took Barton's hand after his tears and mine had ended and I introduced him as my best friend and a man who had just lost his brother. Then we sat on the pier and talked for a very long time.

Even though his visit was initiated by loss and sadness, being with Barton was as much of a tonic for me as I was for him. During the next two days, I poured out my heart to him about everything, including my feelings for Pinky and my waning feelings for Charles and my occasional insecurity over my notoriety and the realization that now I was depended upon by so many.

Barton eased my fears and I like to think I did the same for him. I asked Joseph if it was okay for me to bring him along to the meeting with his family, not knowing that something else remarkable was going to happen because of it.

The visit with Joseph and his family was extraordinary and I took notes during the entire evening. I had purchased gifts for the family, special items that Joseph had told me they needed and wanted. Sewing materials, books, lots of sugar and flour, a new frying pan, some woodworking tools, and plenty of special treats for the children. Their house was not much bigger than mine, and how they all managed was beyond me, but I had never met a more polite or special group of young children. Their house was on a scrap of land with hardened soil, and when Joseph's wife, Carrie, told me what they had given up, I knew I had a story that would touch many, many hearts.

"We had a beautiful home with a view of the ocean that we paid for from selling the plumes." She began. "There were lovely floors and two large bedrooms and the children had shoes and new clothes during those years, but part of my joy had always come from watching the pink and white birds fly so close to the top of the ocean. I don't know why I never thought about the plumes, what was really happening, and how many birds were being killed. One day I was with the youngest girl and we were walking in the early morning on the beach and we came upon a stack of dead birds so high that my baby could not reach the top of it when she stretched out her arms. I picked her up and ran and ran and ran and that was the beginning of the end of the plume hunting for me and our life as we knew it."

Joseph eventually stopped hunting and they lost their home and moved out into the jungle and eked out a living. They were now committed to saving birds and doing whatever they could to let others know how wrong it was.

"Education is the key to the world," Joseph explained. "When you let the world know the whole story, like you are, Miss Julia, well, that's what changes minds. It's knowledge. Right, my children?"

All three of them popped right up to agree and I knew I had an amazing story to tell my readers about sacrifice and doing the right thing, but the night was far from over because Barton was about to become Santa Claus for this lovely family who had cooked us a meal that I know must have cost them a week's wages.

"Joseph, you are a carpenter, a builder, a brick mason, a fixer of many things, are you not?"

"Yes. I also know a bit about farming and the land and there has never been one thing I cannot fix or build."

"I have an offer for you and your family. I would like you to move with your family to my farm and help me build, manage, and run it. I have started building a house for a caretaker and it will be yours, and Carrie will be glad to know it has electricity and an indoor bathroom. I will pay you an excellent wage and your children will attend a fine school."

Carrie and Joseph looked as if they might faint, but Mr. Barton Santa Claus was not yet finished.

"There's one more thing," he said, rising so he could put his hand on my shoulder. "Carrie, your job will be to form an Audubon chapter in our area and to help me find a suitable piece of land to purchase so we can donate it in the memory of my brother as a bird sanctuary."

It took less than five seconds for every person in the room to burst into tears, and then I grabbed everyone's hands and we danced about the little cottage, singing "yes" over and over, but the giving and receiving was hardly over.

Barton was staying at Pinky and Rose's house, on a bed they had made in the kitchen and on Christmas morning there was a strange feeling in the house. Everyone but me was in a hurry to eat and exchange a few gifts and ride out to my house to spend part of the day by the river. I looked around the breakfast table as they were trying to hurry us out the door and thought about each one of us and our relationships and our lives and how accepting and loving we were and how wonderful it might be if the whole world was that way. I gulped down my eggs and bread and bacon and wished that every Christmas and every holiday for the rest of life might be this lovely.

But then we were off, almost at a gallop, to my house and my land and what I was coming to think of as my river as well. I thought they had all gone mad, and I finally stopped to enjoy the stretch of trail just before my house where the view opened up, and suddenly the river was right there as if it has just dropped out of the sky. I wasn't even looking at the house because my eyes always went to the river first. I dismounted, tied up Bertie, and then turned to see all three of them grinning and standing under my porch in front of a Christmas tree and motioning for me to hurry. What was going on?

It became clear the moment I walked under the porch that Joseph and the three of them had conspired to get the house finished by Christmas Day. The outdoor fireplace was stacked with firewood and Joseph had built several chairs and an outdoor table as well, and when I looked up, there was a new wooden bench at the water's edge. There was a sign on the door that said *Julia's Nest*, and I knew right there and then that I was not going to get through the next few minutes without bursting into tears of joy.

The house was more than even I had imagined and I would spend the last few days of December sketching it. The wrought iron stove and the lace curtains and the magnificent roll-top desk and the wooden bed with a covering the color of my beloved cardinal and a small sitting area and the most lovely outhouse with a peephole at eye's level, so when one was taking care of business, there would never be a moment when a bird could not be spotted.

I wish I could have taken the entire day and put it in a glass jar to look at over and over again. There was nothing but love and laughter and new beginnings. There was no dark cloud hanging above us or a talkative bird to warn me about what would be appearing not so many days later, just after the birth of a new year.

Tape Twenty-One

Courage and Light on
the River of Life
Julia's Nest—January 11 to January 25, 1905

There was a brief pause in my life for many lovely days as I settled into Julia's Nest and set up my home and working area. I had never lived alone, yet there I was five miles from the nearest neighbor, ten miles from any kind of civilization, a day away from the train station, and a lifetime away from the world I left behind in Boston.

My first night alone was January 2, the day Barton left for his farm, and after we had moved my trunk and acquired belongings, as well as food and household supplies, into the house. Barton had been such an amazing help and had helped me dig out a small section of land where the canopy of trees did not blind the sun so I could put in a garden. One afternoon he showed up with a wagon filled with plants and flowers that he set about planting here and there, after giving the entire plan much thought. It was clear he had a gift for horticulture and I suspected his citrus business would be thriving as soon as his trees started producing fruit.

We worked like packhorses for several days and then the night before he left we fired up the kitchen stove and he helped me cook a chicken and fresh vegetables, and we baked the first of many loaves of bread that would be coming out of that great black oven. After dinner we sat on the bench by the river talking about our lives and plans and when we would see each other again. I said I would come to him next and see what he was creating in his new world.

I had the sense that something else was going on because he kept lingering and lingering on the bench, and I wanted to go set up a place for him to sleep, as we were spending the night in the house. He kept talking and would pull me back down to sit each time I got up, and soon I knew why.

Two boats came rowing around the bend of trees on the far right side of the river and pulled up to the pier, and the men in the boats started calling to Barton. He ordered me to follow him and we walked out onto the pier. The man in the first boat jumped up, shook Barton's hand, got into the other boat, and then rowed off. Barton had the rope that was tired to the first boat in his hand and was wearing a grin as wide as the river itself.

"Here's your new boat, Julia. It's a swift little craft and you can hug the shore and watch your birds, and when I come back to visit, I expect to test your muscles and see how strong you have become."

"Barton! What a sweet gift and a sweet man you are! I have been dying to row to the island and see what nests are out there and now I can row up to Pelican Island or even across the river."

"I know because you've only talked about it fifty times. I thought I'd better get it for you before I go broke running the farm. Now go get in it and look on the very back."

The boat was very stable, but I wished for the millionth time that I was not wearing a skirt so I could move about more easily. Men still had the upper hand in most things, and I was tempted to ask Barton to leave a pair of his work trousers so I could wear them when I was alone and working about the house and yard. I crawled to the back of the boat and leaned over, and on the back of the boat it said, *Fearless for Feathers—The Julia I.*

I told Barton that if he continued to be this nice to me, I might never let him go. I was thrilled to have a small boat, and when I asked what the number one was for, he said he suspected it would be the first of many boats. Then he turned and looked back at the house and started talking as if he could see into the future.

"I also see a beautiful white house up there some day, with a long garden in front and a set of wide steps and a porch that wraps around the entire house. There will be a big bedroom upstairs with a small veranda so you can sit out there and read, write, and watch your birds any time of the night or day. It's going to be lovely, Julia."

"Is that your seventh sense talking?"

"Yes, but have I been wrong yet?"

"No."

I had to agree that Barton had more than one special gift, and now that he had fallen into my life, I had no intentions of ever letting go of him.

That night I had a lesson in love and tenderness that opened my eyes and heart even more. Life was such a mystery. The big lesson I was learning, day after day, was to remain open to suggestions and other ways of doing things. I sometimes would remember back and be grateful for the times when I did not hesitate to try something new or step out of a comfortable position. I loved thinking about the day I took off my clothes and jumped into the river with Harriet and Margaret, and I could hardly wait to do it in my own river. People who were afraid to jump naked into the river were missing so much! And I might have missed something wonderful too if I had been afraid when Barton dared to ask me a question as we were preparing for bed the last night he was visiting.

I was in my thin cotton nightgown and he had on pajama bottoms and was bare-chested. He approached me and put his hands on my arms.

"Julia, I have been so terribly lonely and sad, and you know who and what I am. Would it be so wrong if I were to sleep with you tonight so we could simply hold each other?"

My heart skipped a beat, for I too had been lonely and craving the sweet touch of someone warm against me, and I could see no reason to deny either one of us the simple pleasure of comfort while sleeping. I put my right hand on his rough cheek and nodded yes, and we blew out the lights and walked to my bed.

I held him in my arms for a while, one spoon against another, and he kept his lips on my hand as he talked about his hopes for the farm and how he would fill his life with the laughter of Joseph's children and charity work once the farm started. Barton was a man filled with great emotion and compassion and I had never known a man who would let himself cry so easily. That night it was as if he were emptying a vessel that had been waiting to be spilled over for a very long time.

Some time during the night we switched positions and when I woke I was cradled in his arms and I could not move for fear of waking him and losing the sweetness of what we had shared all through the night.

When it was time for him to leave, it was my turn to empty my vessel. I promised I would see him before spring, not knowing then it was a promise that would be impossible to keep, and I stood in the road with my arms crossed until he disappeared around the corner.

And then I was alone.

Courage is something that I had always associated with brave men, soldiers, pioneers, and the founding fathers of our nation, but I think the moment Margaret and Harriet started to pry open my eyes, I realized that women were more courageous than men. Giving birth three times also helped me come to that realization, and after all, it was women who birthed boys who turned into men, was it not?

My first night alone at Julia's Nest was a great revelation to me about the necessity for personal bravery. It was one thing to think that everything would be fine but another to not seize upon the many things that might happen to a woman, who was a bit well known, alone in the wilds of Florida. I was fine during my first day when the sun was shining as I went about the tasks of keeping house, working in the garden, my letters, and about ten more things that seemed to need doing every day. There were fish to catch, a report to compile for Thomas, and an announcement to prepare for the Vero newspaper about the Audubon meeting that Rose and I were trying to organize. I was too busy to worry about nightfall until it happened.

Darkness where I lived descended quite fast and I was thankfully in the house when it happened. I was able to light my lamps and make certain the door was latched. The door latching seemed ridiculous to me, but Barton and Pinky had insisted and I would use it for a while in spite of my misgivings. I had my trusty rifle and kitchen knives and a big mouth so I was thinking I would be fine.

But then my mind started to wander and I thought of all the plume hunters who must hate me. I thought about bears and alligators and snakes and evil robbers and crazy men who were running away from the law. I had the windows open and every little sound made me jump with anxiety. Finally, I loaded the rifle and put it on the table and put a knife next to my bed on the nightstand.

I walked around the tiny house like a prison guard checking out every detail. My box of treasures was on the nightstand as well and I had taken the white feathers, strung them together with leather, and they were hanging on the wall so I could look at them when I was lying in bed. I'm not sure why, but I had also hung the wedding photo of Charles and me below the feathers. There were several colorful rugs on the floor that I had purchased from local women and my small kitchen table was about three feet past the little entrance to my make-shift bedroom.

I tried to put a special centerpiece on the table every day—a lovely branch with moss on it, a rock from the edge of the river, a leaf from the trees along the highway, a turtle shell that washed up on shore. Barton had made a hole in the handle of the wooden spoon that I had tucked into my bag the day I left Boston, and I loved looking at it hanging next to the little counter where I prepared food. I had placed empty bottles along the windowsills at the front of the house and there was an assortment of dead but beautiful weeds in each one of them. There was a wall post for hanging my clothes, a rather uncomfortable sitting chair that I hoped to replace if I could ever find anything decent to sit in, and then of course, the amazing view from my two windows. Joseph had decided to enlarge both windows and I was thrilled when I realized I could look out and see the river without opening the door.

The river never really got dark that night and I know this because I did not sleep one wink. I sat by the table, watching for creatures and critters, and failing miserably in my quest to conquer the darkness. The following day I paid a steep price for my long night, as I was useless and ashamed and vowed to remember how I had survived three births, leaving my husband, posing as Nellie Lewis, shooting a rattlesnake, being shot at, and about thirty other things.

I watched the sky lighten, which was very special I must say because it looked as if someone were pulling away the darkness one little inch at a time until finally the sky was a soft glowing ribbon of white. It was spectacular and I threw open the door, set down the rifle, and walked out onto the pier and performed a bit of a ceremony.

The birds were scurrying about and I threw open my arms and welcomed in the day and thanked the night for making me realize it was okay to be frightened. I tossed back my head and closed my eyes and decided to release my anxiety into the morning air so I might be able to live without fear in the beautiful place that had chosen me as much as I had chosen it. I opened my mouth and screamed like I had never screamed before, not even in childbirth, and I let go.

I simply let go.

I screamed for a very long time, until I was gasping for air, and then I surrendered to the night and day and the elements and the river, and I asked for protection and joy and a life that would be long and fruitful. And I added "lots of fun" because I thought that was just as important as anything. Then I walked to the edge of the pier, took off all of my clothes, and jumped in. I swam out into the river and thought about what I had just done as yet another baptism. I was the bird woman who was Fearless for Feathers and who lived in Julia's Nest and I was never, ever going to leave or give up who I was.

Exhausted, I walked up to my house, left the door wide open, and fell into bed, not caring if man or beast came after me.

The baptism worked wonders and allowed me to enjoy where I was, while still being somewhat cautious, and to catch up on much needed correspondence and to continue to work on my property. I was clipping along and almost thinking about a trip to town when Joseph rode up with a sack of letters, and I think also to check on me.

He said his family was preparing for the move to Barton's farm and they hoped to see me before they left the following week. I suggested a picnic and frolic in the river at my house to celebrate all of our new lives, and he agreed. I passed off my letters and included in the mail was a new Fearless for Feathers article that I had completed about Joseph and his family. He placed a rather large bag on the outdoor table and I asked him what it was.

"Mail."

"What? All of that is mail?" I could hardly lift it.

"It's all for you and you may have to get an assistant if you keep answering them all."

"I had no idea!"

"You are a kind lady, Miss Julia. You are also humble and I don't think you realize what a difference you have made and are making and how many people look up to you."

I thought about that for a moment and looked at the bag and then back at him again. "If I keep at it, I won't have time to do anything else. Tell me, Joseph, what have you heard about plume hunters lately. Is it getting better? That's where I really need to make a difference."

He grew quiet and took in a breath. "Yes and no is the answer, which is not the best answer. It's a bit better around here, but until the market doesn't require plumes, there will still be hunters, and I hear rumors of big interest in some newfound rookeries down by the Everglades."

My heart sank, but the news was really no surprise. Changing the world was not going to happen overnight and there were still so many men who relied on plumes as a way of living. Joseph left with my outgoing mail and I ignored the sack of new letters for several days as I went about my work and completed several new sketches. I was getting better and better and had decided to sketch the outside of my house and write my next story about Julia's Nest and my new life as a property owner in the beautiful jungles of Florida.

I was torn about the letters and not sure what to do. I finally sat down and decided to sort them in case there were letters from my family, Margaret, Thomas, or if one believed in miracles, maybe even Charles Briton himself. I was beyond excited when the fourth letter turned out to be from Ruby, and I ripped it open so fast that I accidentally tore it in half and I had to read it in two parts.

> *Dearest Julia,*
>
> *Oh what a thrill to pick up the newspaper when I was at my granny's and see you on the front page! Margaret has talked to us a few times and I know you are aware of what has been happening here. Needless to say, Ella and I miss you so much we have taken to sitting on the front porch and looking down the road in hopes that you will return. But don't! Stay where you are and be the beacon for all of us who are afraid to dare!*

We are getting along okay, but Charles has fallen into a depression that I fear has crippled him. We were both here when Margaret came to talk to him about the will, and I think you would have gone in with not just one, but two wooden spoons to spank both of them. It was loud and long and I have to say I was rooting for Margaret. Ruby and I huddled in the kitchen but by the door so we could listen and before it was over we decided it was our chance to lay down the law in the house as well.

You treated us like real women and honored our opinions and we could not turn back from that so when Charles tried to take out his anger on us, we stood firm. We held hands in the kitchen and I spoke and told him he could no longer yell at us and that he must find a way to keep his temper in check or we would leave.

Oh, Julia! You should have seen his face! I think he knew we were serious, yet he retreated and we giggled into our hands in the kitchen and thought about you and how we would never again let a man or anyone treat us poorly. You have changed our lives and we are both so happy that you have followed the passion in your own heart.

Do not worry about Charles. We heard him crying last night and he has lost a bit of weight and I think he misses you and is beginning to realize what a horrible mistake he has made. He must figure out how to fix his life all by himself.

We are here carrying on, and if there is anything you need us to send you, please ask us. You have made us famous among our friends who have asked us to sign copies of the newspaper article simply because we worked for you!

Guess what? We are both going to an Audubon meeting next week, and I have started a list of all of the birds that have appeared in the backyard since you left.

We miss you so much, but please carry on!

Your Friend,
Ruby, and Ella too, who is now making dinner!

It was such a relief to hear from them, but even though they told me not to worry about Charles, how could I not? Ruby had included her home address in the letter and I sat down immediately to write to her and tell her how honored I was and that I was so grateful they were looking after Charles. I was as honest in the letter as I had been with them in person and told them I felt guilty, but I also realized that Charles had his own life journey and he needed time to look at things differently. I told them that one day they would come to visit me and we would sit on the pier and I would cook for them and they would see birds that would take away their breath. I also thanked them for their gift of friendship and said they were a great comfort to me when I was feeling alone.

The joys of female friendship are so very special and I credit you both for opening up that world to me. Thank you for staying in my life. Much, much love to both of you.

I thought of them in the Brookline kitchen and sweeping the front porch and standing with their arms crossed if and when Charles tried to yell at them. It seemed like a hundred years had passed since I had walked through the house, saying good-bye and then dashed to Boston Harbor, and already images of that life, my former life, were beginning to fade and grow dim. Was it as easy to fall out of love as it was to fall in love?

Maybe another woman would rush back and help Charles and maybe it was wrong for me to be moving on, but I could no longer waste precious time worrying about all of that. I had turned into a caring, self-propelled woman since the day of my marriage, and although I knew I had a duty to the marriage, I believed I had a duty first to myself. Maybe that was more of an inspiration to the women who were reading my articles than it was to the birds I was trying to save.

I went through the rest of the letters to see if by chance there was something from Charles, but there wasn't, and I set all of the letters in the house and went back to my sketching. There were at least a dozen common ground-doves who ran back and forth near the porch all day and I was working on several sketches of them. I loved their soft cooing sounds and the way their heads bobbed up and down. I was already very good at shading and could use one pencil to color in the wings of the small bird so its gray-brown wings with purple spots looked almost real. I was by no means an expert, but I was getting better and better, and I was also experimenting with color.

There were so many birds and so many colors, and I was seeing more and more every day how every field and tree and island was important for the survival of so many of them. The mere thought of cutting down a tree made me terribly sad. I was torn about telling people about the beauty of Florida because I didn't want the land to be eaten up with roads and houses and factories.

What a dilemma the earth faced! It seemed obvious to me that everything would eventually run out if we kept using it up. I also knew that I could drive myself mad if I thought like that constantly and didn't enjoy every moment of wonder when I could, and there were plenty of those.

Because I had no close neighbors, the animals and birds were out and about all of the time, the sky was almost always clear and blue, and the weather was delightful. It was January and I could swim and walk without my shoes on and sleep with the windows open. I knew the rivers in Boston were by now frozen solid and there must be snow on the ground, and I did not miss one bit of that nonsense at all.

I promised myself that I would spend at least two hours a day simply sitting in the quiet and observing my surroundings and all the creatures that shared my world. I took an hour in the morning as the sun was rising and an hour at night when it was setting. It was a gift I hoped to give to myself as often as possible for the rest of my life, and after a few days, I began to see why Edna could care less if she ever put on a pair of shoes again. It would be so easy to become a tree or a bush and disappear into this jungle and never see another human again. I was trying to be careful not to wish that I could be alone forever, and I would end each quiet hour by thinking about the joy of friendship and love. I would think of Charles of the Heart but usually more about Barton and especially of Pinky. I thought of Rose, too, and Joseph and the girls and all the people who were reading my articles and of Thomas and Margaret. My life would be empty without all of them and I knew there was room in my heart for more, so many, many more.

Days passed like this and my skin started to get brown because I was rarely wearing my blouse and swimming in the heat of the day when the sun was hot, and I loved every second of it. I fished and wrote and sketched, and on January 25, just as I was convincing myself that it was time to go to town and get moving again, I heard the unmistakable sound of Pinky's voice calling my name as he galloped up the trail.

My heart froze, I grabbed my blouse and dressed quickly, and when he appeared like a brave knight on a horse and said, "Something has happened," I knew my brief respite was over.

There was work to do and I was about to face the biggest challenge of my life.

Tape Twenty-Two

The Bird Woman Searches
for New Nests
Everglades Journey—January 25 through
the end of February, 1905

It was unfortunate that the days I had been apart from Pinky had not changed my deep affection for him. My love for him was not the same wide-eyed innocent naive rush of intoxication that I had when I saw Charles for the first time. Pinky was a man who treated me as an equal and who saw me in ways that Charles had not been able to see me. I knew it was because both Pinky and I had changed and grown, and I also knew that not everyone could move forward as rapidly as I had when they realize there is more to life than smiling at your husband over dinner.

I thought of my sister who had married so quickly and to a man who was ill-suited for any kind of change. He was a mean man who drank and abused her, and he could never see his way out of the traditions that had locked his family in place for a very long time. My sister could not find the courage to leave and start over. How could I be so different? I married a wealthy man who had given me all the physical comforts available in modern times, yet I left him because I was unfulfilled, empty, and unhappy. I knew many people could not understand that and also many could. How could two sisters be put together so differently?

I knew I could spend the rest of my life pondering that, but all the pondering in the world would not change the fact that I was in love with Pinky, and maybe still a bit in love with Charles. But it was Pinky who was in my life and not Charles, and if they had both been there at the same moment, it would have been no contest at all.

Pinky jumped off his horse and we had a marvelous, yet silent, exchange. It was a lovely "Oh I've missed you, yet I can't say I've missed you" moment when he stood by his horse and I stood under my porch, pushing the last button on my blouse in place. Our eyes locked and time stood still, and if the world had ended in that moment, it would not have mattered because I would have been on the same piece of ground as Pinky Foster.

Thankfully, reality interceded and a bright-green parakeet with a red mask and white beak flew between us and squawked as if it were trying to say, "She's married and so is he," and then landed on the peak of the roof and would not shut up. I started to laugh, even though Pinky looked as if he were bringing me grave news, and I could not stop. He couldn't help himself and he started to laugh also, and I knew this was a release for both of us because what I really wanted to do was throw him to the ground, rip off his clothes, and make love to him.

Oh my! There's a revelation that would make my sister and half of the world see the bird woman in a new light, but passion does not stop at the end of a bird's nest, or anywhere else for that matter. Pinky walked toward me, and I hated being proper and hated loving Rose, too. I also hated that I had a moral compass that could not be subdued by my lust and hated that if I acted on my feelings, so many people I loved and cared for would banish me from their hearts and lives.

The risk of this held so much more weight than what had come before. I now carried the wonderful burden of the birds on my shoulders, and what I thought might be the future of so many species if I stopped my work to satisfy an urge that I could barely suppress. I looked up at the lively green bird on my roof and it was as if it were there to guard me and to make certain I made the right decision. And of course that is exactly what I did.

"Pinky, what is it? Is everything okay?

"I've received news about a massive hunt being planned in the Everglades because the spoonbills are nesting late."

"I love the spoonbills and so many have already been slaughtered!"

"Remember when you told me about the three hunters from the ship?"

"Of course! That's where they were headed, down to the swamps and a very remote lake inland from Miami."

"They've been recruiting hunters from Jacksonville to Miami for months, and I received word that they are planning a massive slaughter. Julia, I'm going to go. Someone must stop them."

Pinky had ridden hard, probably all the way from town, and while I thought about what to do next, I went inside and got him some water so I could slow my beating heart. I loved the roseate spoonbills. They were stunning when they flew with their pink wings a blaze of color across the blue sky. The first time I saw one, or a portion of one, had been in Charles's factory, and their beautiful wings were tucked in a line, one after another, headless, heartless, and I would never forget it. Now that I had seen them in the wild, pushing their spoon-like bills from side to side as they waded through the shallow waters on their stick-like rosy legs, I would do anything to keep someone from shooting them.

I came back outside and Pinky was standing with his arms crossed and looking out at the river. I handed him the water, being very careful not to touch a single inch of his skin, and then I stood next to him and looked out at the water, too.

"Pinky, you know I have to go with you. I can write about this, and I have my rifle and I am not afraid. Will you take me with you?"

There was a line of clouds moving slowly across the tops of the trees across the river that looked like a parade of white, puffy cotton. I couldn't take my eyes off of it, and I wondered if the Wright brothers would ever get their air machines high enough so they could tell us what it felt like to touch a cloud. I could hear Pinky breathing and soon he turned to look at me.

"Are you certain?"

"This is my life now. Yes, I am certain."

"It's dangerous and not like being here, which is civilized compared to life down there. Many men who would not fight in the Civil War fled to the Everglades because it is wild and rough and no one would come to look for them, and many of them are plume hunters. I don't know, Julia. It seems foolish, and I would never forgive myself if something happened."

"I believe it is my choice if you will have me. I will carry my load. You know that."

We both knew there was more to this adventure than me being a woman and Pinky worrying about my safety.

"Would I offend Rose if I went with you, Pinky? Because I would never want to hurt her. She is my friend."

"She knows," he said, and I wasn't certain what she knew. "She's already preparing for me, and for you, to go. She is a woman who understands, as you do, that some things can't be stopped."

I had to assume we were talking about the birds and our work. Otherwise I could never have agreed to go, but I did agree, and within thirty minutes, he was gone and I was alone with so much to do my head was spinning in circles.

We would travel light, take our horses south, and then follow a crude map into the deepest and most dangerous untamed section of Florida in search of illegal plume hunters.

It was a risk, but then again so was living safely and wondering what might have been.

The remainder of the day and night could have stretched for another week because I had so much to do. There was barely time to pack my small bag, the same one I had carried from Boston, and who knew what one needed for weeks in the swamps? Before I prepared myself for the trip, I had to prepare the house and the yard as well. I thought Rose might come by to check on things, but I didn't want to leave anything to chance.

I managed to pull my little boat up onto shore. I actually dragged it all the way up the small incline and propped it against the house so it wouldn't fill with water and float away. My days of walking in Boston were still helping me out because I was used to hard work and enduring hours of physical movement. I staked plants in the garden and made certain my flowers and the bushes Barton had planted were secure. I went about the house tidying up my cupboards and the kitchen, and before I packed my bag, I sat down and wrote as many letters as possible.

The first one was to the newspaper and it was less than two pages long, explaining my sudden departure and where I was going and how I was going to get there. I went through my sketches and found one that I had done of two spoonbills and included it in the envelope. I barely wrote three sentences to Thomas, and the same to Barton, and when I was about to finish with Barton's letter, a peculiar feeling came over me. I closed my eyes and saw something, but everything was fuzzy, as if the far end of a dream had disappeared, and I thought maybe I was looking into the future and that something was going to happen. It was a seventh sense kind of feeling and I jotted it all down for Barton and decided it was some kind of premonition.

Something's going to happen, of course, but I have an odd feeling, Barton. Send me some good luck!

When I finished writing, my hand ached. I had written pages and pages in a very short period of time and I decided at the last moment to also write to Rose. I told her that we would ride fast and that Pinky would come back to her, and I said that if anything happened, she should find Charles and everything I had would be hers.

You have been a true friend to me and I love you, Rose. Thank you for trusting me and for being part of the Audubon.

I told myself if I said these things in a letter, if I wrote them down, then that would make them real and true. I was not invoking The Liar's Brow, but I wrote the letter very slowly.

I ate a very late supper and then started to go though my clothes and pack for… well, who knew for how long? It was no simple ride to the Everglades, days and days I imagined, and we'd be camping again. I started pulling out clothes and I discovered a pair of Barton's trousers that he must have left behind. I looked at them and almost started crying I was so happy. My life in the saddle would be so much easier if I could wear them. Dare I? I dropped my drawers and slid them on and they were a little baggy around the waist and a bit long, but I had belts and I could roll up the legs. I decided I would wear them and be thankful to Barton for the rest of my life.

There was barely room for much more than one change of clothes and a light jacket in case the weather turned, a bit of food, and several boxes of bullets. I decided to take a fishing pole, a knife, and only a few personal items, including my brush, a bar of soap, and of course, my sketching materials and notepad so I could write and take notes as we journeyed south. I knew Pinky would bring matches and what we needed along the trail because he had done that when we traveled from Jacksonville.

I was desperate for a good night's sleep in my comfortable bed before I had to sleep on the ground again, but it was almost impossible to slow down my mind. I sat on the doorstep with my legs outside and my body inside and watched the river for a very long time. I was no longer afraid of the dark and often welcomed it, especially on those nights when I felt so alone. The shadows and the moon and stars dancing on the water made me feel as if I were not alone and that the entire world was just beyond my arm's reach. That night was no different, but I already felt as if I were missing the house, my little boat, the garden, and my days and nights of solitude.

It was very late when I fell asleep and when the light started coming in through the windows, I stayed in bed for a long time, not out of fear, but because I wanted to savor the feeling of comfort as long as possible.

By the time I heard Pinky coming up the road, I was dressed and had eaten and walked around my little kingdom at least a dozen times. I looked at the wedding photo hanging on the wall, and then when I heard Pinky knock on the door, I took the feathers that were hanging above it and put them over my head so I was wearing a leather necklace with feathers that dangled past my breasts.

When I opened the door and Pinky saw what I was wearing, his face almost dropped to the floor.

"You have on men's trousers!"

"Yes, I do."

"And there are feathers around your neck!"

"Yes, there are."

"Are there any more surprises?"

I quickly looked around the house and spied the wooden spoon and thought there might be fifty ways to use it on the trail so I stuck it in my back pocket, turned around to show him my rear end, and said, "Just the spoon."

Pinky roared and I was glad our adventure started out on a light note so we would not have to address anything else. He went through the house to check my windows and then secured the door with a lock, and we hid the key under a rock.

He helped me tie my bag onto Bertie on top of the bedroll I had already attached to the saddle, and then he pulled a heavy tarp over the top of it that, which he said I would also be able to use as a covering when it rained. Before we mounted, he asked me one more time if I was certain this is what I wanted to do. He went on and on about danger and plume hunters, and I assured him I was fine and going along so he could do the dirty work while I sketched it all. Finally, to get him to shut up, I turned Bertie around and started down the trail.

There was no way anyone could keep me from the Everglades. Pinky galloped to catch up and when he reached me, I turned around just in time to catch a last glimpse of my river and the roof of my silent, empty home. Everything disappeared as we turned right and the only thing I could see was a sea of green, and I moved into it without a second thought.

Pinky was gracious enough not to tell me we had to travel close to two hundred fifty miles on horseback to get to Cuthbert Lake. He waited several hours and told me after we had dropped off my letters in town and had clipped off a good ten miles from the distance we had to travel. I should have thought about this, but there hadn't been much time to think about anything, and even if it had been five hundred miles or more, I would have gone. We were quiet for a long time and then we started to talk about the information he had about the plume hunters, who I discovered from Pinky were not so far ahead of us.

Pinky told me they had passed through Vero three days ago and they had been bragging from one town to the next about the spoonbills and a huge order they had from New York. The words New York were a relief to me and I was glad he didn't say Boston. I thought it might also be a good idea to ask him how we were gong to stop them.

Apparently there was a growing network of Audubon supporters and bird lovers who were stationed along our route who Pinky was hoping would help us. I was hoping, too, because I had met the hunters and Pinky also said they had boasted about meeting up with their relatives so there might be as many as eight of them by the time they got to the lake.

It was not prime plume hunting season. Most of the birds nested in spring and that's when so many of them had been killed in the past. The brave hunters would shoot them while they were in their nests, or after the eggs had hatched, because they knew their mothers would not leave their young. Two generations of some of the birds had already been wiped out and I was not about to let that happen again. The spoonbills sometimes nested and laid their eggs in late December and January and that's what the hunters were apparently counting on. They would slip into the Everglades with the help of their relatives who knew the area, shoot hundreds of birds, skin them, take their feathers, and then leave the rotting remains for the babies to stare at while they starved to death.

We talked about this and the all-knowing Pinky asked me if I thought I could shoot a man if I needed to. I had never really thought about it and yet I remember how I had fired into the air when we were at Pelican Island and how I instinctively dropped to the ground. But could I shoot to harm or kill someone?

"You need to think about it, Julia, because these men came a long way and they are determined, and it's terribly remote where we are headed. I don't even want to think about how many men and women are already buried under cypress trees or in hidden graves in the Everglades. It's a place that rules itself, and you and I and whoever enters it needs to be ready."

Pinky was serious and I took my time thinking about this before I answered. I had never really thought about killing anyone and it's not that I hadn't been angry or upset, but in a civilized place, there's not much need to worry about something like that. People yelled and stomped about and, of course, there had been murders in Boston, but not more than a handful. Here I was in Florida, where there were swamps and hideouts and where men who had run off from the Civil War or from other life obligations could hide out forever without being found.

I had the natural instincts of a mother because I was a mother. I fingered the feathers as we walked along and I thought about shooting a man or a woman if I had to, although interestingly enough, I had never heard of a female plume hunter. I knew with all certainty that I could kill to protect my children or anyone that I loved, and did I not love the birds? If someone threatened me or raised a gun in my direction, how brave would it be to let them fire first?

I turned to Pinky to give him my answer and he was looking at me with great intensity.

"What?" I asked him.

"One of the reasons I love you is because you think before you answer and you work out a problem in your mind and your heart first," he said.

The feather around my neck could have pushed me off the horse. Pinky had just said that he loved me! Now what should I do? Mention it? Ignore it? Or keep thinking?

I smiled and so did he, and I didn't have to say a word about love because Pinky and I had a conversation with our eyes. I told him that yes, I could shoot someone if my or his life was threatened, or if someone was breaking the law and refused to stop. We all knew there was a law against plume hunting and killing birds so you could transport them across state lines.

"Good," he said, still smiling, and I felt dizzy and held on to Bertie with both hands as I sealed the moment in my mind and heart.

We camped that night along the road and the two nights following that, and the weather was perfect. I sketched whenever we stopped and the moment we unsaddled the horses at night and without saying a word, Pinky prepared food and took care of the horses so I could work. And it was work that I was doing. I was keeping precise notes about our journey and the nesting sites we passed along the way and I wrote also about Pinky and his life and how he had changed from a plume hunter into a bird lover. I didn't tell him he was in my notes because I didn't want him to say no. I thought if I put him in the newspapers, his business might flourish and he would not have to worry about money or his own future. I was not going to give him the chance to say no, and I also started to sketch him while he sat by the fire or worked on the saddles.

Oh my! The women would go wild when they heard of this Pinky Foster and maybe they would hold up the stories in the newspaper to their own men and say, "Why can't you be like this?" I'm certain the world would also raise its eyebrows when they learned that a married woman was camping in the wilds with the likes of handsome Pinky Foster. Well, every day I cared less and less what anyone but Julia thought about anything. It was very wonderful to simply be there and sit in every moment of every day without the pressure of the rest of the world weighing me down.

I gave the idea of living each moment lots of thought those days on the trail. The world was becoming faster and faster every day. There was talk of airplanes and a train running all the way to the Florida Keys. Telephones were going in everywhere. People were starting to move out of the cities and they were buying automobiles, and I thought all of that might create a kind of distance between what is important and what is not.

The third day on the road we stopped for supplies at a small way station where we loaded up on oats for the horses and some meat, vegetables, and bread for ourselves. Pinky talked to the storeowner for a long time, and I correctly guessed that he was part of the birding network. When he came out of the store, he told me we would now begin to travel off the main highway and on a trail that ran inland and headed toward the Everglades.

"It's going be rough going from here on in." He warned me. "The trail is narrow and your favorite snakes and insects will be everywhere."

"I'm laughing, Pinky. I don't think you can scare me."

"There might be angry plume hunters, too."

"I'm certain I will scare them more than they will scare me."

"Especially when they see those baggy trousers."

"Get on your horse, Mr. Pinky."

We were trying to make light of the danger, and I was not foolish enough to think it wasn't real. But we were also prepared and he was absolutely correct that the going from then on was going to be much harder. The trail narrowed almost immediately and it was as if we'd plunged into the heart of the jungle the moment we left the small store. Pinky had shown me a somewhat crude map that detailed stopping points where we could rest and where settlers had managed to clear out areas and make a living far from the eyes of the rest of the world.

He told me he had been on this trail many times, visiting, and that I should prepare myself because some of the families lived in conditions that were far from acceptable by the standards the rest of the world had set. I had been through the poor neighborhoods in Boston and some of the side streets in my own neighborhood growing up at houses that were no more than brick shacks. There had always been one or two families that were not just very poor, but also very simple in their ways and manners of thinking and living, yet we thought of them as part of our side of town. When someone outside of our circle picked on one of our sons or daughters, one of us would rise up and defend them. Not everyone had been lucky enough to have been born with clear minds and every piece of their mind and body in full working order, but that didn't mean they were not entitled to the same joys and freedoms that the rest of us were allowed.

I thought I was prepared for anything, but the first settlement we reached was unlike anything I had ever seen in my life. We rode from the trail and into a large clearing that was littered with the stumps of the trees that had been cut to bring in a bit of light. A tarpaper shack sat crookedly at the far side of the opening, as if it had been dropped from the sky. It rested on tall stilts and was tipped to one side, and as we approached, I started to count the children: one, two, three, four, five, six, seven, and at eight, I stopped.

Pinky let out a kind of whistle, apparently a backwoods signal, and a man appeared from behind the house, waving but also carrying a rifle. He was thin and his hair hung down to the middle of his back and his beard was just as long. His clothes were tattered and absolutely filthy and the children ran about like wild dogs and were even dirtier. After several moments, a woman emerged from the house and I had to fight hard to stifle a cry. She only had one arm and limped, and her dress was nothing but an old sheet that had been tied around the waist with some rope, and someone had cut a jagged hole in the middle so she could drape it over the top of her head.

Everyone had black, rotted, teeth and Pinky told me to stay on my horse and I watched as the man cautiously approached him as he was taking a parcel off of his saddle. There was a brief exchange—I couldn't hear a word they were saying—and then I saw Pinky slip his hand into his pocket and pull out some money. It was fairly obvious what was happening, but I could hardly wait to have Pinky tell me himself.

We rode on and stopped to water the horses at a lovely stream about a mile from the clearing that was littered with watercress. I could see that it widened as it headed south and there were probably plenty of fish waiting to be caught.

Pinky told me that was the first of many backwoods families who had escaped the rest of the world and landed in this part of Florida. He said many of them had hunted plumes and that he was helping them to change and to farm or even move closer to an area where they could get help.

"Pinky," I said, beside myself with angst, "something needs to be done. Those people are hungry and they need help. What can we do?"

"You can add them to your list of causes, Julia. I help when I can and I have gotten several of the church women in the area to take an interest. They need education and some medical care and I have other men who have been helping them with farming and trying to convince them to move to the coast where fishing can be a fine livelihood."

"What did you bring them?"

"Candy for the children and ribbons and material for clothes. Their needs are endless, but somehow they manage, and I must warn you that on this trail it will be one family after another."

"Why didn't you ask me? I can help."

"Because I knew you would throw yourself into this and there are others who are helping. One cause at a time, Julia."

"But look at you!" I was not about to let him tell me I couldn't do something.

"It takes time and they trust me. It might be years before they accept you, and in the meantime, please feel free to do whatever you can with those of us they do accept."

The next five days were more of the same and I could see that Pinky was correct. People ran when they saw me and if I took on every cause in the world, I would get none of them right. But I knew I could not let these children grow up without hope and that when I could, I would do something.

We were now very deep into the jungle and I had no idea how close we were to the nearest town or any kind of civilization. Pinky had talked to three separate men who planned on meeting us in two days at a rendezvous close to Cuthbert Lake. I had to force myself not to think of all the wilderness families and to focus on writing and my sketching, but of course, there was no way to keep my emotions hidden. I sketched their shacks and their bare feet and the clotheslines with the ragged pants and shirts blowing in the wind. I drew their pitiful gardens and the backs of the children's heads as they sat a table where the only food was watery potato soup. I might not be able to help each family myself, but I realized I had the power to motivate others.

Pinky and I fell into a daily pattern of sorts. We woke at the first sign of light, talking little—except if one of us had been dreaming and needed to talk about the significance of our thoughts—and had a light breakfast, tended to the horses, and were mounted and off within an hour. I had started to sketch while in the saddle, not for accuracy as much as for memory. I could look at my work and quickly recall a place or a bird or a strange marking on a tree or the way Pinky slanted his head to one side when he was thinking or if he was about to tell me something. We stopped as often as possible when there was fresh water so the horses and both of us, and our water containers, would be filled as often as possible. We took a short midday break to eat bread or whatever we had in our side saddles, continued on the rest of the day, and always found a place to set up camp well before nightfall.

This is the time of day I loved the best because we talked as we rolled out our blankets and one of us cooked and we fed the horses. The one thing we didn't talk about was us, yet there was a kind of a unspoken tension between us. Once when I had turned on the light in the kitchen in Dorchester, I held on to the light switch and felt a bit of the current run right though me. My entire body tingled with what I guessed was a small charge of electricity. That's how I felt at night when Pinky and I were poking about the fire and camp area like an old married couple. We slept on either side of the fire, but I would often catch him looking at me, and he would catch me looking at him, and then we would smile and look away.

It was not hard those days to push everything else out of my mind. Charles and Boston and the rest of my life were out there floating under one of the clouds I occasionally saw as the trees opened up and we passed from one thick grove into another. While we were riding and heading to our destination, there were only the birds and Julia and Pinky, and time, in a sense, had been suspended.

I actually lost track of what day it was, and I believe it was around the twelfth or thirteenth day we had been riding when we reached another hut and there were three horses tied up outside of it. I had never seen horses or any animals except a few chickens and dogs at any of the other places we had passed, and this hut looked well constructed. I even spotted curtains on the window when we approached.

Pinky told me this time that I should dismount about the same moment a woman came to the door of the cabin wearing trousers and looking as if she had just skinned half a dozen rattlesnakes with her bare teeth. Needless to say, when she saw me approaching wearing my own trousers, we became instant friends. Within fifteen minutes, I was sitting at real table in a house, not unlike mine, talking about swamps and birds with Vonnie Gelman, a woman whose beauty was not at all tarnished by her sun-browned skin, calloused hands, and a scar that ran from the top of her forehead all the way down the left side of her face.

During the next seven days, while Vonnie's husband Frank joined Pinky and two other men on scouting trips to the Cuthbert Lake, Vonnie and I fished. I also learned how to set a trap for wild pigs, and I gave her several lessons in drawing, an update on world affairs, and a lesson or two about the Audubon and what I was trying to do with my articles and apparently my entire life. I drew her home and her face, which she never tried to hide, and she told me she hadn't spoken of the scar for ten years, but it no longer bothered her because Frank had made her feel beautiful.

The scar was from her father, who attacked her when she was trying to protect her mother. There's no reason, I told myself as she was sharing her story, ever again to think that I had heard or seen everything. She was married to Frank then. He fought her father and ended up killing him, and the two of them fled to Florida and never looked back.

They befriended some local Indians who taught them how to live, survive, and obviously how to thrive in the wilderness. Vonnie had also become a kind of medicine woman apprentice. She now traveled through the swamps and all the way to Miami, administering to the families who lived hidden in the mangroves and remote areas and who saw her as one of them and trusted her.

"It's funny how you can find your place in life without even knowing you were looking for it," she told me. "I've been so very happy living here and learning from the land and finding such great peace and in the sounds of wind and rain, and the birds that you also love. The people I help are very grateful, and when I am with Frank, nothing else seems to matter."

"Do you get lonely?"

"I didn't think so, but the company of a woman, a new friend, has made me think about that. Will you write to me and visit again when you leave, Julia?"

I walked across the room to hug her and she knew my answer was yes. The last thing I thought I'd find in the middle of the swamp was a new friend, a wonderful kindred spirit, and it was impossible to know that something was about to happen that would connect us for the remainder of our lives.

Tape Twenty-Three

A Dangerous Encounter
in the Swamp of Life
Cuthbert Lake, Florida Everglades—
March 1 to March 3

I was flabbergasted when I went back through my sketches and notes and discovered Pinky and I had been gone the entire month of February and it was the first day of March. It had been several weeks since I'd been able to send a letter with anyone, and I'm certain the people who cared about us were sick with worry, but there was not much we could do about that problem. I had been waiting, not so patiently, for a chance to walk the five miles to the lake and see the spoonbills, and this was the day it was going to happen.

Frank and Pinky had set up a little camp in a secluded area on a small knoll overlooking the lake where they had been watching for the plume hunters. Several other men who were not fond of plume hunters had come and gone during the past week, and Pinky thought the hunters might have changed their minds or gotten lost. He was concerned for my safety, but I was tired of waiting and wanted to be able to sketch some of the spoonbills and the area around the lake.

Rumors had been abounding about the lake and a major rookery and a slaughter that had taken place there three years ago. Foolish money-hungry plume hunters who were brazen enough to come back and see if any birds remained had Frank, Pinky, and the bird woman waiting for them.

The first day of March was typical for the Florida days I had become accustomed to for this time of year. It was a hot, sun-drenched day that would only get warmer with each hour. I had also gotten used to the mosquitoes and bugs and dared another snake of any kind to ever come near me, or Pinky for that matter. Vonnie thought my wooden spoon was very funny and useless, and she gave me a sheath for the knife I had been carrying in my bag and told me to keep it attached to my belt at all times. It was now second nature for me to rise from the little bed she had made for me on the floor, make certain my knife was in place, eat breakfast, grab my rifle and sketch pad, and get to work. Pinky and Frank had ridden back the night before and Pinky told me I should come and join them for a few days so I could sketch. He said the spoonbills, white ibis, and little blue herons were everywhere. I was so excited I wanted to run all the way to the lake.

Vonnie stayed behind and the three of us set out on foot in late morning with our bedrolls and cooking equipment. Pinky and I were going to stay by the lake because he wanted me to see the sun rise there and watch as the birds swarmed over the tops of the trees. He said he had never seen anything like it and the rookery was huge, nothing like Pelican Lake. Both men had been talking about the birds, hundreds and hundreds, since we had arrived. But nothing had really prepared me for what I saw the moment we came to the end of the trail and stood behind the pile of tree limbs and dead shrubs they had placed in a semicircle as a place to hide from the hunters and the birds.

I had never seen so many birds in one area in my entire life. My ocean voyage had given me the chance to see countless birds, but not great flocks of them, and the Pelican Island rookery was only a few acres of land, a mere dot in the St. Johns River. Cuthbert Lake itself looked as if it spread out a long ways, at least half a mile if not more, and it was as rugged as it was isolated. There was nothing but mangroves and scrub oaks and cactus and brush so thick it would have been impossible to even see the lake if the men had not built a trail and a small place to camp.

I held up my spyglass while Pinky stood next to me, grinning. He leaned down to whisper in my ear, "I knew you would love this," and his hot breath on the side of my face made me feel that electric charge all the way to my toes.

I stood there for a very long time, watching so many different kinds of birds, all quite happy to share the same area, that my arms grew tired and I rested for a while. Pinky said it was important to stay behind the barrier in case the plume hunters showed up, although there had been no sign of them since we had arrived. He pointed off to our left and I could see a small opening, far enough for a rifle shot to reach, where they would enter if they showed up.

Because the hunters still might arrive, the men hadn't been making a fire at night but had spent hours watching and waiting, and Pinky admitted that he had crawled through the bushes to the other entry point and had seen no sign at all. Frank stayed for part of the morning and then left to go back to his cabin. Pinky and I stood watching for hours and when it started to get dark, we sat on our bedrolls and talked like we had while we were traveling. The moon was a sliver and just enough to make the water glow. When I stood up, I could still see the beautiful pink wings of the spoonbills as they moved about the island that was directly in front of us.

There's nothing quite like listening to the descent of night. There's a moment when the entire world grows still, and it's as if the day has just taken its last breath and then closes its eyes as the night march begins and darkness creeps in, one little step at a time. I think besides watching the birds, there is nothing I like better than watching and listening for this moment. Since my arrival in Florida, I had never seen nightfall so brilliant and pronounced. Maybe it was the sky or the location or the distance from the sun or because I simply had not bothered to pay attention to this moment when I lived in Boston. Here, and at Julia's Nest, there were no streetlights or houses to block the view and each and every nightfall was different.

The first night at Cuthbert with Pinky, the sky turned almost as pink as the spoonbills and then it became shaded as darkness crept in and overtook it. I stamped this vision in my mind's eye because I knew I would one day have to try and paint it. I wanted to paint and draw everything I saw, and starting the next morning, that's exactly what I tried to do.

We decided to stay another night so I could keep drawing and write down everything just the way it was, because I was beginning to see that things and places change as much as people. I was also thinking ahead and had already decided to draw some of the scenes and send them to President Roosevelt. If Pelican Lake could be a bird refuge, then why not Cuthbert Lake, or all of the Everglades for that matter? What about the seashore in places where we already knew hordes of birds nested and the mountains in New York and the plains out West where the buffalo roamed?

These are the things I thought of all afternoon and into the evening, while setting a record for the number of sketches and pages of notes I was writing. The Associated Press had no idea what they were in for when I returned home to write up all my articles. Pinky came and went all day, but I'm certain he was never very far. I had a sense now for when he was close, and who knew how to explain that? It wasn't his smell or noise, but that electric charge that started when he was within half a mile of me.

That night we dined on the last of the fish Vonnie had sent with us and two apples, half a loaf of bread, and the last of our fresh water. We would be going back in the morning and we'd have to decide if we were going to stay or head back home and let Frank stand guard. We gave this decision considerable discussion and thought, and as much as I wanted to stay, I knew it wasn't fair to keep Pinky away from his work at Summer Haven and from Rose. It wasn't as if I didn't have anything to do either, and I thought about the letters, articles, the garden, and the meetings I was trying to arrange. I tried very hard not to think about Charles at all because a full moon was rising and it touched the side of Pinky's face and he looked magnificent.

Is it even possible for a grown woman to call a man magnificent? I would never utter that word out loud, but when the moon swung around the right side of the lake, there was Pinky, looking like he had just fallen off of a huge column in Rome. I took a chance and decided to switch from talking about birds and I asked him about Rose and marriage.

He looked at me strangely and without saying anything, got up and went over to his saddle pack. It was dark and I didn't see what he had until he came back. It was a bottle of wine.

"Pinky, where did you get that?'

"I've had it the entire time, Julia. I thought there might be one night when there was a full moon and we could share it and talk, honestly and openly, about us."

"Us?"

"Yes, us, Julia, because it's beyond obvious that we have a great attraction and that we love each other and, in fact, are in love with each other."

There is no way to prepare for a moment when a man who is, for all intents and purposes, married to a woman you call a dear friend tells you, a married woman, that it's time to talk about "us." He was correct and there was an "us" and it needed talking about, and it also needed as much wine as I could drink in a very short period of time.

Pinky told me he had no idea a man could love two women at the same time. He said he felt as if he were floating when he was with me and that it had taken every ounce of his strength every night we had been together not to kiss me and sleep with me and tell me how much he loved me and what a wonderful woman I was.

I told him pretty much the same thing, and after half the bottle was gone, we were right back where we started. Moral dilemmas are not as much fun as one might think. I didn't allow myself to linger in the past for more than a few minutes, and to think about how innocent I had been a handful of years ago. There was very much at stake to be discussing such an issue with Pinky, but I was way beyond not addressing issues in my life, or anyone else's for that matter.

"Pinky, do you think it would be wrong if we had one kiss? No one would ever know. I would never say a word and it would keep me from wondering for the rest of my life what it might be like to kiss the smart, handsome, sweet, absolutely loveable Pinky Foster."

Pinky laughed and his teeth glowed in the soft moonlight and it looked as if a cloud had settled just below his lips.

"Oh, Julia," he did not so much say as sighed. "I thought you would never ask."

And then he leaned in to kiss me and there was nothing left to talk about, absolutely nothing at all.

I wish I could say it was the birds that woke us the following morning, but it was not. I had fallen asleep next to Pinky and he must have gotten up in the night and covered both of us, but I must have been in deep slumber when he did it. It was a human voice that woke us and not just one or two, but four or five. Pinky sat up quickly, clasped his hand over my mouth, and motioned for me to listen. These men were so dumb they did not realize that even a whisper can tiptoe across the top of water so someone across the lake or pond can hear every word you say.

The plume hunters had arrived.

Pinky dropped his hand and started crawling to his gun. I waited for him to come back and then did the same thing. Pinky turned and slowly rose to his feet. There was no way the men could see him, but he could see them and he quickly motioned for me to stand.

The men were lined up on the shore about two feet from each other and surveying their plume hunting grounds. I was not afraid, but so angry that my hands were shaking. I looked out into the water, and the birds, my birds, were unaware that they were about to be slaughtered. They were primping and stretching and just beginning to think about food and flight. I could almost hear Pinky thinking.

I tapped him on the shoulder and mouthed the words, "What should we do?" to him, and he mouthed back, "You stay here." Then he pointed to the bush where he had crawled through several times. I assumed he was going to take them by surprise. We had talked about this back at Frank's and we had decided that we would confront the hunters, explain the law, ask them to leave politely, and tell them we would not report them if they left and never came back. We would do all of that while holding our rifles against our chests so they could see we were not doves, but protectors.

I put my hand on Pinky's face before he turned to leave and bushed my fingers across his lips, and he smiled, kissed them, and then motioned for me to stay down. Then he disappeared.

Time stopped again, but not for the reason I would have wanted. The light was starting to brighten the sky and it would seem to me that if the men were going to shoot, it would be fairly soon. I was worried, worried for Pinky and for my birds. I never thought to worry for myself.

I could feel my heart beating, hear the blood pumping through my veins, and it felt as if there was nothing inside of my head but air. This was no time to act like a silly girl and I shook my head, took in a breath, and then I heard voices and they were not calm, "please leave" voices. I thought I heard Pinky and then I thought I heard the other men, and then I knew for certain I heard gunfire.

Ten seconds passed and then twenty and there was still gunfire, and I did something that I thought made sense. I fired two shots into the air so the plume hunters would not think Pinky was alone. My idea worked and the shooting stopped. I stepped out from behind the barricade and walked one, two, and then three steps in front of it.

I did not see or hear the bullet. I did not hear Pinky scream and the other gunshots. But as I went down, I threw my hand against my shoulder where the pain was almost as intense and blinding as childbirth and then looked at the blood running down my hand, and I thought the color of the blood was almost as beautiful as the plumes of a roseate spoonbill.

Tape Twenty-Four

Lessons in Life and Love
Vonnie's Cabin—Everglades, Florida—
March 3 through March 27, 1905

O h, the places I went the next six days! I flew over Cuthbert Lake
and I had a lively conversation with the most beautiful flamingo
I had ever seen in my life. I zipped over to visit Barton and we sat
on his unfinished porch and smoked cigars and drank tea and then
whiskey and laughed for hours about absolutely everything. I checked
in on Charles and the girls, and there he was still pouting and walking
back and forth in his office like a big baby. Margaret was busy at work
and Edna was fishing, and mostly, I was at Julia's Nest, working and
working, and once I sailed right across the top of the water and landed
on a tree that was on the island I could see from my pier.

I was totally delirious and had a fever and a gunshot wound the size
of a very large pea in my upper chest, near my shoulder, that had missed
my lung by "the breath of an angel." I woke up screaming, which scared
me as much as it did everyone else, and I saw Pinky first, who looked
terrible because his face was covered in scratches, and then there was
Vonnie and my first words were, "Did you get the dirty bastards?"

Pinky smiled and then knelt down by the bed and cried into my
hair. "I'm so sorry. I'm so sorry," he said over and over.

I tried to talk again, but that's when I realized how much pain I was
in and I winced as I was trying to say, "No need to apologize."

I wanted to move, to raise my hand, and to touch him and say more, but I must have slipped away again for a while. When I came back to stay, it was dark and Vonnie was lying next to me in a bed she must have pulled over to be close. She was asleep and I managed to lift what from that day forward would always be known as my good arm, and I traced the beautiful scar that ran down her face.

She opened her eyes, touched my hand, and said, "Welcome back, dear Julia. You've been on quite a journey."

The journey was far from over, but I was going to live, and most importantly, not one bird had died. Vonnie stayed next to me, barely moving, except for her lips, while she told me the entire story.

I was shot by one of the three men who had been on the steamship with me when I arrived in Florida. Which one remained to be discovered, but they were in jail and so were three of their cousins. Pinky had done what he said he was going to do. He told them not to shoot, that the birds were protected, and he held his gun against his chest. They laughed and started firing and someone spotted me in my trousers, thinking I was a man, and took aim. Pinky went crazy, fired three rounds into the air, one into someone's foot, and then took off running through the horrid, thick, thorny bushes.

Frank had heard the gunshots and rode in on his horse as Pinky was running down the trail with me in his arms. Pinky kept going and yelled for Frank to go get the hunters.

"Pinky ran with me in his arms for five miles?"

Vonnie nodded her head up and down. "He did it so fast Frank thought he was a cougar at first."

"You saved my life, didn't you, Vonnie?"

"I'd say Pinky saved your life, sugar."

"What did you use to save me?"

She smiled and her scar spread out even wider, which I thought made her look even more interesting. "Oh, a little of this and a little of that, but nothing like alligator blood or anything. Don't worry."

We sent Pinky home two days later so the world would not think we had all died, and when he came in to say good-bye, I tried to talk to him about what had happened the night before the shooting.

"Pinky..."

"Shhh," he said. "We had a wonderful night and you need to get better because the world and all the rest of the birds we have not yet saved need you."

I smiled and he bent down to kiss me on the lips and he tasted like blood and life and so much more, and then he was gone. I heard his horse clipping through the trees and I fell asleep dreaming that night only of Pinky.

My recovery was not as swift as both Vonnie and I had hoped, but I was strong because of all my walking and rowing the boat and living like a pioneer. I had to believe, and I did with all of my heart, that Vonnie was a seventh sense miracle who really did save my life. My wound was fairly serious and after I had passed what she called "the hump of healing," she told me I would have died trying to get help from anyone else. Thankfully, the bullet had exited and did not have to be fished out. One can only imagine what that would have been like in a wilderness cabin, but there was much damage and blood loss and an infection from something that must have touched me when I fell to the ground. Vonnie's Indian medicine and her own medical wonders really were what kept me alive.

She applied a rather smelly poultice to my wound every day and made me drink so much water I thought I might swim away. Vonnie had a theory about water and life and how important it was to make certain there was enough of it filtering through the body and all of our organs. "Think of it as an inner bath," she said as she constantly set down one glass after another in front of me. It was not always easy to force myself to drink, but I must admit that the water worked, and I could feel myself becoming stronger every day.

Frank disappeared into the swamps to fish and to scout for other rookeries that might be in danger. We had an endless supply of food: fresh vegetables, meat, and fish that the people Vonnie treated would leave us almost daily. They were like ghosts who would slip through the trees at night or very early in the morning. I caught a glimpse of some of them occasionally, ragged men and women who the rest of the world might consider not much better than animals, but I knew the truth.

Vonnie had such a tender heart toward them and they were grateful for her many kindnesses and for the healing graces of her magical fingers. In another time and place, Vonnie would have been a great doctor, but her talents and gifts still helped so many people. I knew she would never trade her life for another.

My strength came back in little doses, and even though I was desperate to write and sketch, Vonnie made certain that I mostly rested and sat in the sun, and we spent hours together talking about everything, and I mean everything. Apparently my attraction to Pinky, and his to me, had been beyond obvious. She wanted to know what I was going to do about it.

"That's a good question, Vonnie," I said. "I'm not certain I have a choice. I'm married and so is he."

"Are you really married, Julia?"

"I still have Charles in my heart. The space for him has grown smaller, I must admit, but he's in there, though it's true that as each day passes, I think of him less and less. I'm not sure how he would fit into my life here or if he would even be able to love the woman I have become."

"Oh, Julia! There is hardly a man alive who would not want you! Your heart bounces around on your sleeve and you are kind and generous. Even with blood on your face and arms and wearing those damned trousers, you are still very beautiful, too. If Charles does not want you, I would say he is the one not worth wanting."

"Pinky and I talked of love and how it might be possible to love more than one person at a time. I suppose that's a very good excuse to misbehave. I've come to think it's not only possible to love several people at once, but very real as well."

"There are always consequences."

"Rose. Yes. And Charles also, if he ever leaves Boston. My reputation would be last on that list, and I must think of the birds and what will happen to them."

"I have always thought that matters of the heart are no one's business but the owners of the heart in question," Vonnie said. "I think if we knew the secrets of the world, we might all be released to love and live the way we want to without fear of society or anything but our own desires."

That sounded like a wonderful notion to me, but I did what the rest of the world usually does and that was to move forward without any kind of plan, except the one I had been following since the day I decided to leave Boston. I was the bird woman and everything and everyone else would have to take second place in my life. I suppose I had come to think that I was married to each and every bird in the whole world. I was the bride of every winged creature in the universe, and it was my duty to protect all of them. Imagine what the wedding dress must have looked like!

Vonnie didn't laugh when I told her that, but she said even the bride of birds needs someone to warm her nest at night and to feed the physical and emotional needs of her heart, mind, and soul. I understood that, but I also understood how a person could get lost in his or her cause and work, and how passion of that sort could override the others. Vonnie said I was a liar, but I wasn't so sure.

Our conversations went back and forth like this as the days passed, and then I started to sketch again, gradually because I was shocked at how the shooting had taken its toll on my strength. I sat on the porch and then in the yard, and eventually I could walk to the edge of the clearing where the birds were more plentiful. This is where I fell in love with the mockingbird. What a sweet little gray-and-white gift this bird was to the world! I listened to the birds calling and singing back and forth to each other night and day, and I'm certain their voices helped speed my healing.

Frank and Vonnie's cabin was so remote that during the weeks I was recovering, there was no mail sent or delivered. I found that after the second week I was getting a bit anxious and imagined all the letters that might be piling up, my overgrown garden, and more than a few people who might be worried about me. I thought about Julia's Nest often, and even though my forced respite gave me time to think, I knew what I really wanted was to get back to my work.

I asked Vonnie to share some of her doctoring secrets with me and she was quick to say that nothing was a secret. She explained how the Indians had been using herbs and what nature had provided for as long as there had been time. She walked with me through the swamps that were closest to her cabin and showed me roots and bark and plants that the rest of the world might ignore, but she knew they could save a life and in my case, heal a wound. I knew she was a treasure and I asked her what I could do to help the people who lived so poorly and so remotely.

We talked about education and school and books, so the children of these families might have a chance in the world if they wanted to leave the wilderness where they had grown up. We both agreed that a choice in life was one of the most important gifts a person could have. I knew that my growing prominence might give me a chance to raise awareness for these delicate lives and I promised I would do my part to help her cause. I also joked that I would have to live to be a very old woman in order to help all the birds and all the people, but truth be told, I really wasn't joking. Maybe being shot and almost dying had done something to me, but I felt more confident than I had in a long time, and I already was quite confident before being shot by a plume hunter!

When I grew strong enough to walk five miles back to Cuthbert Lake, I also knew it was time to go home. I asked Vonnie to walk with me to look at the lake and to see where I had been shot so I could write about it accurately, and I also wanted to remember the night I had spent with Pinky. Frank was going to ride halfway back to Vero with me, and I was more than ready to face whatever came next.

Vonnie and I walked in silence all the way to the lake, and it was just as I remembered. The pile of trees and shrubs was still in place, and I stepped in front of it to where I knew I had moved to fire the shots and found all of my empty shell casings, which I picked up and slipped into my pocket. Vonnie had taken my bloody shirt, washed it, and then cut it up and made it into a scarf that I had taken to wearing all the time. She called it my badge of courage, but I called it my badge of stupidity. No matter how old a person is, there is much to learn. I had been a fool to step in front of the structure, but I didn't feel like a fool when I thought about Pinky Foster.

We stood by the lake for a long time and I showed her where the men had been standing and the bushes Pinky had crawled through. She used my spyglass to watch the birds. I wondered if I would ever be back, but Vonnie made me promise, and when a dozen spoonbills flew right toward us and then dipped away at the last moment, I knew there was no way I could stay away. When it was time to go, I made certain that she headed down the trail first and I picked up a beautiful stone I had spotted lying in front of the shelter. It was streaked with dark flecks and shaped like a heart. I didn't need a rock to remind me of anything, but Barton would have said Cupid had placed it there and I would be a fool not to take it.

Frank and I left two days later on the first overcast day in more than a month. My heart was like a tangled vine when it was time to mount up and leave, and I held on to Vonnie for so long the horses were getting a bit nervous. I had extracted a promise from her to leave the wilderness in early summer and join me for a week at Julia's Nest, so I knew I would see her again, as she was a woman who would not go back on her word.

I owed her so much, yet I felt as if I had nothing to give her. Before I swung my leg over Bertie, I slipped the gold bracelet Thomas had given me off my wrist and put it on hers.

"We are now sisters for life," I told her, running my hand down her lovely face one last time. "I will see you soon, and for the rest of my life I will be grateful."

I galloped away, not daring to look back, and I was completely ready for whatever waited for me when I opened to door to a place that was truly my home.

Or so I thought.

Tape Twenty-Five

In the Nest for Good
On the Road and Julia's Nest—
March 28 through April 10, 1905

I'm not certain I had ever been as excited to see a place as I was the morning I rode alone up the trail that led to my house. I had been saying "my house... my house" for miles and miles and days on end and trying to remember every last detail of every inch of the house, the pier, the view, the river. It felt as if I had been gone for years, and if you measure years in experiences, I would imagine I had amassed at least several years' worth.

Frank and I rode up the main highway instead of on the back trails, which shortened the trip considerably, and we mailed a few letters at the first small village in hopes that the mail might arrive before I did, but it really didn't matter. Frank wanted to stay with friends along the way, or at inns, and I would not hear of it. I had grown so accustomed to being outside and sleeping under the stars that I wanted it to continue as long as possible.

Vonnie's husband was a man of few words, but we talked a little about the shooting incident and his love of the birds and how he hoped to get an appointment as a warden so he could have more authority. I said I would see what I could do about that, and after two days, I told him that I felt strong and that he should turn back and get on with his life. There was traffic on the road, other horses and carriages, and an occasional car, and I convinced him that after everything I had been through, I would be just fine. He in turn convinced me to retire the trousers for a bit so I would not get shot again. I had gotten so used to wearing them I had forgotten about putting my skirt back on.

"One day, Frank, women will be able to wear trousers and smoke cigars in public," I predicted. "I think maybe Vonnie and I will be in charge of all of that."

"If anyone can do it and change minds, it would be you and my wife. I feel bad for anyone who goes up against you two!"

I was more eager to be alone than I had imagined, and when Frank turned to go the third morning, I smiled at the blue sky and felt like the luckiest woman alive, except for having to wear a skirt again! It had not been terribly hot and the mosquitoes and bugs were not as thick along the highway. Almost every person who passed going either way stopped to ask if I needed anything, and I thought I could amble up and down the road for the rest of my life without a need or worry. I have to admit there were few—well, not a one to be exact—lone women riding north who had one hand on a rifle and who had recently been shot. I'm not sure if it was the rifle or my face, but I had fresh food every night, and water, several sips of whiskey, and more than a few offers of companionship.

I pulled well off the road each night, as Pinky had taught me, to set up camp, being careful each night to keep the fire I made for cooking small so I didn't attract attention. I tried to stop a few hours before nightfall so I could sketch a little before it got too dark and write down notes about what I had seen so I wouldn't forget any of it.

By the second night, I had counted ten varieties of snakes, dozens and dozens of lizards, so many blossoming flowers that I knew it was going to be an early spring, and one man galloping down the road who was asleep on his horse! I could hardly wait to round the next bend because I never knew what might be waiting.

Pinky and I had passed a small way station about a day's ride south from Julia's Nest, and I had decided to stop there on my last night out to take a bath, eat a full meal, and sleep in a bed. I thought it might be good practice for returning to civilization, and I really did need a bath. Some portions of the road were so dusty I felt as if I had been riding through a thick fog.

When Bertie and I pulled in front of the inn, at what I guessed was late afternoon, no one else was there but the innkeeper's wife. She took one look at me and asked if I was all right. I started to laugh because I had no idea what I looked like, and she grabbed a shiny pan off the counter where she was standing to hold it up to my face. I looked like a raccoon with dust covering everything but my eyes because I had been wearing my face covering.

"You've been on the road and we don't see many women alone here," she said, looking from my face to the rifle I was holding. "Are you running from the law?"

I started to laugh again and decided if I told her what I had been through, she might think I was mad. Instead I told her no, I was just a woman on her way home.

And that's exactly who I was.

The following morning was my last on the road, and as anxious as I was to get home, I was also anxious to make every second of every moment of my life count. That is what I thought about the last twenty-five miles. I thought about how I never wanted to wait for anyone or anything again and how just as it was wrong for someone to tell me how to live, it was also wrong for me to tell anyone how to live. I thought about forgiveness and blue sky and how maybe the birds that my father had introduced me to were trying to tell me how much they needed me when I was a little girl. Mostly, I sat in the saddle and breathed in each moment and told myself with each step that I was going to live like that the rest of my life.

People were already hurrying too much and rushing to answer their new phones and to jump into their new cars. Mr. Ford and Mr. Edison were going to make our lives easier, but I wasn't certain our lives would be better. People walked too fast when they went to the store and departed too quickly when they told their children bedtime stories. It wasn't just being shot that made me want to slow down even more, although with all my new causes I couldn't imagine how that might happen, but a yearning not to miss anything blossomed deep within my soul. I knew from my hours of bird watching that sometimes the smallest detail, a singular movement, one long note, a missing feather—those things could signal the beginning or the end of something terribly important. I was not going to miss anything.

My emotions were roiling when I saw the entrance to my property and noticed that the sign on the road had been replaced with one that said *Julia's Nest,* and I guessed it was either the handiwork of Barton, Pinky, or Rose. I watched my familiar trees, bushes, and shrubs appear, and even Bertie knew we were going home because she was frisky and wanted to run, but I wouldn't let her. Everything looked the same, only more vibrant, and I wasn't sure if that was because of the summer rains or because from here on in, everything would look, taste, and smell better to me.

The word joy came to mind and I knew not just the feeling, but the definition as a state of well-being, happiness, or possessing what one desires. I was definitely joyful and thankful when I came to the clearing and saw my beloved river and then turned to see my house, still standing, waiting and welcoming and all in one piece.

Bertie was eager to go into the little stable and drink water, and I unsaddled her and gave her the sweetest oats and then brushed her down before I hugged her and thanked her for bringing me home. Anyone could have seen that I was crying, but they were sweet tears of happiness. I was so absolutely happy that the tears were springing from the deepest part of my heart, the part where my beloved birds lived, and where there was music and light and nothing harmful. It was heaven, my heaven, and my tears were nothing more than an extension of the river of joy that sprang from inside of me.

The key was under the rock, and I unlocked my door and walked into my house and immediately saw the bouquet of fresh-picked flowers, barely wilting. They must have been put there sometime within the last three days. Rose and Pinky must have gotten the letter. There was a bit of food on the counter, and I could tell the dust had been swept from the house. I set down my bag, opened both windows, let the door stay propped open, and then I saw the bags of mail stacked in the corner. I walked over and that's where I found a little note from Rose.

Sweet Rose.

My heart quickened, but I was never going to regret anything again, and I opened up her note and smiled as I read it.

Welcome home! I am checking every few days and we received your letter and I am so glad you are safe and home, my dear friend! The world is waiting for you! Pick up the first newspaper and then you had better rest. You have a lot of work to do. Love, Rose.

There was a stack of newspapers on top of the mail and I picked up the first one. It was a *New York Times* dated March 15, 1905. My face was as big as a giant bird right on the front page and the headline read, "*Bird Woman Shot by Plume Hunters! Condition Unknown! President Roosevelt Investigates!*" I all but staggered to a chair and read the entire article while an early evening breeze pushed in through the front door, as if it had been waiting for weeks to enter. Pinky had found a telegraph station on his route home and sent news to Rose, and Rose had sent news to Thomas, and well, that was like sending a bag of candy to a child and telling him or her they could only look at it. Thomas knew the value of publicity and using the newspapers, and he was probably sorry he hadn't thought of shooting me himself!

It was obvious that my quiet would not last long, so I threw myself into it that night and the following day. I swam and I fished and I took off my feathers and hung them back on the wall, and I placed the heart-shaped rock on the window ledge and promised myself that I would never tell anyone where it was from and why it was significant to me. I sat on the pier, watching the darkness descend the next two nights and talked to the birds as if they could understand every word I said.

When the tide came in, my feet touched the water and I threw back my head and thanked whatever spirits might have helped me to survive, to realize what a precious gift each and every day was, and to live with joy and passion no matter the cost.

My shoulder and arm still ached a bit and I thought the best medicine would be to get to work before hordes of newspaper reporters and Audubon people started parading up the road. There was much work to be done and the bird woman must get to it. I had to write an article about the shooting, contact my Audubon people, make plans to see Barton—well, maybe I would even have to go to Washington D.C. to talk to President Roosevelt about getting more wardens and, without question, more refuges for the birds.

I thought it made sense to start with the letters that Rose had stacked up in the corner near my kitchen table. The task was a bit daunting. It looked as if there were several hundred of them and about twenty newspapers from Miami to Wisconsin. The sun was already high, and I decided to haul everything outside and sit at the table Joseph had made me so I could look directly at the water and keep a watchful eye on the comings and goings of my birds. I thought Rose might be visiting during the day, and I could not bring myself to imagine what my next reunion with Pinky might be like.

Onward, Julia!

There were letters from everywhere—New York and Wyoming and California and several with postmarks from foreign countries. Many of them had bird drawings on the envelopes, and I imagined some of them were stuffed with treasures like found feathers and advice on how to handle plume hunters. I decided to sort them before I started in so I could answer letters from families and friends first. I must admit it was not unlike waking up on Christmas morning to see all the presents under the tree. It was a bit overwhelming, but in a good way.

It was hard not to be distracted by the view and I ended up going back inside to get my notebooks so I could take notes and sketch a bit while I was working. The birds were circling my tiny island in bunches and it got me thinking I should probably name the little slice of land. The first thing that came to mind was *Vonnie's Perch*. I would write and tell her as soon as I caught up.

There were three letters from Barton, one from my sister, another from Edna, one from Margaret, and I still had a huge stack to go through. I looked at the postmark on some of the letters and that's when I realized it was April 10, 1905, exactly one year to the day I had lost my third child. My hand went instinctively to the tip of my womb, and I doubled over remembering that day with such clarity that it was almost as if it had been yesterday.

One year!

It had been exactly one year since the loss of the baby had propelled me into a new life and a new world, and I could hardly remember everything that had happened to me. Boston and feathers and plume hunters and riding in the steamship and gunfire and Pinky and so much more! I promised myself that one day I would write it all down, every great detail, so in seventy years, hopefully after I died of old age, what I had done in one short year might help someone else. I thought of women like Harriet and Bertie who had inspired me to move forward and embrace my passions and to risk, and maybe some parts of my life would do the same for someone else some day.

But first there was work to do. I continued to sort through the letters, determined to make headway before Rose arrived. I got to the middle of the second stack and when I picked up the next letter, my heart caught in my throat and I grew dizzy. The letter was from Charles.

I held it for a long time, wondering what might be inside. It was either the beginning or the end, or maybe just the middle of something. I was not gentle when I finally ripped open the envelope and my hands trembled when I read the simple message.

> *Dearest Julia,*
> *I am coming.*
> *Your Husband,*
> *Charles Briton*

There was no way to know why he was coming or what I would do when he got there. I held the letter against my chest and watched the gulls and the terns and the great blue herons dance together as they approached *Vonnie's Perch*. My heart would not stop thumping against my chest, and I put the letter next to my notepad, picked up my pen, and wrote, *April 10, 1905—The View from Julia's Nest—I received a letter from Charles just now...*

The day was bright and promising, and I had much work to do, a life to live, birds to save, and a heart that was more than ready to embrace whatever might come next.

The Defining Moments of All the Lives

The last tape was twirling round and round, and both my mother and I were unable to move. We had gone through an entire box of tissue, and both of us were now wiping our noses and eyes on the bed sheets. I had never seen my mother cry this much or heard her laugh so hard as she did along the way when Julia said something that was so unmistakably Julia. It was obvious that my mother was not going to be able to move so I got up, went downstairs to get us whiskey, which seemed most appropriate, and called to order us a pizza from the all-night joint in Vero Landing that one of my brother's friends owned. It was four o'clock in the morning and both my mom and I felt as if we could stay up for a solid week.

Mr. Pizza was very quick, and when I came back upstairs, with the entire whiskey bottle tucked under my arm and the pizza in my hands, my mother was pacing. My mind was doing the pacing for me, and I realized I would have to be the one to set the tone for how we walked through the fifty thousand questions we both had. It was finally time for me to put my college degrees to work, and the moment I started to talk was really the beginning of the first day of the rest of my life.

"Mom, what is your biggest question right now?" I asked while pushing a glass into her hand and trying to lure her over to the pizza.

"Well, who in the hell was the father of her child? Did she sleep with Pinky? What in God's name happened when Charles walked up to Julia's Nest for the first time?"

"Mom, that was three questions."

"Well, Jesus, hell, damn! I have a shit load of questions!

This was a side of my mother I had never seen before, and I rather liked it. She was swearing and drinking and confused, and who could blame her? We had all known about The Year, but certainly not everything. Now we both knew that The Year was just as much of a love story as it was about Julia finding her place in the world and then spinning the whole damn universe as if it were a top.

Something was happening to me, too. I felt alive and useful for the first time in years and years. Maybe the last time I had felt as if anyone really cared about me was when Julia and I had spent all that time together and I had hung on her every word. If only I had listened more and understood what she was trying to tell me! What had happened to the little Kelly girl who was supposed to be the family torchbearer?

That night, which was really the following morning, my mother and I finally shut up about 10:00 a.m. as we curled up, a bit drunk and totally exhausted, in Julia's bed. Before we fell asleep, we had discussed so many things and for me, it was as if a clear path to my future had been dropped right through the roof. "Hello, Kelly! We've been waiting for you to arrive."

Every good historian knows that the world before left clues, and that was where we started first. Well, it was actually second, because I had to ask my mother something big, really big. It went like this:

"Mom, I know I have been a pain in your ass for a long time, but I was wondering..."

"I can feel something major coming."

"Yes, it's big, Mom. I was wondering if I could move back in here for a while. We need to sort through all of this and now, don't freak, but it's given me an idea for what I really want to do."

"Sell pizza?"

"Mom, shut up."

"Talk."

"Can I move back in?"

My mother, for once, didn't say a word, but reached across the bed and kissed my fingers, and I swear to God a huge egret swooped in front of the window at that very moment.

What happened after we sobered up would make Julia throw back her head and laugh with great joy.

The first thing I knew we needed to do was to find the clues to make certain Julia had not been sniffing tree bark when she made the tapes. We had easily deduced that she knew it would take her a while to record everything, and so she had started her project in the 1960s when she bought the tape recorder. I found the purchase receipt; the Britons were not that keen on throwing anything away, and I was finally happy about that.

My mom got a bit manic at first and wanted to rip through the entire house, but I fell back into my historical research mode and knew we had to stay organized. We argued about this and finally I had to sit her down and tell her my other big news.

"Mom, I've decided I'm the one who should carry on Julia's legacy. It's what she wanted all along and she left clues for me all over the place, but I was messed up."

My mother was fidgeting and I knew she wouldn't believe me because I had also inherited The Liar's Brow and had used it heavily over the years. It didn't matter that I had actually moved in and was already knee deep in research.

"Are you really going to take over The Briton Birding Journal?" The word skeptical does not begin to describe the look on her face.

"Mom, listen to me. I've been reaccepted into the PhD program I've talked about for fifteen years. My thesis has already been approved. It's about Julia and her life and her history and uncovering what we discovered is part of my research. I'm doing this, Mom. I. Am. Do-ing. This!"

My mother was no longer the same person I knew a few weeks ago, and neither was I. She smiled at me, no yelling, and asked me about the Journal and the birds, and there was about forty-five minutes filled with precise questions and I had answers for all of them.

I was not the birding queen, but I had been born with half a wing; there was no doubt about that. My wing was a mix of the birds and history, and I was going to become an expert in early twentieth century history, with a focus on the environment and women's underlying and terribly important role in the salvation of the world. My mother would remain the queen of the Journal for a time, but we had much to do first.

I convinced my mother that we needed to start with what we did know and that was quite a lot. The back-story was all true. Julia's birth and family and marriage and Margaret and Harriet, all of that happened. We knew that Charles was married to Julia until he died suddenly in 1940, while fishing off the coast of Vero Landing, but was he really my great-grandfather and my mother's grandfather? It was more than possible for her to conceive after the loss of three children, but the father question was not so easy to answer. That would take a bit of searching, and I was up for the challenge. There were a few missing links about the Briton family business that would necessitate a trip to Boston and its archives, but each one of us had received stock in a variety of airplane manufacturing plants when we were born. My mother swore that Charles had made a fortune in the aviation industry after he left Boston, and given what Julia said in the tapes, that made total sense.

Julia's life was unmistakably obvious. She became an Audubon champion and one of the foremost authorities on wildlife refuges and ornithology in the world. She was self-taught but studied with all of the great birders and is credited with the salvation of numerous endangered species. My great-grandmother was presented with honorary doctorate degrees but died wishing she had been able to go to college. Julia traveled the world and lectured and became a much-loved speaker and storyteller. She met presidents and Aldo Leopold and Rachel Carson and every important earth lover and progressive-thinking man and woman in her time. She had huge fundraising parties at Julia's Nest and wrote three birding books, started The Briton Birding Journal in 1935, a folksy, downhome bird lover's magazine that still has a circulation of over two million. Her sketches and drawings sold for thousands of dollars and were sought after for collections all over the world.

But what most people remembered about her was that she was kind. Julia helped so many people, and when not just hundreds, but thousands of letters started pouring in after her funeral, my mother and grandmother started reading them, could not bear it, and boxed them up and stuffed them into the attic.

I was itching to get up there, but before we did that, my mother and I had to keep diagramming the truth. We knew Barton and the man he ended up spending his life with, a lovely dentist who set up an office on

Barton's thriving citrus farm. We also knew how much she loved Barton, and when he died, Julia had to go away by herself for a month because she was overwhelmed with grief. She went to a hotel in Savannah where she said they had once stayed, and when she came back, she had written and illustrated the most lovely children's book about a gentle man with a large heart. My mother recalled Julia saying that Barton was "as close to a soul mate" as any woman could hope to get.

I was curious about every single person in the tapes, especially Rose and Pinky, and my mother said her mother had mentioned how Julia would often disappear, especially after Charles died, for days at a time and return without offering any explanation. That news was enough to make me not sleep at night. I automatically assumed she was running off to see Pinky—who has a name like that anyway?—but I have to admit I had the hots for him even though he must be long dead.

We made a list of people and relatives we wanted to try and find. Pinky, Rose, Vonnie and Frank, Edna, Ella and Ruby were people I had to track down, and the Briton and Kelly relatives would be taken care of when I dragged my mother to Boston.

I had one other person to look for and I was keeping that to myself until the very end. If I told my mother about it, she might never believe me anyway, but I was almost certain I knew where our research was headed and even more certain that everything Julia had spoken about in her tapes was absolutely true.

Julia had never tried to hide the real clues from The Year. When it was finally time to start the scavenger hunt inside of Julia's Nest, we hit pay dirt immediately. The little wooden cigar box that she had carried from Boston to Florida had always sat on her dresser and we had all looked at it now and then. Clara Barton's letter, William Randolph Hurst's business card, and her original wedding announcement were tucked into the box, as were the notes from Thomas Edison and President Roosevelt. All the Briton women also kept jewelry boxes where treasures always rested. Nothing had been touched in Julia's room since before her death and when we lifted the cover of her jewelry box, it was almost as if the other clues were there waiting to laugh at us.

There was a gold Confederate coat button, the one that Barton had given her, an old key that I assumed had been the key to the front door of the house she left in Boston, and a handful of old bullet casings that *she had picked up from Cuthbert Lake after being shot. There was also the strand of pearls Charles had given her on their wedding day.*

I was so thrilled every time we found something that it's a wonder I didn't have a heart attack. It's one thing to dig into history, but when it's your history, something as real as the blood running through your own veins, well, Julia would say it's like seeing your first roseate spoonbill.

My mother and I became more like sisters during this grand research that lasted over a year. The bonding over the reading of all those letters from the funeral kept us in the same room for days and weeks on end, but everything we wanted, mostly everything, had been resting above our heads since Julia's funeral. The letters in the attic were amazing.

Ella and Ruby's children had written thank you letters, and we discovered that Julia had sent Ella money to buy her bakery and Ruby money to buy her farm. Edna had apparently married the man Julia had sent to help her fix up her hut and their descendants still lived on the slice of land, and they would never let anyone build on what had turned into prime waterfront and bird habitat land. Vonnie and Frank stayed near the Everglades their entire lives and Julia gave them money for a medical clinic where Vonnie, and a brave young doctor, worked their magic on at least two generations of families. Frank became a warden and when he died, he was buried in his uniform. I'm certain Julia got him the job.

My mother and I could hardly stand to read some of the letters because they were so absolutely lovely that we would constantly break down and begin sobbing. Julia, apparently with the help of the fortune Charles amassed, helped so many people, and she never, ever talked about it. We were emotional wrecks on and off, yet I had never been happier.

We could find absolutely no information about Jessup Rose and Pinky Foster, and I did my best to get my mother to forget about it because I wanted to find them by myself. When I told her we had to go to Boston so I could meet with some professors and visit the places from the beginning of Julia's year, she thankfully forgot about Pinky and Rose.

We flew to Boston almost eighteen months after my grandmother's death and the night we had listened to the tapes, and then spent an amazing two weeks tracking down relatives and touring the homes in Brookline and Dorchester where Julia had lived. We stopped at an old building where the name Briton was still barely visible above the door, and when I went inside I had the unmistakable feeling that I knew exactly where Julia had seen the dead bird parts in boxes for the first time.

The day we left, we drove slowly to the cemetery where Julia's three babies had been buried. My mother and I threw ourselves on the grass in front of the tiny white grave markers and cried like babies ourselves.

Back in Vero Landing, I lied to my mother, because I was still so damn good at it, and said I was going to lock myself up at a friend's cabin for a week to write and try to finish my doctoral dissertation. I had already found what I needed to connect the last link in Julia's life, but I had to do it on my own. It was clear to me that Julia knew I would find her biggest secret, and what I would do with it remained to be seen.

I had figured out that the person I needed to look for was Nellie Lewis. Julia had really turned into Nellie Lewis, but if I wanted to find out what happened to Pinky and Rose, I needed to find Nellie. My history research and all my contacts did not let me down. It took me a bit of work, but I found a property listing in a remote area about fifty miles south of Vero Landing for a Nellie Lewis.

The drive south was on the same road Julia had taken when she rode home after being shot, and in my mind's eye I could see her trotting up the road, the wind in her hair, her eyes to the sky. I found a small marker at the entrance to the address I had discovered, turned right, and prayed my stomach would follow. The drive was long and winding and not unlike the same drive that led into Julia's Nest.

When I got to the end, there was a simple cabin that looked as if it had been recently remodeled, a lone green pickup truck, a garage off to the side, and about three million birdhouses. I was obviously at the correct location.

The next two days were a revelation that was never really a burden because I knew what Julia would have wanted. I met Rose and Pinky's grandson, a lovely man my mother's age, who took one look at me and said, "You must be Kelly." He sat me down and handed me a hand-carved wooden box that he said Pinky had given to him to hold on to until I showed up. My hands trembled as I opened the box, pulled out the feathers still attached to the leather that Julia had worn around her neck, and the heart-shaped rock Julia had taken from Cuthbert Lake.

And one last note.

> Kelly,
>
> *I knew you would find me and find out my secret. I loved your great-grandfather and you are his descendant, but there was a man I also loved and his name was Pinky Foster. The details of what we were and what we shared you can imagine and then do with them what you will. I needed and wanted one thing, one part of my life, for just myself, and that is why I never told the whole truth about The Year. Pinky and I built this little house and this was my escape, my real world, the real Julia's Nest in so many ways.*
>
> *Pinky was true and real and devoted and always let me be myself. I hope you will find someone like Pinky some day—a true mate, an equal, a man or even a woman—who cares! You must promise me that you will always be yourself—to hell with what the world or anyone in it might think!*
>
> *Your grandfather came around and we forged a unique partnership, but with Pinky it was as if we had been destined to fly in the same high winds, free birds, alive in the spirit of love and great tenderness from the day we were born.*
>
> *Fly, my sweet Kelly! I have loved and treasured you and know that if you have found this, then you are about to find your own nest.*
>
> *Love,*
> *Your Julia*

Pinky's grandson told me that Rose had died very young of breast cancer and that he had only found out about Pinky and Julia's relationship after Pinky's death, not long before Julia died. He wanted me to take Julia's rifle, still engraved with the words, *Julia—The Bird Woman.* The rifle hung above a fieldstone fireplace that I assumed Joseph had made, and there was the damned snakeskin right next to it, framed with the words, *Julia's First Shot.* I left everything there, and I visit the cabin often and have discovered that when the grandson passes, the love nest will become mine.

I never told anyone about the letter or Pinky, and Pinky's grandson was also sworn to secrecy. When I completed my doctoral thesis, titled *The Year*, it was not exactly as it had been in the tapes, but I had my hand on my necessary Liar's Brow the day I turned it in, so everything turned out just as it should.

Not so long after I finished my research, I discovered that I was pregnant and after much soul-searching, I decided it was time for me to build my own permanent nest. Julia was correct. My daughter is the spitting image of her great-great-grandmother, equally as sassy, and when she dreams, she tells me she is always flying through the sky and that her arms turn into wings. I named her Vonnie Rose, but everyone calls her Little Julia.

Today I am Dr. Kelly Briton, a renowned historian, who also carries on the legacy of her great-grandmother and who wants the world to know that we should never, ever, forget the daring and courageous women who brought us to this moment.

In the end, I had my year too, only I just spread it out over many, many years. Julia would not give a damn about that, but she would love that I know how important it is to have *The Year*, no matter how long it takes, and for everyone to have a Pinky Foster as well.

I haven't found my Pinky yet, but I'm having a wonderful time looking, and that's an important message also. Life is a grand adventure, and if you hesitate or surrender, you might miss seeing the most beautiful bird ever, the loveliest sunset, or the best kiss of your life.

Acknowledgements

Thanks to Amy and Jo Johnson for sharing the lives and names of important people from years gone by who have been resurrected via their names in this novel. Thanks also to Justine for sharing her Jessup Rose.

John Marani helped me with Boston information and my amazing research assistant, Liz Webster Riedford, was a miracle worker and never failed to find me exactly what I needed.

My partner, cheerleader, expedition companion and tireless assistant, Madonna Metcalf, let me drag her through swamps, remote hiking trails, bird refugees, libraries, late night exclamations, chapter revisions, history lectures and moments of self-doubt without complaint.

I am beyond grateful to the SparkPress team for all they do to get my work in your hands. My Sparkbabes are wonderful.

And lastly, even though my father was a hunter, his love of wildlife, birding, and stopping in the quiet to hear the soft beating of wings is a gift that I will treasure the rest of my life.

About the Author

© Alison Rosa

Kris Radish is the bestselling author of ten novels and three works of non-fiction. Her empowering books focus on the very *real* issues women face in their lives and she celebrates the important and amazing power of female friendship via her novels and in her yearly retreats held for women from across the globe. She is a former working journalist, editor, university lecturer, bureau chief, nationally syndicated columnist, magazine writer, worm picker, Professional Girl Scout and lifeguard—to name but a few of her past experiences. Radish is also co-owner of the Wine Madonna wine lounge in downtown St.Petersburg, Florida and Radish & Company Boutique where she hosts book groups and special events and does a bit of wine drinking herself. Radish is also working on her eleventh novel and a second book of autobiographical essays.

SELECTED TITLES FROM SPARKPRESS

SparkPress is an independent boutique publisher delivering high-quality, entertaining, and engaging content that enhances readers' lives, with a special focus on female-driven work.
Visit us at www.gosparkpress.com

The Balance Project, by Susie Orman Schnall
$16, 978-1-94071-667-1
With the release of her book on work/life balance, Katherine Whitney has become a media darling and hero to working women everywhere. In reality though, her life is starting to fall apart, and her assistant Lucy is the one holding it all together. When Katherine does something unthinkable to her, Lucy must decide whether to change Katherine's life forever, or continue being her main champion.

The Legacy of Us, by Kristin Contino
$17, 978-1-94071-617-6
Three generations of women are affected by love, loss, and a mysterious necklace that links them.

Bear Witness, by Melissa Clark
$15, 978-1-94071-675-6
What if you witnessed the kidnapping of your best friend? This is when life changed for twelve-year-old Paige Bellen. This book explores the aftermath of a crime in a small community, and what it means when tragedy colors the experience of being a young adult.

9 781940 716510